Ace titles by Moira J. Moore

RESENTING THE HERO
THE HERO STRIKES BACK
HEROES ADRIFT
HEROES AT RISK
HEROES RETURN
HEROES AT ODDS

Heroes at Odds

Moira J. Moore

ACE BOOKS, NEW YORK

THE BERKLEY PUBLISHING GROUP
Published by the Penguin Group
Penguin Group (USA) Inc.
375 Hudson Street, New York, New York 10014, USA

Penguin Group (Canada), 90 Eglinton Avenue East, Suite 700, Toronto, Ontario M4P 2Y3, Canada
(a division of Pearson Penguin Canada Inc.)
Penguin Books Ltd., 80 Strand, London WC2R 0RL, England
Penguin Group Ireland, 25 St. Stephen's Green, Dublin 2, Ireland (a division of Penguin Books Ltd.)
Penguin Group (Australia), 250 Camberwell Road, Camberwell, Victoria 3124, Australia
(a division of Pearson Australia Group Pty. Ltd.)
Penguin Books India Pvt. Ltd., 11 Community Centre, Panchsheel Park, New Delhi—110 017, India
Penguin Group (NZ), 67 Apollo Drive, Rosedale, Auckland 0632, New Zealand
(a division of Pearson New Zealand Ltd.)
Penguin Books (South Africa) (Pty.) Ltd., 24 Sturdee Avenue, Rosebank, Johannesburg 2196,
South Africa

Penguin Books Ltd., Registered Offices: 80 Strand, London WC2R 0RL, England

This is a work of fiction. Names, characters, places, and incidents either are the product of the author's imagination or are used fictitiously, and any resemblance to actual persons, living or dead, business establishments, events, or locales is entirely coincidental. The publisher does not have any control over and does not assume any responsibility for author or third-party websites or their content.

HEROES AT ODDS

An Ace Book / published by arrangement with the author

PRINTING HISTORY
Ace mass-market edition / August 2011

Copyright © 2011 by Moira J. Moore.
Cover art by Eric Williams.
Cover design by Annette Fiore DeFex.

ISBN: 978-0-441-02064-5

ACE
Ace Books are published by The Berkley Publishing Group,
a division of Penguin Group (USA) Inc.,
375 Hudson Street, New York, New York 10014.
ACE and the "A" design are trademarks of Penguin Group (USA) Inc.

PRINTED IN THE UNITED STATES OF AMERICA

10 9 8 7 6 5 4 3 2 1

*To the family and friends who bought my books
to give them away.*

To those who reviewed my books on their blogs.

*To those who invited me to write guest posts
on their blogs, or interviewed me.*

*To the booksellers who put my books
in the hands of their customers.*

*To the librarians who added my books
to their catalogs.*

*To those who created pages about me
on Wikipedia, TV Tropes and other websites
to be tripped over by thousands.*

Thank you, all; this one's for you.

Acknowledgments

I would like to thank my family and friends for all of their support and encouragement. I would like to thank my agent, Jack Byrne, and my editor, Anne Sowards, for all of their hard work.

Chapter One

I signed the letter "Shield Dunleavy Mallorough" and folded the thick document shut, sealing it with wax and stamping it with the Triple S emblem. More of a report than an actual letter, it was full of evasions, half-truths and omissions. To my regret, I had become adept at hiding inconvenient facts. I'd once prided myself on being honest.

I ran my fingertip over the emblem. Three capital Ss, slightly overlapping, slightly descending in degrees of the horizontal. The first S symbolizing "Source," a person able to touch the powerful forces behind earthquakes, tornadoes and other natural disasters, and channel them away, creating stability.

The second S for "Shield," the Source's partner, able to protect the Source from the effects of channeling, the danger of ripping himself apart and being crushed like an eggshell while he worked.

The third S for "Service," the organization that housed and raised and trained Sources and Shields, and then watched over them as they performed their duties.

The Source and Shield Service. The Triple S.

As a Shield, one of my duties was to write reports about the activities of my Source and me, and the conditions of our environment. Circumstances had taught me that it wasn't wise to be completely candid in them. I had come to believe the possible repercussions could be nasty. We could do things Sources and Shields weren't supposed to be able to do. The Triple S suspected this. We'd been subjected to intimidating scrutiny in the past.

Though recently not so much. No visits, no letters complaining of insubstantial reports. Nothing. It was as though we had, as far as the Triple S council was concerned, fallen over the edge of the world.

Which was fine with me.

I pulled out a fresh sheet of paper to begin a much more pleasant piece of correspondence.

A bird screeched just outside my window, making me jump and swear in surprise. Flown Raven was the quietest part of the world in which I'd ever lived. Except for its birds, which were truly obnoxious. If I were crazy enough to believe birds could possess motives, I would think they were going out of their way to startle me.

I had to admit to myself, and no one else, that I wasn't madly in love with Flown Raven. It was a remote community, bizarre in its combination of tradespeople, whalers, fishers and farmers; people who worked very hard and very long and seemed able to crush iron with their bare hands. Any music, theatre and art were largely created by those same people during their scant spare time, which meant these cultural pleasures demonstrated true talent but lacked the complexity and variety to which I had grown accustomed. I had just moved to Flown Raven from High Scape. High Scape was a huge metropolis, with slews of theatres, music halls, sporting events and fabulous urban art. Flown Raven, well, in its way it was a much more staid place.

I wrote a lot more letters in Flown Raven than I had anywhere else. It was something to do.

A few moments later, my Source, Shintaro Ivor Cear Karish, slid into our suite, home from playing cards. I looked at him and smiled. He was so pretty, lean and golden with lightly slanted black eyes and slightly curling black hair. I had once preferred men who would be described as rugged, tall and

broad with strong facial features. Taro taught me to love the fine
and the slight.

There had been a little bit of a distance between us until
very recently. Immediately upon our arrival in Flown Raven,
we had experienced some difficulties, and I had not reacted
well to how those difficulties had been handled, needing a little
time and space to myself. But we had gotten through that, and
I was relieved and pleased.

He leaned down to kiss me.

"Did you not win, then?" I asked.

"Of course, I did. I always win."

That was almost true. "Where's your money?"

"I felt bad for one of the players. She lost all she had. So I
gave her my pot."

He didn't need money. No one in the Triple S did. By law,
we were to be given almost any goods we wished—clothing
and food and even luxury items like jewelry—and a good many
services, from anyone to whom we made the request.

Which, by the way, made us so very popular with merchants and landlords and the like.

Taro used coins merely as markers of how well he was
playing. "Won't that just encourage her to gamble more?"

He shrugged. "Maybe, but at least I'll know I had nothing
to do with her downfall."

"That's good of you." But not unlike him. He was not a
perfect man, of course, but he was a good one, and more con-
siderate than many of the rumors about him properly demonstrated.

He picked up the package destined for the Triple S. "What
does this one say?"

"The usual. Nothing much. Everything's fine."

"They might get suspicious if you always say the same
thing."

"I word it differently every time. I'm very clever, you
know." When it came to writing letters, anyway. I was pretty
sure there were whole arenas of human endeavors in which I
was completely dense.

Hester, our new personal maid, came in without knocking
and curtsied. I would never get used to that. We were living in

the manor of the titleholder, Fiona Keplar, Duchess of Westsea and Taro's cousin. She wasn't required to house us in her private home, we could have lived at the closest tavern, but she was a generous person. And she no doubt knew that an extended stay on our part at the modest tavern would create enormous resentment in the landlord.

"Sir, ma'am, Holder Mallorough, Trader Mika Mallorough, and Trader Dias Mallorough have arrived and are waiting in the sitting room."

I stared at her, my mouth open in absolute shock. "What? Did I—?" Get a letter I had forgotten? No, I couldn't have. A surprise visit?

I made an embarrassing sound, a whoop of joy, and ran from the room, hearing Taro laughing behind me. I nearly took a header down the stairs and I didn't care. My brothers were there. I hadn't seen them since my Matching, which had allowed us only a few moments, and it had been years before that since I'd had a decent conversation with them.

And my mother? Well, I had seen her much more recently. The visit hadn't gone well. She was used to children open to parental guidance. I was used to being left alone. We'd never really resolved that conflict, and she'd cut the visit short because of her distress.

Not that it made me any less pleased with her coming. She was my mother. She was fun. And I had no doubt she would have reconciled herself with the lessons she had learned during our last visit.

Taro followed me. I was pleased he did so without being asked, without feeling he might not be welcome.

My mother was small and thin with dark auburn hair. My brothers were both tall and blond, Dias stocky while Mika was slim. My mother hugged me. Dias squeezed me too tight and I ruffled Mika's hair. "I'm delighted you're here," I said. "Why didn't you let me know you were coming? Are Father and Kaaren here or on their way?"

"Someone had to stay behind to watch our coffers," my mother answered. "Shintaro, lad, it's lovely to see you looking so hale." She wrapped my Source in an embrace. Taro was obviously surprised but hugged back easily enough. He did the same when Dias and Mika embraced him.

"How long are you able to stay?" I asked.

Fiona came into the room then, carrying her son, Stacin. "I was told we have guests."

"My lady," I said formally, and I introduced her to my family.

"Dunleavy, please, not so stiff. I am Fiona." She held out a hand to be shaken, and my mother and brothers politely did so. I had been half afraid that they would try to hug her, too, but they restrained themselves. "And this is my son, Stacin." He hid his face in her neck, and she cuddled him. "I am having rooms prepared for you. I hope you'll agree to stay with us for the duration of your visit with Dunleavy."

My mother smiled broadly. "Thank you," she said. She didn't protest that she didn't want to inconvenience Fiona, as I would have, at which point Fiona would have insisted it was no trouble, and I would then have accepted her offer. I found my mother's easy response a little shocking, but maybe it was a relief to those offering to just get acceptance and a thank you, rather than going through the circles strictly good manners demanded. "That is most generous of you."

"There is plenty of space, and Dunleavy is important to us."

Oh. Really? Fiona had been friendly with me from the moment I'd met her, but she was friendly with everyone.

"Is it possible that we could retire to those rooms to wash up?" my mother asked. "We had a rather hard run."

She did appear a little windblown, though that could be merely a result of the fact that Flown Raven was a windy place. "You rushed? Why?"

She smiled almost sadly and touched my shoulder. But she didn't say anything to me. "My lady?"

"Of course." Fiona pulled on a bell cord. "Holder Mallorough, I've put you in one of the suites facing the east gardens. I have your sons sharing a room. I hope that is acceptable."

"Certainly. Thank you."

One of the maids arrived to take my family to their rooms. My mother and brothers appeared calm as they followed her out, but Dias shot me a strange look before stepping through the door. I frowned, wondering what that was about.

"Anyone for a drink?" Fiona asked rather loudly. "I know I could use one." She went to the liquor bar and, one handed, poured herself a tumbler of whiskey.

Fiona had had a hard time recently. Her husband had died while whaling. Flown Raven had suffered some calamities, including the collapse of the wind rock, a necessary tool and considered a symbol of good luck to the local population. And that population wasn't thrilled to have Fiona as a title-holder, though not because of anything she had done. They thought Taro, the brother of the original duke, should have taken the title. He had refused, and that had created a lot of resentment in a lot of people.

Fiona might not feel awkward if she was the only one drinking, but I would. "Is there any white wine?" I asked.

Taro grimaced. For no good reason. It wasn't as though I was going to make him drink it.

"We haven't any chilled."

"I don't mind. No, no, I'll get it myself." Fiona had been trying to juggle child and whiskey in order to pour me some wine.

So there I stood, sipping at warm wine I didn't want, trying to figure out why my family was there. I had become a pessimist over the past few years. Surprises were rarely pleasant.

Bailey stepped in to announce that the evening meal was ready to be served. The four of us silently moved to the dining room. Tarce, Fiona's brother, was already seated at the table. Next to him was Roshni Radia, the Wind Watcher, who was currently unable to perform her duties, for a couple of different reasons.

It was the first time I had seen her out of the room Fiona had given her. Her leg had been crushed in a rockslide that had destroyed her home. It was a miracle she'd been able to keep it, that it had healed as quickly as it had, and that she would be able to walk on it again. Still, it wouldn't have been easy for her to make it down the stairs to the dining room.

There didn't appear to have been any discussion between the two, which wasn't surprising. Radia had little patience for someone as useless and arrogant as Tarce, and Tarce was so madly infatuated with Radia that he didn't know how to talk to her. It was funny, pathetic and embarrassing all at the same time.

"Roshni," Taro greeted her warmly. "It's lovely to see you downstairs."

Her smile was indulgent as she let him kiss her hand. "It's

lovely to be here. No matter how attractive a room is, it can be tiresome to see nothing but those four walls for weeks."

Tarce was scowling at Taro. He resented Taro's ease of manner. Taro knew this, of course, so to aggravate Tarce further Taro sat on Radia's other side. I shouldn't have found that as entertaining as I did.

"Have you finished with the books yet?" Taro asked Radia. "I'd be happy to bring some more."

Now Tarce looked surprised as well as resentful, because he hadn't thought to do something like that for Radia himself. And if I could see that just by looking at him, so could everyone else. I was terrible at reading people.

"Those books didn't involve flighty stories needing only an evening to completely finish, Source Karish," she responded. "I am still well occupied."

My Source nodded. Tarce glowered. Radia, well, her eyes were gleaming just a bit.

My mother and brothers came in before anyone was compelled to say something unfortunate. I quickly introduced everyone.

Dias approached Radia and, like Taro, kissed her hand just before she could slip her hand away with a look of disapproval. "My sister said you are called a Wind Watcher," he said.

"That is correct."

"And what does a Wind Watcher do?"

Dias was merely being polite. Or something. I'd written of Radia in my letters.

"The wind in Flown Raven can get so fierce that it blows people and livestock off their feet," Radia explained. "It can kill. It is my task to watch the wind and warn everyone when it looks like it will get too strong." Her words were dry but her tone was warm. She was a person who felt true affection for her occupation. Pride in protecting people. I could empathize with that.

"I've never heard of such a position in any other place," Dias said. "It sounds romantic."

Radia raised an eyebrow at him. "It is merely a job that needs to be done."

Dias looked ready to ask another question, but my mother cut him off.

"Take a seat, Dias," my mother told him in a manner that I thought would be more appropriately directed to a child. If it annoyed Dias, though, I couldn't tell it from his face.

A light green soup was served as the first course. I found the food most commonly eaten by the people in Flown Raven a little strange, and not always appealing, but the soup was tasty.

"How long will you be with us, Holder Mallorough?" Fiona asked.

"Well, that will depend on certain circumstances, but I wouldn't feel comfortable staying beyond a couple of weeks."

"That is a long way to travel for such a short visit."

It certainly was. My mother had stayed much longer when she'd visited me in High Scape, and High Scape was closer to Seventh Year, where my family lived.

"It is," my mother agreed, "but it's necessary."

Necessary. A disquieting choice of words.

"Were your travels uneventful?"

My mother chuckled. "Is travel ever uneventful?" And she proceeded to entertain the gathering with stories of a landlady so entranced with Dias that she tried to sneak into his bed, a livery that tried to sell her a donkey, and an incompetent thief who'd tripped over his own feet while trying to snatch her purse.

It was interesting. I would have considered such incidents aggravating. My mother seemed to find them hilarious.

The next course was fish. Fish was a frequent dish in Flown Raven. I could deal with less fish.

Daris, Fiona's older sister, drifted in. I could smell the odor of whiskey surrounding her. Like Fiona and Tarce, she was tall, slim and blond. Like Tarce, she was fairly useless. Her most unique characteristic, besides being perpetually drunk, was fierce bitterness over the fact that Taro had chosen to pass the estate to Fiona instead of her. And a good thing he did. Daris would have been a disaster.

She smiled nastily. "Well, if it isn't the Shield's slip serving family," she sneered. "Come to bask in the significance of their connections."

Slip servers. One of many not so nice names for members of the merchant class. I wasn't sure why this one was supposed to be insulting. What was wrong with giving people pieces of paper detailing what had been bought and sold? I looked at my mother and brothers. None of them seemed disturbed by the term.

Fiona sighed. "Must you always make a fool of yourself?"

"I'm not the one breaking bread with a bunch of pot shiners."

That was a new one. Still didn't bother me. Or my family.

Daris directed her bloodshot eyes to my mother. "I bet you thanked your long bones when your daughter hooked Lord Shintaro Karish."

"We have come to feel grateful for it," my mother said calmly. "He treats her well. We've heard how some Sources can be."

And I'd seen some of them first hand. Sources were people, after all, and some of them were rapists and murderers and every other kind of criminal one could think of. I was well aware of how lucky I was.

"And no doubt your connection to our family has done your business all sorts of good."

"Beg pardon, but is your name Karish?"

"It is not."

"Then we have no connection to your family."

Daris's nostrils flared. I didn't know why she was so offended. Did she want to be thought of as a Karish?

Then again, common sense was not a trait I had seen her display.

I did find it interesting that Mother didn't deny that a connection to the Karish name was helping business. Did that mean it was? I felt uncomfortable with the idea of my family using the Karish name to increase their wealth. It was just good fortune that I bonded with Taro, nothing that I or my family had earned. They shouldn't be able to profit from that.

"And you." Daris nodded at her brother. "Panting after the Wind Watcher. You're ridiculous."

Tarce flushed. I couldn't tell if it was from anger or embarrassment. Radia was concentrating on her fish with great intensity.

"Appreciation of the beautiful is never a cause for embarrassment," Taro said lightly.

Mika smirked. "I think that comment might be a little self-serving."

Taro widened his eyes in feigned innocence. "What can you mean?"

"Tell me, my Lord, how long do you spend examining yourself in the mirror each morning?"

"It's the duty of all to ensure they look their best when they are to appear before others."

He'd tried to convince me of that when we'd first bonded. He'd given up pretty quickly. He was a smart lad.

The rest of the meal passed with Taro and Mika bouncing comments back and forth. Daris drank goblet after goblet of wine and muttered under her breath. Everyone else just ate. I wanted the meal to be over. I wanted to find out why my mother and brothers were here.

When the bowls for the vanilla mousse were scraped clean, my mother said, "Your Grace, we would like to speak to Dunleavy. We have important family business to discuss. Is there someplace where we can talk without being disturbed?"

Aye, I'd been right. Family business that needed to be discussed with me? Someone was dying. Or they were all sliding into destitution. It could be only bad news.

"More ideas on how to make money off our name?" Daris asked with a decided slur.

Everyone ignored her.

"Of course," said Fiona. "Use my office. You'll be assured of privacy there. None of the servants will enter without your permission. Bailey will show you."

This time, Taro chose not to follow us. I wanted him with me. I felt he belonged with me. If this was a family discussion, and Taro was part of my family, as my mother and brothers seemed to think he was, should he not be part of our discussion?

On the other hand, it might be best if I heard whatever was coming on my own, so I would have the chance to rephrase the news to better suit his ears.

Fiona's office was the size of the sitting room in the suite I shared with Taro, and it had the largest desk I had ever seen. The ceiling, walls and floor were built in shades of brown, and when Bailey closed the door upon leaving, the room felt like it was cloaked in silence. It was a restful place. I knew Fiona spent very little time in it.

Although there were enough chairs for all of us, none of us sat.

"I'm going to get right to the point," Mother said, rubbing her hands together in a nervous gesture that seemed unlike her. "Do you remember the Prides?"

"The Prides?"

"Specifically, Cars Pride and his son, Marcus."

I thought a moment. "No. I've never heard those names."

"They are on the way here to see you. I'm surprised we managed to get here first."

"Why?" What was so important they couldn't just send me a letter? What was so awful my family had pushed themselves over half a continent to reach me first?

Mother took a deep breath. "Because you're betrothed to Marcus."

I snickered, because that had to be one of the most ridiculous things I'd ever heard.

But no one was snickering with me.

"I'm being serious," said my mother.

"Please. No one does that anymore."

My mother seemed to contemplate that for a moment. "It isn't surprising that, given your upbringing, you might not be as aware of certain realities as—"

"I live in the real world," I snapped. Yes, I'd spent seventeen years protected in the Shield Academy, but I would wager I'd gone through more extraordinary things in my years since leaving than anyone in my family could imagine. "This does not happen."

"It does, actually. It is much less common now than it was when you were born, and even then it was more the custom to arrange marriages between adults rather than children, but it was done then, and it is still done occasionally now. I could give you some examples, if you wish."

I stared at her. She looked back at me with grim determination. My brothers didn't appear amused. Dias, in particular, looked like he pitied me. This was not a joke. How could this not be a joke? "You betrothed me to someone?" I couldn't believe those words were coming out of my mouth. It was farcical.

"They are a merchant family and—"

"I don't care who they are, how could you—"

"—we were experiencing some—"

"—take such an important—"

"Dunleavy Mallorough!" Mother snapped. "You will show me the respect of listening to me without interruption."

I clamped my lips together and crossed my arms. But I was furious. Oh, I was furious. This was the most idiotic thing I'd ever heard. How was I supposed to show respect to someone who had dredged up such a ridiculous obsolete tradition?

"Our fortunes were at a low ebb. The lowest we'd suffered in generations. The Prides had only recently established their enterprises, but they were doing well. They were new and fresh, and they created so much produce that some suppliers began to deal only with them, needing no one else. You are probably unaware of the practice, but many suppliers to the markets would prefer to deal only with one source rather than many. So we lost some of our connections, which cut down greatly on the markets our produce reached, and our income flow sank so deeply we were facing the possibility of being unable to support our staff, even our own family, without selling off assets we couldn't afford to lose.

"The Prides approached us. They wanted our name. We were established; they were new. They had resources; we had experience. They felt combining our lines would benefit us both. You were an infant. Marcus was only slightly younger. They knew we wouldn't agree to his marrying Kaaren. She was our firstborn; she would be responsible for our enterprise when your father and I were too old to carry the business ourselves. And she was nearly ten. I believe the combination of her status and her age would have given her an advantage over their son that made them uncomfortable. The boys weren't yet born, of course. You were the only suitable child. And we were sliding too close to the edge to refuse their offer."

What I was hearing made no sense. I had been betrothed my whole life and I'd never even known about it? It was impossible. They hadn't told me anything about it. Surely, if this were true, they would have told me at some point. It was a pretty significant fact.

Seriously, this couldn't be happening.

"Papers were drawn and goods were exchanged. But a few years later we learned you were a Shield, and as you know, once that happened, you belonged to the Triple S and the contract was invalidated."

Yes, that was right. Relief unclenched the panic balling in my chest. Of course I wasn't actually betrothed to anyone. The very idea was ludicrous. My knees felt weak. I wanted to sit down. "Then why are they coming here?"

"They don't consider the contract invalidated. We didn't return the payments. The paperwork hasn't been revised. We still use the connections the agreement garnered us."

"Why didn't you return the payments?" I demanded.

"It wasn't required, under the circumstances."

I was appalled. "I would think decency would require it."

"I didn't realize trade was part of the curriculum in the Shield Academy," my mother said coolly.

I felt like I'd been slapped. It hurt. But that wasn't the important issue right then. "They can't expect me to actually marry this man." Of course I wouldn't do it. I didn't care what contracts had been signed. I hadn't signed anything, and as far as I was concerned, I was the only one who could and have it stick.

If these Prides had just sent me a letter, I would have reminded them that, as a Shield, I couldn't be held to obligations created by my family. I would have saved them the trip. And the fact that my family had thought to trade me off like a sack of grain wouldn't be made known to everyone in Flown Raven.

Because it would be made known. To everyone. That was the nature of a small place like Flown Raven.

This was going to be so humiliating.

Taro was going to lose his mind.

"The Prides are desperate, Lee. Things have been going very badly for them. They're in textiles, too, but much of their money was tied to land they owned in the south. Nacin worms have spun in their trees for decades, but a blight has killed almost all of them. The Prides haven't been able to honor all of their trade agreements and their name has started to acquire tarnish. A marriage will make the connection between our families undeniable to the rest of the world. We could act as a form of security for their ventures. And, of course, there is money and goods that we would then have to settle on their family as part of the wedding process."

Perhaps it was callous of me, but I could give a broken stick for whatever troubles the Prides were going through. "And this Marcus fellow, he's just going to go along with this?" Had he no spine?

"Cars has informed us that Marcus is obedient."

Not feeling good about Marcus. "I won't do it. You do understand that, right?"

"Of course. We came to warn you of their coming and to offer our support against them."

"Oh." Couldn't she have started her announcement with that? Something to tell me that she had some odd news to deliver but not to worry because nothing would come of it all? I would have been spared all the anger and panic.

Though my emotional responses were my own fault. It was my responsibility to remain calm in all circumstances. My training in that area had been slipping further and further over the past couple of years.

So just be calm. I was making a fool of myself. "All right."

And the crazy thing was, this wasn't even the first time someone wanted to marry me. What was it with people? I had no title, no land, no business interests. There was absolutely no reason for anyone to want to marry me.

I couldn't believe my parents ever thought to marry me off. They'd negotiated over me like they would a cow. They'd signed paperwork.

"Kaaren's doing well," my mother said. "She was quite upset she had to send Deacon away, but she is recovering her equanimity nicely."

I couldn't help staring at her. She had nearly capsized my emotional equilibrium, and now she wanted to sink into gossip?

Who the hell was Deacon?

I cleared my throat. "If that's all to be said about the Pride matter, I suggest we let Fiona have her office back." Sometimes, when one doesn't know what to do, fall back on strict civility.

So we retired to the suite I shared with Taro, where my mother proceeded to tell me all about what was going on with the family and the business and a bunch of people I'd never met and probably never would. I tried to look as though I really cared, when all I wanted to do was ransack Fiona's library for law texts. Maybe one would clearly state that Shields couldn't be forced to honor family obligations. I could stand before these Prides with the text, show them the relevant section, and send them on their way.

My brothers said nothing. I didn't know them as well as I would have liked, but their ongoing silence struck me as un-characteristic. It was disquieting.

In time, Mother started yawning, her eyes watering. "Time for us to bed down, boys," she announced. "We've had a hard day."

Dias and Mika didn't appear tired, and I expected them to demur. I was surprised when they didn't. They were too old to be going to bed just because their parent told them to, but they got up and left with her.

Interesting.

I sat alone by the fire and tried to settle my mind. Thoughts were jumping in and out and bouncing against each other. It was so hard to focus. It was impossible to remain calm.

What if I hadn't been a Shield? Would I have been already married? Having grown up with that expectation, would I have accepted it with equanimity, or would I be as bitter and resent-ful as I was feeling right then?

And then Taro breezed in. Oh, lords. I had to tell him.

"Your family is very free with their hands," he commented.

"I'm sorry."

"Oh, that wasn't a complaint. I like them."

Yes. Taro liked to touch people, too. Or he used to. He didn't do it as much anymore. I wondered why.

He liked my family at the moment. What would he say once he knew why they were here? "They have told me some dis-turbing news."

I had planned to get it out all at once, I wasn't looking for drama with a significant pause, but Taro interrupted me.

"Is something wrong? Is someone ill?" He reached out to touch my hand.

"No, nothing like that." I pulled in a deep breath. "Apparently, when I was a child my parents entered me into a betrothal with a boy named Marcus Pride. They never invalidated the agreement when they sent me to the Shield Academy, and Marcus Pride and his father are coming here in an attempt to enforce the contract."

He stared at me. "What?"

It was too ridiculous to say again. "You heard me."

Taro's lovely black eyes widened. "You're betrothed." His voice was flat with disbelief.

"Of course not. The agreement became invalid once I was recognized as a Shield."

"So why are they coming here?"

"Apparently they're claiming the contract was never voided. Mother says they're desperate."

Taro's posture stiffened. "Wonderful. That's just wonderful." He started pacing.

"Listen, it's nothing. They'll come here, they'll make their demands, I'll say no, they'll go home. That's it." I almost felt sorry for them, coming all this way for nothing. Almost. They should have written. Or, better yet, just accepted that the contract was void.

Perhaps they had hoped I wouldn't know they had no legal claim, hoped to arrange a quick wedding before I found out differently. If Marcus was so meek, they might assume I would be, too.

I was almost looking forward to proving them wrong.

"Have you met this Marcus Pride?" Taro asked.

"Not that I can remember."

"So what happens if he's moderately handsome and intelligent with a pleasing manner?"

I glared at him. "Don't be absurd."

"Please, the whole situation is absurd."

"I don't disagree. It's going to be humiliating. It won't result in anyone getting married."

Taro knocked his knuckles against the wall before turning and pacing back. "It doesn't make sense. You don't own anything."

"My family does." That was all the Prides would care about.

"Becoming a Triple S member severs family ties."

"I already said that."

He pushed his hands through his hair and then rubbed his face. "I can't believe this."

"Neither can I."

"It's always something."

I frowned. "What's that supposed to mean?"

"There is always someone."

"There is always someone what?"

"Someone . . . interfering. With us."

"I don't know what you mean."

"Yes. You do."

I really didn't, but I had no interest in arguing. "They'll get here, I'll tell them there's no chance, they'll turn around and go back home. Sorted."

"You really think it's going to be that simple? They'll come all the way from . . . wherever they're coming from, and they'll just turn around and leave on your say so?"

"They can stay as long as they want. I won't be marrying anyone."

He just scowled and kept pacing.

"My family is against this. The only pressure I'll be feeling is from a couple of strangers. Do you really think I'll submit to it? You know me better than that."

"If this Marcus is—"

"Who cares what Marcus is? It doesn't matter. And I can tell you this much about him: he's prepared to go through with this asinine marriage plan. How could I possibly respect someone like that?"

"There's nothing wrong with someone who cares about his family and is prepared to sacrifice for them."

My mouth dropped open, I was that shocked. "Have you been drinking?"

"You haven't even met him yet, and you're discounting him. You do that, you know. With people."

"You sound like you want me to give this serious consideration."

"You are naive. You underestimate people all the time. You have no idea what's going to happen."

None of that mattered. "I know that I will not be marrying anyone."

He paced a bit more. "I don't want to talk about this," he said finally.

"Good. Neither do I."

He stomped out through the door, closing it too loudly behind him. I sighed. What a completely wonderful day.

Chapter Two

I was surprised when Holder Ibena Bridge tried to punch her husband in the face. Hiroki, one of Fiona's footmen, grabbed her from behind and swung her away. Another footman, Sam, prevented Trader Andes Bridge, the husband, from charging after them. On the one hand, I shouldn't have been shocked, as they had entered the court room screaming at each other with no noticeable concern for the spectators in the room. On the other hand, well, she had tried to hit him. In front of everyone. If for no other reason, she should be concerned at how it would make her look in front of Fiona, the decision maker. In my experience, violent people weren't granted a lot of credibility.

It was Decision Day, held every week. It was the day when Fiona, as titleholder, heard the complaints and the disputes of her tenants and local aristocrats and ruled on them. Observing the process was a wonderful method of learning who all the residents were and what was going on in the area. I attended frequently, though there was no function for a Shield to perform.

And yes, it was a form of entertainment for me, for which I was a little ashamed. But that day, I was really in need of entertainment. I'd slept badly, Taro was in a mood, and I could barely make myself talk to anyone I was related to. Decision Day was an escape.

Except, the two current parties appeared to be particularly crazy. That was a little too entertaining for me. Issues that private should never be put on display.

"Let go of me!" the woman shrieked, kicking Hiroki in the shin. He impressed me by doing nothing but wincing slightly. "I'll smack the arrogance out of him!"

At the same time, the man was shouting something like, "You suck the value out of everything! The land! The sheep! Me! The sun should have disappeared by now!"

The two footmen pushed them farther apart.

"Both of you shut up before I toss you out!" Fiona shouted. I watched her breathe deeply, clench her teeth for only a moment, and square her shoulders. "Holder Bridge, if you would calmly explain—"

"He's trying to take my land, the lazy bastard!" she cried.

"That land wouldn't be worth half what it is without my efforts, you grasping bitch!"

I could hear snickering from the aristocratic spectators. They thought this was hilarious.

How could the Bridges not care how they appeared to us? They looked ridiculous. I would be humiliated to be seen behaving in such a manner.

Then the holder got Hiroki right in the nose. A good blow if the way Hiroki jerked back was any indication. And the blood started flowing.

"Floor them," Fiona ordered. For a moment, I didn't understand what that meant. The next thing I knew, each footman had a Bridge on his stomach on the floor. The move seemed to knock the parties breathless. It was an appalling example of handling, but I supposed strong measures were needed for the violent. "You are unable to act as adults," said Fiona, "so I'll treat you as children." She paused, and the two parties didn't seem ready to complain. "Now, Trader Bridge, what is your plaint?"

The trader was trying to catch his breath. He looked extremely uncomfortable. "We've been married twenty-six years," he said, his voice unpleasantly scratchy. It was hard to listen to.

"Now that she's tossing me out, she is trying to claim I have no right to the value of the land."

"I see." Fiona ignored the sounds of wordless outrage from Holder Bridge.

"That land would be worthless without me. I am the one who established the trading partners for all the wool we produce. I was the one that brought back the animal specimens to improve the whole flock. I have made the Bridge name synonymous with quality. Your Wind Watcher prefers our wool and weaves in exchange for favors for you. I have brought honor to our family and our titleholder. And now, after I have given her the strongest years of my life, she wants me to leave with nothing."

"I own that land!" the holder exclaimed. "I own that flock. Both of them were handed down to me by my mother. That fool has enjoyed the wealth of them during our marriage, and now that he has decided to slip with another woman, he wants to take with him the value of my land? It's disgusting and wrong."

"What do you say of his claim to improving your land and flock?"

"He did nothing more than what a trader should. It was why I married him."

Well, aye, that was why people married. To share economic connections and political power. Usually. My mother was a holder, and my father was a trader, and I was childish enough to hope that their decision to marry had nothing to do with property.

"Did either of you bring your marriage settlement papers with you?"

"There are no settlement papers," said the holder.

That created a flood of whispers among the spectators. A few days ago, I would have been shocked. How could anyone with property marry without drafting proper settlement papers? It was all fine and romantic to talk about marrying for love, but love didn't last forever. Not the passionate kind. Everyone knew this.

But I could have done with a little less paperwork regarding my own marital state.

"Really?" said Fiona. "You had viable land and healthy live-stock, and you did nothing to protect them before marrying? That leads me to believe that you are not as forward thinking as one might like."

"I was to predict the worthless swine would chase other skirts?" the holder demanded with an appalling lack of respect. She should have been more moderate in her tone and vocabulary, both because Fiona was her titleholder—a good one worthy of esteem—and because Fiona would be making a decision that would have an enormous impact on this woman's life. It was never wise to aggravate the adjudicator.

"You were to predict your own reactions to any failings on the part of your husband. Marriage is a serious business. You don't disrupt it for reasons such as infidelity."

I thought that was a little harsh, despite it being a common opinion. If someone cheated on me, I doubted I would be particularly rational about it.

"My steward shall determine the value of the land and the flock as it was twenty-six years ago, and its value now," Fiona announced. "The value of the assets at the time of marriage shall be the holder's. The remainder of the value shall be divided equally between the two."

Neither party liked that, their objections loud and their slanderous descriptions of Fiona's parentage creative.

Fiona ignored it all. "Holder, you may give the trader his share in funds or in land and sheep. I expect everything to be settled within fourteen days, either by reconciliation or the settlement. Please escort them out."

The two parties were dragged squirming and protesting out of the room. Really, they had no sense of decorum at all. I could hear them even after the heavy door closed behind them.

In my brief time at Flown Raven, I had never witnessed such appalling behavior on Decision Day. The lack of dignity was not, however, completely unprecedented. People had been letting themselves slip further and further from the codes of simple good manners. Did that mean they were going to get worse?

The two footmen returned to the court room. "There are no others, Your Grace," Hiroki announced.

Fiona nodded. "Then I will call this session—"

"A moment, Your Grace," a man I vaguely knew called out, and everyone turned in their seats to look at him. The tall man with shoulder length white hair rose from his seat near Fiona's chair. His proximity to Fiona indicated he was among the highest in rank among the spectators.

"I recognize the Earl of Kent," said Fiona. "Do you have a plaint to deliver?"

"Not quite." He descended down to the floor and stood before Fiona. He was dressed in black from head to toe. It stood out against the lighter colors everyone else wore. "It is more an invitation, one that is in your best interests, and in the best interests of your tenants, to accept."

Hm. Someone who thought he spoke in the best interests of others. That was never good.

Apparently, Fiona didn't think so, either. She leaned back in her chair, palms resting on its arms, long legs crossed. Her eyes narrowed. "How intriguing." Her tone was formal and uninviting.

He smiled. The expression was, on the surface, charming. It made me feel greasy. "All of us here are aware that your coming into the Westsea title was irregular. Source Karish was the natural heir."

Oh, gods, what the hell? Did we have to go through this again? Had he been talking to Taro's mother?

"I can assure you that there was nothing irregular about my assumption of the title," Fiona told him coolly. "It was in all ways legal and legitimate."

"Yet you do not deny that Source Karish would have been a more natural choice."

Really, when were people going to let that go? Fiona had the title. It was done.

"Had he not been a Source, certainly, though, as you are aware, there is no law stating a title must be passed within a family."

"But you have experienced so many difficulties since taking the title," Kent said in the smooth voice of a practiced speaker. "The decrease in your productivity. The loss of your most necessary wind rock. The desertion by so many of your people. Even the death of your poor husband." A melodramatic pause seemed to cause those last words to echo in the large room.

"It's almost as though someone was trying to tell you something."

And right there, I felt he had gone a step too far. "Someone" meaning who? It would have been better just to announce the difficulties without implying someone more powerful was arranging them on purpose. Because who could possibly do that?

"And what is it you are trying to tell me?" Fiona asked, apparently unmoved by Kent's list.

"I am willing to take the responsibility of Westsea off your hands."

The room exploded into the noise of dozens of people trying to talk over each other. There was a mixture of shock, outrage and amusement.

Fiona was flushed with anger.

Don't shout, I thought. It will only make you look as though you've lost control.

She didn't, which relieved me. "How kind of you," she said dryly, her voice more temperate than her expression.

"I have great wealth and I will sell my assets to buy Westsea from you. You will be able to return to Centerfield, where you have been productive. You will be wealthier and more at peace."

How very condescending.

I couldn't imagine how much an estate like Westsea would cost. How could anyone afford to buy it? It just didn't seem possible, to me.

"It is kind of you to worry so about my peace of mind," said Fiona. "But I'll stay as I am."

"If you won't do it for yourself, do if for your people. They need someone they can look to for guidance."

"I lead my people well."

"Are you blind?" And he slid from mildly condescending to outright offensive. "Did you not see what the rest of us did this morning? People coming before you, in disarray and with disrespect. Two of them almost needed to be bound, they so little understood their place."

"And is that what you would have done?" Fiona asked coldly. "Bound them in ropes and chains?"

"With respect, my people know how to behave before me. They are always quiet and orderly."

I really didn't know anything about Kent beyond the fact that his land bordered Fiona's, but I had seen enough to decide I didn't like him. I hated arrogance, in every person. It was one of Taro's less attractive traits, though he didn't descend into it very often.

"I congratulate you on your complete control of your tenants," said Fiona. "But that is not an argument likely to convince me to release my responsibilities."

"Certainly. Don't think of your tenants."

I was pretty sure Fiona wasn't implying the interests of her tenants were irrelevant.

"Think only of yourself, if you wish. You would be much more comfortable at Centerfield."

It never ceased to amaze me how many people thought insulting someone was the way to persuade them to do something. I supposed Kent was trying to humiliate Fiona before the others. Sometimes people agreed to the atrocious when stuck in embarrassing public situations. I didn't believe Fiona was such a person.

"Again, I thank you for your consideration, but it's not necessary."

"You refuse my offer."

Of course she did. Had he really thought she would accept? Who would?

"I do." Her flush had faded.

He sighed, and he didn't appear at all sincere. "That is unfortunate. The other way is far less pleasant."

"And what way would that be?"

"I'm sure you are aware of the monarch's right to give one titleholder's estate to another, should the former be seen to be mismanaging the estate."

That surprised Fiona. "That law hasn't been invoked for generations."

That wasn't quite true. It had happened at least twice in my lifetime.

"It's still in the books."

There were a lot of obsolete laws in the scrolls and books,

and a lot of traditions that should be left behind. Every law I'd been forced to give serious thought to had seemed unnecessarily cumbersome or outright ridiculous.

"And you honestly feel you have the grounds to suggest I'm mismanaging Westsea?" Oddly enough, Fiona sounded more amused than intimidated, and good for her.

But I was worried. The Emperor didn't like Fiona. How did I know this? Well, the fact that he had sent some of his Imperial Guards to spy on her was a big clue.

Or it could be the fact that he had sent an assassin to kill her. I didn't know if we could trust the word of the assassin, who claimed she had the Emperor's protection, but we couldn't just dismiss the possibility, either.

And even if the assassin hadn't been hired by the Emperor, there were so many other ways he was abusing his position that it was impossible to predict what he would do next.

From the day his mother had died, the Emperor had engaged in activities that weren't included in his legitimate authority. He had demanded taxes from titleholders before he was crowned. He had sent Taro and me from our post in High Scape to Flown Raven, a decision only the Triple S was authorized to make. He had forced Taro to kneel before him and swear an oath of fealty, something no member of the Triple S should be required to do.

Sometimes really stupid ideas just popped into my head without any logical origin. This was one such occasion. I wondered, just casually, if the Emperor had put Kent up to this. It seemed to me the sort of thing our Monarch would do.

"I believe the incidents I have already described would lead a prudent titleholder to question her competence."

"What about a titleholder whose tenants burned down his gristmill in protest of the fees he charged for the services?"

I hid my surprise. I hadn't heard anything about that. It seemed to me a very dangerous, destructive and drastic action. People would have to be infuriated to do something like that, something that risked their own livelihoods as much as Kent's.

"That is less damning than having tenants walk away from their land altogether."

"I would say that's a matter of opinion."

"The Emperor's opinion." And Kent smiled unpleasantly.

Was that confirmation of my vague suspicion?

It was so frustrating. I kept hearing about the Emperor. He was meant to be a distant figure, someone spoken of only on some of the larger festival days. I wasn't supposed to have to worry about what he was thinking. Even if he was a grasping, overreaching prat.

"It's not the Emperor's decision, you know," said Fiona. "He merely makes an announcement based on the decision of the Council. The Council is quite a different creature nowadays. Times and standards have changed. And the Council is now comprised of a significant number of the merchant class. Whose indiscretions do you think they would consider more egregious?"

"The merchants are in the minority of the Council."

"And you think the remaining members will be unanimous in supporting you?"

"I think I would know better than you and, more importantly, I'm better known to them. How much time have you spent at court in Erstwhile?"

That, I thought, was a solid blow. For aside from Emperor Gifford's coronation, Fiona hadn't been at Erstwhile at all. That, in my opinion, made her a better titleholder, for she remained with her people and saw to their needs, but she was allowing whatever political power had once been enjoyed by the titleholders of Westsea to be drained away.

Did Kent have the Emperor's favor? Would it really matter if he did? Why would the Emperor care? The only interest I'd seen him show toward the estate was in granting Taro the opportunity to take it back from Fiona. So the question was, did he just not want Fiona to have it, and was therefore willing to see anyone else as the titleholder? If so, he might give Kent his support. But if he wanted Taro to have the estate, I couldn't see him giving it to a third party. He'd have to convince the Council to give the title to Kent, and then turn around and convince them to give it to Taro. That would look ludicrous, indecisive, and it would test the patience of the Council.

"I am confident both the Emperor and the Council will see that my estate is profitable and stable," Fiona said to Kent, and she sounded loose and comfortable. "All is well in hand."

"Your confidence is rooted in ignorance," said Kent. "You

can sell Westsea to me. I can apply to the Emperor to give it to me. Or I can merely take it from you. The latter two will leave you looking ineffective and incompetent. Others will give thought to taking Centerfield from you. They'll be successful, due to your failure with Westsea. You'll be left with nothing."

"Your concern is generous, but I assure you, it's unnecessary."

Kent stood for a moment in silence. He looked about the room, at all the people avidly watching the confrontation. Then he smirked and bowed very slightly. "You must do as you think best. Good day, Your Grace." As he headed for the door, the whispering of the spectators resumed.

I watched them, picking over this juicy bit of news with disapproval and delight. After they left they would be telling everyone they met about it, predicting who would be successful, Westsea or Kent. At least some of them would feel Fiona would fail.

Fiona appeared to be deep in thought, tapping her lips with the tip of her index finger. She didn't look at all alarmed, but I was pretty sure she was merely hiding her emotions with a skill I envied.

I couldn't imagine the stress she had to be under. Kent was an ass, but all the problems that he had mentioned, they and more had happened. A weaker person might have collapsed under the weight of it all. I wouldn't have blamed Fiona if she decided to chuck it all and go back to Centerfield.

Fiona stood, and the whispering stopped. "I thank you all for your attendance." If she was at all perturbed by the events of the day, no one would know it by looking at her. "I bid you all good day."

Everyone was silent as Fiona crossed the room and climbed the stairs to the second floor, Bailey, her butler, following close behind her. I stayed in place. I didn't want her to think I was tagging around after her to get her to talk to me. I was sure she wanted to rage in private.

The mistake in that plan became immediately apparent. Petro Rosen, a pompous squeaking little rat of a man, practically ran to my side. "What does Her Grace plan to do?" he asked.

I hesitated a moment, surprised. Did he really think I knew?

It had just happened. I couldn't look into her mind. "I have no idea, my lord." Not that I would tell him if I did.

Unfortunately, he wasn't the only one to seek information he had no right to expect. "Did Her Grace know Kent was going to challenge her?" some woman whose name I couldn't remember demanded.

Had it looked like Fiona had known? Had the woman not been watching? "I have nothing to tell you," I said quickly. "Excuse me." I headed for the door.

That wasn't good enough. They followed me. "But you're Her Grace's confidante," the woman protested.

Where had they gotten that idea? "I am not."

"You go on those early morning walks with Her Grace and the Wind Watcher."

Ah. It really disturbed me that she knew that. Not that it was a secret or anything, but I hated the fact that they were watching me.

I didn't want these people chasing me. I stopped and looked at them and let my eyes go out of focus. After a few moments, I blinked, shook my head, and I tried to appear as though I'd forgotten they were there. "My greatest apologies. I must see to some Triple S business." Nothing got rid of people faster than claiming I had some Triple S duty to perform. As quickly as I could without actually running, I got out of the room and disappeared into another.

Westsea was one of the wealthiest and most powerful estates in the world. I imagined there were many who craved to have it for those reasons alone. As Fiona's neighbor, Kent would be well aware of the difficulties Fiona had been experiencing. That he had publicly announced his intention to take the estate suggested to me that he was not going to be dissuaded by mere words.

Something more was coming. And it would be aggravating.

I knew I was a selfish person, because right then all I could think of was that I didn't know how I was going to deal with Kent's delusions while I was already burdened by those of my family.

Then I rolled my eyes at myself. It wasn't my responsibility to deal with Kent. My task was being a Shield. How 'bout I stick with that?

Chapter Three

I was not an early riser, one of the ways in which I failed to be the perfect Shield. I liked sleeping. It was often a warm, comforting state. It allowed me to relax in a way I never could while awake. Sometimes a part of me wished I could sleep all the time.

Still, whenever Fiona woke me by tapping me on the shoulder, I got up. It was good for me, and it was an honor to be chosen. Besides, Fiona never really gave me the option of saying no. She just assumed I could have no objection.

I dressed silently and joined Fiona just outside the door to the suite. "Sleep well?" she asked in a low voice.

"Sort of." It had taken me a while to get to sleep after spending most of the day before avoiding everyone I knew, but once I got to sleep I had slept solidly. "How about you?" She was, after all, the one who had received a genuinely horrific surprise the day before.

Fiona shrugged. I took that to mean she had slept poorly. She unwrapped a bundle of cloth. "Have a tree tear."

Tree tears were shiny little balls of onasin sap mixed with honey. They were tasty and sweet and they cleared the mind and bolstered physical strength for a while. They were, I thought,

native to Westsea. At least, I'd never encountered them anywhere else, and I'd been around a fair bit. I loved them. I would
miss them once the Triple S finally decided to transfer Taro and
me to a new post.

We made our quiet way out of the manor and into the cool,
hazy light that was a typical morning in Flown Raven.

There were wisps of fog lying close to the ground, an en-
chanting and serene sight. Sometimes the fog got so thick one
couldn't see more than a cubit into the distance. We never walked
on days that had that much fog. And it was one circumstance in
which I would refuse to walk, even if Fiona were the sort to insist. I had been lost in the fog once, and though it hadn't been for
long and I had not been in real danger, it had been enough to give
me a bit of a fright.

"So your brother has eyes for our Wind Watcher," Fiona
said to me without notice.

"Um," I said intelligently. "I really couldn't say." He'd
flirted with her a little, but I didn't know if that actually meant
anything. "He said nothing to me."

"And I thought Shields were supposed to be perceptive."

"Really?" It never ceased to amaze me, the kinds of rumors
regulars spread about Shields and Sources. Shields weren't
known for being particularly perceptive among members of
the Triple S. Shields focused on themselves and their Sources
and, as a rule, little else. "Whoever told you that?"

Fiona looked at me with curiosity. "So you're saying you're
not perceptive?" she asked.

"I don't believe that's ever been one of my qualities." Unfortunately. I would have gotten into a lot less trouble if I'd
simply been able to see what was right in front of my face.

Fiona looked amused. "Well, believe me when I say he was
most interested in our dear Roshni. It had my beloved brother
grinding his teeth."

"I'm pretty sure Dias already has someone he's interested
in back home," I said, thinking of a letter I'd received from my
mother a few months before.

Fiona looked disappointed. "Then his behavior was ill
done."

Really? I remembered watching my mother flirt with a man
not my father. That had been disturbing. When I had chastised

her for it, she had claimed there was nothing wrong with it. Maybe it was a family trait. One I wasn't particularly proud of. "Did Radia think he was showing genuine interest?"

"I haven't had a chance to talk to her about it."

"Ah." So it was possible that Radia hadn't felt there was anything unusual about Dias's behavior.

"Mika's handsome."

I loved my brothers, but neither of them were what I could call handsome. Not that they were ugly. They were just plain. Like me. Though maybe their blond hair made them more appealing to others. My hair, unforgivably red, always seemed to look a mess.

"He's not betrothed, is he?"

"Not to my knowledge."

"So he's a prospect," said Fiona.

"I'm afraid not," I told her. "He prefers men."

"Damn it," said Fiona.

"Are you seriously trying to find a match for Radia?"

"A match is not necessary. Just a man who will keep her attention for a while."

"I doubt she would appreciate your efforts." Such interference would infuriate me.

"She needs to have children. We need her talent to be passed down."

I could understand that concern, but Radia was not a horse with fine bloodlines. It was offensive to pressure people to have children, especially when the desired outcome was to have those children perform a particular task. "Don't you think you should leave her to it?"

"She's not doing anything about it. That's the problem."

"She will when she wants to."

"I can't just let these things drift. We need a Wind Watcher."

"You have one."

"People need to see that their futures are being taken care of. They need to know there'll be someone to replace Roshni when the time comes."

"This is not something you can control."

Fiona glared at me. I was trying to keep my face expressionless. No, I really had no right to speak on this subject. On the other hand, she was talking to me about it. She had to expect a response.

Then she smiled. "I'm really just trying to put my brother out of his misery. He's painful to watch."

"That he is."

We were approaching the village. It was a small but prosperous place, supported as it was by the many titleholders in the area. Right then it was quiet, but in a short while it would be an orb of noise.

As we usually did on our walks, we went to the miller's first. By the time we reached her, she was always pulling out her first batch of small bread loafs. Warm bread with fresh butter was one of the best things in the world. I'd never truly appreciated that before coming to Flown Raven. Maybe the walk made it taste better.

"I heard your family is visiting," the miller said to me.

"Yes, they are."

"How long will they be staying?"

"A couple of weeks."

"It's always nice to have new faces. Traders, aren't they?"

"Yes."

"Are they looking for any connections here?"

"Not to my knowledge, but then I know almost nothing about such things."

She pursed her lips before asking, "They're your family, aren't they?"

"Aye, but I'm a Shield. I have nothing to do with their enterprises."

She appeared unimpressed. "Huh."

Fiona cleared her throat. "How is everyone doing?" she asked. It sounded like a casual question. I didn't think it was.

The miller shrugged. "Some grumbling, of course. Not like before those bastards tried to kill Healer Browne."

The bastards were the Imperial Guards the Emperor had sent, allegedly looking for evidence of people pretending to cast spells. Healer Nab Browne did cast spells, but I didn't think that had actually been observed by the Guards. The Guards had seen her healing people and had assumed the tools and ingredients she had used were quackery obscuring the attempts to cast spells. They hadn't been able to tell the difference between the ingredients for casting, which they hadn't discovered, and genuine medication, which they had.

They hadn't been planning to kill the healer, just flog her, but the numbers of lashes would have been the end of her. It had been the limit for Fiona, and she'd ordered the Guards away in another example of defiance of the Emperor.

Before that had happened, there had been a lot of people upset about Taro giving away the title, and they had blamed Fiona for that. Her standing up to the Guards had apparently won her some admiration, at least of those who hadn't later decided to leave.

"Anything I need to worry about?" Fiona asked.

The miller shrugged. "Don't think so."

"How about you? Is there something you're concerned about?"

"Nothing worthy of my lady's attention."

That, I thought, was a cagey answer.

Apparently, Fiona thought so, too. "Are you sure?"

"Aye, my lady."

Fiona tried a couple more times to get something out of the miller, but the woman refused to give even so much as a hint, and Fiona eventually had to give up.

We left shortly thereafter. We walked around the village, greeting those who were up and about. Fiona asked them all what was happening in their lives, if there was anything they thought she should know. Most of them claimed to have nothing to worry about.

The fog was burned off by the strengthening sun, and the air became noisier as we made our way back to the manor. The peace of the early morning had been shattered. Everyone was up and moving. The manor was bustling by the time we reached it.

Walking down the hall toward the dining room, we could hear masculine laughter ringing through the air. We entered the room just in time to hear my mother say, "And then he said, 'Not without the duck!'"

An uproarious explosion of merriment ensued. Taro was slapping the table in applause. Tarce was bent over in his chair.

I'd never seen Tarce laugh before. He looked beautiful and

free, the habitual sneer completely gone, his eyes shining. If he looked like that more often, he could probably entice anyone he wanted.

"You all seem in high spirits," Fiona commented as she served herself from the side bar. I headed for the coffee.

"Why should we not?" said Mother. "It is a fine day in a comfortable house with good company and a tasty breakfast. All the ingredients for contentment."

She seemed in far better spirits than she had been the day she'd arrived. A day to rest? Relief in having given me the bad news and therefore passing on the responsibility?

I hated that I resented my mother for being calm while I was a bundle of nerves. That wasn't her fault. She probably assumed I was always as calm as a Shield was supposed to be, and therefore accepting the bad news with grace and equanimity.

"Lee, is that any way to dress when people will see you?" Mother complained.

I looked down at myself. I was wearing a beige shirt of rough cotton and dark brown linen trousers with my sturdiest boots. "It's perfectly sensible wear for an extended walk over uneven terrain."

"You're not on uneven terrain now, are you?" Mother pointed out. "As Taro said, you have a duty to look your best when you're to appear before other people."

Everyone was staring down at their plates, everyone except Mika. He was watching me with curiosity.

I put some bread and cheese on a plate and brought that and my coffee to the table. "It is my custom to change after breakfast." I sat down and began to eat.

It was unkind and, I thought, unlike her to behave this way in front of others.

"I can't see how you ladies can be so hungry," Taro commented, breaking the uncomfortable silence. "I know you stop at the miller's and stuff yourself with freshly baked bread."

"Early morning walks are excellent for increasing the appetite," said Fiona.

"Surely it would be safer to do it later in the day," said Mother. "When there are more people about."

"I have never felt unsafe," Fiona said, sipping at some mint tea. "And there is something special about that time of day, just before to just after sunrise. Quiet and new. I feel I can sense the power of the land, breathe it in, wear it on my skin."

A year before, I would have dismissed Fiona's words as nothing more than sentiment. A poetic way of describing her feelings. Soil didn't have power. Titleholders didn't have profound connections to the land. It was all just fancy and emotion.

I had learned a lot in the past year. I had learned that the casting of spells was real, not merely a means of conning people out of their money. I had had a spell cast on me. I had cast spells myself. I had seen a man suss out emotional vibrations from rooms with a bowl of water. Radia could feel when the wind was coming. Maybe there were other forms of power of which I hadn't yet heard.

Was Fiona's walking about the land at a specific time of day some kind of ritual, some kind of spell? Spells came in all sorts of forms, and not all of them required rhymes. But Fiona had said she couldn't cast spells, that she had tried and failed.

Maybe I was looking for proof of casting where none existed. That was a drastic shift in attitude. I generally felt uneasy with such shifts. They could be kind of painful.

"What have you planned to do today?" Fiona asked my mother. "You're welcome to my horses. I can have one of the servants show you the grounds."

"That is most kind of you," said my mother. "But we'd prefer to stay close to the manor for a few days."

Were we going to tell them who was coming and why? That would be embarrassing and aggravating. Everyone would probably treat the whole thing as a form of entertainment. But I didn't know how we could hide it. The fact that the Prides hadn't sent me a letter suggested to me that they wanted to surprise me. They probably wanted me to be off balance. And they wanted me to feel pressured into fulfilling the contract. The best way to do that was to make it all very public.

"Are you all in good health?" Fiona asked.

"Certainly, but we haven't seen Lee or Shintaro for a good long while, and we would like to catch up."

I sort of thought we already had. That was what all the talking the day they'd arrived had been about, wasn't it? Was there more terrible news waiting for me?

So, what would be worse than being told you're expected

to marry a stranger? Being told you were going to lose a limb? Being told you were expected to move to Seventh Year and actually work in the family business you knew nothing about? Being told you couldn't be a Shield anymore?

And then my mood slid down into the black cavern below my feet. I didn't want to be there. I didn't want the food on my plate. I just wanted to go back to the suite and fume about it all in private. Though that wouldn't do anyone any good.

I would feel better once the Prides got there. They would make their complaint, I would say no, and everyone could go home. I could then focus on things that actually mattered.

Chapter Four

After breakfast, I went to the suite and no one followed me. My mood must have been clearly written on my face, which was something to be ashamed of, but I didn't care. It was nice to be alone. Now, I just needed something to distract me. And I knew what could do that.

The overmantel of the fireplace in our bedchamber had a false front. Fiona had shown it to me. In that overmantel I had hidden books. Books of spells. Originally, those tools of casting had been concealed in the overmantel while the Imperial Guards had been searching for those very articles. But then, I started reading the books myself.

I had learned that I could perform spells. The law didn't recognize the existence of spells. The law said spells were things people only pretended to cast, for the purpose of charlatanry. So pretending to cast spells was illegal while, in theory, actually performing spells was not.

Sometimes the law really didn't make sense.

I was embarrassed by how fascinated I was with the whole subject. There was something about it that seemed lazy and childish to me, as it was a form of wish fulfillment in an attempt to avoid working for what one wanted. And yet, now that I knew spells worked, the nature of them entranced me. Why did words spoken in a spell have more power than when they were spoken in ordinary conversation? So many of the powders and liquids used in spells were nothing more than baking ingredients or healing elixirs. Why did they have power only when combined in a spell? Why could spells be successfully cast in some places but not in others? Why could some people cast spells while others couldn't?

I could cast spells. Fiona said she couldn't. I had no idea whether Taro could. To my knowledge, he hadn't even tried. He didn't really seem interested, which was unfathomable to me. The things that could be accomplished with spells were incredible. And I would wager he would be good at it. He was Shintaro Karish. He could do anything.

I pulled out a book. It had been written one hundred and thirty years before. I couldn't understand the motive behind it being written, as, from what I understood, casting hadn't really worked back then. According to what I had been told and what I had read, after the First Landed had come to our world with their machines, mechanical wonders that could fly and communicate and dig up soil, the magic inherent in the world had blinked out, and had started returning only a couple of generations ago. So why would anyone write a book about spells when no spells worked was beyond me.

But I was glad that the writer, a Lisbe Hut, had been motivated to do so, for her book was interesting. It was about taking shortcuts while casting spells, finding ways to decrease the number of tools and ingredients. Which was brilliant. The biggest liability with casting was all the paraphernalia it required. That was cumbersome, and I could easily imagine situations where a person would find herself without all the necessary tools. Or taking so long to perform the spells that the ability to do any good had passed before the spell was completed.

Not everyone could use the shortcuts, Hut warned. The principal purpose of spells, of assembling the ingredients and speaking the words, was to bring the mind into focus. Not everyone had the required mental discipline to skip the steps and bring the mind to a pinpoint of concentration.

I figured I had as good a chance as anyone. Being a Shield required a lot of discipline and focus. And despite some mishaps, I'd picked up casting pretty quickly.

Not quickly enough, though. Fiona's husband, Dane, had been out whaling during dangerously strong winds. Knowing I had been experimenting with casting, Fiona had pleaded with me to calm the wind. I had tried to calm it and had been completely unsuccessful, resulting in the death of Dane and two other whalers. In time, I had been able to make the spell work, but too late to be any use to Fiona or Dane.

I regretted that intensely. I had liked Dane. He had been a friendly, uncomplicated man dedicated to the best interests of his wife and child. It wasn't fair that he had died.

I never wanted to be caught so useless again. That meant reading, studying, practicing.

All right. Relax. Long breath in, long breath out, long breath in, long breath out. That was it. Let it all go. It would all be sorted.

After concentrating on nothing but my own breathing for a while, the whirling in my mind eased and I could think more clearly. I picked up the book again. I turned the page and found two versions of the same spell.

It was a levitation spell. That could be interesting. And useful. The list of components was rather lengthy considering what the spell was meant to accomplish, but that wasn't unusual. Some casts meant to do little required a long list of ingredients and steps, while some meant to accomplish something significant were simple. Casting didn't always make sense.

I pulled out all of my supplies and sat down on the floor. I always preferred to be on the floor when I cast. It made me feel more stable and connected to my environment.

Lemon juice to rub on the inside of the wrists, mint for under the tongue, resin powder to rub at my throat, red nut oil to be mixed with mustard seed and black pepper in which to dip each of my middle fingers. Once everything had been rubbed and mixed and dabbed as required, I looked at the candle I had laid on the floor. "Candle be air, rise beyond care, fly up above, as wings of a dove." I clenched my hands on my knees to keep from moving them. Gestures mattered while casting. "Rise beyond care. Rise beyond care." I felt a little pull in my mind and a jittery sensation in my stomach. That latter sensation meant casting was being done. I stared at the candle, telling it to rise.

The candle drifted up and hung in the air. Huh. Managed it first time. I let the candle drift down to the floor.

I washed off all the powders, then resumed my position on the floor. I put another mint leaf and some of the resin powder under my tongue. The resin powder tasted foul and I longed to spit it out, but this was the shortcut. "Candle be air, rise above care, fly up above, as wings of a dove."

I felt the same tug in my mind, only harder. Nothing happened. I concentrated on the foul taste in my mouth, letting its sensation soak into my mind. I stared at the candle, stared at it hard, until everything that was not the candle went black. "Rise beyond care."

The candle floated up. I sighed in satisfaction. The candle dropped to the floor. The shortcut required much more intense concentration, but that made sense to me. Fewer tools meant a stronger mental component.

I turned back to the book. There were other spells, and I tried those for which I had the supplies. I was able to perform all the shortcuts, but when it gave me a headache I decided to give them a rest and just read through the rest of the book, noticing several more spells I would like to try.

Suddenly, I felt something through my bond to Taro, from wherever he was. I felt the mental shields that protected his mind come down. That meant a natural disaster, probably an earthquake, was threatening Flown Raven. He needed to open his mind to the forces that made up the earthquake, so he could direct them somewhere harmless and drain the earthquake of its power. But the forces of the earthquake were not the only forces swirling about. My job was to protect Taro's mind from the forces he was not channeling, to calm his mind and heart and blood against the strain channeling put on them.

When we first bonded, I had had no difficulty Shielding Taro, but since then circumstances had seemed to conspire to make channeling difficult for us. At one point, a rogue Source had learned how to cause disasters, rather than calm them, and those events had been difficult to channel. At another point, I'd been ill. The most recent source of trouble had been our transfer to Flown Raven. Taro had been born in Flown Raven. It was the policy of the Triple S that Sources were never posted at their place of birth. They tended to have trouble channeling.

And we had had trouble. The forces had rushed through Taro so quickly and so hard that Taro had barely been able to control them, and I had been barely able to Shield him. I had been close to admitting to the Triple S that we needed to be transferred, something Taro, for some reason, hadn't wanted done.

Fiona owned a book that had been printed by the First Landed, those people from another world who had landed on our world to build some kind of colony. Most of what they'd brought to our world had been destroyed and buried by natural disasters, but this book had been discovered on Fiona's land after an earthquake. It was a book of spells, mostly designed to deal with weather as well as natural disasters. Academic Reid, who had translated the book, had guessed that the spells hadn't worked for the First Landed. And perhaps they hadn't. But they worked for me, provided I used them through Taro. When he opened his mind to the forces, it gave me access to them that I didn't have on my own. When I cast the spells then, they worked.

I kept the necessary ingredients in my purse at all times. I was never without my purse. I pulled the purse off my belt, sat on the floor, and dumped all the ingredients.

I rubbed dark orange hannan powder on my left inner wrist. "Soil to obey me," I said. I rubbed white icin powder into the hannan. "Air to subdue soil." From a vial I poured whale oil on the powders. "Water shape soil." I picked up a red handled knife. "I call to you all." Very carefully, I made a shallow cut on my wrist. "Bide by me." I sprinkled dirt into my palm and made a fist. "I hold the soil still. Soil trembles no more. Bide by me."

Through Taro I could feel the forces rushing about, straining his heart, pushing at his mind. It was invigorating, and it could be frightening. The forces could get too strong. They had the power to kill a Source. If the Source died, so did the Shield, and the natural disaster would be free to wreak destruction.

As I spoke the words of the spell, I felt something moving within me, something slow and soothing. It flowed from me and through our bond into Taro, calming and slowing the forces. The power of the forces thinned and stretched out, making them easier to handle. It meant it took longer than usual to channel the event, but at least no one's brains were in danger of exploding.

With the use of the spell, the channeling went as channeling was supposed to. The forces flowed through Taro. His blood and mind and heart suffered only the usual amount of strain. I had no fear of being forced to lower my Shields. It was all good, and not a single tremor touched the ground. Job done, we each allowed our Shields to slide back into their natural states.

And then something hit the window with a thud that made me jump. "Son of a—" I stood and moved to the window. The wind was sounding pretty brutal out there. I listened for Radia's horn but couldn't hear it.

When the wind got strong enough, the Wind Watcher—Radia—was to blow a horn called a fischen to warn everyone in Flown Raven. She wasn't quite capable of it right then, and Tarce had volunteered to take care of that duty. I now saw the flaw in that arrangement. What if Tarce wasn't close to Radia, didn't receive a message in time?

I cleaned up my casting tools and went to Radia's room. She was sitting in a chair by the window, reading what looked like a novel. She smiled as I entered. "Shield Mallorough! Good afternoon."

I suddenly felt bad that I wasn't there to visit her, and that I hadn't been visiting her often enough at all. I sat down. "I'm just wondering, do you think the fischen needs to be blown? Because I'll do it if it does."

"No, no. The wind is not so strong."

"It sounds strong."

She smiled again. "Trust me."

Ah, yes. Sometimes I could be arrogant, such as challenging someone else's ability to do their job. "Are your needs being seen to?"

She looked rueful then. "Lord Tarce is a frequent visitor. I have more than enough of . . . everything."

"Including his company?"

"I would never say such a thing."

"But you would feel it?"

She just gave me a look. She was more mature than I.

"Did Dias annoy you?" I asked.

She smiled. "He's charming."

"He isn't free, you know."

"Shield Mallorough, we were only talking."

"I know." I was a simple person. I didn't really comprehend the practice of flirting with no intention of seeking a romantic attachment. What was the point?

Though Taro seemed to like it.

Radia smiled again. "You're so very serious."

It was entertaining that she, in particular, accused me of that crime. She'd always struck me as a fairly somber person. "Then I am in good company."

She didn't dispute it.

She looked down and plucked at a loose thread on the arm of her chair. "I understand you can cast spells."

I did not like to hear that. "Do you?"

She didn't pause at my chilly tone. "Normally, I wouldn't discuss such . . . delicate matters. But it's the wind rock. No one can lift it into the arch. No one knows how it was done the first time."

The wind rock was the outward sign that the wind was too strong. A massive slab of stone suspended in an arch of the same material, if the wind could move it, the fischen must be blown.

Many also considered it a talisman of good luck. No one had been able to tell me why, merely that it was a belief created through many generations.

The wind rock had been knocked down by the same rock slide that had destroyed Radia's home. "There are no records?" That was shocking. The post of Wind Watcher was so important. Vital. How could there be no records?

"There are, but nothing that addressed the creation of the rock. Too far back, I suppose."

"I see."

"If the rock can't be raised, everyone will be devastated. And most of them will blame Her Grace. They will claim it is proof she's not fit to be the titleholder."

Damn it, we were supposed to be past the stage of the tenants grumbling under Fiona's rule. "I don't think I could do anything about that. It's so heavy. It's huge."

"Does that matter? For a spell?"

"I don't know. Wouldn't it?"

Radia shrugged. "Not my sphere of knowledge."

Not really mine, either.

The door flew open. To my utter shock, the Dowager Duchess, Taro's mother, was standing there glaring at me. "Where is Shintaro?" she demanded.

It took me a moment to collect myself enough to answer. "I don't—"

The door was slammed closed.

"My Lady," I heard Bailey through the door. "If you would let me see to your comfort in the parlor."

I didn't hear a response.

Radia and I exchanged looks of alarm. "Excuse me," I said, and I left.

"My lady, please."

I followed the racket up to my suite. The Dowager had barged right in, a young man I didn't recognize with her.

Taro's mother. A horrible, horrible woman. I hated her more than any other person I knew, because of how she treated Taro. To my knowledge, she had never contacted Taro, ever, before his brother had died, and after he died it had been only to criticize him, give him ridiculous or demeaning orders, or try to browbeat him into seeking the Westsea title. And every time Taro had to deal with her, he came back twisted into knots and furious and, though he would never admit it, feeling less of himself.

Except for the last time. A few weeks ago, Taro finally laid into her, and it had been glorious to see. He had been calm and firm as he let her know she had no influence over him and never would, that he would do nothing she wanted, ever, simply because she wanted it. He would not seek the title, no matter what she did. He would never trust a word she said. I had been so proud of him. She had been floored, and we hadn't heard from her since. I had hoped we'd endured the last of her interference.

"Ah, hell," Taro said from behind me, making me start. I disliked it when he snuck up on me. "Think we can still escape?"

"Never," I whispered in dismay. The Dowager had stormed the castle, so to speak. We wouldn't get rid of her until she said what she wanted to say.

I didn't see the Dowager herself, but her companion turned to face us, and his appearance made me pause for a moment. He was stunning. Dark brown hair cut short, the greenest eyes I'd ever seen, gorgeous cheekbones. He smiled, showing off beautiful teeth. He was tall and broad in the shoulders and his hands were long and capable looking.

The Dowager did like her men young and beautiful.

Taro strode to the door leading to our bedchamber. "Just what are you looking for, Your Grace?" he demanded.

"That is an appalling way to greet someone," I heard the Dowager say, and then she came into the sitting room. "What kind of manners are those?"

One marvel about the Dowager was that she had no problem demanding exquisite courtesy from others while displaying none herself. It was magnificent in its consistent hypocrisy. I almost admired her for it. Such indifference to the feelings of others surely took years of practice.

Taro and his mother looked more alike than any two people I had ever met, and that included twins. She was short and slim, with black hair untouched by gray, slightly slanted black eyes, delicate features and golden skin. There were few lines on her face, perhaps because her face was usually expressionless.

"Not nearly as bad as the lack of manners that would allow a person to rifle through someone else's things," I said. In times past I had remained silent in the face of the Dowager's attacks. It hadn't been my place to speak, and I hadn't wanted to exacerbate the friction in a relationship that might possibly improve. But the stunts she had pulled since we had come to Flown Raven, including spreading rumors that I'd been sleeping with another man, and Taro's ultimate decision that he would have nothing more to do with her, left me feeling free to say what I liked.

Of course, I knew whatever words I said would bounce right off her skull, and I might as well save my breath.

She smiled, and I thought the shock it caused would stop my heart.

"Shintaro, Dunleavy," she said with a warmth that might have fooled someone who didn't know her. "This is Linder Hart. He is the son of a dear friend of mine in Tree Valley. He's gone through a difficult time, and he's come out here to rest and reflect. I was hoping that during his stay here, you would take care of him, Shintaro. Everyone else his age will be busy."

Was that a stealthy insult? Like Taro should be ashamed of not having a lot to do all day? Was I being paranoid? Was there such a thing as being too suspicious when one was dealing with the Dowager?

"I see," Taro said dubiously.

"How enthusiastic," the Dowager drawled. "Can you not assume the cloak of interest for Linder's sake?"

"It all depends on why you want me to do this," said Taro. With good reason. The last time the Dowager had a gorgeous young guest, the plan was to seduce Taro away from me. How did we know this wasn't more of the same?

I still wasn't sure why the Dowager wanted to separate us. While she was attempting to lure Taro away with a toothsome young woman, she had been trying to convince me to leave Taro, providing examples of when Sources and Shields had been granted by the Triple S the right not to work with each other. That contradicted everything I'd ever heard about what the Triple S expected from their Pairs, whether the two liked each other or not. I had been tempted to ask the Triple S about it, just to find out, but Taro would probably not be thrilled about it if he learned of my inquiries. He preferred to keep our contact with the Triple S council to a minimum, and I had no problem acting in concert with that wish.

"Merely because I've been assured over and over again by several people that my son is compassionate, and good company."

I felt badly for Linder, standing there silently while the Dowager and Taro argued over him. I wasn't sure what to think of him. I'd despised the Dowager's last guest on sight, beautiful and elegant and everything I was not. But then, she'd known she was there to separate Taro and me, going so far as to show up naked in the bed I shared with Taro. Linder looked a little like he didn't know why he was there. It made me think he was an unwitting accomplice to the Dowager's scheme.

Because there was no doubt this was part of a scheme. Last time, she'd tried to use a woman to seduce Taro away from me. This time, she was trying a man. Never let it be said that the Dowager wasn't thorough. She was prepared to test every option in her quest to have Taro take the title.

"Linder," Taro said suddenly. "I won't be sleeping with you. Neither will Lee. As long as you accept that, everything will be fine."

I couldn't help the small noise I made in my throat in reaction to that blunt assertion. Taro was usually more delicate.

Linder looked confused.

"Shintaro, really," the Dowager chastised him.

"Don't even start. You know you've tried it before."

"I'm sure I don't know what you mean," the Dowager drawled.

Taro didn't actually roll his eyes, but he looked like he really wanted to. Neat trick.

"Are you not going to ring for refreshments?" the Dowager asked.

Taro sighed and pulled on the bell.

Really? We were actually going to entertain them? Really?

"Shall we be seated?" the Dowager suggested, and so we all sat. Hester came in and Taro asked for tea and biscuits.

"Linder's mother gambled away her family's entire estate," the Dowager announced.

Yes, I was sure Linder was thrilled to have that information just tossed to strangers like that. I didn't know where to look. Would he prefer we pretend we hadn't heard? Would he think us disgustingly callous if we didn't express sympathy?

The Dowager, as usual, didn't need any response from anyone else. "I have offered him respite here, away from wagging tongues. And I thought, with all of the titleholders in the area, he might be able to find a place with a family here."

I frowned. I almost asked what kind of place she had in mind, with him looking as he did. To my knowledge, people didn't like hiring attractive servants. It lured the youngsters in the family away from more advantageous society.

Then again, maybe Linder would still be considered an appealing connection. That the money was all gone didn't necessarily mean the family was considered worthless.

"What kind of talents do you have?" Taro asked him.

"I am well educated," he said, and his voice was disappointing. Rather thin. "And I have a great deal of experience drafting documents. Correspondence, survey maps, contracts. Our family's solicitor is—was—close to retirement, and Mother didn't want to hire a replacement."

That sounded surprisingly useful for an aristocrat. Although . . . was he an aristocrat? Merchants had solicitors, too.

And it wasn't too terribly far-fetched that the Dowager was honestly trying to help him. She did have friends, hard as that was to believe. And I had no doubt she had firm connections in Flown Raven and the extended area. I could almost believe she really was acting only in Linder's best interest.

Except, if all that were true, she would feel no need to introduce him to us.

Hester came in with the tea tray. The Dowager assumed responsibility for serving us. I was supposed to do that, as the Dowager was a guest, but she couldn't be expected to observe the niceties when she could be dominating everyone's attention.

"Linder has an interest in bench dancing, Dunleavy," the Dowager commented. "I told him you were an accomplished dancer."

Well, I was a Shield. Shields were taught to dance the benches from a very early age, an age when children were particularly stupid when it came to figuring out what was dangerous. And I was good at it, though many professional dancers could easily defeat me.

Linder smiled at me. It was a pretty smile, and it appeared genuine. I couldn't be anything other than friendly. "I do enjoy bench dancing. There's no opportunity to do it here, though." And I missed it. It had been so long since I'd properly danced, I had probably lost much of my skill at it.

"Why not?"

"Well, as far as I know, there are no dancers here. No benches and no bars. No one to handle the bars."

"As far as you know? Does that mean you haven't asked?"

"Well, aye, that's right."

He grinned. "So you can't know for sure."

"I suppose not."

"Lovely." The Dowager clapped her hands together in apparent enthusiasm. "That's something the two of you can investigate together."

I could only stare at her.

"Seriously, she's not sleeping with you," Taro told Linder.

He couldn't really think I was the Dowager's target this time. What would I want with someone like Linder when I had Taro?

Linder looked embarrassed. No doubt the poor boy didn't know what to say. Really, who would?

"Shintaro, you're being impossible," the Dowager told him coldly. Taro didn't even glance at her.

There was a knock on the door. "It's us," Dias called through. I got up and opened the door. It was my two brothers, but not my mother. "We have company."

"So?" said Dias. "Are you ashamed of us?"

Not ashamed. Just wary about how they would behave in front of the Dowager. And what the Dowager would say to them. Insults dripped off her lips like grease, and those insults were often well aimed. My brothers would no doubt respond with insults of their own, and the tension in the room would escalate into something unbearable.

"Your Grace, Linder, these are my brothers, Traders Dias and Mika Mallorough. Dias and Mika, this is Her Grace, the Dowager Duchess of Westsea, and Linder Hart." Did Linder have a title?

The Dowager favored them with a cool nod. Linder grinned. "I wasn't aware Pairs were allowed to keep their family with them," he said.

"These are special circumstances," I told them. "My brothers are merely visiting."

Dias and Mika pulled two chairs into the conversational circle. "Shame on you, Lee," Mika scolded me. "I'm sure I told you to bring any handsome men to me." He winked at Linder.

Zaire, that was ridiculous.

Linder didn't seem to think so. Mika was another recipient of one of Linder's pretty smiles.

And I developed a brilliant idea. "Mika, Dias, Linder is new to the area and has few acquaintances. Perhaps you can keep him entertained."

"We wouldn't dream of imposing on your time," the Dowager said quickly.

Ha! Scuppered that plan, didn't I?

"Not at all," said Mika with a broad smile. "The more the merrier."

Linder smiled a lot, but there seemed to be a particular warmth to the smile he gave to Mika right then. "Thank you. I appreciate it."

He sounded sincere. I still didn't know what to think of him. But the Dowager Duchess looked irritated and sour. I was prepared to like him just for that.

Chapter Five

My brothers, Taro, and Linder immersed themselves in a discussion about gambling. Apparently my brothers were avid gamblers. I thought Linder was insane to engage in the activity that had caused his mother to lose his home, but no one was paying attention to me.

No one was paying attention to the Dowager, either. She scowled. I bit back laughter.

This was fun.

Hester returned to the room with a message from Nab Browne. The healer wanted to see me. I was a little irritated with being summoned, and I'd been enjoying the show the boys had been putting on, but I let myself be pulled away. Whatever Browne wanted, it was probably important. I made my way to Browne's cottage with a quick pace.

I knocked on Browne's door. I heard footsteps within the small cottage. Browne had a habit of dragging me in once she opened the door. No matter how quickly I stepped in, it wasn't quick enough. So, as usual, she grabbed my sleeve and pulled me in. And, as usual, she had all the curtains tightly tied together. It couldn't be because she was trying to hide the fact that I was there. I was certain everyone knew I visited her fairly often. It could only be to make sure people couldn't see exactly what we were doing. She sold her services as a spell caster. It wouldn't help her business if people could watch her through her windows and figure out how to cast spells on their own.

Nab Browne was younger than I would have expected a healer to be, slightly taller than I, with blond hair usually worn in a long braid. She was levelheaded and intelligent. It wasn't long ago that the Imperial Guards had tried to have her flogged, yet here she was, continuing to use spells as though none of it had happened.

"Please, have a seat," she said. "I want to talk to you about a few things."

I sat at the table and accepted a mug of tea.

"There are a group of casters in the area," Browne explained. "All within a half-day's ride. We meet once a month in the early morning. Our next meeting is in three days, at dawn. I think you should come to the meeting."

"Why?" Was it a good idea for casters to meet on a regular basis? I had no doubt that at some point, Imperial Guards would be coming back to hunt for spell casters. The ones who had already been here had no doubt spells were being used in the area. Surely a group of casters holding regular meetings would be easier to spot?

"You appear to have some skill at it," said Browne. "You may be a very powerful caster. And if that's the case, you shouldn't be left free to stumble around on your own."

I wouldn't call what I was doing stumbling around. There was a certain amount of trial and error, of course, but that was to be expected in learning any kind of skill. "I really don't think that's necessary."

"You are a Shield. Are there not certain rules and ethics about what you do?"

"Of course."

"Yet you do not think casting requires similar rules?"

Well, actually, I did. Not everyone could cast, but those who could were left free to do whatever they could manage. I didn't trust the common sense of the average person. I knew that was arrogant, but I'd seen too many people do too many stupid things.

But I didn't need to be watched. I knew enough to be

careful. However, I couldn't say that without revealing my arrogance.

"Besides, it is a wonderful forum for learning. We share difficulties and new ideas. And gossip."

I had to grin at that. If others were going to talk about me, it was only fair that I talk about them. "All right."

"Good. Come here first. I'll take you to Sonal Snow's homestead. That's where the meeting will be held this month."

"Excellent. Thank you." I set my empty mug on the table and shifted to rise to my feet.

"Just one more matter," said Browne.

I settled back on the chair.

"You will recall that the first time you came to me for assistance, we came to an understanding that I would provide you with supplies and advice, and in exchange you would help me when I asked for it."

"Aye," I said uneasily. I hadn't been thrilled with the agreement when we'd made it. I wasn't even sure why I was driven to make it. I had found the idea of casting interesting, but not essential. I hadn't known at the time how helpful being able to cast would prove to be. Yet I had made the agreement. I couldn't renege.

Browne rose to her feet and took a small bag from a shelf. "This was found on the shore." In the bag was a small rock, about the size of the last joint of my pinky. It was a translucent blue. "You've seen something like this before," she guessed. Possibly from my lack of reaction.

"I might have," I said.

She chuckled. "You might have. How convincing. The rumor is that there is a whole cave full of stones like these."

There was. I had been to that cave. I'd been stuck in that cave, with Fiona, in the dark, for hours. Academic Reid had explored the cave as well. I wondered if he had been the source of the rumor. I doubted Fiona would have told anyone—she'd been determined to keep it a secret—or Dane, and I knew I hadn't. Well, other than Taro. That didn't count.

"There is also a rumor that you and Her Grace spent some time in that cave."

Really, why did people talk about us so much? "Half the ridge collapsed. The cave might not even exist anymore."

"If you look for it and can't find it, then of course nothing more can be done."

"And if I find this cave?"

Browne pulled another bag from the shelf, this one the size of a person's head. "I want you to collect some more rocks for me."

"I can't do that," I objected. "Everything in that cave belongs to Her Grace. I refuse to steal for you."

"This is not a precious stone. If the others in the cave are like this, they're of no value to Her Grace."

"How do you know whether it's a precious stone or not?" Fiona didn't even know that.

"I just do."

What an irritating response, but if I asked her again, she would probably just give the same answer. I disliked conversational circles. "Then what do you want them for?"

"Look." She blew on the stone, and then she whistled at it, a long, low, single note.

To my utter shock, the stone began to glow. A moment later, an aura developed around it, white light slightly tinged with blue. Browne reached up and took a hair pin from her hair. She stopped whistling to draw breath, and the aura blinked out, but it appeared again as soon as she resumed whistling. She put the tip of the pin against the aura and pushed. The tips of her fingers whitened with the effort of pushing the pin, but it didn't penetrate the aura.

I'd never seen anything quite like it. It amazed me, the different things casting could do. "How did you learn to do that?"

"I experimented. Casting isn't just about doing what's already been done. It's about finding new ways of doing things."

"But how did you even think of whistling at it?"

She shrugged. "Sometimes things react to vibration."

Actually, I had seen that, humming at a bowl of water. Though that practitioner had said that wasn't casting. Maybe this wasn't casting, either. "Can I try?"

"Certainly." She put the small stone in my hand.

I blew on it, and I needed her to whistle for me so I could imitate the right pitch. Once I reached it, I felt a tingle in my hand and the aura appeared around the stone. It was amazing. "What else can it do?"

"I don't know. I only just received it."

"From who?" I demanded.

"I'm not prepared to tell you that."

"So why are you telling me this?"

"I want you to get more for me."

I scowled at her.

Browne laughed. "You don't need to be so tense, dear. I'm not your enemy or opponent. Nor am I Her Grace's opponent. You might remember that I have good reason to be grateful to her. I swore an oath of loyalty to her. I take that oath seriously."

Still, I hesitated. I was very sure Fiona would not want this.

Browne raised an eyebrow. "Do you not take your oaths seriously?"

She had a point, damn it. I would have been furious if someone had suggested I might give my word and then refuse to honor it. "I will go to Her Grace and ask to be able to take some of the stones for you. I will do my best to persuade her. That is as far as I will go. If she refuses, I will find some other way to repay you." I would requisition some jewelry and give it to her. We weren't supposed to do that, requisition items to give to other people, unless they were our children or partners, but it was less dangerous than other things Browne might require of me.

"I suppose I can accept that," said Browne.

"Can I borrow this so I can demonstrate its properties?" Browne didn't look thrilled with that. "I think it would go a long way in convincing her. I promise you you'll get it back."

Browne nodded. "All right."

I left then, the stone in my purse. The sky had gone black and the night air was damp and cool. Sometimes, I liked the chronically brisk weather of Flown Raven. It was refreshing. Taro hated it. He often found it too cold.

Bailey met me in the foyer of the manor. "I'm afraid you missed the evening meal, ma'am."

"That's all right." I could fix myself something simple in the kitchen. "Do you happen to know where Her Grace is?"

"I believe Her Grace has retired to her suite."

"Thank you." I wasn't comfortable with the idea of disturbing Fiona in her private rooms, but it was the best way to ensure that we wouldn't be overheard. I felt the properties of the stones should be kept quiet, at least for now. I went to her door and knocked loudly. I heard a faint voice telling me to come in. I entered and passed through the sitting room to the bedchamber.

Fiona was sitting on her bed, her back resting against the headboard, her sleeping son draped across her lap. She was looking down at him with a soft smile, stroking his blond hair. "He should be in his bed," she said in a low voice. "But sometimes I like to keep him with me."

He was a beautiful child, and delightful. I should be watching her with him, taking notes. While it was unlikely that I could conceive, the act of channeling tending to counteract the reproductive processes of both men and women, Shields and Sources, the less frequent occurrences of events in Flown Raven meant I had a chance.

"I come with a request from Healer Browne," I said.

"Why could she not speak to me herself?"

"I think she felt you would be more likely to grant the request if it came from me." And maybe I should have asked as though I were the one making the request.

"That's nonsense. I have great respect for Healer Browne."

Feeling awkward, I said, "She's heard about the crystal cave. She wants some of the crystals."

Fiona frowned. "I imagine everyone would want some of the crystals, if they learned about the cave. I can't give them to one without giving some to everyone, and I'm not prepared to do that."

"A titleholder can't favor people?"

"Not if she doesn't want to sow discord."

"Browne doesn't want them for whatever monetary value they might have."

"Why else could she want them?"

I took the stone out of my purse, held it up, and whistled. When its aura appeared, I pushed against it with my finger. The aura was a cool, solid surface.

Fiona gasped. "Let me try." She held out her hand. I gave the stone to her. She whistled at various pitches, including the correct one, and nothing happened. She sighed with disappointment. "Why can't I do any of this? I'm the titleholder. My connection to the land should give me the ability to do this."

I had nothing to say to that.

"All right," she said. "I'll take you there. Assuming the cave survived the ridge collapsing."

"Thank you."

"How much is she expecting?"

"She gave me a bag to fill."

"Hm."

"It's not large."

"I'll take you in, in a couple of days. Will that satisfy her?"

"I believe so. Thank you."

She merely smiled and looked down at her son.

I had disturbed her long enough. "Have a good evening."

I went down to the kitchen for some bread and cheese and then went back up to the suite I shared with Taro.

Taro was in our sitting room, playing a card game for one, looking bored out of his mind. "Where did you take off to?" he asked.

"Browne wants some of the crystals from the cave. I asked Fiona if she would allow it, and she agreed."

"What does Nab want with them?"

"Apparently they might be useful for casting." I sat on the table beside Taro's web of cards. "So who do you think Linder is for? You or me?"

"Whoever would have him, I think." He grinned. "And it looks like your brother will. I adore Mika, by the way."

"Why does your mother want us separated so badly? She wasn't anything like this when we first bonded. I mean, she didn't like me, but she didn't try to interfere with the bond."

"She thinks I'm too much under your influence."

"But she sees how we work. She knows that's not true."

He snickered.

I slapped his shoulder. "Even if it were true, why would she care?"

"She thinks if you leave, I'll be open to trying to get the title back."

"If I leave, then, I would just take you with me."

"Not if you have a handsome, smiling young man to take with you."

"I already have a handsome, smiling young man."

He rolled his eyes.

"I wish there were something we could do about her." I sighed.

"Let's kill her," Taro suggested.

"That's in very poor taste."

"Yet appealing, all the same."

It kind of was. Any permanent removal would be alluring. "Maybe we could pretend to have a rift."

"What would that accomplish?"

"She might take a step back?"

"We couldn't keep it up indefinitely, and then she'd take a step forward."

"Do you know of any friends of hers that you could invite out here, someone who would distract her?"

"Zaire, she's filled my ears with so many names of friends and connections that I couldn't fish out just one."

"Maybe we could convince Fiona to send her away."

"Aye, but then she might go to Erstwhile. There's something going on between her and the Emperor. I don't want to encourage whatever scheme they're planning. I want to keep an eye on her."

I raised an eyebrow at him. Us? Keep an eye on her?

"I know, I know." He sighed. "She's just so annoying. And she never quits. I told her she couldn't do anything to convince me to fall into her plans. She brings in Linder anyway. When he doesn't accomplish what she wants, she'll try something else."

"We just have to wait it out. We'll be transferred in a couple of years."

"The council said they thought it was to their advantage to keep us here. Whatever that means."

"I don't think it means we'll be stuck here forever."

"We have no way of knowing."

"I can ask."

"You think they'll tell you the truth?"

Here was the thing. The Triple S had raised us, taken care of us, taught us, to the best of their ability, what we needed to know. But Taro had been leery of the Triple S since before we'd met. According to him, the council called Pairs back to Shidonee's Gap at times, and then those Pairs were never seen again. It was why Taro didn't want the Triple S council to know about his special talents. He could cause events, not just stop them. His touch could ease pain. I felt he could actually heal to some extent, though he denied that.

The Triple S council was suspicious. They had questioned us about strange occurrences they had heard about, occurrences that were related to Taro's use of his skills. And we'd had to lie in response.

Still . . . "It can't hurt to ask."

"They'll want to know why you're asking."

"We could tell them your mother was trying to drag us into local politics."

"Which we would be expected to ignore. We are adults, Lee."

"You know, I've seen a whole lot of adults do a lot of childish things. Why can't we do that occasionally?"

"Because we're better than them."

I just looked at him.

He grinned back. "Still think we shouldn't kill her?"

"Stop tempting me."

His eyes gleamed with humor. "Never." He pulled my leg closer to him and peeled off my boot. "Think we can convince someone to lug up the big bath?"

"Feeling the need for cleansing, do you?"

"Not at all."

I smiled.

Chapter Six

As usual, Taro was gone when I woke the next morning. I took advantage of his absence in order to stretch out fully on the bed, on my stomach, each hand and foot directed to a corner of the mattress. I dozed for a while, and every time I opened my eyes the air got a little lighter.

In time, though, hunger and a need for coffee prompted me to rise. As did the two obnoxious birds screaming at each other right outside my window. I would have thrown a nice heavy book at them if I hadn't thought books were too important to endure such handling.

Dias was the only one in the sitting room, sipping on coffee and tearing a croissant apart. "Morning, darling," he greeted me.

"Good morning." I filled my own cup with the dark blood of life and intelligence. "Did you sleep well?"

"Wonderfully. This house is very quiet." He popped a piece of pastry into his mouth. "I didn't see much of you yesterday," he said.

"I was busy."

"Doing what?"

"Nothing that I want to talk about in front of so many

people." Maids were constantly coming in and going out, topping up dishes and making sure the beverages were still hot.

He waved a hand in dismissal. "It is part of a servant's job to keep his master's secrets."

Oh, that was right, he was used to servants. At the Academy, we had been careful about what we said in front of the people who cooked and cleaned for us. We believed they would report everything we did to the professors or the headmistress. I understood wealthy people treated their own servants differently, as though they weren't there at all. That didn't mean I was going to talk about anything in front of these servants. I had seen that they were prepared to gossip about me, and I didn't like it. "Maybe later."

He shrugged. "Fine. We'll talk about something else."

"Excellent." I sat at the table across from him.

He snagged one of my croissants from my plate. "You weren't deliberately avoiding us because of how Mother was acting yesterday at breakfast?"

Actually, I'd forgotten all about that. "No."

"You seemed upset."

I didn't know if upset was quite the right word. "I was annoyed. She treated me like a child."

"Well, of course, she did. You are her child."

"But not *a* child. I'm an adult. I haven't lived under her roof for nearly twenty years. And she never criticized what I wore or told me what to do when she visited me at the Academy."

"You wore a uniform," he pointed out.

That was true.

"You just have to remember that Mother wants what's best for you."

"I'm able to decide what's best for me. And even if I weren't, I'm an adult. No one tells me what to wear. I don't understand why you let her tell you when to go to bed. That's ridiculous."

"I'm used to it."

"But you are too old to be letting her manage the minutiae of your life."

"Every time I've gone against her, it's turned out to be disastrous."

Disastrous? Really? "In what way?"

He thought about it for a few moments. "I knew this man, Del Finit, who was the son of one of our competitors. Mother told me not to socialize with him, but I didn't like being told who my friends could be, so I spent a great deal of time with him. It turned out that Finit was using me to get information about a supply of dark weave that Father was trying to buy. Finit's father was able to underbid Father. We'd been relying on having that weave and we had a couple bad years after that."

Hm. That would cause a bit of paranoia about social connections, I supposed, but . . . "Nothing I do can endanger them in that way."

"Father mentioned something about a Trader Fines."

I froze. "What about him?"

"Apparently he feels that he did you a great service in High Scape. Among other things, that it was through him that you found a healer who could treat you when you were poisoned."

"I see." I had been hoping that being transferred away from High Scape would be the end of any contact with Trader Fines and his crazy group of ash users. They'd tricked us into rubbing paste made from human ashes into our hands, the motive being that such an activity, illegal as it was, would prevent Taro and me from reporting Fines and his associates to the authorities for their criminal behavior. The thought of it still had the power to nauseate me.

"He contacted Father to share transport connections. Father had him investigated and didn't like what he saw."

"What did he see?"

"There are rumors that Fines is willing to go to lengths that, while not actually illegal, may be seen as unethical." Dias frowned. "I'm not sure. He won't tell us exactly what that entails. Which is aggravating. Anyway, Fines has been telling people throughout the merchant community that Father lacks honor and is ungrateful to those who assist him."

"And that's enough to do damage?"

"Reciprocation is a vital part of doing business."

Damn it. "I had no idea that could be used against the family."

"If Mother had been around, she would have been able to tell you what the implications of accepting help from a trader might be."

"I suppose she might have." And to be honest, I would have appreciated her insight. I'd had no idea how to handle Trader Fines and his cohorts. "But the family is still doing well, right? Despite this difficulty?" I didn't know what I'd do with myself if I had done real damage to my family's fortunes.

"Well enough."

Not the most reassuring of responses, but better than it could have been.

The others drifted in, Taro and Tarce and Fiona, my mother and Mika. I enjoyed their chatter, all of them—except Tarce—expert conversationalists who could make each other laugh. It was like watching a play.

Then Bailey walked into the dining room and ruined it all. "My lady, there are a Trader Cars Pride and a Trader Marcus Pride here to see Shield Mallorough."

I couldn't help sighing. I'd been hoping my mother had been exaggerating the persistence of the Prides, as unlikely as that would be. Or that something had happened to keep the Prides from coming. Nothing dangerous, of course. Just something like changing their minds, or Marcus tripping over someone he'd rather marry.

"I've put them in the front room."

My brothers, mother and I rose from the table. I looked at Taro, who had made no move. "Will you come?"

He appeared surprised. "Of course."

"They asked to see Shield Mallorough alone," said Bailey.

"Then they're going to be disappointed," said Mother.

That they would. I didn't need my family for moral support. I could say no all by myself. It was their reaction for which I wanted witnesses. Not that I assumed the Prides would be violent or anything like it. It was just that I didn't know them, and I would feel more comfortable with others there who could account for exactly what was said by them.

Two men were standing in the front room. The younger one was of average height, blond hair tied back, with brown eyes, slim and erect. The older man was gray, with a beard and a potbelly, taller than his son. They both faced the door as we walked in.

I didn't bother to introduce myself. "Yes?" I asked as coolly as I could.

The older man said, "You're Dunleavy Mallorough?"

"I am."

"I am Cars Pride. This is—"

"I know who you are," I interrupted.

"We requested that you come alone."

"I know," I answered, taking a seat. I made no effort to introduce anyone, I didn't invite anyone to sit down, and I didn't suggest to Bailey that he bring tea. After all, I was not the hostess of this manor.

Bailey withdrew without asking if he should bring refreshments. He was a smart man. I'd always liked him.

Taro sat beside me on the settee. He put his arm along the back of the settee, just above my shoulders. Claiming his significance to me in an unmistakable but not inappropriate manner. I appreciated the gesture.

The others, including the Prides, took chairs about the room. I think my mother had wanted the settee, as it was directly opposite the Prides, but I was angry with her. She'd done all of this. She'd colluded with these people in the past. I would have as my support the person who was closest to me, the person who meant the most to me. The person whose place Marcus Pride was trying to take.

"Speak," I ordered. We might as well get this over with.

Cars scowled. That was the kind of reaction I expected. "As your mother is present, I have no doubt you already know our purpose for being here."

I assumed a frown. "I have trouble believing that what she says about you is true. You couldn't possibly expect me to marry your son. Don't you know who I am?"

"The daughter of William and Teshia Mallorough and the subject of a contract sworn with me."

"That contract no longer exists."

Cars pulled a folded document out from the inside pocket of his waistcoat. "This is a copy right here."

It occurred to me that I should have taken a look at a copy myself, assuming Mother had brought one with her. "I misspoke. The contract is voided."

"You have an obligation to fulfill."

"The only obligation I have is to my Source." And he should know that. No matter what people heard about Pairs, ridiculous rumors and suspicions, what people were right about was the fact that the Pair bond was more important to Shields and Sources than any other relationship.

"This obligation," he waved the document, "was created before you were a Shield."

"My dear man." I tried to drawl those words as Taro did when he wanted to appear arrogant and obnoxious. "The law is that all Sources and Shields are released from any contracts made on their behalf before they are diagnosed. There can't be a conflict of obligations." I smiled, hoping I looked condescending. "You don't seem to understand how this works."

"I will not allow Triple S sophistry deprive me of a contract I made in good faith and have relied on since. I expect you to obey your mother and meet your commitments."

"My mother has not told me to marry your son." Not that that would have persuaded me to do so. I wondered if my mother was aware of that.

Cars glared at my mother. "I'd assumed that was why you were here. To inform her of her responsibilities."

My mother was not intimidated. "I told you that my daughter would not be marrying your son. I've said it in every letter I sent you. I said it when we met."

"I had hoped further consideration would have revived your sense of honor. Or the desire to protect your name, if nothing else."

"Give over, Cars. You're in the wrong here and you know it. And I think our name can withstand a little tarnishing."

Cars looked at me. "Maybe your family is refusing to comply with the contract because they know you won't. Maybe it is you who has no honor."

"I don't really expect you to understand, but my only means of achieving honor is to Shield my Source. My most important duty is to my Source. I could never get married. I must be able to move as my Source does, and the demands on my time preclude marriage." That wasn't strictly true. I could marry someone who was willing to move according to the demands of the Triple S. It would just be complicated and inconvenient.

Cars snorted in derision. "What can a Shield know of demands? You flit about from place to place, everything handed to you without your working for it"—I felt Taro stiffen beside me: he hated that particular accusation—"expending a bit of effort here and there controlling natural disasters that only you say exist in the first place. You don't have to work from dawn to dusk, day after day, like everyone else does. So maybe that explains why you can't understand the importance of meeting your commitments. But your mother doesn't have the same excuse."

"How about we stop wasting time?" I suggested. "The answer is no. The answer will always be no. Go home."

There was a short silence before Cars turned to my mother. "You didn't tell me your daughter was so ill-mannered."

I was delighted he thought so. "There are those to whom manners should be shown, and those to whom one needn't bother." Hey, that was a good one. Really obnoxious.

Marcus scowled. It was good to finally see some kind of reaction from him.

"You're just a slip server like the rest of us, girl," said Cars. "Being a Shield only makes you a freak. It certainly doesn't make you better than us."

A freak? Surprise knocked my head back. He thought Shields were freaks? I hadn't come across that opinion before. I would have to think about that later. Right now it was working in my favor. "If you so misunderstand my qualities, surely you don't want your son to marry me."

"I don't want you for yourself," Cars sneered. "You are merely the connection to your family. If it weren't for that, I wouldn't let my son near you. Everyone knows you're a whore."

Huh. Well, it wasn't the first time I'd heard that. Unfortunately.

To my shock, Taro leapt up, pulled the larger man to his feet, and punched him in the mouth. I could only stare at him. That really wasn't like him. And it was totally unnecessary. What did we care what a stranger thought of me?

Then it got even more ridiculous. Marcus got up to shove Taro away. Dias shoved Marcus, Marcus shoved back. Dias fell against a small table, sending the porcelain figurine flying. It shattered against the wall.

Well, this was humiliating.

"Isn't this charming?" a loud voice said, piercing the ruckus. It was enough to get everyone's attention.

Daris entered the room from the stairs, with her ever present aroma of alcohol. "Really, Dunleavy, your family has brought such an air of gentility to our home."

Wonderful. Our childish antics had been witnessed. And by Daris, a drunkard. But what she said was true. It was terrible that everyone's behavior had disintegrated so thoroughly.

"If you don't mind," said my mother. "This is family business."

She shrugged. "This is my home."

She had a point, damn her. Anyone could wander in and we had no right to stop them.

"Perhaps we can go to your private quarters," Cars said to me.

That was not happening. I was not letting these people into our personal space. I wasn't sure guests were supposed to go up there. And, of course, once they were there, it would be difficult to get them out without causing a horrific scene.

"There's no need," said my mother. "There's nothing more to be said. I'm not going to have my daughter slandered in that way."

Cars drew breath to say something that was no doubt offensive.

"I apologize for what my father said," said Marcus, looking directly at me. "It was unforgivable."

Well, that was interesting.

"Don't you dare apologize for me," Cars snapped.

"How could you expect them to invite us into their family when we demonstrate that we don't know how to conduct ourselves?"

It seemed that Marcus had a spine after all.

"None of you know how to behave." Daris seemed to be looking around for something.

"You are the very mirror of deportment," said Taro to her.

"I've never needed physical restraint."

"No, you merely inspire the need in others."

"We are veering from the point," Cars complained. "You, girl." Was that how he talked to people? No wonder his family was failing. "Will you do the honorable thing and marry my son?"

"I will not marry your son."

"Then your family will face the consequences."

What did that mean?

"Your wife would not like what you're doing, Cars," my mother said gently.

That seemed to infuriate Cars. "Don't you dare speak of Lendi!"

"She was a good woman, and very sensible."

"It's disgusting that you are attempting to use her as a reason to evade your duty."

"I know her death has hit you hard and has made business more difficult for you, but—"

"Stop talking about my wife!" Cars roared.

Was that what this was about? I was aware that the loss of a spouse could have a devastating impact on a family's business. Had the death of this woman caused the financial difficulties the Prides were experiencing? Or was her loss merely making Cars irrational?

Marcus had lost a parent. His family were losing their prosperity, his livelihood. I felt sorry for him. That changed nothing. "I will not marry you."

Cars clenched his fists. "You honestly think you can say no and that will be the end of it?"

"That should be all that I need to do."

"If you refuse to honor your parents' agreement, everyone shall know that the word of a Mallorough means nothing."

"That is unfortunate, but not enough to convince me to marry." Besides, surely no one would hold a voided contract against a family who had lost the relevant family member to the Triple S. It was just a threat.

But the expression I was seeing on my mother's face made me wonder whether I was underestimating the validity of the threat. She was frowning, concerned, but not, I thought, about me.

I would hate it if my actions caused serious hardship to my family, but I was not going to let that force me into marriage. The very idea of it was preposterous. "It's unfortunate that you came all this way for nothing," I said to Cars, "but if you had written to me I would have given you the same answer and saved you the trouble. Nothing you say can change my mind. Now, if you will excuse me." I stood and crossed the room to the door.

"We are not finished here," said Cars.

"I am." I opened the door. Cars strode over to me. "Do not follow me."

"This isn't finished," he insisted.

"Do I have to call for some footmen to help you leave?" Taro demanded. "Because I will."

Cars stopped, but he looked furious. "I can't believe none of you have any understanding of commitment and obligation. How can you live like this?"

He sounded desperate. I had no doubt he knew as well as anyone that I couldn't be held to a contract created before I was sent to the Academy. And he had to know his son, if he married me, would have to travel with me, follow me wherever I was sent by the Triple S. Whatever function Marcus served for his family's business, he would no longer be able to perform it. Marrying him to me would cause a loss as well as a gain.

Cars could think of nothing else to do. I was sure of it.

"I'm sorry," I told him. "I really am. But it just isn't possible."

"This is entirely possible," he retorted. "You just don't want to do it."

No, I didn't want to do it. He spoke as though my wishes were irrelevant. But no one should be forced to marry anyone.

And Taro should not have to put up with it.

And I was wondering why, if this contract was so damned important, they didn't seek to marry Marcus to one of my brothers once they realized I could not be bound. If the whole thing was so damned important to everyone, throw Mika at them.

There was nothing more to say. So I left.

Cars didn't follow. Taro did.

I went to our suite, Taro following me. I didn't sit down. I couldn't stay still. I paced, which was Taro's habit. Maybe I'd gotten it from him.

"It's going to be all right," he said.

"It's not going to be all right," I snapped. "You heard them. They're going to ruin my family's reputation if I don't marry

Marcus. And from the look I saw on my mother's face, that's a real possibility."

"So what are you saying?" he asked stiffly. "You're thinking of saying yes?"

I stared at him. "Is your mind wandering?"

"What am I supposed to think?"

"That this is a mess and it's probably not going to be that simple to fix."

"Just because it will be difficult and annoying and embarrassing doesn't mean the end result is going to be anything other than what you want it to be."

I had to admit, "That's true."

"So just think of it as a learning opportunity."

"An opportunity to learn what?"

"How to convince a regular not to marry you."

"When will I ever need to do that again?"

"You hadn't anticipated having to do it once, did you? The future is unpredictable. Embrace the uncertainty."

I scowled at him. "You're not cute."

"I have it on excellent authority that I'm fantastic."

"I expected you to be more, well, angry, about this."

He waved a hand. "I've grown weary of melodrama."

I didn't blame him. So. No melodrama. I'd just keep saying no until the Prides accepted it and left. How hard could that be?

Chapter Seven

Fiona silently shook me awake before dawn the next day. I wondered how she always managed to wake so early. I dressed without waking Taro. I went down to the kitchen, where Fiona was waiting with a rope, two buckets and two lanterns.

We were going to the crystal cave to chip out some rocks for Browne. We were going early in the morning in the hope of avoiding any interested onlookers.

"Thank you for doing this," I said, taking a lantern and a bucket. The bucket held a pick and some burlap.

"It may end up benefitting me in time. It's not like I have anything else to do with the crystals. Except maybe sell them, but now that I've seen they have some"—she made a kind of circular gesture with her hand—"casting properties, or something, I'm not comfortable with just sending them out to strangers without knowing what they are."

Fiona and I stepped out into the cool, damp morning. The silence at that time of day was soothing to my ears. We crossed the gardens and, before I could help myself, I looked at the Dowager's dark manor. Was she sleeping? Was she dreaming of annoying little schemes for making Taro's life more difficult? Would Linder turn into an ass under the weight of her proximity?

We took the thin curving path through the ridge. The shape of the ridge had been drastically changed by the rock slide, and the path through the ridge had had to be cleared out. That had been a nightmare of a task that had shredded the hands, knees and feet of everyone involved. The other rocks had been left where they fell. We carefully walked on them, around a bend of the ridge, and from there we climbed up to the location of the cave. I slipped several times, and that was painful.

We reached the mouth of the cave. At least that much had survived the rock slide.

Fiona tied the rope to an iron ring hammered at the bottom of the mouth of the cave, the rope a means to make sure we could find our way back. I followed her into the cave, the faint daylight quickly fading away. It wasn't long before all we had for light was the yellow glow of the lanterns.

I was a little nervous about this. The last time I had been in this cave, someone had stolen the rope and the lantern had been dropped and doused. We had to wait for Fiona's husband to come looking for us. It had taken him hours to decide to come for us, hours with Fiona and me sitting in the dark, to which our eyes never adjusted. It had been frightening.

So maybe this wasn't the greatest idea I'd ever had.

Taro did know we were doing this, right? I thought I remembered telling him at some point the evening before.

After a few bends in the path, a cavern opened up, glittering with crystals of white and blue. It was just as breathtaking as it had been the first time I had seen it.

"I'm going to keep a hold on the rope," said Fiona, clearly having learned from our last experience in the cave. "I'll chip away here. You can go deeper into the cavern. What size crystal does she want?"

"I think a variety of sizes would be best." I hefted the handle of my pick. It did seem a shame to defile the cave by hacking at it, but the amount we were prepared to take probably wouldn't be too scarring. I found a long crystal and swung at its base. The pick bounced with such force that I dropped it.

The vibration hurt my hand. "This is going to be more difficult than I anticipated."

"We'll just have to put our backs into it." She swung at a crystal and it popped out of the wall.

She didn't have to do anything. She was doing a favor for me to help me repay the favor I owed to Browne. I was creating a situation in which I was becoming beholden to more and more people. That wasn't good. A Shield was supposed to be unfettered. Except to her Source, of course.

I chipped away at the crystals for a while. I worked up a fine sweat. It was boring work. And I could see that it was going to take a while.

Then, out of nowhere, Fiona said, "Kent asked me to marry him."

My arm kept swinging the pick without mental direction while I thought about that. "What?"

"You heard me."

"Aye, but . . . what?"

"Aye."

"How hard did you hit him?"

"Don't I wish."

"Seriously, what was he thinking? You're still in mourning."

"He is aware of my responsibilities."

"Your responsibilities?"

"To marry someone."

"You have a duty to marry?" I was shocked, but oddly relieved. Crazy people were harassing her to marry, too.

"It makes for a more stable estate."

"How?"

"No one knows. That's just the way it works. Estates with married titleholders tend to prosper, those without tend not to."

Huh. "But you don't have to actually marry anyone, do you?"

"I'm not sure what you mean."

"You could just take a lover." Ah, there was a good chunk of crystal. I wondered if it mattered what color we chose.

"No, that's not good enough."

"Why not?"

"A wedding is a ritual. Rituals have power. The best, closest lover in the world doesn't have the power of a spouse."

I supposed that made a certain sense. Sort of. "So you will get married in time?"

Fiona paused in her hammering to push hair out of her face with her forearm. "Aye, I suppose I will."

The Emperor wasn't married. He had been, but his wife had died before he gained the title. Did his single state mean all of us would prosper less? And if Kent believed it, why hadn't he married before now?

"But not to Kent," I said to Fiona.

"No, not to Kent. There is a darkness within him that I have no desire to examine more closely."

I agreed, though I wouldn't have put it so poetically. He was an avaricious pig, and he deserved to have something unpleasant done to him for trying to take Fiona's estate from her. "How does this work, his getting the estate from the Emperor?"

"He has to go to the Emperor and make his plaint. He has to bring with him a token from the land he wants to take, a clump of dirt or a branch or something. He has to bring some kind of proof that I'm experiencing difficulty. Testimony is enough, so he could bring someone I've annoyed, a title-holder in the area who holds a grudge against me or enjoys meddling in people's affairs, or even someone who wants a chance to meet the Emperor. Kent has to convince the Emperor he has a prima facie case. If he doesn't, Kent gets fined for wasting the Emperor's time and he can never petition for anyone else's estate ever again. If he does, the council conducts a more thorough investigation and gives the Emperor their decision."

"If Kent can achieve his goal that way, why would he ask you to marry him?"

"It would be easier than convincing the Emperor to give Westsea to him."

"But you would still be the titleholder. The title is what he wants, isn't it?"

"Maybe he feels he would be the power behind the title-holder."

"Doesn't really know you, does he?"

"It would seem not."

It was weird how life worked sometimes. Both of us getting

unwanted marriage proposals. "How did he react when you refused?"

"He was quite the gentleman about it. Told me he would give me time to think about it and come to my senses."

"I do not admire people who will not accept a negative answer."

"Some people feel that's a sign of strength."

"Some people are idiots."

Once we filled the buckets—Browne would be getting more than she'd asked for—and covered the tops with burlap, we found our way back through the cave, the rope right where it should have been. The bright sunlight pierced our eyes as we stepped from the shadows of the cave. "What an unusually pleasant day," said Fiona, shielding her eyes with her hand.

I blinked and waited for my eyes to adjust. "Thank you for helping me."

"That's what friends are for." She paused. "What the hell?"

"Hm?" I blinked again and was then able to see a whole slew of fishers standing about on the shore. They didn't appear to be getting ready to work.

As we walked toward the water, I could see fish lying dead on the rocky shore, silver and flat. Thousands, it looked like.

I could smell them, too. Yikes.

Then I noticed within me the jittery feeling that told me a spell had been cast. I moved closer to the fish and the sensation grew stronger. The fish were either the tools of a spell, or the result of one.

Fiona kind of groaned and rubbed the back of her neck. She didn't seem surprised, though.

"What's this?" I asked.

"It happens."

"What? The fish just jump out of the water and die here?"

"It's fish rot. They die in the water and the tide brings them in."

"How often does it happen?"

"Couple times a year."

"This seems like a lot of fish." And there was a spell involved. I was sure of it.

"It is," said one of the fishers with a scowl. "I've never seen anything like this."

There was really nothing Fiona could say to that. Maybe it was true. She'd lived in Flown Raven only a few years.

"I thought Lady Daris would have told you," the tenant continued.

"I can't believe she's aware of this," Fiona replied.

"She's been here."

"She isn't one for wandering away from the manor."

The tenant wasn't impressed with being doubted. "I've seen her myself."

"Of course, Aven," Fiona said quickly, to avoid causing offence. "I'm just surprised." She bent down and picked up one of the fish.

I suppressed a grimace. Better her than me.

We bid Aven and the others good day, and once I thought we were out of earshot, I asked Fiona, "Can Daris cast?"

Fiona snickered. "You need focus and concentration to cast, don't you? Daris is always too drunk to have either."

"All right, but there's something about these fish that involves casting."

She frowned. "Are you sure?"

"Completely. I don't know the nature of the spell, you should probably get Healer Browne to look at it, but there's definitely something there."

"So you're saying a spell was deliberately used on the fish."

"Or the fish were used to cast the spell."

"Why would anyone do that?"

"I have no idea. I'm not suggesting it has to be nefarious. But someone is using spells that have an impact on your resources, and you don't know about it. That can't be good."

"No, I don't believe it is." She gave me her bucket. "Can you take these to Healer Browne and ask her to come back with you?"

The buckets were heavy and their handles bit into my hands. "Of course."

I walked toward the village. People were up and working, bustling about and talking. I was reminded anew how busy the average person was, how hard they had to work. I was happy to be a Shield, but something about all the activity in which regulars engaged was appealing, every day seeing the results of one's labor, a chair created or a furrow of seed planted. I wondered if I was missing something by being apart from it.

I heard shouting then, sharp and panicked. I spun toward the noise. I saw six horses pounding through the street, their riders clearly lacking any concern for who they might be endangering. In fact, it looked almost as though they were deliberately aiming for people. But that couldn't be.

And I froze. Screams filled my ears. I saw the hooves pounding into the ground, so hard I thought I could feel it. My eyes were assaulted with fast shapes and shattering lines.

Then everything seemed to slow down. Sound reached me only through a muffling sensation. I couldn't feel anything, not even the ground under my feet. I felt like I couldn't concentrate on anything, my mind filled with fog.

I couldn't breathe.

The world flipped again. The sound of glass smashing became brutally loud. Sunlight pierced my eyes. I could feel the mist of the morning air against my skin.

The horses were bearing down on me.

My brain kicked in and I leapt off the street.

People were desperately clawing out of the way. There were so many people and the street was narrow. One man dove against a wall in an effort to avoid the horses and seemed to knock himself out. A small child was trampled. Another man threw himself against the side of a wagon trying to stay clear. One of the riders slashed a woman in the face with his crop. Who were these bastards?

They were laughing.

Once they reached the end of the street, I expected them to turn around and take another pass, because that seemed to be the sort of people they were. Instead, they galloped away. It was baffling. What motive could they have for doing this? Who were they?

I ran to Browne's cottage. I had to put down one of the buckets in order to pound on her door. Apparently I hadn't dropped them when my life was in danger. My priorities were excellent.

"I have a patient!" I heard from within the cottage.

"You have more out here!" I snapped back.

A few moments later she was at the door. "What?" she demanded irritably.

"There are people trampled by horses out here."

She frowned. "More than one."

"Aye."

She turned back into her cottage. "Just take that tea, Alia. You're fine."

"You might as well take these," I said, giving her the buckets.

She glanced at them briefly. "Oh. Thank you. Come on, Alia." She took the buckets and set them down beside the door. Then she stepped aside to let a heavily pregnant woman out. Browne disappeared briefly and reappeared with a pouch. "Let's get going."

A young man ran up. "Healer—"

"I know, I'm coming," she interjected.

The four people I had seen injured had been grouped together. The man who had jumped into the wagon and the woman who had been whipped were standing, though the man's arm was held strangely. The boy and the other man were laid out on the ground, pain etched on their bloody faces. The boy, about six, was crying.

It was just unfathomable to me. Why would anyone do this? How could they get pleasure from doing something like this? "Who were they?" I asked.

"That's Colm," said Browne, pointing at the boy. "That's Radek."

"No. The riders."

No one answered. I assumed that meant no one knew.

Browne knelt beside the boy. She touched him gently and asked him questions about how he felt. He was having difficulty answering and his breathing was wet. "Someone carry Colm back to my cottage," she said. "Lay him on the table. Be very gentle with him." A young man stepped forward, and though he was obviously taking care, Colm cried out when he was lifted. "You need to be brave just a few more moments, Colm. Then I'm going to make you feel much better." Browne knelt beside the man. "Where does it hurt?" she asked him.

"My head, Healer," he groaned.

"Anywhere else?"

"I don't—I can't—"

"All right. Don't worry."

Browne put her hand lightly on his temple. I saw her whispering, but I couldn't determine what she was saying. "You'll be fine," she told him. "I'll have you taken to mine, Radek, but you'll have to wait until I've seen to Colm."

Another man stepped forward and helped Radek to his feet.

Browne grabbed my arm and pulled me off to one side. "Go to Her Grace and tell her what happened."

"Will they all be all right?"

"I can't be sure, but I believe they will."

"Has anything like this happened before?"

"Not to my knowledge," she said in a hurried, distracted tone. "Please go tell Her Grace."

"Of course." Who the hell were those riders? How could they be punished if no one knew who they were? And they needed to be punished. There was no excuse for what they did.

"Hurry," she said. "They might be coming back."

I nodded and started running. The horrible images of what I had seen kept going through my mind again and again. I kept hearing that terrible laughter. It made the back of my neck shiver.

I was seriously out of breath by the time I reached the manor. One of the results of the lack of bench dancing in my schedule. "Bailey!" I gasped, my lungs working painfully. I bent over, my hands on my knees. "Where's Her Grace?"

"She's out overseeing some irrigation on one of the farming lots."

I swore. I wasn't able to run anymore. What if those riders came back? Were they likely to? The villagers would be ready for them this time. They could throw things at the riders, if nothing else.

"I can send one of the footmen out to her," said Bailey. "Shall I do so?"

"Aye, but I need to talk to him first."

"Of course. If you would like to recover yourself in the sitting room, we will be with you shortly."

I nodded, didn't bother to speak again, and headed to the

sitting room. Where I didn't sit down on the nice furniture, because I was sweaty. A few moments later, Hiroki came in.

"You wanted to see me, ma'am?"

"You need to go to Her Grace and tell her six riders drove through the village, trampling people. Four were injured, one a child. I don't know if anyone recognized the riders."

Hiroki, his eyes widened in surprise, nodded. "Anything else, ma'am?"

"No, you can go. And hurry, please."

He left.

I sighed. What a day, and it wasn't even half over yet.

Two awful things happening in one day. The fish were the result of a spell, and it didn't make sense. Destroying resources was never smart. As for the trampling, well, it wasn't as though criminal activities never happened in Flown Raven. Taro and I had been robbed on our way to Flown Raven, which, granted, was not nearly as severe as what the villagers had experienced. And the riders hadn't taken anything. They'd reaped no benefits from their actions.

So, was the same person behind both events?

I went up to my suite to bathe and get melodramatic in private about the events of the day. And the first thing I saw was the flower arrangement on one of the end tables. Bright yellow flowers in a brown straight-sided vase. A small brown cake was supported by the blossoms, and a pair of earrings hung off the lip of the vase. At the foot of the vase lay a card with the name "Marcus Pride."

I groaned. This was a token meant to ask to start negotiations for marriage. It was something aristocrats did. It didn't make sense for Marcus to send this to me. We were both merchant class. And it seemed kind of redundant. Wasn't the contract a sort of marriage proposal? A proposal I'd refused?

"So what are you going to do?"

I looked up. Taro was leaning against the doorway to the bedchamber, arms crossed, eyebrow raised.

"What do you think I'm going to do?" I snapped. "I'm sending it back."

"Are you sure you want to?"

Oh, he was being aggravating just for the hell of it. "Of course, I'm sure. Don't be ridiculous."

"He's your class."

"So?"

"He's handsome without being too terribly handsome."

I actually didn't find Marcus physically appealing. "You're being a prat, Taro."

"I'm merely pointing out the facts."

"The fact is that I love you." Though it wasn't something I particularly felt like saying right then.

"Maybe you're just one of those people who feel they should love whoever they're sleeping with."

"No, I'm not one of those people." That was a little naive, and I was offended that he would accuse me of it. "You know, I've had a really bad morning. I had to watch six idiots drive their horses through town. Four people were injured, including a child. I don't need this." I pointed at the vase. "Or that."

I looked at Taro, waiting for his next stupid remark.

He surprised me. "Were you hurt at all?"

Oh. I hadn't been expecting that. "No. I was well away from the danger."

"Were the riders caught?"

"I don't know. Not to my knowledge."

He sighed and rubbed his face. "It's one thing after another. Why can't everyone just leave Fiona alone? What is it about this place that makes everyone so insane?"

"It's a large and wealthy estate?"

"There are others as big and wealthy."

"Not a lot, and no others are next to Kent."

"What does that have to do with anything?"

"Just that he's causing trouble for her."

"You think Kent is behind these riders?"

"Didn't think so before." Surely he wouldn't go that far. I didn't think it would improve his chances of getting a positive ruling from the Emperor. Something like anonymous riders attacking the village, that wasn't Fiona's fault. It couldn't be held against her. "I don't know. It's not like he's the only one unnaturally interested in Westsea. The Dowager is unbalanced about it. Daris wants it. The Emperor is unusually interested in it. But all of them, I would think, would want the resources to be healthy and plentiful and the tenants able to work. Something else is going on."

But I couldn't determine what that might be. My thoughts were going in circles and I couldn't make sense of them.

Taro's response was forestalled by a knock on the door. A knock meant it was one among Fiona, my mother or my brothers. The servants just walked in whenever they felt like it.

I opened the door. My brothers were standing in the hall and they surged past me. "Is Taro here?" Mika asked, and I gestured at Taro.

"What is this?" Dias was looking at the engagement token with a curled lip.

"It's an invitation to negotiate a marriage contract."

Dias snickered. "From who?"

"Who do you think it's from?" I snapped. "Read the card. Marcus Pride."

Mika laughed. "Sister, dear, who would have thought you would be so very desired by so many?"

"Shut up."

Mika laughed again.

Dias put an arm around Taro's shoulders, visibly startling my Source. "We're here to invite you on a jaunt."

"What kind of jaunt?"

Mika put a finger to his lips. "Shh. It's a secret."

"We're in the middle of something here," Taro objected.

"Nothing that can't wait," said Mika.

I agreed. Some entertainment would be good for Taro. "Just don't go to the village, aye?" And I told them about the riders. They appeared disturbed.

"Is there anything we can do?" Mika asked.

"I doubt it. They're being taken care of by the healer." I didn't know if anyone was looking for the riders, but if they were, I doubted my brothers would be of any use. They didn't know anyone in the area.

"Then we will do nothing to offend the sensibilities of the villagers," said Mika. "We're just taking this lad out for some fun. He's too serious."

"You think everyone's too serious." I could have used some fun, too, but I wasn't invited. "Have a good time."

Dias grinned and pulled Taro out of the room. Mika bowed to me then followed them.

It was good that my brothers had taken an interest in Taro.

They were sort of family to him. He would benefit from exposure to a family that wasn't a nest of poisonous snakes.

I looked at the engagement token with a sigh. It was ugly and irritating. I got one of the footmen to take the token back to Marcus Pride.

Chapter Eight

I had buried myself in a book when I heard another knock on the door. I suppressed a sigh. I didn't really want to see anyone. I played with the idea of not answering. A third knock forced me to my feet.

It was Marcus. Surprised the hell out of me.

"How did you get up here?" I demanded. "Someone should have sat you somewhere and brought me to you."

Marcus shrugged. "I bribed a maid to let me up. Because I'm pretty sure you would have refused to see me if I'd given you any warning that I was here."

I glared at him.

"Was I wrong?" he asked.

No, he was not. I stood to the side to let him in. "Have a seat."

He did. "You sent the opening volley back."

I took a chair opposite his. "You couldn't have expected anything different."

He rubbed his eyes, and I noticed that he was pale and looked exhausted. "We really need this marriage to go through."

I felt a touch of sympathy, which was inconvenient.

"I'm sorry you're in a difficult situation, I really am, but I'm not going to marry you to get you out of it."

"It's not just my father and me, you know. It's my sisters. It's my blind uncle. It's our servants. It's all of our workers. It's everyone who relies on us for their livelihoods."

Yes, I knew that. I didn't know much about my family's business, but I knew it involved a lot of people. A lot of people depending on the success of the holders and traders. "I'm sorry for that." I knew what it was like to have to rely on money and not have enough of it. Flatwell had taught me that. "I belong to the Triple S. My place is with Taro and where the Triple S chooses to put me. There's no changing that."

"I'm not disputing that. Obviously I would travel with you wherever you're posted."

I felt my eyebrows fly up in surprise. "And you're really willing to accept that? To give up your home? I'm assuming you've been training to be a trader all your life. You wouldn't be able to do that if you traveled with us."

"Yes, I understand that. Though, in following you to your various posts, I might meet people I wouldn't otherwise. I might be able to make contacts that will be advantageous to my family. And yours, incidentally."

I was shocked. I really was. Shocked and baffled. I didn't think I could ever give up so much for the betterment of my family. I guess that made me the lesser person. "I can appreciate what you're willing to sacrifice, but it doesn't matter. I won't marry you."

•   "I won't interfere with your relationship with Lord Shintaro," Marcus added.

I stared at him. He couldn't be saying what I thought he was saying. "What?"

"You heard me. And I would expect the same freedom from you."

I couldn't believe this. He was prepared to marry me but leave me free to sleep with other people. "That's insane."

"We need this marriage," he repeated.

That badly? Really? What was wrong with them? How could business possibly be that bad? If it were that bad, wouldn't it be better to just let the thing sink and start all over?

"I'm not going to marry you." I was getting tired of saying it. I resented him for making me say it.

"Why not?" he demanded. "I just told you I wouldn't interfere with your duties to the Triple S or your ties to Shintaro Karish. What more do you want?"

Well done. He was able to make me feel like an ungrateful wench with just a few sentences when I really wasn't at fault. He should be a politician. Or a teacher.

"Is it because of my father?" Marcus asked. "I'm sorry about the things he said. I can promise you he's not usually like this. He's just so worried about our family right now. Once we are married he will treat you with the respect you deserve."

He was speaking as though our marriage were a sure thing. That irked me. "I can't marry you."

"How far do I have to bend?" he demanded bitterly.

"You shouldn't have to bend at all, should you? That's proof that I'm totally inappropriate. Why don't you find a spouse from some other merchant family?"

"No one will have us," he admitted angrily. "No one wants to be aligned to a descending family."

"How do you know that? Have you even tried?" After all, his family had made the contract with ours when we were having difficulties.

"Yes," he spat.

Aha. "So you didn't think this marriage contract was binding, either."

Marcus's eyes widened as he recognized his misstep. "No. That's not what I meant."

"Not what you meant to say, perhaps." I suddenly felt a lot better about refusing him. I was his last choice. The agreement had been forgotten or disregarded until they had run out of options. "I won't marry you. No matter what you say, what you promise, or what you threaten." I hated the idea of my family name being blackened, but I couldn't let it force me to marry against my will. "You and your father might as well pack up and go home."

Marcus scowled. "We won't go back. We'll stay in the village and do whatever we have to, to make your life difficult until you agree to marry me."

"How romantic." It was like something out of a poem, really.

"Oh, you're not about romance, Dunleavy. I know that. And clearly the well-being of your family won't move you. But what about you? Your own best interests?"

"There is no way marrying you is in my best interests."

"This is about your honor, too. Your good name. You can't be willing to lose that."

"The only thing I have to do to keep my good name is to Shield well." And not break any laws. "And I do Shield well."

He pushed out a breath in exasperation. "Will you not see reason?"

"This isn't about reason. It's merely what you want."

"I mean what I say. I'll stay in Flown Raven until you agree to marry me."

"You can't stay in Flown Raven. You'll run out of money eventually."

"We'll manage. We're determined."

"Aye, well, so am I."

He squared his shoulders. "You're only making things harder for yourself," he warned me.

So here was the thing. He was making demands he had no right to make. He was kind of obnoxious. And yet, there was something about him that wasn't entirely unappealing. I could be obnoxious, too, when I was worried about things.

I felt Taro's protections go down, and I was horrified. He was channeling an event. I needed to Shield him. But Marcus was right there. I couldn't cast in front of him. "You need to leave."

"What's wrong?" he asked.

"You need to leave."

"Why are you so pale?"

There was no help for it. I had to get to work.

I raised my Shields around Taro, and my mind was sunk into turmoil. Unnatural sensations whirled around me. My skin felt battered by cold gray waves, the screams of sea birds pierced my ears, salt flowed into my eyes, my ears, my mouth. The onslaught was all I could think about. It confused me.

Where was I? I needed to get to the supplies in our room, but I didn't know how to get there. I didn't know how to move my feet.

Blood pounded through Taro's veins, his heart beating too quickly and too violently. It seemed ready to burst right out of his chest. Fluid flowed over his brain, sparking and curdling. He was dying.

It was too much. I felt like I was gagging.

I couldn't lose my concentration. I had to keep my Shields up. Taro relied on me.

But the water was pounding at my Shields. I could practically feel cracks developing, pulsing liquid escaping through them.

This was all in my head. There was no water. There were no walls.

Hold on, hold on, hold on.

I could barely breathe through all the salt in my nose and mouth.

There was no salt, but I couldn't help trying to spit it out.

I pressed my palms against the sides of my head. I had to stay calm. Think only of the Shields. Hang on to the Shields. Taro was all that mattered. Taro needed the Shields.

Was I keeping him safe? I couldn't tell. I could barely feel him through the onslaught. That was so very, very bad. I should be better at this.

All I could do was hang on, barely keeping my Shields up, as the forces rushed on and on.

And then, thank gods, they were gone. I found myself curled up on the floor, panting, trying very hard not to vomit.

Marcus was standing over me, a hand on my shoulder, his eyes wide.

That's right. I'd had an audience.

Oh, no, that wasn't humiliating.

"What's wrong?" he asked. "Is it some kind of fit? Do you need a healer?"

I was drenched with sweat and I would swear I could still feel the sting of salt in my nose. I got up shakily. "No. It was just a channeling."

It was the kind of event that Taro had been channeling while we were still in High Scape, unaware that he had been channeling an event as far away as Flown Raven. This was the first water event we'd channeled since coming to Flown Raven, though. All the other events had involved earthquakes.

He looked appalled. "And this is what it's like? This happens to you every time?"

"No, not every time." And I had no interest in discussing such things with him.

"I had no idea it was so difficult. I thought you just had to, I don't know, wave your hand or just think about it for a moment. But this is . . ."

"None of your concern," I said sharply, standing a little unsteadily.

"It will be my concern, eventually."

"No, it never will."

"What happens if you're in the middle of something else when you have to do this?"

I closed my eyes and pinched the bridge of my nose. "Please leave." I was struck with inspiration. "There are duties I have to perform. As I do after every channeling. Things it's not appropriate for regulars to see."

"Regulars." The corner of his mouth quirked up. "Is that what you call people who aren't Shields?"

It was what everyone in the Triple S called everyone who wasn't a member. I thought everyone knew that. And I was not going to get dragged into a discussion about it. "Please."

He went to the door. Thank Zaire. But then he turned back. Damn. "This isn't the end of it," he warned me. Or possibly threatened me.

I just glared at him. Words, I knew, would have been a waste of air.

He finally left.

Chapter Nine

I felt tired and gritty and exposed, like my skull had been sliced off and my brain left open to the air. Part of me longed for a bath, but I was stopped by the ridiculous and repulsive image of soapy water seeping into my head. I was ashamed of myself for being so hysterical. I was frustrated for allowing myself to become so unbalanced while channeling. This was what I had been trained to do, damn it. I sat on the floor, my legs crossed, and closed my eyes.

Long breath in, long breath out. Time to calm down. Time to call serenity, smooth and light.

But the door burst open before I could accomplish anything substantial.

"What happened?" Taro demanded.

My mind was still stuck on breathing. "I don't understand."

"That channeling. It was horrific. Did the spell not work?"

"Oh, that." I rubbed my forehead. "Marcus was here. I didn't want to cast in front of him."

Taro cocked an eyebrow. "Marcus was here."

"Um, aye." Perhaps I shouldn't have said that so casually, as though Marcus being in my room wasn't odd. "He was trying to convince me to change my mind."

"And you brought him up here to listen to him try to change your mind."

"Of course not. He bribed a maid to bring him here. Then I figured I'd better hear him out."

"Why? What could he say that he hasn't already said?"

For some reason, I felt uncomfortable revealing Marcus's confidences. He seemed to be doing his best to be accommodating, the only one to do so in this whole mess. But I thought it was important to be as honest as possible with Taro during this ridiculous upheaval. "The way he put it was that he would never interfere with our relationship."

"What the hell does that mean?"

"Please, Taro. You know what it means."

"But if he isn't going to insist on a proper marriage, why is he really doing this? There must be other merchant families he can marry into and have a real marriage."

"He's tried, apparently. No other family would have him." And that had to have been a harsh blow to his pride.

"Damn it."

"It doesn't matter, Taro. I'm still saying no."

"He's desperate, Lee. You know as well as I do that desperate people can do some truly atrocious things."

I barely knew the man, but I couldn't help thinking Marcus was not the sort to do anything illegal or abominable. "All we can do is keep an eye out, right?"

"Or get Fiona to toss them out."

"They're not staying in the manor, are they?" I did not want to be running into them—either of them, but especially Cars—on a daily basis.

"No, they've taken rooms at the Red Barrel, but Fiona can order them off her land."

"Really." What an excellent idea. "I wonder why she didn't think of that herself."

"Well, it's none of her business, is it? Besides, she has other things on her mind."

"Of course." Though I doubted that if I were to ask Fiona to employ her authority in that matter, it would cause her any additional stress.

Unless it was something more complicated than simply

ordering them to go. Maybe there was a ritual required. Sometimes it seemed to me that almost everything required a ritual.

"I think I gave your brothers a bit of a scare," Taro said. "They were with me when I channeled. Apparently, I put on quite a show." He looked embarrassed. "And then I had to pretend to be angry with them so they wouldn't follow me here. Tell them it was Triple S business and that you are particularly delicate just after channeling, and that their presence would harm you."

My eyebrows rose. "That's an interesting lie." Why did I have to be the delicate one? Why couldn't he be delicate?

"So the next time you see them you might want to reassure them."

"Thanks," I said, a little sourly. I rose to my feet, wondering how I was supposed to convince my brothers I was fine despite the fact that my Source had told them I turned into a fragile flower every time I channeled.

Shortly thereafter, the bells announced the evening meal. Taro and I went to the dining room. Fiona was the only one there, standing by one of the windows, staring out into the darkening sky.

I felt badly for her. Everything seemed to be going wrong. When she had first taken the title, she'd had the Dowager Duchess harassing her, attempting to take over the responsibilities and privileges belonging to Fiona, only ceasing when Taro was transferred into Flown Raven. Since then, the Dowager had done her best to create a schism between Fiona and her people, whipping them up into a frenzy of disobedience, making it clear to absolutely everyone that she thought Fiona was not the true or legitimate titleholder of Westsea. Then Fiona had had someone trying to kill her. Her husband had died, and a devastating rockslide had destroyed lives and homes and knocked over the wind rock. And now she had another titleholder going after her estate. She didn't deserve it, and there didn't seem to be anyone about to give her support. Certainly not her sister. Maybe her brother was able to ease her, though I hadn't seen anything to suggest he might be a useful pillar.

Maybe Fiona really did need a spouse.

Upon our entrance, Fiona turned from the window with a smile. It was forced and a little hard to look at.

I hated to ask, but I needed to know. "The people injured in the village—"

"They will all live," Fiona said. "In time, they will all recover fully."

"Does anyone know who the riders were? Where they came from?"

Fiona shook her head and poured herself some wine. "I have a couple of men looking into it. They're very clever."

"Can I help?" I had no idea what I could do, but it never hurt to ask.

"Lokian—he's the clever one—he's pretty obnoxious. He enjoys Bon's help, but he considers everyone else a useless interference."

"Ah," I said, and then couldn't think of anything to add. I wished I were the type who could cheer people up. I looked at Taro. When he looked back at me, an expression of inquiry on his face, I tried to tell him silently to flirt with her. People usually enjoyed it when he flirted with them.

Then again, she was his cousin. That would be weird.

Mika and Dias were in next, Mika carrying Radia. He seemed to have no trouble doing so. Radia was a small woman, but carrying her down all those stairs couldn't have been easy.

"Are you all right?" Dias asked me, putting an arm around my shoulders. "Taro said channeling makes you very weak. You look well, though."

Annoyance at Taro for making me the weak one in the Pair rose up again and was firmly stomped down. "I am. Some events are more difficult than others, that's all."

"No one's ever told me channeling is painful," Mika said as he helped Radia into a chair. "Why do they keep that information away from us?"

"You're making it sound nefarious." Thank you very much, Taro. "Sometimes it's difficult. It's not painful, though."

"I don't like it," Mika declared.

Aw, he was being protective. That was so sweet. "Trust me, all right? I know what I'm doing." I tapped him lightly on the cheek.

He grumbled, but he sat down. Not as stubborn as certain others in my life. That was kind of a relief.

My mother came in. She looked at me and said, "You look lovely, Lee," making me wish I'd dressed in my shabbiest clothes and left my hair uncombed.

I could be immature at times.

And then Tarce entered the room. He scowled at Dias, who was seated on one side of Radia, and Mika, who was seated on the other. I wondered if my brothers were deliberately trying to aggravate him. It was a little mean-spirited of them. And yet, I thought it good for him. I had the feeling he had been over-indulged in the past.

Foiled in any hopes he'd had of sitting beside Radia, he chose to sit exactly across from her. "I imagine you miss your loom, Wind Watcher," he said. He seemed awkward, but at least he wasn't trying to act the cool inscrutable lord.

"Very much." Radia sighed.

Radia had had a lot of spare time even before her tower and wind rock had been destroyed. She had spent some of that time weaving the most astounding tapestries. So beautiful, Fiona had used them in trade with other titleholders. So beautiful, I was reminded anew how much I envied people who could create things with their hands.

"I have arranged for a loom like the one you had to be delivered here."

Interesting.

Radia looked shocked speechless. She opened her mouth but nothing came out. Then she cleared her throat and said, "Thank you, my lord. That is exceedingly generous." And then she grinned beautifully.

"You are an essential person to the people of Flown Raven, and we owe you a great deal. It pleases me to bring you pleasure." And he smiled.

Who was this man?

I noticed a slightly smug expression on Taro's face. That made me suspicious. Something was going on.

"You're right, Tarce," said Fiona. "I should have done that myself. Thank you for catching my lapse."

Tarce nodded. He seemed embarrassed. He shouldn't have brought it up at the table if he hadn't wanted attention.

The meal was served. It was, as usual, excellently prepared. It involved, as usual, fish.

We were in the final course when Bailey came into the room and whispered into Fiona's ear. Fiona scowled and nodded and Bailey left. No one asked her what Bailey had said, though I wanted to.

Once the final course was finished, Fiona announced, "Traders Cars and Marcus Pride request our attendance in the front room."

Damn it, not again. Hadn't they marred my day enough? Why couldn't they just leave me alone? "Who is 'our'?" I asked.

"They said everyone in the house, but I don't think we need to disturb the servants."

"Actually, no one needs to be disturbed. Mother and I will go and deal with them."

"I'm going," Taro said firmly.

"I think it would be best if I went, as a witness to what happens," said Fiona.

"You're not getting rid of us, Sister," said Mika.

So I just had to reconcile myself to the fact that I was about to be humiliated in front of an audience.

Marcus was standing in the middle of the front parlor. Cars stood a little behind him. Marcus was holding a large bronze platter in his left hand, a rapier in his right. I heard Taro's quickly indrawn breath and had a feeling I really wasn't going to like what happened next.

Once the door was closed behind Dias, Marcus hit the bronze platter with the rapier three times. "I challenge you to the Suitor's Run," he said to Taro.

Aye, I hated the sound of that. I'd never heard of it. I spent the space of a breath hoping it was something Marcus had just made up.

"That is a challenge between two High Landed," said Taro. "Of which you are not. That's why you're using a plate instead of an emblem."

And there went that faint hope.

"There is no law against the challenging of a High Landed by those of a different class. I've checked."

So they had come planning to do this? Well, yes, they must

have. Why else would they be carrying a bronze platter around?
"Explain this ritual to me," I ordered.

"What it sounds like," Taro spat as he glared at Marcus.
"Two people seeking to marry a third. The two compete in
three tests. Whoever wins marries the . . ." He hesitated.

Aye, it was as bad as I'd thought. "The what?" I demanded.
"The prize?"

"Technically, the person sought is called just that. The
Sought."

"But surely the Sought doesn't actually have to marry the
winner."

"Well, no, he or she does. It's the purpose of the Run. Usually the Sought is trying to get out of a prior obligation."

"I don't have a prior obligation."

"Ignoring the truth doesn't make it any less true," Cars
announced.

"That's assuming the false premise that there is only one
truth," I countered.

"Oy, philosophy," Mika muttered, and I glared at him.

"If we don't do this, they'll keep after you," said Taro.

I stared at him. "Tell me you aren't taking this seriously."

"They'll ruin your family."

"They can't." Surely my family was stronger than that.

"You said yourself that Marcus had tried to connect with
other merchant families and they wouldn't have them. This is
probably their only chance."

Cars frowned at his son. "Why are you telling her our family business?"

Marcus didn't respond. He didn't even look at Cars. He was
watching Taro.

Hey! This was about me. "Mother? They can't actually ruin
you, can they?"

"Of course not," she said heartily.

Too heartily. I didn't believe her.

Ah hell. This was getting more unbelievable by the moment. Why were all these crazy people pulling these outmoded
formalities into the real world? There was no longer any place
for them.

"When I win," Taro said to Marcus, "you'll accept that the
contract is dead."

"When I win," Marcus responded, "every clause in the contract is to be satisfied in full."

"Stop this!" I snapped. "I'm not going to marry anyone, no matter who wins what."

"Then we will ruin your family," said Cars. "We can do it, you know. We're an example. We made the mistake of allying our very successful business interests to the Mallorough's ailing enterprise. We've done nothing but slide further and further into debt while the Malloroughs rise and shine, having accepted the benefits of our contract but giving nothing in return. We will make sure everyone sees the contract, make copies and have them mailed to everyone we know and nailed to posts in every market we can find." He looked at my mother. "It will add to the ill will created by Trader Fines's words of your family. Anything we say will merely confirm everyone's growing suspicions."

No one claimed this was impossible.

"Excuse me," Taro said before leaving the room.

I didn't stare after him, but I couldn't believe he deserted me. I was aware this whole discussion was infuriating for him, but still, to just leave like that.

I looked at my mother, at my brothers, waiting for one of them to say something to stop this nonsense. My mother met my gaze; my brothers could not. No one said anything.

"I don't care what the circumstances are," I said. "I'm not marrying anyone."

But, and I couldn't believe this, I suddenly felt less certain about that. This was stupid and old-fashioned, but the idea of my family being ruined was awful. How badly would I regret not marrying Marcus once they were left with nothing?

Would it really be so terrible if I were married, if I could still move about as a Shield and didn't have to sleep with my supposed husband?

I was appalled by my own thoughts. I was going insane. All this absurdity was pushing me over the tipping point.

Taro returned with a dinner knife. He tapped Marcus's bronze plate with the blade three times. "I accept the challenge."

"Taro! No!" I hissed. Why was he giving this farce legitimacy by accepting the challenge? All I had to do was keep saying no. Marcus couldn't afford to hang around until I said yes, which I never would, no matter what he claimed.

Unless he managed to find himself some kind of employment. I hadn't thought of that. If Linder thought he could find a position in the area, maybe it was possible that Marcus could, too.

"It's done, Dunleavy," Fiona said.

I couldn't believe what I was hearing. Were they all drunk? "Nothing's done. It's just words."

"Words are all it takes," Fiona said.

"I'm doing this, Lee," Taro told me. "Nothing you say can talk me out of it."

"This is my life!"

"It's my life, too."

Never before had I so longed for the gift of rhetoric and persuasion. I looked at everyone in the room. No one was prepared to speak up for me. I was almost numb with bewilderment. I had to get out of there. "I'm disgusted with all of you."

I had no memory of leaving the room, climbing the stairs, or entering my suite. I became aware of my surroundings only as I paced in our sitting room, my thoughts racing. I couldn't help but talk to myself, repeating demands of how they could do this, swearing every other word.

This was just foul.

Taro came in, and I was alarmed at how much I wanted to hit him. Not just a tap on the back of his head or a swat on the shoulder. I wanted to really hit him. It scared me.

"They're settling the fine details of the tests," he said.

"Then we should be there." Not that I wanted that, to have any part of shaping this fiasco, but it would be less degrading than letting anyone else determine what was going to happen.

"No. That's part of their role. The contract is between your mother and his mother. Well, his father now, as his mother is dead. It's not between you and him, or me and him."

"That's not right. This is about me." About Marcus, too, but I didn't care about him. Maybe that made me selfish. Right then, I didn't care about that, either.

"That is how the Suitor's Run works."

"How do you even know what a Suitor's Run is? I've never heard of it."

He shrugged. "A couple of the professors at the Academy were 'ristos before being sent in. They felt those of us from

High Landed families should know all of the traditions. They were remarkably thorough."

Oh, what did it matter, anyway? I sighed and sat on one of the settees, holding my knees to my chest.

Really, how was this happening in my life? It was absurd.

Taro sat beside me and took my hand. "I'm going to win," he said.

"You have no way of knowing that."

"Do you have no faith in me?"

"Don't even try that."

"The first two tests are physical, Lee. I've been spending over two years running and riding and lifting things. What has Marcus been doing?"

I was not reassured. "We have no way of knowing. Maybe he runs three leagues every morning before breakfast."

"Trust me. Have I ever disappointed you?"

"No," I admitted sullenly.

"And I really think the Prides know what they were talking about, when they said they could ruin your family. Your mother acted like it was true. I don't want that to happen to them. They're your family."

I didn't want them to be ruined, either, but this was all so unfair.

Life was unfair. I would whine about it no more. But I was not going to marry anyone. I didn't care how the tests worked out. Making me marry a stranger to save the family business was prostitution, even if no sex was involved. Not that there was anything wrong with prostitution, if that was what someone wanted to do. I didn't.

Taro put an arm around my shoulders and gave me a gentle squeeze. "It'll be all right, I promise."

I leaned my head on his shoulder.

We sat in silence for a long while, long after the sun had sunk.

Someone knocked on the door. I groaned. Taro got up to answer it.

"Good evening!" I heard Mika exclaim. "Where's our sister?"

My brothers, both of them dressed in their nightgowns,

walked into the bedchamber. I'd had no idea it was so late. Mika was carrying a flask of wine and four mugs, and Dias had a small sack. He snagged up a lit candle from a side table. Taro and I followed my brothers into our bedchamber and watched them climb onto our bed. "What are you doing?" I asked.

"We do this all the time with Kaaren at home." Dias pulled bread and cheese out of the bag. "After the house was asleep, we would meet in one of our bedrooms and talk about whatever would make us smile."

I experienced a swift jolt of envy. My brothers and sister had been sent from home to boarding schools, of course, but they still had had much more time with each other than I'd had. They'd grown up together, lived together, shared experiences and habits. I'd had friends at the Academy, and we'd developed our own traditions, but it wasn't quite the same.

"I'm not your brother," Taro said from where he stood in the doorway.

"You've put up with our sister daily for years, and you will for the rest of your life," said Mika. "So you're our brother whether you like it or not. Come on."

At first, Taro looked shocked. Then he went sort of expressionless, and I didn't know what that meant, but he joined my brothers on the bed. I climbed on, too, feeling like a child. But then, it wasn't always a bad thing, to act like a child.

"So, Sister." Mika poured wine into the mugs and handed them out. "How does it feel to be the prize to be battled over by two such handsome young men?"

"Degrading," I muttered.

"Must you bring that up?" Taro complained. "We're trying to forget about it for a bit."

"Good luck with that," said Dias.

"Maybe you don't know that brothers are supposed to torture each other," Mika told Taro.

I kicked Mika. Taro knew all about brothers torturing each other.

"Don't hit me," Mika remonstrated. "Unless you want to be tortured, too."

"Why does anyone have to be tortured?" I asked plaintively.

"That's what siblings do."

So maybe I didn't envy them so much after all.

"Did you see Lord Tarce at supper?" Dias said, pulling apart the bread he had brought. "Who unwrapped the stick from his spine?"

"He was never that bad," said Taro.

I looked at him. "Are you serious?" I bit into my chunk of bread. This was a good idea. I was suddenly starving.

"He's been pursued by people all his life because of who his parents were, who his sister is. He doesn't know how to act."

Dias laughed. "We've heard the stories, Shintaro. You've always been inundated with attention. It hasn't turned you into a stiff prat."

"Perhaps Tarce has more pride than I ever had," Taro muttered.

None of us knew what to say to that, so we spent a moment in uncomfortable silence.

Then Mika hit Dias in the back of the head. "Nice job of depressing everyone."

"Hey, he's the one who got all serious on us. Why don't you hit him?"

"Only I am allowed to hit him," I told them.

Taro raised an eyebrow.

Though, really, none of us should be hitting anyone else.

And then, out of nowhere, Mika said, "Did anyone tell you about the time Dias was caught having sex with a supplier's daughter under a table during supper?"

It was like pulling on the reins of a galloping horse. It took a few moments for the change in direction to really sink in. Because what had made Mika think of that?

Dias leapt on him, covering Mika's mouth with a hand. Mika pulled Dias's hand away and then it became a struggle as the two of them fought over where Dias's hand would go.

It was infantile, yet it made me smile and exchange an amused glance with Taro as we avoided the thrashing limbs of my brothers.

"The dinner was for potential suppliers," Mika gasped out.

"No!" Dias managed to sit on Mika's chest but his attempts to cover Mika's mouth were still thwarted by Mika's hands. "Mother and Father were hosting a house party to attract new connections."

"Shut up!"

"And one had a lovely young daughter."

"How young?" I demanded.

Mika scowled at me. "Not that young. Don't be disgusting."

"Sorry. The wording threw me."

"Anyway, when she and Dias met, it was lust at first sight. The introductions were barely finished before they disappeared. Mother was annoyed because she'd wanted Dias to observe the discussions, but no one could find him or the woman anywhere. Until supper, when after everyone had been seated we could hear these very odd noises from under the table cloth."

If one could be said to tackle another person, while both were sitting, that was what Dias did to Mika. They rolled on the bed, and Taro grabbed everyone's mugs and held them out of spilling range.

I pulled my leg up to my chest, wrapped an arm around it, rested my chin on my knee and watched my brothers act like fools. Taro was smirking. It was fun.

Mika was finally able to hold Dias down and finish the story, which, really, I could predict, but Mika was rather good with his words, after he got started and warmed up. I could even laugh at his description of Dias and his friend under the table, and how furious Mother had been at the shenanigans. Then Dias told a story of how Kaaren had disappeared for two weeks, our parents frantic until Kaaren came back with tales of her and eight others moving from house to house playing cards and smoking blue dust, unmoved by our parents' worry and fury.

I told them of a time at the Shield Academy when I had gotten sick of the soup being served for the fourth day in a row and, in an attempt to make my own, had ruined a pot and made a mess it took hours to clean. Taro told us of the time he had fainted after channeling under the guidance of a teaching Pair. It was a story I hadn't heard before, and I'd thought we had talked about everything during our long shifts at the Observation Post in High Scape.

I couldn't say how long we sat on our bed, talking. And laughing. It certainly felt very late when Dias and Mika excused themselves.

Why couldn't we have transferred to my family's site? Seventh Year wasn't Taro's place of birth, so channeling would have been easy. There would be no power plays to watch. Taro wouldn't have been torn about by his proximity to his mother. It would have all been so easy.

Maybe next time.

Chapter Ten

I was up before the sun again, having never slept solidly that night. I'd kept waking up to make sure I didn't oversleep. I tore myself from the warm blankets on our bed and dressed quietly, tying my hair back from my face. I lit a lantern and made my way out of the silent, dark manor. I tripped three times by the time I reached Browne's cottage.

I didn't know if the meeting was going to be held at all, with people being injured the day before. As I knocked on Browne's door, I thought that I might be rousing her from much needed sleep. She had probably been working hard dealing with the people hurt by the riders.

But the door opened immediately. "Shield Mallorough, fair morning."

"Fair morning, Healer Browne."

I was pulled into the cottage. "Have some tea," she said.

Three lanterns were lit and the stove was heated. I could smell the tea as Browne poured, some kind of mint mixed with something sweet. I accepted a cup and sat at the table. "I wasn't sure you would be up for this," I commented.

"Why ever not?" Browne poured herself a cup of tea and joined me at the table.

"Yesterday was a very busy day for you."

Browne took a sip of tea. "Everyone is settled with their families. Everyone will heal."

"Your talent seems exceptional." The tea was wonderful, lightly sweet.

"I had excellent teachers."

"Really? In a place as remote as this?"

"It's not remote," she responded with surprise.

I was a Shield. I was supposed to be endowed with some measure of tact. "I'm sorry. It's just so far away from everywhere I've ever been."

She smirked. "And that makes it remote?"

All right, so I felt like an idiot.

"There have always been people passing through here. I mean, obviously most of the tenant families have been here for generations, but there have always been teachers, artists, tradespeople, all sorts moving in and out."

Huh. That was surprising.

"I've always lived here, but there have been three other healers here in my lifetime. Very different in their approaches, their areas of skill. I learned a great deal from all of them."

"Did one of them teach you about casting?"

"No." She took another sip of tea. "I had a partner. We worked together, seeing to the needs of the people. She died six years ago of the sweating disease. There was nothing I could do for her. None of my skills as a healer were of any use. It was why I started exploring spells. The range for healing seemed greater."

"How did you start, though? Did you find some books?"

"No. I was seeing to a patient with a bad fever. Rock vine sickness. And I was losing the battle. His father had a suggestion. A spell he'd tried before they brought me in. It hadn't worked for him. He thought I should give it a try."

"And it worked? Your first spell?"

"I'm very good," she said without a trace of arrogance. "After that, I went looking for people and any other source of information. There's a lot to be had, around here."

"But it's dangerous, people letting other people know of their interest in casting."

"Not so much here. There has always been casting here, though for a long time the spells weren't very strong. But yes, we do have to take care. We usually don't approach anyone unless we're fairly confident they're trustworthy."

Yet people were talking to me about it. What had I done to prove to them I was trustworthy?

There was a knock on the door. "Come," Browne called. The door opened and two people entered, a young woman and a middle-aged man. They were both wearing odd, bright yellow robes. Browne and I rose to our feet. "Shield Mallorough, this is Whaler Spencer Yonhap and Fisher Penelope Tye. They're going with us." Browne withdrew into the other room and returned wearing her own yellow robe. We headed out.

It was still dark. So much earlier than I should be awake. And what about those casters taking a half-day's ride? How were they handling it?

I couldn't imagine how one rode a horse in the dark.

Someone came out of a cottage and trotted over to us. He was young, not yet twenty, I guessed, with the exaggerated slimness of youth and a messy mop of red hair. He was wearing a yellow robe, too. "Shield Mallorough, have you met Sewer Ivor Chan?"

"No, I don't believe I have."

"Actually, we have met," said Chan, and that was embarrassing. I hated forgetting people. "We helped you arrange for clothing. We had difficulty with your Shield braid. We'd never had to weave those before."

"My apologies." I was apologizing for forgetting him, not for putting him to the trouble of weaving my Shield braid.

He understood that. "You haven't been here long, and I imagine you've had to meet a lot of people."

That was true. And it hadn't helped that everyone had known who I was before we met, due to gossip.

"How is your father, Ivor?" Browne asked.

"The ointment helps, Healer Browne, but it is still difficult for him to sew."

"He shouldn't be sewing. He should be leaving that to the younger members of the family and enjoying his freedom."

"He gets angry whenever we suggest that. I think it makes him feel useless."

Browne shook her head. "There's nothing more I can do for him."

"I understand. There's nothing I can do for him, either. But he keeps asking."

Could they afford not to have their father work? One thing I had noticed about the villagers, everyone from young children to the elderly had to work very hard. And every chore I'd witnessed had looked brutal. Bending the back without relent, or ripping up fingers. I couldn't imagine doing such work.

I could sort of understand why regulars resented me. My life had to look so easy to them. They didn't know we risked our lives every time we channeled, or, more likely, they simply couldn't understand it at a real level.

Then again, there were others who risked their lives without enjoying the freedom members of the Triple S had. Soldiers, for one. Runners, too. They really had a reason to resent us.

We were heading away from the village, away from the area I usually visited. The sky was lightening a little. The morning felt fresh and vibrant.

"How long has this group been meeting?" I asked.

"Forever," said Chan.

"Not quite," said Browne. "But a few generations."

"How many are in it?"

"Usually there are twenty."

"Usually?"

"Three live in Kent. They have missed the last four meetings."

Interesting. Had they been ordered not to come? "Have they told you why they no longer wish to attend? Is it a permanent breach?"

"There has been no word from them."

We were walking by farmland. We were going to the residence of a tenant farmer, I supposed. For some reason, the idea of a farmer spell caster felt incongruous. Farming was all about hard work in the solid, heavy ground. Casting was about avoiding hard work. Air instead of soil. Words instead of implements of wood and iron. Though I supposed those that worked the hardest most deserved the ease of casting.

There was a group of people standing beside a farmhouse, most of them with lanterns. They were all wearing yellow robes, and they stood in a warped circle. No one was talking. The silence was creepy.

"You didn't tell me to wear a robe," I said to Browne. Not that I had such a garment. Not that I wanted to wear one, either. They were ugly.

My voice sounded very loud. I winced.

"You aren't a member of the group," Browne whispered. "Hurry. We're late."

There were no greetings exchanged. Once the others saw Browne, Tye, Yonhap and Chan, they straightened out the circle, setting their lanterns on the ground before them. They were, for the most part, evenly spaced. There were three spaces twice the size of the others, and I wondered if those were the places for the missing casters.

No one invited me to join the circle, so I stood to one side, feeling awkward.

They started humming, in harmony. It was a strong sound. I could practically feel it, and it hovered over the edge between attractive and disturbing. It wasn't quite music, it was something more than noise. I didn't know how, but it somehow felt welcoming. I almost wished I could participate.

They continued to hum as the sun crept up from the horizon. In my fancy, I imagined that the humming was calling the sun into place. My mind felt clouded and for just a moment, I believed that was what was actually happening.

I shook my head. Clearly I hadn't had enough sleep.

When the sun was fully in the sky, the humming stopped, and my ears and mind felt empty for a moment or two. Everyone moved closer together and Browne gestured at me to stand beside her.

And what followed was a list of names for everyone in the circle, a rush of introductions I had little hope of remembering.

Everyone joined hands, except for me. Although I stood next to Browne, she and the person on my other side reached around me to join hands. I still stood outside the circle.

"By what is this woman called?" an older man who had been introduced as Farmer Trudeau Mitloehner demanded.

I looked at Browne with a frown. Surely she hadn't brought me without asking the others first? Surely I wasn't the only one who distrusted those who inflicted surprises on others.

"Shield Dunleavy Mallorough," Browne answered a little loudly. "She is a caster seeking guidance and wisdom."

Hm. I didn't know about that. That was presumptuous of her. I was just interested in what they were doing. I really didn't trust them to guide me. I'd gotten in trouble with that sort of thing before.

"What does she bring before us?"

"Intelligence, curiosity, and goodwill."

"What will she take from us?"

"Knowledge."

"What must we fear from her?"

"Nothing."

"Shield Dunleavy Mallorough," Mitloehner said to me. "What do you bring to us?"

Ah, damn it to hell, why hadn't Browne warned me? "The desire to learn."

"What will you take from us?"

"Wisdom." I hoped. I was making this up as I went along.

"What have we to fear from you?"

"Nothing."

"And what if we should do what you disapprove?"

"It is not my place to interfere."

At that, the old man really stared at me. Really. It was hard not to look away, and I wondered what he saw, if he saw the rest of my incomplete answer, the fact that I would interfere if I thought they were doing something horrific. It didn't matter whether it was any of my business or not. Sometimes people had to stand up for things.

But apparently he saw none of that in my face. Maybe I wasn't a total loss as a Shield.

The man nodded. Everyone sat down, except for him, and I followed suit. The old man came to me and upended the contents of a pouch onto the grass in front of me. "Make a blade of grass into a rose," he said.

"Excuse me?" I said.

"You heard me."

"Why?"

"Because we ask it."

I looked at Browne. She nodded.

A test, then. One I would fail. "I don't know how to do that."

Mitloehner frowned. "I thought you were instructing her," he accused Browne.

"I never said that. She asks me questions from time to time, but she is largely self-taught."

"Those left to learn in the dark tend to stumble away from essential ground, leaving it undiscovered."

Well, that sounded pompous.

"I wouldn't presume to instruct another," said Browne.

"But you presume to bring this woman to join our circle."

"I didn't come here with the intention of joining anything," I objected. "I have obligations."

"So do we all," said Mitloehner. "Nab has her patients. We all have families. We have shops or farms. You think these are not just as demanding?"

I didn't know how to answer that. "I am not able to balance obligations as you are all able to do, apparently." That was surely the safest answer.

"And you have no interest in trying?"

I didn't know yet, so there was no point in talking about it. "I can't create a rose from grass." That, at least, was the truth.

What a worthless spell. Not that I had anything against worthless spells. The first spell I had successfully performed had had no value. It just seemed to me an odd choice for a test.

"Take a look at what we have. There are many spells possible from these supplies."

I looked them over. I picked vislock powder, a dried hinen leaf, and a human tooth. I took up the mortar and pestle and ground the ingredients together. I poured the powder into my palm and knelt behind Browne, who either knew what I was doing or trusted me a whole lot more than I deserved, as she didn't turn around to face me. "Darken the eye, blanket the mind, let thoughts go to rest, and silence all voice. Wait for my call." I blew the powder into the back of her head.

She slumped to the side and rolled onto her face, asleep. I shifted her so she wouldn't be breathing in dirt.

"Can she be roused?" Mitloehner asked.

I shook Browne and her eyes immediately blinked open. She rubbed them and looked at me. "Excellent work, Shield Mallorough."

"How do we know she didn't pretend to fall asleep?" a young woman, Maid Faye Berlusconi, demanded.

Browne sat up. "What have I done to make you think I'm a liar?"

"That's not what I meant," the woman stammered.

"Well, that's what you said."

"Enough," said Mitloehner. "Shield Mallorough, when did you start studying casting?"

"When I moved here."

"What spell did you first successfully perform?"

"An illusion, changing the color of a blade of grass."

"What is the most complicated spell you have ever performed?"

I didn't know how to answer that. The most complicated spells I had performed had been while channeling or controlling the wind. Even those weren't as complicated as other spells I'd found in various books, they just required a lot of focus. And I didn't want to tell anyone that I was doing it.

So, another spell that was complicated. "I've been able to make things rise in the air."

"Levitation," the old man said. "That requires a great deal of concentration." He pursed his lips. "When did you decide to become a Shield?"

How was that for a change of subject? "I didn't decide. I was discovered to be a Shield when I was four and I was sent to the Shield Academy."

"So you had no choice in the matter."

"Correct."

"Do you resent this?"

"No." I never seriously thought about doing something different. I was grateful to be a Shield. I loved doing it. I couldn't imagine being anything else.

"You must know a great many secrets. Because of your position as a Shield."

"I wouldn't say that," I hedged. I probably did, but not because I was a Shield.

The old man smiled. "Even now, you keep them."

If he wanted to believe I was discreet, that was fine with me. Discretion had always been a characteristic I admired.

"Shield Mallorough, please leave us."

"You mean, go home?" Then this had been kind of a waste of time, hadn't it? I could have slept in.

"No, just stand away so we may talk."

Oh. "All right." So I stood and walked until I couldn't hear them. They seemed to trust that I had gone far enough, for I could see them discussing something with great animation.

I supposed they were discussing whether I should be asked to join their group. They hadn't bothered to canvas my opinion on the matter. That was arrogant of them, and I thought I might refuse to join for that reason. I already belonged to a fairly exclusive group. I had no need to join another.

I didn't even know if I wanted to work with them. They hadn't shown me what they could do. I didn't know if I could learn anything from them. And I wasn't comfortable showing strangers what I had already discovered on my own. They might talk to others about it.

But I stood there and waited. I could be wrong. They might want something else entirely, and I might as well find out.

It was taking them a long time to come to their decision. The sun rose higher. I was glad Browne had insisted we drink the tea before we left her cottage. I was getting hungry.

In time, I was called back to the circle, and I sat down with the others. I looked about the circle and saw some expressions of disapproval. None of them knew me. Of what could they disapprove?

Of course, the reverse was true as well. They didn't know me, so of what could they approve?

"We may invite you to join our circle," Mitloehner announced.

He paused, and I gathered that I was expected to say something. "I am honored." I wasn't, but that was a safe, polite response.

"Would you, if you became part of this circle, hold your loyalty to this circle above all others?"

"Of course not." My first duty was to my Source, my second to the Triple S. They had to know that.

Berlusconi said, "Then you can't join our circle."

"I see." That was annoying, but not unexpected. "I understand."

My mild reply seemed to irritate them. "Why did you bring her here?" Berlusconi demanded of Browne.

"Trudeau told me to," Browne retorted.

"A Shield would be a positive addition to our group," said Mitloehner.

"And it's our duty to teach her," Browne added.

"Not if she doesn't want to be taught," Berlusconi insisted.

"I don't object to being taught," I protested. "But I'm not going to make any oath of loyalty to this group. I have obligations that can't be superseded by anything else." And nothing they said was going to make me feel badly about that. They didn't understand what it was to be a member of the Triple S. They couldn't. Having a Source was different from having family or a regular work partner. Those could be left. It would take a dishonorable dog to do it, but they could. I could never leave my Source, and I neither could nor would place anything above him.

"She needs appropriate instruction," said Browne. "It's our duty to make sure she doesn't cause damage in her ignorance."

"Either she joins our group and shows this circle the honor it's due," said Berlusconi, "or she swears not to cast."

"I'm not going to do either," I said. "You don't seem to understand. I'm a Shield. I can't let anyone have control over me. You wouldn't like it if I could, because you aren't the first person to try, and the first person who did was not a nice man." Before I could decide against elaborating on that last statement, I realized they weren't listening to me. Heads turned and when I followed their line of sight I saw six riders approaching at a gallop.

Something was wrong. Obviously. But something about their charge struck me as odd. They seemed to be racing right toward us. Surely, if there were some sort of emergency, they would be heading toward the village or the manor.

Unless they needed medical aid, and knew Browne would be there. Perhaps this circle wasn't as secret as I had been led to believe. Perhaps it wasn't a secret at all, and residents in the area were snickering at the self-important casters sneaking about in the predawn with their yellow robes.

Ah well. It wasn't as though I'd ever had any dignity.

I stood as everyone else did.

The riders were getting close. They weren't slowing down. No greetings were called out by anyone. I looked around at the members of the circle. There were no expressions of recognition.

I felt a trickle of alarm.

Were they going to run us down? Should we scatter? Would moving be more dangerous?

I didn't know what to do. Neither did anyone else, from the looks of it.

At what felt like the last moment, the riders veered off just slightly. They didn't leave us, though. They rode around us, again and again. They said nothing. It was eerie.

"Who are you?" Mitloehner demanded, his voice loud and commanding. It was, unfortunately, completely without effect.

I noticed the riders reaching into their purses. That couldn't be good.

Pulling their hands from their purses, they threw fistfuls of something at us. I couldn't see it, but something landed against my cheek. It felt like coarse sand, except when I rubbed my cheek, the sand didn't come off. Then the riders began to shout in unison. I couldn't quite understand what they were saying, but I heard the word "slumber," and a couple of other words that rhymed. I felt the strange buzzing sensation that meant a spell was being cast. At us. I had no idea what to do.

They were casters, but no one those in the circle recognized. So who were these people? Where had they come from?

I was suddenly dizzy, the ground spinning around me. It was hard to stay balanced, hard to stand. I had to take a step or two to stay upright. What the hell?

I couldn't see anything; my surroundings were moving too quickly.

Damn it, I was getting nauseous. I closed my eyes, but that only made the ground spin faster and harder. I was forced to open them again.

I watched the ground tilt and slide and wheel about. It hurt my eyes. A roaring filled my ears and I couldn't smell anything. I collapsed without really feeling it, I was so involved in what was going on in my head.

Then everything went black.

When I could open my eyes again, the sun was considerably higher in the sky and I felt awful, the area behind my eyes tight with pain, nausea clenching in my throat and coiling in my stomach.

Everyone else was stretched out on the ground, too, and all of them were just beginning to rouse.

And then I saw the knives planted in the ground, blade down, in front of every member of the circle, including me. The knives were perfectly straight, leading me to believe that they hadn't been thrown, but that the riders had gotten off their horses and walked around us, thrusting the knives into the ground.

The riders had been walking around us while we were helpless. They could have done anything to us.

Which was the message they were attempting to convey, I supposed.

The riders were nowhere to be seen.

"What was the point of all that?" one of the young men, introduced as Groom Jonat Miyoung, asked. "What were they trying to do?"

"Scare us," Mitloehner answered.

"Scare us from what?"

"That might be something we have to discover."

"None of you recognized any of them?" I asked.

Everyone shook their head or muttered no.

"So you've got strangers who know about your circle."

Some nodded grimly, some looked surprised.

"Shield Mallorough," Mitloehner said stiffly. "Did you talk to anyone about our circle?"

"You just said I exercised discretion," I reminded him.

"That's not a no."

"No."

"Not even to your Source?"

"Not even to my Source." My own answer surprised me. I hadn't even thought of telling Taro. And now he had no idea where I was. That was not only stupid, but thoughtless. I hadn't expected to be gone so long. He might be worried.

"Have any of you been speaking to people you shouldn't?" Mitloehner asked in a manner guaranteed to put everyone on the defensive.

And it did. "You have no need to be an insulting ass," one woman snapped, while one man gasped, "How dare you accuse us of this? We know how important secrecy is. Just as much as you."

"Shut up, everyone!" Browne shouted. "It was obviously Olson Hopkins, Matt India and Cowell Woodcock. The Kent casters," she informed me in an aside.

"I can't believe any of them would contribute to anything like this," said a very young woman, barely past adolescence. "They're good people. Olson was hilarious."

Not that I was qualified to judge any of the Kent casters—I hadn't met any of them—but it was possible to be both funny and a bastard.

"I'm not saying they knew about this," said Browne. "But it's possible, and likely, that they told Kent about us."

"So what if they did?" a woman asked. "Are you claiming Kent sent these people out to do this to us? Why would he?"

No one answered. I had no doubt they all knew Kent wanted the Westsea estate, but couldn't understand why he would choose to order a relatively harmless attack. What would that accomplish?

A warning to Fiona that no one under her authority was safe, not even casters? A warning purely for the casters, that they shouldn't—I didn't know what—that they shouldn't interfere in Kent's plans?

That would depend on what his plans were.

I was tempted to stomp over to Kent to demand what he thought he was doing, which was a stupid idea. He wouldn't tell me.

My headache was preventing me from thinking clearly.

"We need to tell Her Grace," said Browne.

"About the attack?"

"About everything."

"About the circle?"

"She doesn't know?" I demanded incredulously.

"We thought it best that she didn't," Browne told me. "We don't want news of our work to become common knowledge. It might create unfortunate complications."

Like the fact that everyone would want to know what they were doing. The people of Westsea had already demonstrated their willingness to shield their spell casters from the persecution of outsiders, but maybe the idea of a group of casters working together would appear more sinister to them. If Fiona didn't know about the casters, she couldn't be accused of harboring dangerous people.

On the other hand, if Fiona didn't know something odd was happening on her land, right under her nose, it might be seen as further evidence that she was incompetent.

"We have no proof that Kent had anything to do with this," Mitloehner objected.

"That doesn't matter," Browne responded. "Someone knows about us. Strangers. And they used a cast I've never seen or even read about before. They came on this land and attacked us. Her Grace has to be told."

I agreed. It was only sensible.

"This is something we must decide as a group," Mitloehner announced. "Shield Mallorough, will you be bound by the resolution of this group?"

"I will." I supposed. I thought they'd be idiotic if they didn't tell Fiona, but maybe they really didn't know just how accepting of spell casters she was.

And if they did decide to reveal themselves to Fiona, Fiona might decide to tell them about the spell on the dead fish. The circle might be able to determine the exact nature of the spell, maybe even who cast it.

Though I was becoming convinced that Kent was behind it all. If the riders were under his direction, he had people who knew spells Browne's circle did not. These people might have been working on such spells for weeks or months or longer, which meant Browne's casters were suffering from a severe disadvantage.

"Then please leave us. Healer Browne will contact you with our decision."

I nodded and got to my feet. "It was a pleasure meeting you," I lied, because, really, I felt awful. And I hated walking when I was nauseous. The constant threat of vomiting was just nasty.

Chapter Eleven

It was late afternoon. I couldn't believe we'd all spent so much time sleeping. And that no one from Snow's family had come looking for us. Or maybe he hadn't any family. But how could a man run a farm without family and without workers?

Maybe Taro hadn't started worrying about me. It wasn't as though I never went off on my own without telling him, or that he didn't do the same. I was tempted to try hunting him down, but it would get ridiculous, both of us going from place to place looking for each other. So I told Bailey I was back and that I would be in my suite.

I was desperate for a bath, and anxious to look through Fiona's books for a spell resembling the one used on the casters' circle. A spell that could put almost twenty people to sleep that quickly for that long scared the hell out of me.

The walk to the manor had given me enough time to change my mind about complying with the circle's decision about whether to tell Fiona about the attack. I was thinking that it was too stupid not to tell Fiona of that kind of weapon, and I'd have to go against the wishes of the circle if they chose to keep Fiona in the dark. To do otherwise would be irresponsible.

My mother was in our suite, in the sitting room, sipping tea and reading a novel. She put it aside as I entered. "Where have you been?"

I had been gone for hours without telling anyone where I was. It was expected that someone would want to know where I had been. Yet I was annoyed to be asked by my mother. How illogical was that? "I was visiting with a friend."

"Which friend?"

"Healer Nab Browne."

"Are you ill?"

"No, not at all."

Her gaze was noticeable as it dropped down to my stomach, and I resisted the urge to place my hand over it. I knew exactly what I suspected.

And I did not want to discuss anything even approaching pregnancy with my mother. I wouldn't even if I actually were pregnant. I would expect her to keep her mouth shut until I presented her with the infant. "I didn't need her in a professional capacity. She's a friend."

Mother sighed. "You went on a social call dressed like that?"

Lords. "It's a bit of a walk, Mother. Perhaps you need to recognize that I am a very practical person and leave it at that."

Not that I really expected her to do so. I just had to try.

To my surprise, my mother didn't chastise me. "Could you sit down? There are a few things I wish to discuss."

On the other hand, maybe I'd prefer that she continue to harangue me about my clothes. It was probably one of the least irksome subjects of the ones she might choose to inflict on me. I sat and waited for what I expected to be an uncomfortable conversation.

"I've heard things," she said. "Things about you and Shintaro."

I had no doubt she had, being the mother of Lord Shintaro Karish's Shield. Possibly people were speaking of how well we performed our duties, but I was sure there were also less complimentary stories about us as well. "I see."

"I'd dismissed a lot of them, people can believe the most ridiculous things, but then I come here and see that you and Shintaro—that you—well—"

Were sleeping together. I really didn't need her to go any further. "I understand," I said quickly.

She nodded gratefully. "I had no idea until I was told by mere acquaintances, instead of you. That disturbs me."

It was true. I hadn't written to them about the change in the relationship between Taro and me. But how was I supposed to do that? Mother, Father, your little girl is sleeping with her Source. Isn't that grand?

"And there is that year you won't tell us anything about."

I said nothing. I wasn't going to get into that discussion.

"It makes me wonder what else you're not telling me."

What was I supposed to do, tell them every single thing that happened to me? They had no idea how long that would take. And it would make them worry, needlessly.

While it would have been nice to get their advice regarding Fines and his crazy group, there hadn't been time for a letter to reach them and for an answer to get back to me during the course of my association with them. That really was the issue. By the time any news reached them, the events would have been over. They would have been concerned for no reason.

"It makes me feel that all of those rumors I've heard about you might possibly be true," she continued.

"Despite knowing me."

"But I don't know you that well, do I?"

That wasn't entirely inaccurate. "So what are these rumors?" I could just imagine, and I didn't want to hear, but I supposed I must. "Perhaps I can put your mind at ease." Though a petty part of me didn't want to bother, wanted to just let her believe whatever she believed, if she were that way inclined.

"They really aren't fit for polite company."

Oh, aye, this sounded wonderful. "We're not company. We're family." Why was I pushing this so hard? It wasn't as though I would enjoy hearing any of this.

My mother took a deep breath. "There are stories about Shintaro leading you into drinking excessively and using medicines that create hallucinations."

All right. Not wonderful, not something I wanted my parents to hear, but not nearly as bad as I had thought. "I rarely drink to excess." I couldn't claim to have never gotten drunk. I hadn't really put any limits on myself when I was off duty in High Scape. "And I have never used hallucinogenic medication." That stuff could do permanent damage to a person's mind.

I'd be useless as a Shield, which would mean that Taro would be useless as a Source.

My mother didn't look like she believed me. That was annoying.

She flushed; rather uncharacteristic of her, I thought. "There is talk that you and Shintaro have engaged in . . . engaged in . . ."

I couldn't help her out this time as I didn't know where she was going.

"That you, with more than one man, and more than one woman . . ." She made a gesture, obviously hoping she needn't go any further. I really wanted to smile, enjoying her discomfort. I instead raised my eyebrows in inquiry. "Intercourse . . . in . . . with several . . . participants."

Ah. I almost laughed. "No. There's been none of that." Not that I had a problem with it, as long as everyone was a consenting adult, and I wouldn't be surprised if Taro had engaged in that sort of thing in the past, but such group activities didn't interest me.

My mother cleared her throat. "We have been hearing stories about High Scape, about people trying to use spells." For a moment, her mouth quirked into a smile. "I have to admit that I'm astonished that there are people who actually believe in such things."

I should have told her that spells were real, but I felt she had more rumors to relay, and I didn't want to prompt her into a tangent. She would learn that soon enough. She couldn't help learning, staying in Flown Raven.

The amusement faded from her face. "Some say that you . . . got with child and then . . . expelled the child . . . for use in a spell."

My mouth dropped open. "That's disgusting!" I exclaimed. Then another thought hit me. "And you thought that could possibly be true?"

"Of course not!"

But she didn't sound as certain as I would have liked. I didn't know what to do. "That's appalling! You just believe everything anyone tells you about me?" How could she?

"We do not!" she snapped. "But it is bad enough that people are saying such things at all. You're a merchant's daughter. Something like that could destroy your family."

What worried her more, my reputation or that of the family? Had she been this hard when she'd visited me in High Scape? She had nagged me about my clothes, and had tried to create a romantic relationship between myself and a man I'd had no interest in, but I'd never doubted she genuinely cared about me. This time, though, she seemed concerned about me only as far as I was a member of the family. I didn't understand this. What had changed? Or perhaps this contract and the Prides were putting her under unusual strain. "There's nothing to be done about it. I can't control other people's tongues."

"You could act to avoid such rumors from ever starting."

"And how does one do that?" I demanded.

"By doing the things a normal person does."

"Normal? You mean to behave in a way a regular would?"

"A regular," she huffed. "Are you unaware how offensive that term is?"

It appeared I could do nothing right that day. "How can it be offensive?" I asked with genuine bewilderment. "No one has ever said so to me before."

She opened her mouth to say something that I had no doubt I wouldn't like, but she was halted by a thud from out in the corridor. This was followed by loud laughter. Then the door flew open so forcefully I feared for the wall it slammed against.

My brothers and Taro spilled into the room. The sour stench of ale spilled in with them. All three of them were hammered.

"Mother!" Dias greeted cheerfully. "Lee!"

"Lee, my love," Taro corrected him.

My mother stared at them. "What kind of behavior is this?"

"It's fun!" Dias declared, throwing his arms wide, thereby releasing Taro, who would have collapsed if Mika hadn't caught him. "You remember fun, Mother."

"This is disgusting!" my mother exclaimed.

"Oh, relax, Mother," Dias sneered. "There are no ledgers here. No suppliers. No workers. Nothing to do but enjoy ourselves. I've heard stories about how much you liked to enjoy yourself when you were younger. Do try not to be a hypocrite."

So, Dias wasn't a fun drunk.

Taro put a finger to his lips. "Shhh!" He leaned in to whisper in a voice we could all hear. "We can't let them know we've been drinking. They'll get mad."

Mika rolled his eyes. "I did try to get them to slow down, but there was no reasoning with them."

Ah, Mika was sober. I was glad one of them had been sensible.

Taro took a few wobbly steps before slumping into a settee. "I am not drunk," he announced.

If an event happened in the next few hours, we were all dead. Alcohol shattered a Source's concentration and altered the way his mind worked, making it difficult to Shield. I couldn't believe Taro had been so irresponsible.

"So what do you have to say, eh?" Dias challenged my mother. "Going to punish me?"

I frowned at him. I really hoped that was just the drink talking. The idea of my mother punishing my adult brother was disturbing. And what kind of punishment would it be?

"You're embarrassing yourself, Dias," said my mother.

"No, my dear mother, I'm embarrassing you. Isn't that the greater crime?"

Mother didn't answer that. "Who saw you?"

"Everyone!" Dias grinned. "Even the Prides. That makes it the worst of all, doesn't it?"

"How old are you?" my mother asked Dias. "Is this any way to conduct yourself?"

Dias dropped into the settee beside Taro. The piece of furniture creaked under the onslaught. Dias threw an arm around Taro's shoulders and pulled him close. "Taro's older than me." Taro grinned and leaned his head on Dias's shoulder.

"Shintaro's not my responsibility."

"Neither am I!" Dias shouted.

I couldn't help wincing. Really didn't want to witness some contretemps among my family, especially when one of the parties was drunk. That just couldn't end well.

"All right," said Mika, reaching for Dias's hand. "How about you sleep this off?"

"Back off, Mika," Dias snapped, pulling away. "I'm not your responsibility, either."

"Shhh, shhh, shhh." That was Taro again. "They'll know."

"They already know, Taro," Dias said impatiently.

"Not if we don't tell them," said Taro in a solemn tone.

"You're being stupid, Dias," said Mika. "And you're making a fool of yourself."

"And the gods forbid we should make fools of ourselves. Now you're starting to sound like Lee." He turned to look at me. "This is all your fault, you know," he accused me.

How did I become a part of this?

"Their perfect little girl," said Dias. "So obedient and calm. Why couldn't we all be like that?"

That was the first time I'd ever heard anything like that. My mother, when she'd visited me in High Scape, had admitted she was uneasy with me because I was cool and detached.

Taro laughed. "Obedient?" he sputtered. "Who the hell told you that?"

Actually, I was obedient, though I really didn't like to think of myself that way. I always did whatever anyone told me: the Triple S, the Emperor, the Empress before him. I didn't think I had a choice but to be obedient. So I didn't know what Taro was talking about.

"Mother," Dias said with some bitterness. "Before she was sent to her Shield Academy, she was quiet and easy and never made any trouble."

"You were two when I was sent to the Academy," I reminded him.

"That didn't stop the parents from talking about you."

All right, I could understand why he'd find that irksome.

"And then all our visits thereafter, how polite you were, how you never kicked at the restrictions placed on you."

He really resented me for this. It baffled me.

"Mother's been trying to get her to change her clothing since we got here," Mika reminded him. "And she hasn't."

"And what does Mother do when Lee throws her orders back in her face? Nothing."

I hadn't thrown anything in anyone's face. "So you're annoyed with me for being obedient, and you're annoyed with me for being disobedient. Make up your mind. You don't get to ride both horses."

"And what do you have to do?" Dias demanded. "Snap your fingers every once in a while to stop a storm or something. Ridiculous."

By Zaire, he was one of those people who thought we did nothing. My own brother.

He'd seen something of what Taro went through when he channeled. He had been worried about me because of it. This didn't make sense.

"Hey hey hey!" Yes, that roused Taro. "That's not true. You don't know what you're talking about."

"Oh, please. Have you ever had to get up before dawn because you had to work?"

"We did. And in the middle of the night, too. All sorts of times. In High Scape."

"And here?"

"Here we're on duty all the time," I said. "Day or night."

Dias snorted. "You're on duty now, are you?"

"We are." I looked at Taro. "And you'd better hope nothing happens now, because he's pretty much useless. Thank you ever so much for bringing him to this."

"Trying to blame this on me, are you?"

"He's not drunk so much since he got here."

"Maybe he needed to escape from your perfection, too."

Bastard.

"Shut up, Di," said Mika.

"You go to hell," Dias snapped back.

"Mika, take him to your room," my mother ordered.

"I'm not going anywhere," said Dias. "Get us some wine, Lee."

Like hell I would.

Mother gasped suddenly, her eyebrows raised. "Oh, Zaire." She looked at me. "Shintaro doesn't get drunk. You mean that."

"Never when he might have to channel. Never. He has a high sense of responsibility." I looked at my Source, sprawled in the settee and smiling happily at nothing. "Less than half a candle mark ago, I would have thought this"—I waved a hand at Taro, and he waved back—"impossible."

"And Dias isn't usually so . . ."

"Obnoxious?" I suggested.

"Not even when he drinks to excess."

"Ah." It could be just the influence of Flown Raven. It seemed to have an odd effect on people. Taro had been a mess when we first arrived. "Our situation is a little stressful."

"No, that's not it. It's about the contract."

"The marriage contract?"

"Aye. It had some odd clauses. Clauses I'd never seen, not in any other contract I'd signed or witnessed. I didn't think anything of it, at the time. I had no prior knowledge of family contracts. It didn't seem strange to me that they would be written differently from business contracts."

I was curious and irritated. "What in the world could any contract have to do with everyone's behavior right now?"

"It says something like"—she frowned, trying to remember the words—"when the parties are to marry, the groom and his family are to be housed, clothed and fed by the bride's family. Failure to meet this obligation on the bride's family's part will result in weakness and disharmony within the bride's family." She looked at my brothers and my Source.

I didn't know anything about contracts, but a clause like that sounded absurd.

And yet, in this very short time, Mother was, I thought, uncharacteristically critical, Dias was, apparently, uncharacteristically hostile, and Taro was uncharacteristically drunk.

"How could such a clause be enforced?"

"I had no idea. I still don't. I only know that the Prides came here to complete the contract, and we did not house them. They are rooming at a tavern in the village. And now, look at what we have."

"I don't have a home," I reminded her.

"We have to hope our presence in the manor enables us to consider it ours for the purposes of the contract. I'll ask Her Grace if she'll allow the Prides to room here."

"You can't possibly think it will make a difference."

"It wouldn't cause any harm."

Hester walked in. "Her Grace requests the presence of Holder Mallorough," she announced.

"Get us some wine," Dias ordered.

"That won't be necessary," I told her.

"Lee!" Dias shouted.

He really needed to calm down. "You can go now," I said to the maid.

"Her Grace is waiting for you in her office," Hester said before she left the room.

I rose to my feet as my mother did. "I'm going, too."

"It's only to be the signatories of the contract."

"Cars isn't a signatory, his wife was."

"She's dead. Adaptations must be made."

"So my attendance can be another adaptation."

"Fine," my mother snapped. "Mika, make sure these two don't drink any more. They're already an embarrassment to us all." I followed her out of the room, and as soon as the door closed behind us she asked me in a low voice, "What is Taro like hungover?"

"Usually it only takes a hot meal to perk him up, but I've never seen him this drunk before."

"So you don't know whether he'll be fit to run a race tomorrow."

Hell. I hadn't thought of that. "No, I don't."

"Damn it."

Fiona and Cars Pride were in her office, bent over her desk. A map covered the entire surface.

"What is she doing here?" Cars demanded, glaring at me.

"I came to observe."

"Well, you can't observe. Get out."

"Cars Pride," Fiona snapped. "You will be civil or you will leave."

"You don't see Marcus here, do you? We know how to follow legal procedure."

Fiona was clearly working to hold on to her patience. "I'm afraid you'll have to leave, Shield Mallorough."

"I understand," I said. I didn't really, but I wasn't going to make things difficult for Fiona. "I'm really just here to request that tomorrow's race be postponed a day."

"No," Cars responded bluntly.

"Why?" Fiona asked.

"Taro's indisposed."

"Indisposed?"

"He's drunk," Cars announced.

Fiona looked at me. I nodded. "You don't think he will be able to participate tomorrow?"

I hesitated. I didn't know how well Taro could run while hungover. I wouldn't have wanted to do it.

And Cars saw my hesitation, of course. "Then he forfeits," he said with satisfaction. "The first test goes to Marcus."

"No!" I said quickly. "There's no reason why the test can't be delayed."

"Except that tomorrow was the date agreed upon and we don't agree to change it. Especially for the reason you're seeking the change. It's not our fault Karish is so irresponsible."

He wasn't irresponsible. My brothers did something to him. Or something did. I needed to get a look at that contract. "Then tomorrow it is." Was there a point? Could Taro possibly win?

"Then, if you would please excuse us." Fiona gestured toward the door.

Fine, fine. I couldn't believe Cars wouldn't allow the delay. After all, he was seeking to become part of our family. Wouldn't he want to be less of an ass?

The race was going to happen no matter how hungover Taro might be. This would not be pretty.

All right, stop worrying. He won't let you down. It'll be fine.

It'll be fine.

Chapter Twelve

I slept poorly. I was worried. I tried to talk myself out of my concern. It was only the first test of three. If Taro lost it, he would win the next two, I had no doubt. And if he lost all three, I still wouldn't marry Marcus, because the very idea of me marrying anyone was stupid. And my family would just have to handle the damage to their reputation. They were the ones responsible for this mess.

Though maybe the Cars would sue my family if Marcus won and I failed to marry him. They seemed the sort to do that.

But that wasn't the only thing keeping me awake. I couldn't stop thinking of what Dias had said, the accusations he had made. I couldn't believe he held such opinions of me. He barely knew me and I was his sister. Shouldn't he be starting from a position of liking me? And he'd never even asked me what being a Shield was like, not since we were young children. Why would he hold such thoughts and not talk to me about them?

Thinking while stuck in bed had to be one of the biggest wastes of time.

It was a good hour before dawn when Taro groaned and scrubbed at his face. "Oh, gods," he mumbled.

"Good morning, darling," I said in the sweetest voice I could fake.

"Not morning, yet," he muttered.

"Ah, but it will be soon, and you have a race to run."

After a few long moments, he said, "Mm?"

"You're running a race in a couple of hours. Isn't that grand?" I could tell by looking at him that my words were making no impression. I waited.

In a little while he said, "Oh gods."

"Feeling wonderful yet?"

"Oh gods."

"It's going to be a beautiful day."

"Woman, leave me alone."

"Normally, I might." It would depend on how much he'd annoyed me the night before. "But you have to run a race in not too long."

His eyes still closed, his brow furrowed in a frown. Even needing a shave he was too cute. "A what?"

"A race."

"A race?"

"A race."

His eyes opened. They were bloodshot. "A what?"

"You have to run a race," I said slowly. Why were we bothering? He was going to lose.

"Today?"

"In a couple of hours."

He groaned again. "Do it tomorrow."

"That's not an option. You run it today or you forfeit."

"Hm?"

"If you don't run today, Marcus wins this test. You remember the tests? The ones you agreed to?"

He closed his eyes and rolled over, pulling a pillow over his face.

"Oh, no no no. You are getting up and you are getting ready for this race." I left the bed to yank on the bed cord. "You don't really have clothes for this. What do you want to wear?"

After a short pause, Taro said, "You are an evil woman."

"I love you, too, dear."

When Hester came to our door, I asked for coffee and ale, which she clearly found strange but didn't question, as well as hot water. While she was gone, I let Taro fall back to sleep as I dressed and tried to figure out what Taro would want to wear. I did not have anything near his flair for clothing. I didn't know whether he'd want to be practical or whether he'd want to make some kind of visual impact. I didn't know much about clothes, but I did know the visual could have an influence on people's minds, and if Taro could find a way to intimidate Marcus through the power of clothing, I was all for it.

Hester returned with the coffee and ale and I sent her away again. I brought the tray of beverages and mugs to the bedchamber. "All right, Shintaro Ivor Cear Karish, it's time to sit up." There was no response. I took his pillow away and shook his shoulder. He batted at my hands. "Up, Taro."

"My eyes roll in sand," he muttered.

"Have some of this ale and you'll feel much better."

"Oh gods."

"You have that stupid race today, Taro. We have to get you conscious for it."

"Can't we postpone it?"

Patience patience patience. "No, Taro. You either run today or you forfeit. Do you want to forfeit?" Because I couldn't force him to run.

He kind of writhed on the bed before finally sitting up. "No."

"Here." I handed him the mug of ale.

He took it with a grimace. "Gods."

"Wait 'til you see what comes next."

He didn't ask. He drank some of the ale, and declared himself ready to shave. Once he had done so, he dressed in one of his looser pairs of trousers, a white shirt with slightly flowing sleeves, and a dark blue waistcoat. His hair, as always, was tightly tied back.

He looked good. As usual. A little pale, though. "Now have some of this."

"What?"

"Coffee."

"I am not touching coffee!"

"Have you ever even tried it?"

"Of course I've tried it. I wouldn't say I didn't like it if I'd never tasted it."

"Then you know nothing wakes you up like coffee. Drink."

With an expression of distaste, he took the mug of glorious coffee and bolted it down in three large gulps. "Gods, that's foul." He thrust the mug back into my hand.

"And you call yourself an aristocrat." Aristocrats were known to linger over their ridiculously expensive coffee.

"I never call myself an aristocrat."

That was true. I called him an aristocrat, especially when I wanted to annoy him. He seemed to find it insulting. I couldn't quite grasp why. Sure, most aristocrats were useless, but there wasn't anything actually wrong with them.

Except Taro's mother. She was evil. So was the Emperor.

"How do you feel?"

"Vile."

"That's my boy."

He glared at me.

Hey. I had to get my amusement where I could. This was all a humiliating mess.

The race would begin and end at the front steps of the manor. There were people already waiting, tenants and a few of the local gentry. People who clearly didn't have enough to do. Fiona was present to arbitrate. Marcus and Cars were standing still, ignoring everyone. Marcus, of course, looked hale. Not a trace of a hangover about him.

"Good morning, Dunleavy, Shintaro," Marcus greeted us, and Cars nodded. Taro and I nodded back.

My mother and Mika were there. I supposed Dias was too hungover to attend. Tarce was standing beside Radia, who was seated in a chair that had been brought down for her. I didn't like it. I understood the need for witnesses, but did there have to be so many? Did they have to include people we didn't actually deal with on a daily basis?

I wondered why Browne was lurking off to the side. Did she think anyone would need her services? It was only a foot race.

One of Fiona's servants was digging a long, very narrow and shallow ditch into the ground. "Source Shintaro Karish, Trader Marcus Pride," Fiona called out. "This is where you will begin, and this is where you must cross to complete the race. I have placed people along the route of the race." She pointed out the maid standing some distance away in one direction, and the footman off in the other. "Every stretch of the route will be under someone's eyes."

"How dare you assume my son will cheat?" Cars blustered. "He has at least as much honor as any 'risto."

"I will not allow any room for allegations of misconduct," Fiona said coolly. "If this outrages your son's delicate sensibilities, he can withdraw and forfeit."

"I should have never agreed to your being the arbiter," he mumbled. "You're his cousin, aren't you?"

Where did Marcus get his good manners? Certainly not from his father. A fact of which Marcus was clearly aware. "I have no objection to further witnesses," he said quickly. "Nor to you, my lady, acting as arbiter."

"Don't let these people intimidate you, Marcus," said Cars.

"*I* am not intimidated."

All right, I had to admit the arch demeanor in which he addressed his father appealed to me.

"May I continue?" Fiona's tone was glacial.

"Please do." Marcus spoke before his father could. "I apologize for the interruption."

Fiona nodded. "You will not touch each other," she said. "The competitor who touches the other forfeits the race. Any attempt to sabotage, of course, has an identical result. Accidental injury will not be a reason to halt the race."

I stopped listening to Fiona's list of rules when I noticed the Dowager Duchess on her way across the grounds. Oh, wonderful. It only needed this. I wondered if we could get the race started before Taro noticed her.

Linder was with her. So were two other men, young and handsome. A puerile portion of my brain wondered just what positions they had in her household.

And then Taro did notice her. I saw his head turn to look at her. He didn't sigh or swear or groan. He just turned his head again to look back at Fiona. Good lad.

"Do you understand the rules?" Fiona asked.

"I do," said Taro.

"I do," said Marcus.

"Do you consent to participating in this, the first of three tests, to determine who Shield Mallorough will marry?"

"I do."

"I do."

"I call on all those present," said Fiona, "to bear witness to this trial. Those of the east bring balance. Those of the west bring length of sight. Those of the north bring endurance. Those of the south bring grace. All must favor the outcome of this trial."

And, again, I felt the strange jittery sensation of a spell being cast. That had been happening a lot recently. I looked around. Who was casting a spell, what kind, and why? Unease filled me. I didn't see any obvious signs of casting. I looked at Browne, the only other caster I knew who was in the group. She was looking straight back at me, frowning, her lips pressed together.

So she was feeling something, too.

"Take your places," said Fiona, and Taro and Marcus stood at the ditch, facing north. "Three, two, start." The two men took off. To my disappointment, Marcus quickly outpaced Taro and was a significant distance beyond him when they ran out of sight.

This was going to humiliate Taro. That was something I really hadn't contemplated when this had all started. Of course, I hadn't been thinking of anyone at all, except myself.

It was just the beginning. I shouldn't be so pessimistic.

The Dowager Duchess headed straight to me. Of course, she did. When Taro wasn't around, I was her favorite target. I took a deep breath, fortifying myself against her obnoxious arrogance.

"I hope you're proud of yourself," she said.

"Always," I answered.

"Do you take pleasure in watching my son make an idiot of himself?"

"Not as much as you do, I imagine." The Dowager Duchess trying to imply she felt protective toward her son. Who was she trying to fool?

"The House of Karish competing for a woman like a peasant chasing after a greased pig."

I almost smiled. I found the visual funny. "This is a ritual of aristocrats."

"The House of Karish has never demeaned itself in this way. You have brought us to this."

I didn't respond to this because it was sort of true. My family was responsible for this. To an extent. But to be brutally honest, Taro stepped into this mess unnecessarily, and with no prodding from me. I wasn't going to say that, though. She'd accuse me of blaming him for this spectacle.

"This is what you wanted all along, isn't it?"

"Being married off to a stranger? I can really say no."

"Having my son make sport of himself for your amusement."

"You're the one with a history of denigrating him, not I."

But I couldn't disagree. It had never been intentional on my part, but Taro had often been subjected to degrading circumstances because of me. It wasn't fair, and if I could figure out a way to stop it this time, I would.

"You are insufferable," she announced. "Linder, remain with the Shield."

That seemed to surprise Linder, but he nodded. What, was he supposed to guard me in some way? Keep me from doing something? How did she expect him to hamper my behavior?

The Dowager left, and good riddance to her.

I stood with Linder for a few moments, feeling awkward. "What do you think of all this?" I asked him without thought. It wasn't as though I actually wanted to discuss this whole fiasco, especially with a stranger. I just couldn't bear to be silent at that moment.

Linder frowned, and it was kind of cute. "It doesn't seem terribly dignified."

"No, it does not."

"No doubt that is why the Dowager disapproves of it so."

She didn't approve of anything Taro did unless whatever he did was under her order. "No doubt. Though I'm surprised she came to watch if it offends her so greatly."

He looked surprised. "He's her son."

So he was under the impression that the Dowager actually felt affection for her son. I wondered how he had come to that conclusion. It would have been interesting to know how the Dowager spoke of Taro to other people.

I heard Fiona's voice, a little lower than those around us, snapping at someone. I couldn't hear the words, but she was clearly annoyed with the fisher standing beside her.

"I know this is none of my business," Linder said delicately. "But it seems to me that Lady Westsea is having a great deal of difficulty with . . . things. She would benefit from the Dowager's guidance, would she not?"

Dear, sweet, misguided child. "It is none of my business, either."

"You care about Lady Westsea, though, don't you? You want her to be well?"

"Of course."

"Then she should be encouraged to seek advice, shouldn't she?"

"I wouldn't dream of interfering," I told him. "I can't believe you would."

"I know my place, I really do. But people are so worried about their livelihoods. I know what that feels like."

Still, he was a visitor to Flown Raven. He should keep his mind on his own concerns.

"I know I shouldn't tell you this, but I've been handling her correspondence. She thought it would be good practice for any position I might get." He leaned closer. "She has received correspondence from the Emperor."

And that was when I decided he shouldn't actually be anyone's solicitor, if he couldn't be discreet. Though that didn't stop me from asking, "What did it say?"

"That correspondence, she hasn't let me see, and all the letters were sent before I came here."

Unfortunate. I would have loved to be able to learn what foul information the Dowager and the Emperor sent back and forth to each other.

"But it speaks well of her, does it not, that she is in his confidence?"

It was alarming. Perhaps it meant that when she claimed to know what the Emperor was thinking or planning, she was telling the truth. That made the fact that she was claiming the Emperor was willing to support Taro should he seek to retake the title a whole lot more disturbing.

"So Lady Westsea should be encouraged to seek the Dowager's counsel, don't you think?"

I thought Linder was a poor judge of character.

Browne sidled up beside me. "May I speak with you a moment, Shield Mallorough?"

"Of course." I looked to Linder. "Excuse me." I let Browne lead me a small distance from the rest of the crowd.

"You know there's some kind of cast involved in this," she whispered.

"Aye, but how, exactly? I'm not doing anything. Lady Westsea can't. Do you think the Prides are?" Were they cheating?

"I can't get a feeling for a particular person or even direction," said Browne. "It seems more . . ."

I waited for her to finish, but she didn't. "More what?"

Her sigh was, I thought, prompted by frustration. "What is this all about?"

"I assumed everyone knew," I answered dryly.

"I've heard stories, of course. I'd like to know what you know."

Fine. "It's a marriage contract. They gave my family goods and the use of their connections. Once Marcus and I were adults, we were to get married."

"And what happens if you don't? Get married?"

"My family's reputation would be ruined."

"That's all?"

"That seems to be enough, according to them."

She thought about that for a moment. "It was my understanding that a person's personal obligations were terminated if they're called to one of the academies."

"Aye."

"But the Prides would have darkened the Mallorough name anyway? Wouldn't that have fired back on them, under the circumstances?"

"I don't know."

"I'm pretty sure everyone knows a Shield can't be held to a marriage contract."

"My family fears people won't."

"Then what's the point of all this?" She waved a hand at the starting ditch of the race.

"If Taro wins, I won't have to marry Marcus."

"But you don't have to marry him. Everyone already knows that."

"Marcus offered the challenge to either void the contract or enforce it. Taro felt compelled to accept."

"Reviving the contract," Browne murmured.

"What do you mean?"

"The contract was dead. It would have stayed dead if you had just sent them away. I think the tests resurrected it."

An additional layer of unease coated my chest. "I don't understand."

"Just what I said. A contract can lapse if both parties don't enforce its particulars for a long enough period of time, but can be resurrected if the parties then resume enforcing the contract."

While I was busy being horrified, I latched on to something irrelevant. "How do you know that?"

She shrugged. "I dabbled with the idea of being a solicitor for a while. Decided it was too boring."

I didn't feel any better learning that she probably knew what she was talking about. "It doesn't matter. I'm not going to marry Marcus, either way."

"I really doubt it's that simple. There's a spell involved. I don't think that's normal."

"My parents don't believe spells actually work."

"Perhaps it doesn't matter if they do. Perhaps the contract and its enforcement have some kind of spell written through it. What was the process of creating this marriage contract?"

"I don't know. I assumed it was just a normal contract written up by a normal solicitor."

"There was probably more to it than that. I think whoever designed the contract might have been a caster. There is a ritual in creating contracts. The laws are specific about wording, who can draft contracts, how they're signed. From what I understand, only a certain kind of paper can be used, only a certain kind of ink. It all has the making of a spell. Changing the terms would have an element of casting, too. But none of you really know what you're doing. The end results could be unpredictable."

"But we all agreed to the new terms."

"Did you use a ritual?"

"No. Well, yes. There was some kind of ritual involved when Marcus challenged Taro. Apparently, it was traditional." Only Marcus hadn't had a proper emblem. Because he wasn't an aristocrat. "It wasn't exactly how tradition dictated, though."

"Listen, I'm just guessing. I do believe your being sent to the Shield Academy may have successfully severed the contract. The academies are places of power on their own. It's possible, even likely, that if you had left things alone, the contract would be void. By agreeing to these tests, you have resurrected the power of the contract. Possibly in its original terms."

I glared at her. "Are you saying that if Taro loses the tests, I'll have to marry Marcus or my family might suffer serious repercussions enforced by a spell?"

"Or the spell involved might force you to marry Marcus."

"How could it do that? It can't force me to show up for the ceremony, or say things I don't want to say." Could it?

"I can't be sure, of course, but that would be my guess."

Browne was a smart, smart person. Damn it.

My mother was standing a little off by herself, staring intently in the direction from which the runners would appear. I would ask her how the contract had been created. Later. When I could yell at her in private.

Dias wasn't anywhere in sight.

Mika and Linder were together, laughing, the heartless bastards. Linder put his hand on the small of Mika's back, and Mika leaned into him. Hmm.

Marcus came into view, Taro nowhere near him. That was disappointing, even though I'd been expecting it. Some of the spectators starting cheering, which surprised me. What did they care who won? And if they did care, why didn't they support Taro? He was less of a stranger to them than was Marcus.

Or maybe they would have cheered for whoever came first regardless of who it was. Fickle lot.

Marcus crossed the ditch. "I declare Marcus Pride has crossed the termination mark and has successfully completed this test," Fiona announced.

Marcus, slightly out of breath even though he probably hadn't needed to push himself as hard as he did, walked over to stand beside his father. Cars slapped him on the back in congratulations. Then everyone watched for Taro.

He didn't show.

This was really embarrassing.

Taro really put up with a lot of trash because of me. Here he was putting himself on display for crowds of strangers because of something stupid my parents did. It just wasn't fair.

How could I show my appreciation?

And then, finally, Taro came into view. He had clearly been running as fast as he could, but looked to be at the end of whatever strength he'd had. Should I cheer for him? No one else had. Even the conversations had stopped and we were watching Taro stumble along in silence. Would my lone voice raised in support just sound pathetic? Just make the lack of everyone else's support more noticeable?

I stayed silent. So did everyone else.

Taro crossed the ditch. "I declare Shintaro Karish has crossed the termination mark and successfully completed this test," said Fiona. "As arbiter, I find Marcus Pride the winner of this test."

And I felt that jittery sensation again.

Ah, hell.

Chapter Thirteen

"Mother," I whispered, ignoring everyone else in the area. "Do you have a copy of the contract with you?"

"Of course."

"Can you bring it to my suite?"

"Certainly." She strode back into the manor.

I stepped over to Taro, wrapped my arm around his and rested my forehead against his shoulder.

"I'm sorry," he murmured.

"There are two more tests."

"I got drunk yesterday," he said with disgust.

I wasn't sure what to say to that. "Aye, you did."

"I'm sorry."

I rubbed his arm. "I don't blame you."

"How can you not?"

"I am a beneficent and wondrous person and you should worship me." That got a smile out of him, at least, weak as it was. "Can you go up to our suite? Mother is going to show me the contract."

He nodded and kissed my forehead and left.

Mika was deep in conversation with Linder. "I envy you," Mika was saying. "I've never been there."

"I thought traders traveled everywhere."

"In time, perhaps. My father travels a lot. He's been taking my brother about more frequently, but never to Red Swan."

"You wouldn't believe how much—"

"Excuse me, gentlemen," I broke in. "Mika, I'm sorry to interrupt, but I really need to speak to you and Dias and Mother. Can you go up to my suite?"

Mika looked mildly annoyed, but he nodded. "I'll catch up with you later, aye?" he said to Linder.

"Of course." Linder stroked Mika's cheek, smiled at me and followed the Dowager back to her house.

That had happened quickly.

"Where's Dias?" I asked Mika.

"In bed, the last I saw him."

"This late? Really?"

"He's enjoying sleeping late here. We're not often able to do that at home."

"Huh. Could you dig him out?"

"Yes, Mother," he muttered.

"Thank you, my love."

Finally, I approached Fiona. "My lady," I said quietly. "I have a favor to ask. Another one."

Fiona seemed weary, but she said, "Certainly."

Which made me feel worse about asking. "Our contract dictates that my family provide housing for the Prides at this time. Your manor is the closest thing we have to a home."

"You want me to invite them to stay with us?"

"It is a great deal to ask, I know."

She shrugged. "Sure."

People who didn't ask troublesome questions were fantastic. "Thank you."

Taro and my mother were in the suite when I got there. Taro was pacing, his expression grim. Blaming himself for his loss. And yes, technically, it was his fault, but I couldn't really hold him responsible. His intoxication was just so uncharacteristic. Something was odd about the whole thing.

My mother was holding a scroll. "Is that it?" I asked her.

She held it out to me. "Don't expect to understand all of it. Some of the language is dense."

The scroll was thicker than I would have liked. Just to

check, I unrolled it, to see how long it was. I had to stretch my arms wide. It was ridiculous.

After a knock, Mika and Dias came in. I felt the tension in the room crank up. "I'm ready to hear you," said my mother, and she was saying it to Dias.

"Oh?" was all my brother said as he dropped into a chair.

There was a stiff pause as I tried to think of a way to divert the potential argument without revealing how irritated I was that they were going to indulge in one in the first place. We had important matters to discuss.

Before I could act, my mother ran out of patience. "You have appalling behavior to apologize for, boy."

"I'm not a boy," Dias snapped.

"You've certainly been acting like one."

"You always say that. The accusation is getting stale."

"I'm entitled to some respect."

"And I'm entitled to some freedom."

"You have to earn freedom."

"Just like you have to earn respect," said my brother, and I had to admit I agreed with him.

"Not as a parent."

"As anything."

"I'm not even concerned about your reprehensible manner toward me yesterday—"

"I said nothing I'm ashamed of."

"—but you got Taro drunk—"

Taro stopped pacing to lean against the wall. "I got myself drunk."

"—and he lost the race today."

Taro pinched the bridge of his nose as Dias stared at him. "You lost?" he demanded.

"I would have lost anyway. He was fast. Faster than I could ever run, hungover or not."

"Getting drunk didn't help," said my mother.

"Getting drunk was entirely my fault."

"And you have a habit, do you, of getting drunk in the middle of the day?"

Taro hesitated. He didn't want to incriminate my brothers. He didn't want to get in the middle of their argument. He was a smart man.

"When was the last time you got drunk, Shintaro?" my mother asked.

She had no right to ask him that. Taro agreed. His smile was slight. "I don't remember."

"This one makes a regular habit of it." Mother thrust a thumb at Dias.

I didn't like this. What was she hoping to accomplish? If she merely wanted to give him a dressing down, it should be done in private.

"Why are you attacking him?" I asked her. "You said yourself there was a clause in this contract that stated we would suffer weakness and disharmony if we failed to provide the Prides with housing."

"So what if there is? It's just a weird coincidence."

"Do you really believe a solicitor would put language in a contract that had no use or meaning?"

"You clearly haven't read any contracts."

That was true. Still, it didn't make sense to make a contract longer than necessary. Unless . . . "Are solicitors paid by the word?"

Mother looked pained. "Of course not."

"Then every word must be significant. We were supposed to house the Prides. We didn't, and now you two are at each other's throats."

"We always are," Dias said flippantly.

"In front of others?" I asked.

Dias frowned, clearly thinking about it.

"Taro does not get drunk when he might have to channel," I declared.

Taro scowled.

"How do you explain that?" I asked my mother.

"How do you?" Mother countered.

Oy, this was going to be awkward. "I believe the contract is supported by a spell."

Mother stared at me. Dias snickered. Mika raised his eyebrows.

"What happened to you?" Mother demanded. "You've always been so sensible."

"Spells are real. Casting is real. And I have reason to believe that casting was involved in the creation of the contract."

My mother and my brothers all stared at me. "Are *you* drunk?" my mother asked.

Of course, they couldn't just take my word for it. "Excuse me." I went to the bedchamber and closed the door behind me. I unlocked the overmantel and took out the ingredients I would need. After putting the overmantel back together, I returned to the sitting room.

I hesitated for just a moment. I was showing my ability to cast to people who didn't believe in spells, who might be shocked. But surely there was no danger. This was my family.

"Choose something," I told my mother. "Anything you can easily pick up with your hands."

With a sigh of impatience, she stood and picked up a small vase.

"Put it anywhere you like in the room, as long as it's in sight."

She merely moved it from one table top to another.

With the ingredients I needed, and the words I'd learned, I made the vase rise from the table top. I heard gasps and a "What the hell are you doing?" from my mother. I set the vase back down.

"I don't know all that spells can do," I said. "That's only the most minor of tasks. But I have good reason to believe that the contract has the power of a cast supporting it."

"What have you been doing?" my mother demanded. She looked at Taro. "What have you gotten her into?"

"Hey hey hey! This has nothing to do with Taro." How dare she blame Taro for this? For anything? "He can't perform spells. Only some people can perform them. I'm one of them. And spells work only in certain places. Flown Raven is one of them. And more than that, I can feel when spells are being cast. I felt something this morning, during the race."

Mother closed her eyes for a moment. "All I wanted—" She cut herself off, then started again. "It isn't enough that you're a Shield. You have to be involved in . . . in . . . that sort of thing as well?"

Amazing. She'd learned about spells and decided there was something wrong with casting them in under a minute. And since when did she have a problem with my being a Shield?

She'd always acted as though she were proud of me for it. All those visits, the letters, nothing had hinted that my family was disturbed by my status, or annoyed or disappointed.

Was this yet another effect of the contract?

Please let it be just another effect of the contract.

I took a seat and let the scroll open to the floor. I read the first paragraph. It was about two trees, one an ancient specimen, the other a young stripling, braiding their branches in order to create healthier, more glorious fruit. It was poetry of the saccharin sort, and while its meaning was clear, it wasn't the sort of thing I'd expect to see in a contract. Not even a marriage contract, which might tempt one to emotional terms of expression.

What followed was more mundane language, listing my mother and Marcus's mother as the parties of the contract, Marcus and me the fruit of it, and summarizing the purpose of the contract, which was to join our families and finances through marriage. It listed the payments the Prides were to make, the connections they were to share. These same ideas were repeated in the following paragraphs, to a degree I thought unnecessary, though the exact wording changed with each iteration.

From there, the language swerved back into metaphor. Should the Prides fail in their payments, no future grafting would be successful. I read those words out loud. "What does that mean?"

"I understood that to mean connections with other families," my mother said. "Marriages or financial alliances."

There followed a list of communications and meetings that were to take place, gifts to be exchanged, certain trading processes, which I didn't understand, to be completed. None of this occurred, I assumed, as I had been sent away by then. For each requirement, there was a punishment—described in bad poetry—for those who failed to fulfill it. "Do you remember your wells drying up when I was around six?" I asked my mother.

"No."

"You don't even have to think about it?"

"No," Mother snapped. "We never experienced dry wells on any of our properties. To my knowledge."

"And what about clause number—" I cut myself off. I couldn't ask my mother if she had ever miscarried, not in front of the boys.

But my mother appeared to know what I was referring to. "No."

That provision was horribly harsh. And there was a comparative punishment on the Prides' side, namely Cars suffering sterility. I wouldn't be able to find out whether that happened. There was no way I was asking him.

The obligations and forfeits went on. It was quite a list. I went through each item and each sanction. According to Mother, none of the conditions had been met after the initial gifts and contacts had been provided by the Prides, and none of the punishments had occurred. Which was probably one reason why my parents had been able to dismiss the contract as invalid.

And then Marcus had extended his challenge, and Taro had accepted. I couldn't be sure the sanction for failing to provide the Prides with housing had actually come to fruition. While I had never witnessed the bickering I had seen between Dias and Mother, I'd never really seen a lot of them throughout my life. But I couldn't dismiss it altogether. I'd seen what spells could do.

And the tension was still there, though Mika seemed to have escaped most of it.

The list ended with the wedding. If Marcus didn't comply, he would lose the person most important to him. The contract didn't say how. If I didn't . . . "What does it mean, that I would lose my identity?"

"There are certain sanctions that are described in very vague terms," Mother said. "The matchmaker said the nature of such provisions would be determined by future events. I thought it might refer to your status as a merchant's daughter. That something would happen to separate you from the family."

Something had, though I had never considered that a negative event. "How could you see these clauses and not think something was odd?"

Mother shrugged. "Every contract includes consequences for failing to comply."

"Things like wells drying up? Losing identities? That's normal? How were these sanctions to be enforced?"

"It didn't matter. We weren't going to fail to meet our obligations. We never had before."

That seemed overconfident and careless. But then, it had been over twenty years before that the contract had been created. Maybe my parents had been less savvy back then. "How was the marriage contract created?" I asked.

"Their solicitor contacted our solicitor," said my mother.

"Was your solicitor new to the position?"

"No. She had been with us for, I don't know, about four years at that point."

"What about the Pride solicitor?"

"I have no idea. I had no reason to ask."

"Was there anything unusual about how they contacted your solicitor?"

"No. Their solicitor sent our solicitor a letter. She showed it to us. There was nothing that struck me as strange."

"All right. So what was the next step?"

"We agreed on a matchmaker, and he—"

"Why would you need a matchmaker when the two parties had already been chosen?"

"Matchmakers also draft marriage contracts."

"Huh." I never knew that. "I would have thought your solicitors would draft the contract."

"The solicitors draft business contracts. They know nothing about marriage contracts."

"I see." A contract was a contract, wasn't it? "How was the matchmaker chosen?"

"He was recommended by our solicitor, and the Prides agreed to our choice. Matchmaker Jong-il was well known for producing excellent contracts."

"What made his contracts so particularly sought after?"

"They could never be broken. That was the reputation, anyway."

Oh, hell. Oh, hell. "And then what?"

"I and Holder Pride met with the matchmaker to sign the contract."

"And how was that done?"

She looked surprised to be asked, and then she thought about it for a few moments. "After we entered the room, we stood on opposite ends of it. At the matchmaker's prompt, we each announced our full titles and names. We took one step forward. We each named the child to be bound by the agreement. After another step, we announced what each of us wanted from the contract, and the next step, our obligations under the contract. And so on, until we met at a small table in the middle of the room. There were three goblets on the table. One goblet had red wine, the other white, the third one was empty. We each took a sip from the goblet closest to us. The matchmaker then poured the wine from both goblets into the empty one. Holder Pride and I each took a sip from that goblet. Then we signed the contract."

I stared at her. "You went through all that and you didn't think it was strange?" I demanded incredulously.

Mother looked impatient. "It's a ritual, Lee. All important events have ritual. Births, deaths, weddings. That's just the way of things."

That was true, I supposed. If I had heard of this ritual before I had learned spells were real, I would have thought it nothing more than another ridiculously elaborate procedure to do something relatively simple. "So that's all normal?"

"It's not identical to how a business contract is finalized, but there are similarities. The only significant difference was that there were no witnesses. Usually people who are not signatories observe the proceedings and sign the document as proof that everything was aboveboard. But the matchmaker didn't allow anyone else in the room."

"Did he say why?"

"Only that it went against tradition to do so. Something along the lines of a marriage contract being much more intimate than business arrangements, and as in most intimate situations, the fewer the participants, the better."

My stupid mind went to examples of intimate situations that my mother probably hadn't intended. I could be immature at times.

"What is this all about, Dunleavy?" my mother asked.

I told them what Browne told me, leaving out her identity.

Taro looked horrified, learning that his actions might have resurrected a contract that could have been left dead.

Mother appeared disheartened as well. "And you believe this woman?"

I nodded. "I can sometimes feel when spells are being cast. Have been cast. I felt something when the race was finished."

Taro suddenly tilted his head, frowning. Listening to something by the looks of it.

"What's going on?" Mother asked the room at large.

I could hear it, then. People running around the house, pounding through the halls, talking and shouting over each other. Mika opened the door. "What's going on?" I heard him ask.

"The village is on fire!" someone female answered.

"Hey! Wait!" my brother said, but no one answered.

My gods. It just didn't stop. One piece of bad luck after another. How much was Fiona supposed to take? How much were her tenants?

I headed for the door.

"Where are you going?" my mother asked.

"To see what I can do to help."

"That's not one of your responsibilities."

I stared at her, appalled.

She seemed a little appalled, too. "No, you're right. But fighting fires is dangerous. Can you really blame me for wishing you to stay out of it?"

I chose not to respond to that, and the others followed me out of the room. We all ran through the halls and down the stairs. Once we were outside, we could see people riding from the stable toward the village. I had no doubt Fiona was already on her way.

I could see the smoke against the sky, shades from white through gray to black. A fine dust floated in the air, and I could smell the bitter scent of burning wood. People were running, but one man was standing in the middle of everything, shouting, "You're all idiots!" His face was red and he was waving his arms, almost hopping about. He looked ridiculous. "It's all hopeless! Good fortune has been drained from this land! You are charging to your deaths!"

A woman paused by him and slapped him, a solid crack against the cheek. I didn't know who was more shocked, him or me. He put a hand to his cheek and stared at her. "You're making a fool of yourself," she sneered. "Do something or get out of the way."

"You're going to risk your life for a titleholder who can't protect us."

"*She's* not a coward." And then she ran off.

He didn't move. He just watched her go.

I started running. My boys ran ahead of me. I did my best to keep up, but it wasn't long before my breath was burning in my throat and I was working hard to keep my legs moving. I'd be useless by the time I got there.

I ran over a swell on the ground and then down the following incline. That was when I could see the dye maker's cottage, built a little distance away from the rest of the village. The roof was gone; the glass had popped out from the window frames. Some of the flames were pure pink. The smell was horrific.

There were a handful of people throwing buckets of water that accomplished nothing. The dye maker was one of them, tears pouring down her cheeks. Though that may have been due to the smoke rather than despair. The smoke hovered thick and low to the ground. It made my eyes sting and I couldn't help coughing, thereby dragging in more smoke.

Feeling any contribution I made to the effort to save the dye maker's home would be useless, I moved on to the rest of the village.

There were dozens of bucket lines, manned by everyone but the youngest of children. The tiny, temporary streaks of water looked pathetic against flames that stretched up so high into the sky. I had a feeling everyone was motivated more by desperation than any real belief they were going to be successful.

The heat was blistering; my skin seemed to ring with it, stretching painfully over my bones.

I noticed that not all of the cottages were on fire. I also realized that the cottages that were on fire weren't necessarily next to each other. One cottage would be on fire, the next one wouldn't and the one after that would be. How did that work?

Marcus and Cars were in one of the lines, hauling water. I found that particularly decent of them. I saw Daris, too. That floored me. She didn't seem to be too useful, though. She kept dropping the buckets.

I joined a bucket line. I accepted a bucket from one person, than ran to the next. The buckets were heavy, the contents slopping against me, the constant running was exhausting, and I was sure it wasn't doing any good. If only it would rain.

If only it would rain.

I knew of a spell that could call rain. I didn't have the ingredients for it on me and, in my experience, I could successfully cast weather spells only when working through Taro as he channeled. I was currently useless.

I shouldn't have run to the village when I heard about the fire. I should have stayed behind and kept Taro with me and performed the spell in our suite. It would have been a hell of a lot more useful than carrying little buckets of water.

Why couldn't I ever plan ahead, think things through?

Take the bucket, pass it along.

How did these fires start, anyway? Had someone been cooking something and left the fire unattended? Was it something to do with the smithy? Was there any way to find out? And if the person who was the source of the fire was found, what would happen to them? Would they be held responsible by law? Would they be in danger from the other tenants?

The water splashing up from the buckets soaked my skirt, wrapping the material tightly around my legs. The ground became muddy and slippery. I fell more than once.

More tenants showed up, this time fishers and whalers. They didn't use buckets, but larger items I'd never seen before. Shiny material hung from a square frame, the wooden edges a cubit in length each. The whalers seemed to handle them with ease, but I couldn't imagine trying to carry them.

They carried much more water than the buckets, and they were just as ineffective.

It was hard to breathe. I felt like the dark thick smoke was coating my throat and filling my lungs. My eyes were densely filled with tears, so much so I could barely see, but I couldn't spare the time to wipe them, and if I could, I wouldn't want to. My hands were filthy.

Roofs were gone, walls were crumbling into black chunks. People were giving up. Some dropped their buckets and stared.

Others sat on the muddy ground and cried. A few screamed about how much they had lost. Those who kept working became slower and sloppier in their efforts. I doubted anyone really thought any of the cottages or their contents could be saved. They just didn't want to face giving up.

I kept carrying water until someone told me to stop. I didn't want to stop, though I ached in every muscle I had and my hands were chafed and bleeding, but as I looked up I realized everyone else had abandoned their attempts to contain the flames. We watched the burning cottages disintegrate.

What was it like to lose everything, things that took coin or trade to acquire, to replace? How would they recover from it? I was aware that many people in the village bartered for what they needed. How could they barter when they had nothing?

I found Fiona. She was giving orders about people billeting with their neighbors and getting food from the manor. I waited until she was alone before asking, "Was anyone killed?"

She sighed and rubbed the back of her neck. "No, thank Zaire."

I thought that incredibly good fortune until I remembered that having absolutely nothing could destroy lives, too. "What can be done for the people who have lost everything?"

"I'll give them something, their neighbors will give them something, and the rest they'll get on credit. They'll be all right. In time."

It was good to know people wouldn't be cast out starving in the street. "Do you know how the fires started?"

"Riders came by and started them," Fiona said curtly.

"What?" On purpose? "Seriously?"

"That's what the villagers said. The same riders who trampled Colm and Radek and the others."

Did they not hurt enough people the first time? They had to come back and do more damage? "Does this happen a lot to titleholders? People just attacking the tenants? What do they get out of it?"

"I've heard of marauders, especially on country estates. Some do it for theft, some for entertainment, but I think these are different. I think someone is trying to convince me that I can't protect my people. Just another burden I can't shoulder."

"You think this is all Kent."

Fiona glanced about for listeners before saying, "Lokian is dead sure it is. Bon can be charming and can get people to speak more than they normally would. Then Lokian puts everything they say together, and what it all means is that Kent is deliberately creating an environment of chaos and distrust."

"I thought he was going to petition the Emperor."

"So did I. It's possible he seeks to garner more evidence of my weakness. All the 'ristos in the area will hear of this, and Kent might be able to get one of them to speak against me in front of the Emperor."

"What will you do?"

"I don't know yet. If I could prove Kent is behind this, I should be able to complain to the Emperor, and he would— well, might—pass down sanctions. But he has no love for me, and he won't act against a titleholder of Kent's status on the basis of the opinions of two of my tenants."

That anyone could doubt it was Kent behind all of these events immediately after he had threatened to take Westsea from Fiona was ludicrous. No one with any intelligence could doubt they were all connected.

Unfortunately, I had no faith that the Emperor would be reasonable.

However, while the Emperor could dismiss the opinions of tenants, it wouldn't be so easy to do so when it was a Source speaking. From somewhere an erroneous belief had sprouted that Sources couldn't lie. Perhaps it was time we took advantage of it.

The current difficulty with that was that Taro had seen nothing for himself, nothing of the perpetrators. Until he did, he couldn't tell anyone anything.

"Or, legally, technically," Fiona continued, "I can launch an attack on his estate."

I frowned. "You mean, what, some kind of battle?"

"It's traditional."

"From a hundred years ago!"

"It's still legal."

Had her difficulties bruised her brain? "You can't ask farmers and fishers to fight."

"You haven't been here long. Some of these people brawl for fun."

"That's not the same thing."

She sighed again. "This isn't something you need to worry about, Dunleavy."

A polite way to tell me to mind my own business. All I could do was hope that Fiona's head would clear once she was no longer so exhausted. I nodded and went looking for my family.

They were all coated black, wet, and round-shouldered with fatigue. We were of no use to anyone there, not competent enough to safely dig through rubble, not familiar enough to anyone to provide any real emotional support, so we left. Taro started shivering during the walk back to the manor, and my brothers and mother looked miserable. I was proud of them for working so hard, but melancholy over our lack of success. It was just wrong that so much damage could be done in such a short period of time.

It felt like it took hours to reach the manor, and I was ready to lie down anywhere, as filthy and wet and cold as I was. The stairs up to my suite seemed like one challenge too many. All that stopped me from just sitting on the steps and falling asleep was that I tried to have as few regulars as possible seeing me completely wrecked.

Then, once Taro and I were back in our suite, I was afraid to touch anything or sit anywhere. I would create stains that would never wash out. I had no doubt Fiona's servants were all in a similar state, and I wouldn't dream of bothering them with requests for assistance at that time. So Taro and I scrubbed ourselves with the cold water in the water closet, scraping our skin raw, and threw our clothes into the empty fireplace, to be burned once they dried out. I didn't think either the smell or the filth could be soaked out of them.

I told Taro of Fiona's suspicions, and he collapsed into a chair. "I'm sick of this," he muttered. "There has to be something we can do."

"Like what?"

"I don't know. Something. Distract Kent with some troubles of his own. We're able to do things Shields and Sources can't normally do."

How Taro had changed. He had gone from almost fearing his extra abilities and using them in only the most dire of circumstances, to volunteering to utilize them when not strictly necessary. I wondered if I should worry about that. "That could kill people," I pointed out.

"Not if we do it right."

"And what does doing it right involve?"

"Go there some night, destroy something specific. Give Kent something else to worry about. But we'll be careful, make sure no one is harmed."

"I don't like it."

"Why not? We have to do something."

"I agree, but it feels wrong. Dishonorable."

"Who cares? Kent isn't bothering to be noble."

"And don't we despise him for it?"

"He's hurting innocent people. He's going to kill someone if this keeps up."

"I know, I know. I just really hate the idea of you using your abilities this way."

"I've done things like this before."

Not quite. Not really.

"I'm going to do it whether you like it or not," he declared.

I glared at him.

He raised his eyebrows in an expression of challenge.

He wasn't going to budge. "Fine," I snapped.

He nodded, looking a little smug. Aggravating creature.

"When?" I let my tone remain sharp. He should know how irritated I was.

"Not tonight," he answered, to my relief. "I feel half-dead. But soon."

It was a bad, bad idea. I just hoped we didn't kill anyone. Or destroy anyone's livelihood. Or create any other problems with unforeseeable consequences I didn't have it in me to imagine right then.

Chapter Fourteen

I'd been sick. I'd been exhausted. I'd been in pain. I'd even been poisoned.

Yet I'd never experienced quite the sort of discomfort I was feeling upon reluctantly waking from warm, deep, black sleep the next morning. Each muscle I had was twisting and pulling with every movement, no matter how slight, and when I wasn't moving, the muscles hardened into sharp unnatural shapes that seemed to scrape against the inside of my skin. It was ridiculous. The body wasn't meant to feel that way.

Sun was streaming through the window, a rather rare occurrence in Flown Raven, one that seemed to mock how devastated so many people were feeling. Or maybe it would warm them. Gray skies and drizzle were depressing to many.

Taro was still in bed, asleep. He seemed to almost sink into the mattress with his unmoving fatigue. There were dark smudges streaked here and there on his face, missed during his ablutions the day before.

He was one of those people who was a particular kind of attractive when they were dirty.

Of course he was.

He smelled like smoke. I smelled like smoke. We were

probably drenching the sheets in the smell of smoke. Maybe even the whole suite. Was that something that could be aired out of a place?

I wasn't going to be able to go back to sleep, damn it. Might as well get up. I rolled over, I sat up, I twisted to put my feet on the floor. Every movement was careful and slow and painful.

All right. Get moving. Theoretically, it would loosen things up.

I got as far as the sitting room and sank into a chair with a sigh. Had I ever been so drained before? It was such an effort to raise even a hand.

There was no warm, soft, brown aroma of coffee. Because Hester, I had no doubt, felt as awful as I did. If I wanted coffee, I'd have to go down to the kitchen and make it myself. Which I could do, except the kitchen was so very far away, and getting there involved so many more stairs than were necessary.

There had to be a spell that could make coffee out of thin air. Everyone would love it.

And not long after I was thinking about coffee, I was thinking about food. I realized I was so hungry my stomach was folding in on itself. But getting food involved all the same difficulties as getting coffee.

I leaned my head against the back of the chair. I stared at the ceiling and tried to count in my head how many steps it was from the suite to the kitchen. I had almost convinced myself the food and coffee would be worth the effort when I remembered I would then have to climb back up the stairs, and that was the end of that.

I might have fallen asleep again, as I was unnaturally startled by the knock on the door. I glared at the slab of wood, knowing manners dictated that I should open it myself. Manners could go sink. As far as I was concerned, everyone should be too uncomfortable to be visiting. They didn't deserve etiquette. "Enter."

Then I felt awful as the door was opened and Radia shuffled in, supporting herself with a cane. I stood up and took a step.

She waved me down. "I know what happened and the toll it's taken on everyone."

Still, I waited until she sat before sitting myself. "I'm sorry I have nothing to offer you." I looked at the bell pull. "I could call for something." I really didn't want to. The servants had more important things to do, such as rest, than bring food to me.

"No, no. Lord Tarce brought me a tray."

"Did he?" Love could drive people to ignore all sorts of difficulties.

"He can be exquisitely courteous when he cares to be," Radia said blandly.

"Did he prepare the tray himself?"

"I chose not to ask."

I hoped he hadn't browbeaten a servant into doing it for him. That would have been nothing short of an abuse of his position, as far as I was concerned.

It would have been nice to have someone so in love with me that he could push himself through physical impediments merely to provide me with sustenance. My fellow was still asleep.

Then again, I wasn't prepared to fetch food, either, so I couldn't complain.

Radia looked uncomfortable, then, which was uncharacteristic of her. "I have lived in Flown Raven all my life," she said.

"Yes, I know."

"So I am aware of certain secrets in the community that aren't actually secrets."

"I see."

"We are a very protective group, here. It may take a while for a newcomer to be accepted, but once they are, they become very valuable to us. We might argue. We might resent each other. We might even hate each other. But most of us would never betray another to outsiders."

All right, so I did see. "Most of you."

Radia shrugged. "There are no absolutes."

"Hm."

"As well as being aware of the activities of so many others, there are many who take me into their confidence. Much more than I would like. There are some things I really don't need to know about my neighbors."

I could sympathize with that, a little. "One of the liabilities of being discreet and trustworthy."

"And you feel I have those attributes?"

"From what I've seen." I hadn't known her long, but everything about her felt like she was someone solid and dependable.

Radia paused, appearing to collect her thoughts. "I know about the group of casters. The ones who live around here."

I didn't know how to react to that. I wasn't prepared to confirm the existence of the circle. Denying it would be a lie. I didn't want to lie to Radia.

"Lady Westsea is going through an extremely trying time," she said.

"As are her tenants," I responded.

"Aye, and I'm worried about how much more they can take before they snap."

"And do what?"

She shrugged. "Leave, I suppose."

"But they just went through the fealty ceremony swearing loyalty to Her Grace."

"I worry that might not keep them here. Not when they're plagued with one mishap after another."

I supposed I could understand that. When things were unrelentingly bad, a fresh start became attractive, even when changing meant leaving home and property behind. "But you have something in mind to address all that."

"I think if the rock were hung again, it would contribute to restoring everyone's confidence in the viability of Westsea."

Oh, right. I'd forgotten about that possibility, with all of the mess that had been happening since she had first mentioned it.

"Is this something you would be willing to discuss with the other casters?"

I didn't want to. It would feel like I was asking a favor, and I didn't like the idea of becoming even more beholden to them. But I agreed that raising the rock would lift everyone's spirits, and Fiona deserved all the help she could get. "I'll ask, but I don't doubt they'll be concerned about being watched performing a spell with such obvious effects. No one would be able to pretend the casters were a secret anymore."

"Perhaps it could be done at night, when most would be in bed."

"I suppose, but even if we can lift the rock, I doubt very much that we can muster the fine control needed to maneuver the hooks into the chains."

"That is something I can handle, I believe."

"How?"

"Mainly I'm thinking of having a couple of people on the arch manipulating the chains."

Not a job I would have wanted. The arch was high and not broad. And I could envision hands and fingers being crushed between the heavy iron articles. "More people who will see us casting."

"I promise I will choose well."

I was too tired to be contemplating anything more difficult than what dress I would wear that day. I'd spent every ounce of strength I'd had the day before. Could I not be granted a few days just to wrap my brain in cotton and not deal with anything?

"You will ask them?"

"I will ask them. As soon as I can."

"And if they are reluctant, will you try to persuade them?"

I heard some swearing from the bedchamber. Taro was awake. "I will present to them your arguments, but as your arguments, not mine."

"You don't sound like you're in full agreement with the idea."

"I will have to see what the task will entail before I agree to it."

She smiled. "You're the sort who, when asked if you will do someone a favor, demands to know the nature of the favor before committing to it."

"Of course. To agree to do something before knowing what will be expected of you is just stupid."

"That's my girl," Taro said from the door between our bedchamber and the sitting room. He was leaning against the doorway, and it looked like that was the only thing keeping him standing. "Morning, Roshni."

"Good morning, Source Karish." Radia's smile turned into a smirk. "You look terrible."

He blew her a kiss before crossing the room to take my hand. Immediately, most of the pain drained out of me, and I almost sighed with relief. Some Pairs, when they touched, could ease each other's pain. We, fortunately, were one such Pair.

With my hand, he prompted me to move to a settee, where

he could sit beside me with an arm around my shoulders. It felt lovely.

"It must be something important if you were going to limp all the way here," he said.

"I was asking Shield Mallorough if she and the other casters could help hang the wind rock."

"You mean Nab? It seems a massive job for two people."

"I'm hoping it is something all the casters can handle."

Taro frowned. "What casters?"

During the resultant silence I realized I still hadn't told Taro about the circle of casters. Lovely.

Radia was a perceptive woman. "I need to get back to my room."

Taro jumped up to help her stand, and the pain slammed back into me. "I'll see you to your room."

"No, no. It's good for me to manage on my own. Thank you for your time, Shield Mallorough."

Taro held the door open for her, and after he closed it behind her he looked at me with a raised brow.

I had promised the others not to tell anyone about them. Not even Taro. Sort of. I thought.

Actually, I couldn't quite remember whether I'd promised or not. I didn't care. I owed Taro a far higher duty than I owed the circle. And I liked him more. "There are a number of casters in the area who meet once a month or so to practice casting. Browne took me to a meeting the other day. They're supposed to be a secret, but from what Radia says, it's a secret everyone knows."

"I see." He sat beside me and put his arm around my shoulders. The pain once more seeped away. "I'm sure you have an excellent reason for not telling me."

"Uh, I forgot."

"You forgot?"

"I only just met them, and things have been going on since then."

"I see."

"I thought you would be more annoyed."

He winced. "Well . . ."

Ah. His was the forgiveness of the person needing the same in reciprocation. "So what have you been hiding from me?"

"The next test is steeplechasing."

"Yes." Of all the tests to be performed, that was the most dangerous one. And the most stupid. Suicidal idiots leaping horses over walls and across ponds. I was terrified Taro was going to fall and break his neck.

"It won't be the first time I've done it."

"When would you have been doing it?" Was that sort of thing taught at the Source Academy?

"Since we got here."

I glared at him. "You what?"

"It's what everyone does here." His tone was just a shade too calm to be considered defensive, but just a shade.

"How often have you done it?" I demanded.

"I don't know. Every other day or so."

"So all this time I thought you were gambling—"

"I was, strictly speaking. We were betting on the winners."

"You were risking our lives for a bet?"

"Don't you take that path with me. Casting is just as dangerous, in its own way."

I grit my teeth. He was right. Sort of.

"And it's just as well I've had the practice, isn't it?"

I was angry, but I was aware I had no real right to be. It wasn't as though I could tell Taro what to do. Long breath in. Long breath out.

"Lords, the breathing. I'd rather you hit me."

He shouldn't tempt me.

It was time to push my thoughts in a more profitable direction. I could sit there, feeling exhausted and sorry for myself, or I could do something useful for the people in the manor who were worse off than I. "If we help each other, we could get to the kitchen and get some tea and food together. For everyone, maybe." Though that thought could be ridiculously optimistic.

Taro snickered. "You're not thinking of cooking, are you?"

"No. Neither are you." Unlike me, Taro could actually cook well. "I'm thinking bread and cheese and fruit. And then maybe get it all to people. That's going to be the hard part."

"It feels to me that getting dressed is going to be the hard part."

The twisting and bending required to dress did feel a little on the brutal side, while getting down the stairs, holding hands, wasn't so bad. I imagined we were far better off than everyone else in the manor, which meant we would see to everyone else, if we could. But while I wasn't in much pain when I touched Taro, I was still exhausted, and there was no way I was going to be able to carry dishes to everyone else. Maybe we could just put something to eat and drink together in the dining room, and somehow call everyone down. It would be good for everyone if they started moving a bit.

But, to my surprise, the kitchen wasn't empty when we reached it. Bailey, a couple of footmen, a handful of maids, the cook and a few of the kitchen staff were chopping and frying and setting up trays. It smelled fabulous, and I was instantly starving again.

"Source, Shield," Bailey greeted us. "We can have a tray brought to your suite shortly."

"Actually, we were wondering if we could help," said Taro.

Everyone in the room stopped what they were doing, turned, and stared. The reaction was not appropriate to Taro's statement. Had we done something wrong? Violated some protocol?

"That's not the sort of work you should be doing, my lord," said the cook before turning back to his pot.

Taro's mouth tightened. He had always hated being addressed as a lord. "In difficult times, everyone should be doing whatever they can."

"And you did that, Source Karish," said Bailey. "We saw you in the village yesterday."

"There you go," said Taro.

"Is it common for Sources and Shields to engage in activities so far beneath them?"

"How can rendering assistance possibly be beneath anyone?" Taro asked with a shock I shared.

"I think there are many who would find it easy to answer that question in detail."

"They wouldn't be people I'd respect," said Taro. "Lady Westsea was there, too. Did you see her?"

"Of course."

"So she and I are of like mind in the matter. What can we do to help?"

"Stay out of our way," Bailey responded with a wry smile.

It was interesting. The demands of the day seemed to be causing certain very proper people to lower their guard a little. It was nice. "If you would sit there." He nodded at a small square table set directly against the wall where, I believed, cutlery was polished and knives were sharpened. "We can see to you."

"We didn't come here to create more work for you," Taro objected.

"My lord," Bailey said patiently. "I can't know exactly what Pairs do, but you are all that can protect us from the earthquakes and the tsunami, which have the potential to destroy everything and kill us all. It is in our best interests to make sure you are properly cared for. Yesterday, you and Shield Mallorough did your best to help people who are really only strangers to you, and that was a noble and wondrous thing. But today it is time we all resumed our proper places." He pointed at the table. "Sit."

He said it with such authority that we sat without thought. The cook filled two bowls with stew, a footman poured tea for Taro and coffee for me, and Bailey served us dark bread and cheese. It looked marvelous and smelled marvelous and tasted marvelous, and once we were done I didn't want to leave. I was tempted to put my head down on the table and go back to sleep. That would look too slovenly, though, so I let myself be prodded to my feet by my Source and led back to our suite.

But on the stairs we were stopped by another maid, who told us Fiona wanted us in her office. I bit back a groan and followed Taro back down to Fiona's office. Just before we knocked on her door, I heard Cars loudly announce, "It's finished."

Damn it. For a few lovely hours I'd managed to forget about the existence of the Prides.

We entered upon Fiona's bidding, and found both of the Prides and my mother there. Everyone looked irritable, which was suitable, as that was how I felt.

"Thank you for coming," Fiona said wearily. I didn't know exactly why the Prides were speaking to her, but it was probably the last thing she needed to be dealing with right then. "I thought it best that we were all together so I can clear this up quickly."

"There is nothing to clear up!" Cars objected. "Marcus was

at the field at the appointed time." Marcus, looking a little gray, covered his eyes with one hand. "Source Karish was not, thereby forfeiting the test. Marcus wins the challenge. The contract is to be fulfilled."

And that was the downside of forgetting about the Prides. I'd forgotten about the test as well. Even as Taro had been telling me about steeplechasing, I didn't remember that the test was to be held today.

Good afternoon, panic.

"You are being ridiculous," Fiona told Cars. "Neither your son nor Source Karish are in a fit state to be steeplechasing. Just look at them. It would have been too dangerous."

"Marcus was prepared to take the risk. He was there."

"I wasn't," said Fiona.

"With all due respect, my lady, that isn't relevant."

"With all due respect, Trader, it is. You and Holder Mallorough instated me as the adjudicator for the tests. I was not there today to initiate the test nor to determine the winner. No one forfeited anything."

"You are favoring Source Karish," Cars accused her.

"I am favoring good sense and common decency. Neither party is in a healthy state to engage in such a challenging ride. I have far more pressing matters to attend to right now. And it would offend my tenants to have a race the day after their livelihoods were destroyed."

"This isn't about them!"

"It is taking place on my land, and everything here is about them."

"These are not trivial matters to be delayed!" Cars objected.

"They are to the tenants. This is a form of entertainment to them. That's what happens when you choose to conduct your affairs in such a public manner."

It was not gratifying to hear my life, any part of it, described in such a way, but it wasn't as though I thought these tests were anything short of ludicrous.

"You have no right—"

"You are performing this challenge at my indulgence," she interrupted him in a hard voice. "I will not allow you to slither around the spirit of the agreement by demanding unreasonable compliance under trying circumstances. I am well aware you dragged your son to the field fully believing that no one else would show up and hoping to take advantage of that fact. You know we were all working in the village yesterday."

"As was my son," Cars reminded her.

"And you knew he would not have to ride today. Your actions were disingenuous. You will accomplish nothing by treating me like a fool."

"You are favoring him!"

"Enough, Father!" Marcus snapped.

Cars turned to glare at him. "Don't you—"

"We both knew we were twisting the meaning of the challenge by going out there today. It didn't work, and I'm ashamed of us even if you aren't."

"You don't get anywhere if you're not prepared to insist on your rights."

"Just because you have the right to do something doesn't mean you should. Sometimes honor is more important."

"That is not your decision to make!" Cars hissed at his son.

"But it is mine," Fiona interjected. "And I have made it. Accept it with good grace or I'll have you removed."

Cars's glare was poisonous. It seemed he had even less respect for aristocratic titles than I did and was even less interested in hiding it. "May we know when the test will be held?"

"When I feel like it. You can go."

Cars gave her a shallow bow that managed to appear sarcastic. Marcus's was deeper and more fluid, though he seemed at one point in danger of overbalancing and falling on his face. It must have been hell to ride all the way out to the site of the test. I'd barely made it to the kitchen.

"I'm terribly sorry you've been disturbed in this way," my mother said to Fiona.

Fiona shrugged. "They are not under your control."

"This is our family business. I would have preferred to have this all take place elsewhere."

Fiona gave her a tired smile. "Family is rarely convenient."

Fiona was looking pale, her face lined, and I had no doubt she had many more important things to attend to before she could get more rest. That she had been dragged into our sordid personal affairs was humiliating. After murmuring my appreciation, I led my mother and Taro out of the office.

"Nothing like knowing you'd have Cars as a father-in-law to inspire me to do well on the tests," Taro said in a low voice.

"He wasn't always like this," said my mother. "When I first knew him, while we were negotiating the contract and through the first couple of years after, he was a warm, friendly man. Desperation can make anyone unpleasant."

But a person who could remain calm and respectful while dealing with adversity, wasn't that the sort of person to admire?

Who was I to talk? I was a mess when I was stressed. "I'd love to not have to think about this for the rest of the day."

"I think you should go back to bed." Mother looked me over critically. "You look terrible."

So did she, really, but I was too polite to say so, and too ready to go back to bed to stand around talking about anything less than vital. Because while I was no longer in dire need of food and coffee, it wasn't feasible to hold on to Taro all day, and I was very, very tired.

I hoped Fiona didn't announce the next test anytime soon. I felt I could sleep for a week.

Chapter Fifteen

I visited Browne the next day. She was nearly buried under her enormous mass of patients, for while no one had died, many had burns and broken limbs and horrible hacking coughs. Her cottage had survived the fire untouched, but it couldn't accommodate the number of injured, so she had established a temporary infirmary in the assembly room, a large building the size of a barn where the villagers danced and had public meetings.

Browne wasn't the only one attending to the injured. A handful of men and women were there to bring water and soup and change bandages. They were all pale and they moved slowly. I was still barely able to put one foot in front of the other, myself. "Do you have someone young and spritely I could send to the manor to fetch Karish?" I asked Browne. "He is excellent with injured people."

"He has a hand for healing, does he?"

Yes, but not in the way she meant, and I wasn't going to tell her. "He can put them at their ease. Make them smile. Sometimes he's able to help them sleep. He's really very good. If either of us had thought about the injured, he would already be here."

Browne nodded and sent a six-year-old girl out to the manor.

"What can I do to help?" I asked.

Instead of answering me immediately, she took me out of the building and around the corner for some privacy. "What do you need to say?"

I passed along Radia's request.

Upon hearing it, Browne looked weary and impatient. "The Wind Watcher feels it's important to do this now?"

"She didn't say so, but I would imagine the sooner the better. Given the circumstances." Something as traumatic as the fire would leave a huge scar in everyone's memory. Some unexpected good fortune might ease that pain a little. "Can it be done?"

Browne blew a stray lock of blond hair off her face. "I've never heard of anyone levitating anything that big before."

"Does the size matter, if it's moved with a spell?"

"I don't know. I've never thought about it. Even when we heard that it was impossible to hang the rock, no one in the circle suggested there might be something we could do." She frowned and looked off to the distance. "I'll have to play with the idea a bit and talk to the others."

I looked at her for a few moments. "You don't seem upset that Radia knows about the circle. I promise I didn't tell her."

She shrugged. "She is the Wind Watcher. She knows everything."

I contemplated telling Browne that, according to Radia, everyone knew about the circle of casters.

"Give me a couple of days," she said.

I nodded. "In the meantime, is there anything I can do here?"

"There are always bandages that need cleaning."

Ick.

Taro arrived not much later, taking in the rows of injured before kneeling beside the one who had been most badly burned, a young boy. Browne had assured me that she would be able to smooth away the disfiguring scarring in time, but in the meantime he was in some pain and very frightened. I watched Taro take his uninjured hand in a gentle grip and smile at him, his words inaudible from my distance. After a few moments, I saw the boy smile back, I thought I saw him giggle, and not long after, Taro rested his free hand lightly over the boy's eyes. I was pretty sure the boy was asleep by the time Taro left him.

Taro's next patient was a young man. From Taro's mannerisms, I knew he was flirting shamelessly. I grinned and went back to scrubbing bodily fluids out of strips of cotton.

"What is he doing?" Browne asked a short while later.

"He's just making them feel better."

"How?"

"He's very good with people."

"That's it?"

I looked at her and hoped my expression was blank. "What else could it be?"

She raised an eyebrow at me but chose not to pursue that line of questioning. "This will confirm to everyone that Source Karish should have been the titleholder."

"What? How?"

"He is here, tending to the injured."

"Lady Westsea can't dedicate any significant time to work like this. She's got a thousand other things she needs to be doing. And isn't that a sign of good leadership, knowing when to delegate?"

"All that people will know is that he's out here where people can see him, and she is invisible. For all they know, she's lying about reading a novel and drinking chocolate."

"I happen to know she plans on spending at least part of today visiting people, learning what they need."

"That might have been more effective if Source Karish hadn't chosen to do this."

"You want us to leave?"

"No. I could use the help and your Source is clearly making people comfortable." She pursed her lips for a moment. "I may be calling for you over the next couple of days," she said, and it seemed to me that everyone in this place had a love for abruptly changing the subject. "I need you to be available to come."

"Barring a natural disaster, I will be."

Taro and I stayed with Browne for the rest of the day. It was hard work, and I was reminded anew just how easy the life of a Shield was. I played with the idea of doing something useful with my spare time, but what that could be didn't come quickly to mind. I didn't have a lot of useful skills.

When we got back to the manor, I was ready to crawl into bed and maybe sleep for a few days, but upon entering our suite we found my brothers sitting on the floor, looking as tired and dirty as we. They were drinking wine and eating fruit and they had a couple of small wrapped boxes near their feet. "Boys." I sighed.

"We've got chocolate," said Dias, holding up one of the boxes.

"We're not children."

"So only children like chocolate?"

Taro loved chocolate. I didn't dislike it, but I didn't crave it, either.

"Eating chocolate makes you relax," Mika informed me. "So does drinking wine. Take some floor."

I gave in. "Is there a reason we can't use the furniture?"

"Sitting on the floor fosters an air of intimacy," said Dias.

Something about his choice of words struck me as uncharacteristic, though I couldn't say why.

"And the floor is easier to clean," Mika added prosaically.

They had both red and white wine, and the chocolate they offered was quite nice, hard little balls with soft tasty centers. And sitting on the floor, drinking wine that I liked and eating with my fingers, did make me feel better.

"So," Mika drawled. "What *were* you doing that year you disappeared?"

Well, that question had come out of nowhere.

Taro frowned and straightened his spine and shoulders. "What is this?" he asked coolly. "You are trying to lure us into revealing information you're not entitled to? With chocolate and wine? Are you amateurs?"

"Well done," Dias said with admiration. "Very lord of the manor."

"Very pretty," Mika agreed.

"Don't be idiots," I snapped. "We've already informed you we can't tell you anything about that."

"Because it's Triple S business."

"Yes."

Mika pointed at me. "You're lying."

And he was right, of course. He wasn't supposed to be able to read me. We barely saw each other while we were growing up.

"Your manners are exquisite." The sarcasm lay thick through Taro's words.

"We're family."

"So you don't need to treat your sister with courtesy?"

"No," said Dias. "I mean, yes, we must treat her with courtesy, if you want to be all stiff and unfriendly about it. But what I'm talking about is that one of the jobs a family has is to guard your blind side."

"I don't have a blind side," I said. And if I did, well, I felt that was for Taro to guard.

My brothers ignored my comment. "Now, I appreciate that neither of you really understands that," said Mika as he poured himself another glass of white. "You grew up in the academies. You never got to learn how families are supposed to work. But one of the things we do is keep your secrets."

"We have no secrets that need keeping," I said.

Mika rolled his eyes while Dias put a hand on Taro's knee. "I understand you have always had difficulties with your family, and we don't want to dredge any of that up."

Taro glared at me, but before I could say I'd never discussed his family affairs with anyone, Mika said, "No, we've learned nothing from Lee. People talk, right?"

Taro tightened his jaw and his hands, and chose not to answer.

"I suppose what we're saying is that we think the secrets you're keeping aren't your own," said Mika. "And it can be dangerous to be the only ones holding the vital secrets of someone else. They may decide you're a stray thread that needs cutting."

It was a horrifying idea. I didn't want to think about it.

"What are you trying to say?" Taro demanded.

"Let me put it this way," Mika said. "Since his coronation, Emperor Gifford has had fifteen titleholders executed for treason."

That was the first I'd heard of it. "Is that a lot?" It seemed like a lot, but what did I know?

Mika looked disgusted. "Of course it's a lot. What's the matter with you?"

"I don't know about such things."

"And that's what we're talking about," said Dias. "You don't keep an ear out to what's going on for the rest of us. And maybe you shouldn't. Maybe you're supposed to stay above it all. Or, at least, to the side of it all. But that's what a family is supposed to do, fill in the gaps for you. We can watch these things for you."

"But why do we need them watched?" Taro asked.

"You don't understand," Mika said. "Things have changed a lot since Emperor Gifford took the crown. Old laws that have faded past practicality dredged back into common use. New laws that are enforced inconsistently. Those who are in favor with the Emperor are spared anything, those not are condemned on the slightest of evidence. If you can even call it evidence. Those fifteen titleholders, most of them were known for being loyal to the Empress, and they were convicted on nothing more than the testimony of the friends of the Emperor."

"And that's horrible," said Taro. "I'm serious. That's tragic perversion of the law, and I feel badly for these people and their families. But it really has nothing to do with us."

That sounded callous, but it was true. What could we do about it?

"One of the rumors about your absence for that year," said Mika, "was that you were sent by the Empress to assassinate someone."

I choked and my nose became clogged with wine.

"And you brought back their daughter to be brainwashed by the Triple S and crafted into an assassin in her own right."

I couldn't speak. I almost couldn't breathe, the shock was that intense. I mean, what the hell? Where did that trash come from?

It had been idiotic, I supposed, hoping Aryne would escape everyone's notice. She was the grandchild of the Empress's deceased sister, a sister most people hadn't known existed. But we'd had to take Aryne to Erstwhile, she'd met the Empress, and people had known she was there. But I was sure no one else had known she was a relative of the royal family, and I'd really believed everyone had forgotten about her.

Taro's eyes were wide with surprise. He looked as incapable of speech as I felt.

"That's not true, is it?" Dias asked almost diffidently.

That got my voice working. "Of course not! How could you think it was?"

"You weren't saying anything!"

"Let's just say I'm just a little dismayed that people might think I've murdered someone." As soon as the words were out of my mouth, I wanted to cringe. Because I had murdered Creol.

"Only stupid people," Mika tried to assure me.

Still, it wasn't Creol they were talking about, and . . . "The fact that anyone—"

"There are a whole slew of rumors about you two," Dias interrupted. "All kinds of incredible things."

"I can't believe this." Assassins. My gods. "Why the hell—I mean—why us?"

Dias smiled. "You're famous, big sister. Or infamous, at least."

"That makes no sense. There are actors and writers and politicians and notorious 'ristos."

"And the Stallion of the Triple S." Dias grinned at Taro.

Taro growled.

I looked down at the floor so there would be no possibility of sending an accusatory stare Taro's way. I'd known this was going to happen. Well, not that anyone would ever think I was some kind of assassin, because that was ridiculous, but that complete strangers would be talking about us, because it seemed everyone knew who Taro was and found him a fascinating topic for conversation. I'd known that catching people's interest as Taro's Shield was inevitable, from the moment we bonded. I'd been worried people would claim that I was sleeping with Taro. Well, I was sleeping with Taro. Couldn't we go back to rumors about that?

"The problem is," said Mika, "that there are all sorts of rumors flying around about the Triple S, not just you two. Rumors that Sources and Shields are learning more than just how to settle disasters. There are rumors that some Pairs can actually start them and are using that ability to blackmail cities and villages into giving them money."

"Pairs don't need money," Taro reminded them in a voice still hollow with alarm.

"I didn't say the rumors made sense. Rumors often don't. But those are the stories that are circulating. And they're causing people to question the motives of the Triple S. People are thinking that the Triple S isn't as neutral and benevolent as we've been led to believe."

I just couldn't understand it. How had all this happened?

"So our concern," Mika continued, "is that you did perform some special task for the Empress, and the Emperor will use that as a reason to do something to you. Like arrest you."

"Only the Triple S can sanction us," I murmured.

"And only the Triple S can decide where you're posted. Isn't that what you told us?"

Yes, I understood. If the Emperor was willing to ignore one custom, he'd ignore another.

Zaire. I couldn't believe any of this.

"There's more, you know," said Mika. "Pairs seem to be disappearing. Some dismiss it as a rumor. They say the Pairs have merely been transferred and people have just lost touch with them. But others are not so sanguine. It seems to be happening a lot more frequently as time goes by, and the Pairs that go missing are reported to be among the most talented. I can't think it's normal for talented Pairs to be taken . . . what do you call it? . . . off the roster."

"Only, you two haven't disappeared," Dias added. "So we don't know what to think. You're very talented, right?"

Taro said nothing. I shrugged.

"And we're just saying it might be safer if the two of you weren't the only ones to know the truth."

Maybe I was too tired or had had too much wine, but that seemed to make a lot of sense. There had been so many secrets, and I was weary of keeping them. This wasn't what I'd wanted or planned for myself. I'd always valued honesty. I'd always hoped to be an honest person. I'd lost all ability to be that.

I suddenly felt like I'd been carrying an invisible weight on my shoulders for years, a weight that grew heavier and harder to stand up under as time went by. A weight I wasn't sure I could carry on my own for much longer.

I was so tired.

To my disgust and dismay, I felt tears coat my eyes.

"Hey, no, no." Dias put a hand under my chin and raised my face. "This was meant to ease you, not make you feel worse."

Taro took my hand.

"That bad, are they?" Mika asked.

"What?" Taro laced our fingers together.

"The secrets you hold."

Neither Taro nor I responded to that. I had no idea what to say, really. I blinked my tears away and struggled with making sense of what I'd been told.

"You both look exhausted." Mika rose to his feet and Dias followed. "Just think about it, all right? We might be able to help." He kissed my forehead and clasped Taro's shoulder, Dias echoing his gestures, and they both left.

They left the chocolate behind. I popped one in my mouth in the ridiculous hope it would calm me as it had just a short while earlier.

We sat in silence for a few moments, Taro rubbing my arm. "Are you all right?" he asked. "This isn't you."

"I really want to tell them," I admitted.

"We can't," he said.

"I know."

"We promised the Empress."

"I know."

"And I fully believe she left people with orders to, well, deal with us if we spoke to anyone even after her death."

"I agree."

"But you still want to tell them."

"Yes."

"But—"

I shrugged. "I have no sensible reason."

"So let's hear your insensible one."

I hesitated.

"I already know you're not logical all the time. Admit to your foolish fantasies."

Foolish fantasies. Aye, they were. "It's just what Mika said. We have secrets that only the wrong sort of people know." And after having that pointed out, I felt vulnerable. "It feels like we've been separated from everyone else, like we're all by ourselves in forces I don't understand and maybe don't even know about, and I never expected to feel that way."

"Think how it feels to—" Taro cut himself off.

"To what?"

He shook his head. "Nothing that makes sense. I was just thinking out loud."

I suspected it was something more than that, but I couldn't imagine what, and I wasn't going to push. I chose, instead, to complain. "All I wanted to do was Shield, you know. Be a Shield, be a good one, and in my free time bench dance and read history texts and go to plays. That's all I wanted."

"And that's what you would have gotten if I hadn't Chosen you."

I forced myself to chuckle, and I had no doubt it sounded fake. "Think highly of yourself, don't you?"

Except he was right. Our first assignment had been High Scape, such an important city with such an impossible number of natural events that a newly minted Pair would never, under normal circumstances, be posted there. I was dead sure it was because of Taro that we were, and from that situation all of the crazy aspects of our lives flowed.

Sometimes, I heard about other Pairs, stories about saving settlements from vicious disasters just at the last moment, stories about neglect and licentiousness, stories of arrogance and demanding from merchants the best of luxury items. I'd never heard any accusations of them being assassins, though. That was reserved for Taro and me. We were just that special.

I had killed Creol. Deliberately. A rogue Source who could create natural disasters and had been using that ability to try to tear High Scape apart. He'd had no concern for the people he'd killed. He'd had no concern for anything, from what I'd seen. I hadn't been able to think of any way to stop him, and there hadn't been a lot of time to devise or execute any options, so I'd killed him.

Was I as bad as an assassin? Worse?

There were people who knew what I'd done, but they were people so discredited that no one was prepared to believe what they said. Almost no one. The Triple S council was suspicious that something strange had happened. They just weren't sure what, and neither Taro nor I were about to tell them.

I could never tell my brothers that. They couldn't help but see me as some kind of monster. That was how I saw myself. There had to have been a better way to deal with Creol.

But it would be wonderful if we could tell them something of the rest. "I'd like it if there were others who knew some of what we know. Especially about Aryne. And the Triple S's interest in your other abilities. It seems those are both secrets that could result in our disappearing in one way or another. If that happened, it would be nice if someone else knew why." And maybe do something about it?

Were these really the thoughts tumbling through my mind? Weren't we supposed to be avoiding the melodramatic?

"Do you think they could keep it to themselves?" Taro asked.

"I don't know. I don't know them well enough."

"What about your parents?"

"No." That answer just shot out of me, no thought required. I had no idea why I felt so opposed to telling my parents while feeling tempted to tell my brothers. There was no logical reason for it.

Maybe because my mother had demanded to know, while my brothers had offered to listen.

"It's up to you whether we tell them or not," said Taro.

"Don't do that," I objected. "This involves you, too."

"They're your family. You know them better than I."

Not by much. "So you're not opposed to telling someone just on principle."

After a hesitation, he said, "No, I suppose not."

"Huh." That surprised me. He was almost rabid about not telling the Triple S council anything. I would have thought that distrust would apply to everyone.

"You're too tired to be making important decisions," he said. "Let's go to bed and think about it in the morning."

I didn't want to think about it at all. I almost resented the fact that the possibility had been raised. I would worry about it until I made a decision, and then I would worry about the decision itself, and whether I'd made the right one. There was just no way I could forget about it, no matter what I did.

Chapter Sixteen

Two days later, my idiotic Source and I were slipping out of the manor in the middle of the night, dressed darkly and carrying lanterns. We were on our way to Kent to destroy some property. I was so proud.

I had been hoping Taro would talk himself out of his insane scheme to visit destruction upon Kent. I was dead sure anything we did would make things worse for Fiona. But Taro had remained resolute and I hadn't been able to think of a way to stop him. So there we were, doing something so half-witted I was delighted no one who mattered would ever know about it.

We hadn't gone far, though, when we heard footsteps behind us. We turned around swiftly. Then I had to hold back an oath or two behind my tightly clenched teeth.

"Where are we going?" Dias asked in a low voice.

"You're going back to bed," I told him.

"Aye, good luck with that."

"I'm pretty sure whatever you're doing isn't sanctioned by anyone," Mika added. "Or you wouldn't be doing it in secret."

I remembered being that naive. Then the Empress sent us to Flatwell to look for Aryne. No one had been allowed to know about that. "It's Triple S business."

"It is not," Mika objected. "Or, at least, it's not the usual kind of Triple S business."

I looked at Taro, waiting for him to say something. He was always more persuasive than I. But it seemed he had chosen to remain silent, possibly out of the misguided belief that I held some sway over my brothers.

We'd have to try this another night. I wasn't opposed to that. It gave Taro more time to change his mind.

And apparently Mika could see the thoughts in my head, because he said, "We'll just follow you then, too."

"Are you watching me?"

"Yes."

I hadn't expected him to admit it. I didn't know what to say. I felt I should be offended to learn he was spying on me, but I wasn't. It was almost nice to know. How odd.

"So we should get going, yes?" Mika prompted.

Yes. I supposed. I thought taking my brothers along was a terrible idea. I didn't want any witnesses to what we were going to do. When it came down to it, I really didn't know them.

That shouldn't have been so disheartening. I was no different than any other Shield or Source. In fact, I knew my family far better than most members of the Triple S knew theirs. Taro hadn't seen any of his family the entire time he'd been in the Source Academy, though his example was far to the other extreme of behavior from families. My parents had made a real effort to make sure I knew them. I understood I was important to them.

That didn't mean I could predict how my brothers would conduct themselves, especially in situations that were not quite legal.

Mika slung an arm around my shoulder. "You know Deacon?"

"No." Other than that Mother had mentioned him.

"He wanted to marry Kaaren."

"All right." Why hadn't I been told? That was important, wasn't it?

"He was an ass."

"Ah."

"Kaaren isn't really a keen judge of character. It's a good thing she's going to be a holder. If she were a trader the whole family would be wearing bedsheets."

"All right," I repeated. Why was he telling me this?

"But Kaaren was enamored, and our parents were impressed. His family were prosperous suppliers. Everyone thought an alliance was a grand idea."

"And you didn't?" I asked. "Just because he was . . . What? Pompous?" An annoying but not unforgivable flaw.

"Because he hired a prostitute and beat her almost to death."

I stared at him. "And no one would believe her?"

"His father and brother vouched for his appearance elsewhere."

"But you believed her."

"Unlike our sister, I'm an excellent judge of character."

"What did you do?" Taro asked.

"You didn't beat him almost to death, did you?" The idea made me sick, even if the man deserved it.

"No, much as I would have liked to. That would have made him a figure for sympathy. No, I broke into their solicitor's office and read their books. I sent correspondence to every connection they had, other suppliers, holders and traders, a few politicians and some relatives. Anonymously, of course. I told them that the family business was absolutely riddled with debt and that their finances were being examined by a royal auditor, that their product was poisoned, and that Deacon violated animals. I knew enough of their details to be persuasive, apparently."

"He destroyed the entire family in a matter of weeks," Dias added proudly.

I was breathless for a few moments. I didn't know how to feel. I was impressed and horrified all at once.

"Kaaren became disgusted with them, of course. As did Mother and Father. So that was the end of that."

"And no one ever found out?" I asked.

"Not yet." Mika squeezed my shoulders. "The point is, sometimes we have to do underhanded things to protect the people we love."

I understood what he was trying to do, I really did. He told me something that he had done, something illegal with enormous repercussions should others know, to make me feel comfortable about performing an illegal act of my own before him.

Mika gave me another squeeze. "Where are we going?"

Taro took the decision out of my hands. "Kent's estate," he said. "You know those rumors that we can create events as well as stop them? They're true. At least, they are for us."

My brothers didn't appear to be surprised.

"What are you going to do?" Dias asked.

"Won't know until we get there. But I'm aiming for something dramatic. A warning. It's less than he deserves, but right now I just want him to stop. It'll be up to Fiona to decide what the long term consequences for his actions should be."

"It's always good to start small," Mika agreed. "No need to kill a fly with a sledgehammer when a news circular will do."

This comment made me wonder if breaking into a solicitor's office was the only nefarious stunt Mika had ever performed. Right then wasn't the appropriate moment to ask, but I would keep it in mind.

Though we kept a brisk pace, it took longer to get to the border between Westsea and Kent than I was comfortable with. And stepping over that border was a little disconcerting, because the ground changed, almost immediately. There was a sort of roll to it, and it felt harder beneath my feet. And then, after a while and out of nowhere—or so it seemed—a large rock outcropping appeared. It was ragged and high, and I could see us ripping our hands and clothes to shreds attempting to climb it. We didn't have to climb, though, as a narrow passage had been chipped through it. Created by human hands, I was sure, not by water, as had been the breach through the rock behind Fiona's manor.

That would have been a nasty job, cutting through all that rock. And moving through the very narrow passage was disturbing. I couldn't get rid of the unfounded fear that it could easily fall together and crush me.

It wasn't much longer before we got to the manor. It was an ugly mixture of a handful of ill-suited architectural styles. It was also smaller than Fiona's. By a lot. Maybe that was part of Kent's problem.

At the back of the manor was a garden, more elaborate than Fiona's and sprinkled with statues of nudes that were, to my untrained eyes, grossly exaggerated. It was closer to the manor than I liked. What if someone saw us?

"This will do," Taro whispered.

"In what way?" Dias asked.

"You'll see."

"Do you need us to do anything?"

"No. Oh, well, possibly. If someone comes running, it would be good if you could let us know. We'll be distracted."

"Yes," said Dias. "I remember."

"Lee?"

"I'm ready."

Rearranging soil had become the easiest form of channeling. There was something wrong with that, I was sure, given that we weren't supposed to be able to do anything like that. But it was almost effortless. He lowered his shields, I raised mine, I felt Taro pull in the forces, and the ground began to tremble. I heard exclamations—though quiet—of shock from my brothers.

The ground didn't tremble much, though. Taro had become adept at keeping the movement of the ground very precise. I was sure there was nothing happening beyond the confines of the garden.

The noise could have been a problem, though. There was no hiding the faint rumble as the soil broke apart and heaved, the crack of the stone paths as they were pressed into pieces, the splintering of the trunks of the trees. I was sure someone was going to wake and come running.

But no one did, and I wondered at it. How could they not hear this?

It was quickly done. Most of the garden was well beneath the ground when Taro stopped. All except the heads of the statues. Taro kept them in view, little white globes gleaming in the moonlight.

"That is strangely disturbing," Dias murmured.

I agreed.

"Is that it?" Dias asked.

"Unless he's a complete idiot," Taro whispered, "he won't be able to dismiss this as something natural. He'll know someone did it, in retaliation for his actions. He'll know it's a warning. At the same time, he won't be able to blame Fiona for this. It's an accusation that will sound too ridiculous to too many people."

"What if he doesn't perceive this as a warning?" Mika reached out and touched a stone head. "Or what if he doesn't care?"

"Then we'll have to come up with something more drastic," Taro said grimly. "Let's go. Kent is supposed to know I've done it, but I don't want anyone to see me doing it. If he can say he saw me, it will give whatever accusations he may make more veracity."

So we left, apparently unnoticed. Once more, Mika put an arm around me. It felt nice. I didn't experience the instant relaxation inherent in Taro's touch, but it was fortifying nonetheless. This was my brother. He knew one of my secrets. I knew one of his. There was an odd sense of safety about that.

Chapter Seventeen

All the casters—except the casters from Kent—met in the pre-dawn in Farmer Biden Netan's barn. This was not a place where the circle had met before, and that was why it was chosen. They were hoping to avoid another attack with the new location and an earlier than normal date. I hoped there were no casters within the circle secretly communicating with one of the Kent casters. No one, within my hearing, had addressed that possibility, but I hoped they had when I wasn't around. It was an obvious problem.

On our walk over, Browne had said she had informed the rest of the circle of Radia's request, and they had spent the last couple of days thinking about it. I had spent those same days practicing my levitation spells on ever larger objects, from candlesticks to platters to the furniture in our suite, locking the door so no maid could swan in without notice. At first, I noticed no difference in the level of concentration and effort required, but when I moved from the vanity to the bed, the pull on my mind was much deeper. I also had to be much more careful about the manner in which the bed rose, making sure it didn't hit anything on the way up or down. It required a precision of focus that almost approached that which I needed for Shielding.

The first time I raised the bed, it exhausted me and brought on a faint headache. I left it for a couple of hours and raised it again. That time, it was easier and less draining. I left it for the day. The next morning, I did it again, and it was easier still. So I moved down to the dining room, locked all the doors, and raised the dining table. That also required a leap of concentration and raw effort, but as I did it again and again, it became easier and easier.

Maybe I could work up to raising the rock on my own.

What would happen if I dropped it? Could it possibly crack? It hadn't, as far as I knew, in the original collapse of the arch, but that didn't mean damage was impossible. I didn't want to be responsible for that. At least, not all by myself.

As before, the members of the circle hummed while the sun rose. As before, the humming was a little eerie but also appealing. The shivers along my upper back were almost pleasant.

"All right," Mitloehner said once they had finished. "What have we got?"

"I can probably estimate the weight of the rock," said Mason Lamine Hefez. "We can find items that together approximate the weight of the rock. We practice levitating the objects, and then we practice raising them all together, each item raised by a different person. And then, when we raise the rock, each person will focus on a different portion of the rock."

That seemed complicated.

"It is more logical to lessen the weight of the rock," Tanner Cheon Thatcher suggested.

"How the hell do we do that?" Berlusconi demanded incredulously.

Thatcher sniffed. "There's no need to be obnoxious."

"I've never seen or even heard of a spell like that. Have you? Has anyone?"

"That doesn't mean one doesn't exist."

"I don't know that we have time to look for one," said Browne.

"My suggestion suffers from the same flaw," said Carpenter Iyad Coulter. "I'm wondering if we could shrink the rock to a more manageable size. But I've never heard of a spell like that, either."

"That doesn't mean we can't create one," Chandler Danith Thaksin suggested.

Mitloehner glared at her. "We're not addressing this."

His tone was hard and almost angry. I gathered they had discussed the possibility of creating a spell before, and it had been a contentious subject.

"I don't know that we have time to create a spell, either," Browne said loudly in a clear attempt to divert them from an argument.

"What's the rush, anyway?" Thaksin asked.

"The Wind Watcher feels the sooner it's accomplished, the better it is for everyone."

I was inspired to add, "Wind Watcher Radia is healing quickly. I understand her mind is turning increasingly to her duties. I believe it weighs on her that she hasn't been able to meet her obligations."

These seemed to be sufficient motives for everyone to make raising the rock a priority.

"Any other suggestions?" Mitloehner asked.

No one had anything further to say.

"Then we'll try Lamine's suggestion."

There followed a search for items that, in combination, would weigh the same as the rock. This meant pretty much ransacking the house and the barn. Looking over the results, I didn't think we had nearly enough.

It became clear that I was the only one prepared to use the shortened cast for levitation, so I tripped everyone up on their first attempt.

It didn't matter. There were far too many objects. No one could concentrate on more than one item at a time. We tried again and again, until tempers started getting really short, with no success.

"I think we're going about this all wrong," Miyoung declared. "Maybe we shouldn't try separating the weight of the rock between us. To be honest, I can't even be sure how that would work. But maybe if we all worked together to lift the rock as a whole, we'd be more successful."

I couldn't see how that was noticeably different from all of the casters working together with each caster focusing on one part of the rock, but I had virtually no experience in casting, compared to the others. And I wasn't exactly the most creative person ever born.

"It would require speaking the spell in perfect unison," Thatcher mused. "We have no practice in this."

"It's impossible," Berlusconi protested.

Of course it wasn't impossible. Just a little difficult, maybe, considering how many people were involved. "Not necessarily," I found myself saying.

"You have some wisdom on this matter the rest of us lack, do you, Shield?"

Berlusconi's voice was laced with bitterness. There were some issues there. I didn't care. "Shields are exposed to a whole lot of music, different instruments, different voices, different styles, while we're at the Academy." Because Shields could be sensitive to music, driven to acts that we would never even contemplate in our right minds. So exposure was considered the best way to learn to deal with it. "People don't seem to have trouble using words in unison when they're singing."

"Singing spells," Berlusconi scoffed. "That's ridiculous."

I shrugged. That people could more easily articulate words in unison while singing was a fact. Whether it would lead to an effective spell was something someone more experienced than I would have to decide. "You all hum together. That's what made me think of it."

Browne smiled wryly. "I don't know that any of us have the skill to compose a song, especially in the course of a few days."

"Well, no, take the melody from another song."

"I can't sing," Berlusconi announced.

"That might not matter," said Browne.

"We have no idea what impact singing the words might have on the spell," Berlusconi protested.

"That's why we'll be practicing," Browne pointed out.

The next step was finding a song that best fit the words of the spell. The selection everyone agreed upon turned out to be a bawdy drinking song. That was hilarious.

Then we all had to spend time singing it. It took longer than I would have expected. I had never heard the song before, so I had to learn the melody, which had a few weird twists. Some of the casters found the song so distasteful they seemed unable to force out even the spell to the melody. Others were so familiar with the song they had trouble refraining from falling into the original lyrics. And finally, everyone sang at different pitches. Working out the harmonies took a ridiculous amount of time.

I feared Berlusconi, who clearly felt some irritation with the whole process, would deliberately try to sabotage our efforts. She did not. Her voice was lovely. I had to wonder why she'd lied about it.

The practicing of the words extended into the afternoon. I couldn't believe these hardworking people were able to spend so much time away from their occupations, especially the servants. To me, that supported the opinion that the other residents in the area knew of the circle and were providing them with the time they needed. I thought that possibility was interesting.

Finally, we were able to sing the spell, everyone in unison, everyone in harmony.

And it felt fabulous. The notes sizzled up and down my spine, my heart started racing, and I felt . . . light. Like I could lift off the ground myself. It was gorgeous.

But I couldn't let it consume me. I had to contribute to the spell. I had to focus.

One of the benefits—perhaps the only one—of all the difficult times I had had Shielding in the past was that I could think through almost overwhelming physical sensation. I sang the words. I would not let myself fall into singing them by rote. I put power behind them.

Our first attempt to raise a chair resulted in the chair being pulled apart. That wasn't promising. Our second had a plow flying—flying!—uncontrollably and nearly taking out a side of the barn. After some debate we decided trying to levitate an animal might be a bad idea.

"I think everyone's had enough for today," said Browne, and I was happy to hear it. I had a nasty headache brewing behind my eyes.

"Fine," said Mitloehner. "We'll reconvene here tomorrow. Same time."

I returned to the manor. I went to the kitchen and got myself a small cold meal. I was relieved as I went up to my suite that I didn't meet a single member of my family. I didn't want to talk; I wanted to sleep. I was clumsy with fatigue as I changed into my nightgown. I was asleep as soon as I lay down on the bed.

I woke briefly when Taro slipped into bed.

I woke again when the sunlight was beaming through the windows. After a few moments, I remembered where I was expected to be and that I was very late. Damn it. I threw on my clothes, drank a cup of horribly cold coffee, and borrowed one of Fiona's horses in order to reach Netan's barn as quickly as possible.

When I stepped inside, the group was singing, and even though I wasn't singing with them, I felt that glorious sense of vibrancy and excitement. They were holding a table several cubits above the floor. It was being held in place, steady and upright.

They lowered the table, and it looked like one force was in control. Everyone really was working in unison. It was impressive.

Once the table was back on the floor, everyone stopped singing and turned to glare at me.

"Good morning," I greeted them.

"You're late," Mitloehner accused me.

Should I lie and claim I'd been engrossed in Triple S business? Should I be honest and admit I'd slept late? I didn't care for either option. "I apologize."

There was a bit of a pause. They were waiting for me to provide an excuse. I didn't.

"We need everyone to be disciplined about this," Mitloehner scolded.

I gestured at the table. "You don't need me." And I didn't know how I felt about that. I really would have preferred not to be involved. It was neither my business nor my place to participate in such things. On the other hand, well, I loved being a part of the singing. That was marvelous.

"It's a table," Mitloehner pointed out with dry sarcasm. "The wind rock will take a little more effort."

That told me.

We raised the table. At first, my participation caused some serious wobbling, but it didn't take me long to adjust to the influences of the others, and the table rose easily and steadily. We practiced shifting it around while it was in the air, upside down, slanted, fitting it on top of the beams in the ceiling. And when we felt comfortable with the table, we moved on to the plow. After some work, we were able to manipulate it just as easily.

None of us could think of anything heavier than a plow. Except maybe buildings, but of course we couldn't play with those, if for no other reason than that they were usually pretty firmly attached to the ground.

"I think we have to try the rock next," Browne said.

"That's an enormous leap to be making," Berlusconi protested.

Browne huffed with impatience. Perhaps Berlusconi was a consistently annoying person who could crack even Browne's composure. "You have a better suggestion, then?"

"Almost anything would be better."

"Please, provide us with an example."

Color appeared high on Berlusconi's cheeks as she pressed her lips together.

"Who believes we should attempt the rock next?" Mitloehner asked.

Twelve people, including Mitloehner, raised their hands.

"The majority calls aye, the decision is made," Mitloehner announced. "We'll meet at the rock at midnight." He gave me a baleful look. "Everyone will be there."

"Of course," I responded.

The group broke up after that. Browne walked with me to my mount. "Is Mitloehner in charge?" I asked her.

"It's a circle. No one is in charge."

"Mitloehner speaks a lot."

"He is the oldest, and he has been practicing casting longer than the rest of us. We give him the respect he's due."

"Is he the most talented of all the casters?"

Browne paused a moment before saying, "That's not really something that's easily quantified."

I didn't believe that. Surely there were those who could cast more spells, more complicated spells, than others. "You're the most powerful of the circle, aren't you?"

"There's no way to determine that."

I smiled. Yes, she was.

I rode back to the manor at a quick pace. When I returned the horse to the stable, I saw Mika and Linder not very well concealed in a corner, kissing with intense enthusiasm. I grinned. I didn't know Linder, really, but he seemed a decent fellow. And I was pleased Mika was enjoying himself, even if he was the only one, in all this mess.

It was petty of me, but what I liked most was the fact that the Dowager's heavy-handed plan was being so thoroughly undermined. I was tempted to find her, drag her into the stable, and make her watch. Except that that would be kind of perverted.

Knowing I would never be able to make myself wake in time for midnight should I go to bed at a regular hour, that I would instead have to stay awake from sundown until then, I decided to get a few hours' rest in the daylight. One of the things about casting in a group, it seemed to take a lot of stamina. I fell asleep quickly.

I was awakened by arguing.

"Just leave!" Taro snapped.

"Not until I'm sure you've heard what I have to say."

As soon as I heard that voice, *that* voice, I groaned and turned over in the bed, staring up and knowing I didn't want to get up.

Taro's mother.

"Keep it down. Lee is trying to sleep."

"Is that woman all you can think about? Always, you bring her. Always, you speak of her. You are too much under her influence. Even the Emperor thinks so."

What was the man's problem? Why did he have the mental space to care about Taro and what kind of influence I did or did not have over him? He was the ruler of the whole damn world. He had more important things to worry about.

I shouldn't be eavesdropping.

They shouldn't be talking right in our sitting room.

"You would have me bow to your influence instead," said Taro.

He didn't object to her assertion that I had too much influence over him. I didn't like that. Of course I had no control
over him, nor should I.

Maybe he thought it wasn't worth denying. That he thought
she wasn't worth the effort of correcting. That was by far the
more comfortable interpretation of his behavior.

"If you were the titleholder," the Dowager said, "people
would show you the respect you deserve."

"The only person I know of who shows me insufficient respect is the person standing before me."

"I'm your mother."

And, according to her, his mother didn't need to show him
any respect. I doubted that would change even if he were to
take the title.

A part of me felt I should go out there and support Taro.
The other part of me knew I would just make things worse.
Maybe he, and the Dowager, would feel my interference meant
I didn't think Taro could take care of things himself.

"It is your Shield who is poisoning your mind against claiming the title."

I rolled my eyes. The title was gone. Why could she not
understand that?

"It's always been her. I don't know how she's doing it,
but she's been cutting you off at the knees since you were
bonded."

"Why are you so desperate to create discord between us?"
Taro demanded. "You're not even developing any new ideas.
First that Lady Simone, a 'risto, now Linder, who would have
been called a trader had his mother not purchased a title. Who
is he supposed to appeal to?"

Her Grace ignored all of that. "If you would just fall in with
His Majesty's plans you would have far more power than you
could ever enjoy as a Source."

"I don't believe for a moment that you care about how
much power I have. I don't think the Emperor cares, either. I
know this is all about you. I'm pretty sure the Emperor would
forget all about me if you would just stop nagging him about
me."

That didn't even slow the woman down. "It's not as though

you will be able to keep her," the Dowager said in a sharp shift of subject.

What did that mean?

"You have to win the next two tests to win the challenge. The final test is a test of the mind. You know you'll never win that."

I sat up, gasping in shock. Bitch! There was nothing wrong with Taro's mind. There was no reason why he couldn't win the final test.

"She will be marrying the Pride boy. She will bow to the needs of her family. And so she should. You need to do the same."

"Get out," Taro snapped.

"She is making time with Linder, you know."

Taro laughed, as he should. No one could miss that Linder was lusting after Mika.

"You don't understand people, Shintaro. You don't understand how avarice can drive them."

"Get out."

"You can't trust her, Shintaro. She has her own interests."

What interests? What could I possibly want that would entail my controlling Taro? Unless she felt my controlling Taro was an end in and of itself.

"Get out."

"You're being terribly immature."

I kind of agreed, but there really was no good way to deal with that woman.

"Get out."

"Do grow up, Shintaro."

I heard the door open and close. Finally. I got out of bed and wandered into the sitting room. Taro was sprawled in a settee staring at the ceiling. "Are you all right?" I asked him.

"Aye," he answered in a listless tone.

I raised my eyebrows at him, because I didn't believe him. "You said you weren't going to listen to her anymore."

"I find her very hard to ignore," he admitted.

"She is very . . . encroaching."

"Encroaching."

"She just takes over the air around you."

"And sucks it right out of you."

"Maybe that's why I feel so dazed around her and can never think of what to say to her."

"Can we talk about something else?"

"Certainly." As far as I was concerned, we could never talk about the Dowager again. Speaking of her didn't accomplish anything.

"Where have you been?"

"Practicing lifting things. We're going to try the rock tonight."

"Isn't that a little soon?"

"We've gone as far as we can with dry runs, and everyone thinks we should take a hit with the real thing."

"Can I come watch?"

Taro rarely expressed any kind of interest in casting. "The circle thinks you don't know about them."

"Really?"

I couldn't be sure. I thought it was unreasonable of them to expect me to hide anything from Taro. "They're at least pretending they do."

"Do you think you could levitate the Dowager? Maybe that would scare the arrogance out of her."

"Oh, gods," I gasped out on a chuckle. I really, really wanted to do it. I wondered if she would scream. It would be hilarious. "Maybe I would turn her upside down, too."

"That would be fantastic," Taro said. Then he sighed. "But it would make it undeniable that you can cast. I don't want her knowing that."

"Neither do I, but it would be fun."

He sighed again.

"You all right?" I asked.

He stared up at the ceiling for a moment. "I'm going to find a card game."

"Good." He was skilled with cards. It would make him feel better. And he wasn't nearly as tense as he had been in the past, after an encounter with his mother. Maybe he wasn't quite at the point where his mother's poison could just slide off without harm, but he was getting there. And he didn't need me fussing over him. "Can you wake me at sundown?"

"Of course."

I kissed him. "Have fun."

I went back to bed. I spent an enjoyable time visualizing lifting the Dowager off her feet, swinging her around, listening to her shriek. Then I fell asleep.

Chapter Eighteen

It was the full moon, which was a poetic coincidence. It silvered all the curves and lines and shadowed the hollows. It was pretty. Lanterns cast a yellow glow here and there, but the greatest source of illumination was the moon. It made me fanciful. I imagined the silver light had secret effects that would keep those who slumbered in their beds, and would shield us from prying eyes. Which was just stupid. If anything, the light would make us easier to see.

There were spells that were supposed to be performed under different phases of the moon. That struck me as unrealistic, but from what I understood, the moon had an effect on the tides. Perhaps it had an effect on other things, things I didn't know anything about.

I looked at the arch, which had been rebuilt after the rock slide. I hadn't bothered to look before, as I had little reason to visit the shoreline. I couldn't imagine how an arch big enough and strong enough to support a rock that size could be built with human hands. In the bright light I did see not large stones piled on top of each other, which was what I had expected, but smaller stones, uniform in size and shape, interlocking. I ran a fingertip along the lines between the stones. I couldn't fit even a nail between them.

I imagined it all had to do with balance and directing force and weight, but the arch really didn't look sturdy enough to do its job. If we got the rock that high and the arch collapsed, not only would it be dangerous for those casting the spell—and those who would be handling the chains used to hang the rock—but it would create a mess no one could ignore. The tenants would see it as another sign of bad luck.

But the attempt had to be made.

The rock lay where it had first collapsed the day of the rock slide, tilted half on its side. It looked enormous. It seemed impossible that mere words could move it. I almost felt stupid being part of the group that was going to try.

It was decided that we would stand in a circle around the rock. Mitloehner waved out the beat of the song with his hand and we started singing. We went through the cast, went through it again, and went through it again.

The rock didn't so much as shift.

Hell.

Mitloehner stopped us with another wave. Then we stood around and stared at the damn rock.

I'd really thought that was going to work.

"We need ideas," said Mitloehner.

"Maybe if we all touch the rock," Thatcher suggested.

So we tried that, singing the cast again and again, and accomplishing nothing.

I didn't expect to feel this frustrated. "Maybe we could raise everyone's singing up a few notes."

"What could that possibly accomplish?" Berlusconi demanded.

"I don't know. He was asking for ideas. It's an idea." Maybe singing in higher notes would enable us to lift the rock higher. It made at least as much sense as relying on the moon.

"Let's give it a try," Mitloehner said.

So we gave it a try. It was a mess. Transposing the notes in a consistent manner and remaining in harmony was beyond the abilities of just about everyone, including me. I loved music, and it had a powerful effect on me, but I'd never been much of a singer.

"Is there anything causing it to stick to the ground?" Yonhap asked. So we looked, but as far as we could tell there was nothing adhesive under the rock.

"Maybe if we held hands while we sing," Coutler suggested. It was how they began their meetings. So we tried that, with no result.

I couldn't believe it was all going to be useless. We'd already worked so hard. And success would have been so good for morale.

Maybe we should try to find a way to make it lighter, after all.

"Maybe we're just too tired," said Browne. "We've been pouring a lot into this, while carrying on with our other duties."

I'd had no other duties to fulfill over the course of this project. What was my excuse?

I *was* tired, though. "What I wouldn't do for coffee," I complained.

Then I pressed my lips together. I hadn't meant to say that out loud.

Browne snapped her fingers and stared at me. "That might work."

"Coffee?" Mitloehner asked with understandable confusion.

"No, not quite. But I have something that might help. Wait here, I'll be as quick as I can." She took off at a trot.

I almost sat on the rock before remembering it was a good luck talisman, and sat on the ground instead.

"So, Shield," said Berlusconi. "Where does your Source think you are?"

My, she was an annoying person. I thought quickly. "He believes I am interested in healing. He thinks I am helping Browne with a patient." I would have to remember to tell him that.

"Shouldn't you be with him?" Berlusconi demanded. "How can you do your job if you're way out here?"

"We don't have to be together to channel."

She crossed her arms. "Really."

I looked at her in silence for a few moments. I should not be getting irritated with her. If I were as disciplined as a Shield should be, her words would flow around me without making even the slightest impression. But, on the other hand, sometimes just letting things go meant you had to deal with ever-increasing amounts of them. "What is your problem?" I asked her.

She appeared taken aback by the question, but recovered herself enough to hiss, "I had to earn my place in this circle!"

"How?" What did earning her way in entail?

"None of your damn business."

I shrugged. "All right."

"And then you come here out of nowhere and just slide in like we owed you something."

"I didn't ask to be a part of this. Browne didn't even tell me what she had in mind when she first brought me."

"Just because you're a Shield, you think you can have whatever you want."

"In fact, I'm not a part of this circle."

"You come here and flounce about sneering at us."

"How have I been sneering at you?"

"You're from a big city. People like you think people like us are stupid."

I wasn't going to bother responding to that. I didn't think the residents of Flown Raven were stupid. I didn't act as though I thought they were stupid. I had too much respect for how hard they worked.

"Too good to talk to me, are you?"

"Well, you're hardly original, are you?" I drawled. I'd heard most of her complaints before, from other people.

"Oh, don't you sound grand? It's your Source who's the 'risto, darling, not you."

"So you're not normally this obnoxious? It's just me who inspires this dip into bad manners?"

"That's enough," Mitloehner snapped.

"This isn't circle business," Berlusconi retorted. "I owe you no respect."

"You were just complaining that she got into the circle without earning her place," Thatcher reminded her. "That's circle business."

Mitloehner spoke over them both. "I know we can't help making a lot of noise, but we're not going to create more noise than necessary. We don't want people coming to investigate."

Berlusconi said nothing more.

Browne returned with a small bag. "All right, this is kyrra powder." She shook the bag. "I use it when I know I won't have the chance to sleep for a couple of days."

A couple of days? That couldn't be good for a person.

"What use is a powder that will keep us all awake?" Mitloehner asked.

"The reason it keeps a person awake is that it increases vigor and focuses the mind for several hours. With multiple doses, it is possible to stay up for a few days."

"I've never heard of this." Mitloehner was almost accusatory. "I could have used something like that many, many times."

I could have, too, especially for some of the long night shifts in High Scape.

"I've never given this to anyone before. People can come to crave it, and the more one takes it, the more exhausted one feels when the effects wear off. Other discomforts include blinding headaches and intense thirst. To alleviate their discomfort, a person will take more kyrra, will soon get hit by the side effects again, take more kyrra, and so on. I don't know what would happen to a person who took kyrra constantly for an indefinite period of time, but it can't be good. So I don't give it to anyone. I'm suggesting this only because I believe these circumstances warrant it."

"Because you think this increased vigor will help us raise the rock," said Mitloehner.

"It's the only thing I can think of." She held up the bag. "Just understand, you won't be able to sleep tonight, and you will have a headache when the effects wear off, and you will be thirstier than you've ever been in your life."

"Does anyone object to using this . . . kyrra?" Mitloehner asked.

I wasn't the only one to look at Berlusconi, but she didn't speak.

"All right, palms out." Browne poured a little bit of powder into Thatcher's hand. "Just a warning, it's quite bitter."

Thatcher licked his palm and two moments later, the grimace on his face was truly spectacular.

"Don't spit it out!" Browne ordered him.

I watched him swallow. "Gods, woman!" he griped.

Everyone else assumed expressions of disgust before tasting the powder, extending the tips of their tongues reluctantly. I decided to do what I would do when entering a body of cold water. Just jump in. I stroked my palm with the flat of my tongue.

It was bitter, but I'd had worse. Shields tended to feel physical sensations less acutely than the average person, and that included taste. In the Academy, this had been described as a liability, but I'd always been grateful for it, myself. Being sensitive seemed to equate to being uncomfortable.

It didn't take long for the effects to become evident. My blood seemed to start racing. I had the almost uncontrollable urge to run, or climb something, or push against something. And my mind, that was strange. At first it whirled around unpleasantly, as though there were four rats in my brain all running and dancing in different directions. Then it suddenly settled. The focus that resulted was, at first, unwieldy. I looked at the moonlight, and it was all I could see, the silver, bouncing particles filling my eyes. And then, without any direction from my thoughts, my gaze shifted to Thatcher. I'd never paid much attention to him, he was just one in a relatively large group, but I realized right then that his cheekbones were magnificent, gloriously highlighted by the moonlight.

The next thing I knew, Browne had me by the arm and was guiding me to stand somewhere. Then she snapped her fingers in front of my face. "Look at the rock," she ordered.

So I looked at the rock.

After a while, my mind seemed to balance, and I became aware of the singing. It filled my ears, and I was pulled into it. I could sing the words, put force behind them, and look at the rock, the lines and angles of it etching dark borders in my eyes. Everything else just didn't exist.

And the rock moved.

The excitement that created made my heart race even faster, but while I noted the change, the fact of it bounced against the edge of my focus and disappeared. I watched the rock rise higher.

This was fascinating.

At one point, a voice hovering around the edge of my mind

came to penetrate my thoughts. It was Browne, telling us to lower the rock. This order didn't make sense to me, but I obeyed it.

I had no idea how long we practiced raising and lowering the rock. It couldn't have been too long. It wasn't yet dawn when Mitloehner called a halt and told us to return the following midnight. I didn't think we should stop. I was pretty sure I could work a few hours more, and we could get the damn thing done. I was not, however, compelled to dispute the decision. It was easier to just follow along.

I ran back to the manor. It was pure pleasure. Working the muscles in my arms and legs, feeling my lungs expand, cool air brushing over my face and playing in my hair. Why didn't I do this, run for the joy of it? I wouldn't have thought of running as something so sensual. It was something one did to get away from someone. But it felt so good, I almost kept on running instead of entering the manor.

But I didn't think it would look good, my running around for no reason. Normal people didn't do that. The residents didn't need to be thinking their Shield was odd. Or they might panic, thinking there was something wrong. Better to be more circumspect.

I was a little loud climbing the stairs. I couldn't slow down. I hoped I didn't wake anyone.

The suite was too small. The sitting room had too much furniture, tables and chairs and settees. Nowhere near enough room to pace, but I couldn't bear to sit still. So I chose a settee and walked around and around and around it.

The door to the bedchamber opened. I heard it but I was counting my footsteps so I didn't look up. I knew it was Taro.

"What are you doing?" he demanded.

"It takes nine steps to circumvent this settee," I told him. "Though if I stretch my stride . . ."

"You're pacing."

"I'd go around the room, but there's all this trash about. Why do we need twelve pieces of furniture just for people to sit on? We'd never have that many people up here."

"What's going on?"

"I mean, even if we had you and me and your mother and my mother and my brothers and Fiona and Stacin and the

Prides up here, we still wouldn't need all this furniture. And we'd never have all of them up here at the same time. Can you imagine your mother having a conversation with Dias? My gods, it would be hilarious. One would end up slapping the other. I think your mother would hit harder than Dias. Do we have any water?"

"What the hell is wrong with you?"

"Oh, you should have seen it. That rock is huge, just huge, and we made it dance. It was fabulous. All the light and the words and notes swirling through my head and the rock went higher and higher and I couldn't feel my feet. Seriously, I need some water."

Taro stood in front of me, halting my progress. He grabbed me by the shoulders and shook me once. "What happened to you?"

"It wasn't working. It wasn't working and it wasn't working and it wasn't working. We sang and we touched and we— oh!—we didn't dance. Do you think it would have worked if we'd danced? Dancing is very powerful, you know. Clears the mind and works the breathing and it's all movement to a purpose, you know. I bet that would have worked. I wonder—"

"What's wrong with you?" Taro roared.

"Sh sh sh! Don't be so loud, you'll wake everyone. And they work so hard, have you noticed? Up so early and working so hard and barely able to stop even to eat and they can't stop until it's dark and then they sleep and then they have to get up and do it all over again. Do you ever feel badly about it, Shintaro? They work so hard and we do so little."

Taro cupped my face in his hands and leaned his forehead against mine. "What. Happened?"

"It wasn't working, you see. We tried and we tried and we tried and we couldn't move the rock. We just weren't strong enough. So Browne went back to her cottage and Berlusconi really doesn't like me because I am a Shield but she doesn't seem to like Browne, either, and was generally being—"

"Why did Browne leave you? Did she decide it wasn't a good plan? Did she leave you there to do something she considered dangerous?"

"She needed to get this kyrra powder that really wakes a person—"

"She gave you a drug?" Taro demanded angrily.

"No no no, it's not a drug. It's a medicine. Browne uses it all the time when she has to work really really hard. And you know how hard she works. You were—"

"You can't Shield, you realize that. If an event were to come—"

"I would be able to handle it with ease. Because the kyrra turns the mind into a needle, really, I could do anything. I could probably Shield without the spell, which would be excellent, because carrying around the ingredients is a real pain in the—"

"So the rock is up? This is all over?"

"No no no, this was just practice. We'll have to do it again tomorrow, so Radia can get people to chain the rock to the arch. Have you seen the arch? It's so narrow. I can't imagine it can actually hold the rock, but of course I don't know anything about it. Have you ever studied anything about building things? Because I think that would be really good information to have."

"You're not doing this again tomorrow."

I pulled away from him. "Of course I am. Water water water." There was the jug, gleaming white in the lightening air of dawn. I poured myself a glass and it was cool and shivery going down my throat.

"You are not. Look at yourself. I've never seen you like this."

"It's because of the rock, you know. It has to go up. Radia's going spare because she can't do her duty. How would you feel if something was preventing you from channeling? If you were here in Flown Raven and earthquakes were happening and you couldn't do anything about it? I mean, you were born a Source. What if you never found a Shield and couldn't do what you do best? Like Creol. Sometimes I almost feel sorry for him, you know. I couldn't bear that, myself. Knowing what you can do but not being able to do it."

"Please lie down."

There was no way I could lie down. I had to move move move. And talk. There were so many thoughts tumbling through my mind and I had to speak them.

Hester came in with the morning tray.

"Good morning," I greeted her. I felt fabulous. "Is it a good morning for you? How early did you have to get up?"

She didn't answer me. She just looked at me, her eyes kind of wide. That was rude.

"Because I was just thinking—I do that a lot, you know, thinking, though that always seems to get me in trouble, because I always seem to think about the wrong things—that you're here to wake us up, so when did you—no, wait, you don't always bring us the tray. How do you decide when to do that?"

Instead of answering, she silently backed out of the room, closing the door behind her.

"Now that's *really* rude."

I smelled coffee on the tray. A headache just exploded into my skull, and my throat became painfully dry. The nausea created by the headache made it difficult to drink the water, and the water didn't seem to help my throat at all. I felt disgusting.

Suddenly, it felt like every particle of strength I had just rushed out of me. I kind of collapsed into a chair. "Whoa." The room was tilting, and I had the most foul taste in my mouth.

All right, this wasn't good. In fact, it was pretty nasty. How could Browne go through this on a regular basis?

"Ready to be sensible?" Taro drawled.

"Ready to sleep." If I could. My skull was pierced with pain. I pressed the sides of my head with my palms. "My gods."

Taro stood beside me and put his hand on my shoulder. The pain flowed away. Oh, thank Zaire. "So you're not going to take that dross again."

The thought of having any more of the powder made my stomach slosh unpleasantly. "Just tonight, to get the rock up. Then never again, I promise."

"You didn't see yourself, Lee. You were like a crazy person. And your eyes, they couldn't settle anywhere. And it was like the air around you was crackling. It wasn't right."

"One more time."

"The rock isn't your responsibility."

"You would do the same, if you could."

"No, I wouldn't."

"Liar."

"All right," he conceded. "But this involves my family."

"Exactly. They're your family." That couldn't be difficult for him to understand. After all, he was jumping through hoops because of the mess my family had created.

He frowned. "I don't like you doing this."

"I don't like doing it, either. This is not fun." Actually, working with the rock had been fantastic. Anything after that had been alarming. And weird.

Though I still felt that, under the influence of the kyrra, I could channel without the spell. I wondered if it were possible to create a powder that was slightly less powerful, but had none of the side effects. On the other hand, I wasn't thrilled with the idea of taking a drug in order to perform my duties. It disturbed me as using a spell did not. That didn't make any sense. "Just one more time."

Taro clearly didn't approve. I waited for further argument. Instead, he said, "Will you sleep now?"

"Will you lie with me? I have a vicious headache."

"I'll stay with you until you fall asleep."

It took me a little longer to fall asleep than I'd expected. I was tired, but my mind was still circulating a little too quickly. Taro didn't move, and his proximity was reassuring and comforting.

I opened my eyes and couldn't quite decide whether I'd actually slept or not. It was late afternoon. Taro was gone. My mouth tasted putrid. I felt loose and tired as I left the bed to get some water. Normally, I was craving coffee as soon as I woke, at any time, but the thought of drinking any made my stomach curl in protest. I drank some water, splashed some more on my face, and changed my clothes.

I spent the whole day in my room, staring into space, feeling too vile to do anything. No one came to bother me. I suspected Taro had something to do with that.

I was just about feeling normal when it was time to head back out. I joined Radia, who was being assisted by two tall and broad-shouldered men introduced to me as Shipwright Neil Vejajiv, who was wearing a leather bag over one shoulder, and Sawyer Olan Ridden. Despite their size and strength, they didn't carry Radia but supported her while she kind of walked between them. It was awkward and slow, and Radia was sweating and keeping any vocalizations of discomfort behind tightly clenched teeth.

Getting through the small twisting path that breached the high stone ridge behind the manor was particularly challenging, as Radia and the two men couldn't walk through three across. Then the rocky shore on the other side of the ridge caused slippage under everyone's feet.

Everyone else from the circle was at the arch, as well as a few other men I didn't recognize. Everyone greeted the Wind Watcher with respect. There was a folding chair set up a short distance away. The shipwright and the sawyer helped Radia settle into it.

Four men climbed up the arch with a lot of slipping and quick grasps for purchase and balance. No one was used to doing this, and that was alarming.

The chains meant to hold up the rock were enormous. Used for ships, I'd been told. From the looks of it, the way the men handled them, they were damn heavy. I really couldn't imagine how the men would be able to maneuver them in order to hang the rock, but that part of the process was not my responsibility.

Browne handed out the kyrra powder. It seemed to me that everyone was even less enthusiastic about licking their palms than they had been the night before. All I could think about was the headache I was going to have the next morning.

And that wasn't what I should be thinking about. I had a task to perform. I licked the powder off my palm.

This time I was ready for the effects, and perhaps that was why they didn't seem to overwhelm me to the same extent. The clarity of mind felt a little more natural. I looked at the rock, and I could be aware of other forces in my environment without being distracted by them.

And when we started to sing, I could keep the words clear in my mind and direct them with the proper pressure. As the rock lifted, I almost felt like I was touching it with my mind. A sensation that was just plain weird.

However, the hard part was not, at that point, lifting the rock, but holding it close enough to the top of the arch to be reached by the chains, yet not so close that the men on the arch lacked the room to work. Holding it in the precisely correct location was challenging, and tiring.

The first time the men tried to loop the chains, one of them shrieked and jerked his arm back and almost fell off the arch, caught by the front of his shirt by one of his fellows. He had to be helped down while we lowered the rock. Browne examined his hand, bound his two broken fingers, and gave him something for the pain. Then she was back with the circle, and we raised the rock again.

We held it. And held it. And held it.

I was aware of Coulter stumbling over the words. This caused the rock to wobble, and the men trying to thread through the chains swore and pulled back.

Thatcher, standing beside Coulter, put his hand over the other man's mouth. Shutting him up caused the rock to straighten.

We held it and we held it and we held it.

The weight seemed to be more draining on the mind than it had been the night before. Perhaps that had something to do with the kyrra powder feeling a little less powerful.

The men trying to thread the chains through the gaps in the rock were shaking and sweating. Could they get it done?

And then they did. The huge chains were pushed through and pulled up and some sort of fastening hammered into place. Mitloehner put up a hand, and we stopped singing.

The rock held.

I let out a long breath in relief.

The others laughed and applauded and I ended up getting hugged by a lot of people without really thinking about it. Some of the laughter was a little hysterical, perhaps because of the kyrra powder, but also, I remembered, because at least some of them probably believed the rock was a talisman for good luck. And all of them put their hands on the rock, bowing their heads and closing their eyes. I felt a bit awkward being the only person not to engage in these actions, but to imitate their behavior without sharing their beliefs would be lip service, and that was insulting.

The near silence after the constant singing and jangling of the chains was soothing. I could hear the waves flowing in the darkness, a sound I'd always enjoyed. It was calming to my mind which, while not as frantic as the night before, was still whirling more quickly than it should.

The shipwright opened his bag and began pulling out and distributing mugs. "I believe this moment deserves some recognition. This is the best wine from Her Grace's cellar."

Hm. Her Grace wasn't supposed to know about this. How did he get his hands on it?

"No," Browne said quickly. "It will react badly with the kyrra."

Radia looked disappointed. "Even just a sip?"

Browne thought for a moment and then nodded with reluctance. "All right. Just a sip."

The shipwright took this instruction seriously, pouring very little wine into each mug. When everyone had been served, Radia stood and raised her mug. "To luck returning to the land."

"Aye!" everyone else responded, and we all took a sip. I couldn't really taste what I was drinking; my tongue still felt coated with kyrra. That seemed a great waste of good wine, but probably there was some symbolism involved that was more important.

"I'm sure you're all aware that none of us is to admit to having anything to do with the raising of the rock," said Mitloehner.

"How else could it be explained?" Berlusconi challenged him.

She was really annoying.

"It's not up to us to explain. Let everyone think what they will."

We broke up shortly after that. I really felt like swimming, but knew that was careless. The currents of the water were strong, and I risked losing all my strength midstroke. Then I would drown, and that couldn't be pleasant. And it would be rude to leave Radia to go back to the manor with only her escort.

It felt like it took days to get to the manor. I ran up the stairs and into my suite. I paced. Taro came out and watched me pace. He gave me water but didn't try to talk to me. I didn't need him to. My mind spilled out plenty of fuel for a monologue.

It didn't take as long for the strength to drain out of me, but the headache was just as bad. That didn't seem fair.

Kyrra was certainly an amazing substance. There had been many periods in my life when I could have used something like that. But the aftereffects were unpleasant. I couldn't imagine being tempted to use it again.

Chapter Nineteen

The next thing I was aware of was someone shaking my shoulder. "Please stop." If I was still so exhausted, it had to be too early to get up.

"The test is about your future," said Taro. "I would think you would want to witness it."

I pulled a deep breath in through my nose and opened my eyes. That was harder than it should have been. It was daylight, though. I must have slept through the day and then through the night. The kyrra powder was truly powerful stuff.

"How are you feeling?"

I had to think about that. "Take your hand away." He lifted his hand from my shoulder. Nothing changed. "All right."

"You don't sound too sure of that."

I sat up. My body was sluggish, and I felt as though there were some strange barrier between my eyes and mind and the rest of the world. "I think I'm just tired."

"Hester just brought some coffee," Taro said, leaving the bed. "You missed quite the ceremony yesterday. Fiona celebrated the raising of the rock. Luxury food and ale for everyone, and a couple of fiddlers."

"What's her explanation for the raising of the rock?"

"That she brought in people who could handle such work. From Misconception Bay, which handily explained why it took as long as it did to have the rock hung."

Misconception Bay was a good distance away. "And do people believe that?"

He shrugged. "No one seemed to question it. I don't think anyone cares. I've never seen so many of her tenants so happy before."

That was excellent. Well worth the effort and the discomfort caused by the kyrra powder.

I dragged myself out of bed and stumbled toward my wardrobe. I should have been picking out my best morning clothes. People might be watching me, when they weren't watching the test. I should try to look my best. But my best would take far too much effort, so I dressed in trousers and a shirt and let my hair fall loose. Yes, my mother wouldn't approve, not that I really cared, but maybe Marcus would be so put off, some part of him would be disinclined to win the race.

"How are you feeling?" I asked Taro.

"I'm good."

"Not tired or nervous or anything?"

He smiled at me. "Don't worry. I'm good at this."

Taro was not a braggart.

"Fiona wants us all to meet in the back parlor," Taro told me.

I did not go near the coffee. The smell of it almost made me gag.

Fiona wasn't alone in the parlor. She had Stacin with her, along with Tarce, my brothers, and my mother.

"You're not wearing that?" were the first words out of my mother's mouth.

Really, how often was she going to hit that drum? "Good morning, everyone."

"Good morning, Dunleavy," Fiona said in a soothing, calm voice that was a welcome relief in the midst of annoying triviality. "I thought it would be the best way to show support for Shintaro if we appear in a group. It will make us more visible."

"That's an excellent idea. Thank you."

"How are you feeling, Shintaro?" Fiona asked.

"I will win."

Fiona grinned at him. "Then let's get going."

We rode down to the test site. As with the foot race, there was a huge crowd waiting. I bit down on the urge to tell them to mind their own business.

I drew up beside Fiona. "I confess I don't understand why these particular activities are chosen for these tests."

"Running is about health," said Fiona. "Winning a race demonstrates hardiness of the body. A horse is a symbol of wealth. The ability to control the horse is a sign of being able to competently handle one's funds."

"Taro doesn't have any funds." And controlling a horse had nothing to do with managing money.

"That doesn't matter. It's traditional."

"You know, tradition is really annoying."

She chuckled. "That's strange, coming from you."

"What do you mean?" I had no great admiration for tradition.

"The Triple S is full of tradition, is it not?"

"No. Not really."

Fiona glanced at me but was too distracted to question me. She dismounted and handed me the reins to her horse. "Time to get things started." She tapped my boot and wound her way through the horses and people and down to the riding field.

Taro and Marcus lined up their horses side by side. I couldn't believe this kind of race was meant to have two or more horses running at the same time. The field looked so cramped, filled with all of the walls and ponds to leap over.

Gods, this was all so stupid.

Fiona stood a little to one side and raised her hand. Silence fell over the crowd. "Neither party is to touch the other, the violation of this rule resulting in the forfeit of the test. Any form of sabotage will result in forfeiting the test. Accidental injury will not be a reason to halt the test. Do you understand the rules?"

"I do," said Taro.

"I do," said Marcus.

"Do you consent to participating in this, the second of three tests, to determine who Shield Mallorough will marry?"

"I do."

"I do."

"I call on all those present to bear witness to this trial. Those of the east bring balance. Those of the west bring length of sight. Those of the north bring endurance. Those of the south bring grace. All must favor the outcome of the test."

And the spell was cast.

Fiona dropped her hand. "Three, two, start!"

The two horses sprang from their marks. I wondered who'd provided the horses. They didn't look familiar, so I didn't think they were Fiona's. How could they know the horses were equally adept at leaping over the obstacles? Was that even considered an issue in such an event? Maybe picking the right horse was part of the challenge.

The horses raced for the first hurdle, a short wall of wood obscured and heightened by brush. Some care for sparing the animal injury if it jumped just shy of the top, but dangerous enough just the same with the speed at which the animals were moving.

Both horses flew over the hurdle. One down, nineteen to go. I could see all of the jumps from my vantage, and all seemed ridiculously high. And it wasn't just the height of the jumps that was alarming. So much to jump over, so little space, it all looked very crowded. I wondered that the horses could gather any speed at all. Then again, maybe it was better that the horses couldn't go too fast. Or did more speed make for a smoother ride? I'd ridden my fair share, but only as a means of getting from one place to another. I knew nothing about sport. Taro had always been interested in racing, watching it, gambling on it. I'd always found it dull, watching horses—or people, or dogs, whatever—running around in circles. This, though, was a little too interesting for my tastes.

I watched the horses arc over the second obstacle. I heard people gasping around me. It appeared that hurdle was particularly challenging. It did look a little higher than the others, but I would think the third more dangerous, coming closely after the second at a sharp angle.

Did Marcus shift a little too much in his saddle? Did he fumble the reins? It was hard to tell. His horse leapt true, though.

The next obstacle was a water hazard, and it looked wide to

me. I thought Marcus's horse struggled to clear it, though clear it he did.

Yet, still, Taro was pulling ahead. I saw Marcus rise a little further forward in his stirrups. I was pretty sure that wouldn't do him any good.

Marcus seemed to catch up in time to jump over the next hurdle with Taro. It was hard to see from my angle, but the two horses seemed awfully close to each other. The participants weren't supposed to touch each other. What happened if their horses did?

Assuming such an occurrence didn't result in the animals getting entangled and falling and everyone involved dying.

I could hear gasps and cheers from the others. Who were they cheering for? They couldn't really care. Whether I had to marry Marcus or not would have absolutely no impact on the lives of anyone else. So how did they decide who to be loyal to? Taro, because he had been born in Flown Raven? Marcus, because as a regular he was more like them than a Source?

Marcus fell behind again, just slightly, and again he shifted forward in his saddle. Is that why the gait of his horse hitched just the slightest bit? And was that why his horse clipped a cannon against the top of the hurdle?

It was gut wrenching, watching horse and rider fall down. I thought I could almost hear the impact. I was sure that had to have killed Marcus, though I couldn't see the position in which he landed.

Taro kept on riding. Was he aware of what had happened? Should he stop if he did? He would forfeit if he did, but Marcus must have forfeited by falling. What would happen if they both forfeited? They would have both lost, technically.

If Marcus wasn't dead.

I was dismayed at the possibility of him dying.

But then the horse awkwardly climbed to its feet and one of the people who had run onto the—what did one call it? a field? a pitch?—caught its reins and calmed it down. Two of the others on the field ran to Marcus but he was already on one knee before they reached him. Everyone cheered.

And Taro slowed his horse and turned it around, trotting back to the hurdle at which Marcus had fallen. When he had reached it, he dismounted and stood beside Marcus, offering a hand to help him up. The cheering got louder.

No one seemed to worry about the rule concerning touching.

Marcus got to his feet and put a hand to his head. There was some discussion among the people on the field, including Fiona, who had run out to join them. No doubt they were asking Marcus if he was hurt. Then there was some pointing about the field, and I guessed that Marcus had claimed he was fine and could continue the race.

Which Taro had been guaranteed to win had he continued. It was wonderful that he behaved with such generosity and honor. I kind of wished it wasn't the shape of my life that was vulnerable to his generosity and honor, though.

After a few more moments of discussion, the two men mounted their horses and arranged them just after the last hurdle they had ridden over. Or, in Marcus's case, fallen over. Then Fiona called them to start, and they charged at the next hurdle. It seemed to me a ridiculous risk. Surely the horses didn't have enough space to work up the speed necessary to jump so high?

Yet they did, though it clearly required great effort, the force of the movement pushing both riders back in their saddles. And then they were off, and they seemed to be back on track.

But it quickly became apparent that Marcus had felt the effects of his fall more deeply than he'd admitted, for he swiftly fell behind. By the third hurdle it was no longer a matter of two horses in unison, and by the sixth Taro was in the clear lead.

People were still cheering, but I could hear that they were rooting for Marcus. Because he was losing? Weren't people supposed to admire those who won?

The end of the race was anticlimactic. No one was surprised when Taro prevailed. I was pleased that he received a good bit of applause as he crossed the finish line. It would have been horrible for him to go to all that effort and receive no positive response.

Fiona declared Taro the winner of the test.

I closed my eyes in relief. Thank Zaire.

I hadn't realized how very worried I'd been that this challenge would be won by Marcus, and that that would have been the end of it.

I opened my eyes when I heard the others begin to applaud, and I joined in enthusiastically. I would never question how Taro chose to spend his free time again. He was a brilliant man.

I dismounted, giving my fistful of reins to a neighbor, and jogged down to the field, followed by my mother, my brothers, and Browne. Cars was already there. As we approached, I could hear him berating Marcus for losing. Ass.

There were a lot of reasons why I wasn't going to be marrying Marcus, but Cars was a significant one. Cars was not as bad as Taro's mother—no one could be—but at least Taro's mother seemed to have things to do that took her away from our immediate presence. I had a feeling Cars was very much in Marcus's life, and I couldn't imagine associating with him on a regular basis without having to work real hard to resist the impulse to poison his tea.

Taro dismounted and I went to him, rising to my toes to kiss him on the cheek. "You are marvelous."

He grinned.

Yes, we were back on track.

"Do shut up," I heard Browne say to Cars, and that was kind of funny.

Cars's face grew even redder. "How dare you—"

"Your son has an enormous lump near his temple and his eyes are glazed."

Taro frowned. "Is he badly injured?"

Browne didn't answer, instead asking Marcus to follow her finger with his eyes. He seemed to be having trouble with it.

"What's wrong with him?" Cars asked in a suddenly milder tone.

"I'm not sure, yet. I'd like to get him somewhere quiet and take a more thorough look at him."

"So let's get him back to the manor," Fiona ordered.

"The tavern's closer," said Cars.

"The manor's quieter and there's more room. Healer Browne can easily stay if she needs to, without being disturbed, and my staff can bring her anything she or Trader Pride requires. Tarce, see if you can quickly get hold of a carriage or wagon."

"We will do the race again when you are better," said Taro.

I couldn't help glaring at him. There was honorable and then there was just ridiculous.

"You can't do it again," said Fiona. "The test was completed by both parties. It's done."

"He was injured!" Cars objected.

"And if Source Karish had been the injured party, you would have me make the same decision?"

Cars opened his mouth, and I was dead sure he was going to lie. Fiona apparently was, too. She raised her eyebrows at him, daring him. He closed his mouth.

Heh.

"I know you're supposed to conduct the final test tomorrow," said Browne. "But I don't advise you to. Maybe not for a few days, depending on what's going on with your head."

"We will wait until he is sound before proceeding to the final test," Taro announced.

I held back a sigh. The challenge was supposed to require only three days. It was taking a couple of weeks, instead. That couldn't be a good thing. Variation from a regular schedule rarely was.

Chapter Twenty

Shortly after we returned to the manor, I learned that Marcus had a concussion, but that it wasn't severe, and he needed to rest for only a few days. I was surprised at the strength of the relief I felt. It would have been awful if he'd died. Certainly, it would have made my life easier if he had, but he seemed to be a decent man, and the world could always stand to have more of those.

A little while later, I was beginning to wonder if I'd been the one to get hit on the head. The headache that developed over the course of the afternoon was piercing and brought on an intense level of nausea. Most alarming, when Taro touched me it subdued only a fraction of the pain. I still ended up throwing up, which made me feel like my skull was going to shatter.

"It's that damn drug," Taro groused.

"That doesn't make sense. I was feeling better."

"Drugs have unpredictable results. You said Nab told you what the effects were. Did she include vomiting?"

"No. And talking about vomiting is making it more likely that I'll need to do it again." I breathed shallowly through my nose.

"Could you Shield now, if you had to?"

"Of course." I would have to, wouldn't I?

Though, when I contemplated casting the spell, I found it very difficult to remember the words. That wasn't good.

"I don't believe you."

I shrugged.

"I'm getting Nab."

"It's just a headache."

"She caused it. She can alleviate it." He kissed my forehead. "I'll be back as soon as I can."

I couldn't even bear to lie down. I sat in a chair, holding my head in my hands, breathing carefully.

Returning as soon as he could wasn't quite soon enough. I ended up throwing up again, and had to concede Taro might have been right.

It was a bizarre reaction. Maybe it had something to do with my being poisoned a few months before. My current symptoms felt similar to what I'd felt then. But I couldn't believe something from the poison could have remained in my body for so long.

I seemed to get sick and injured a lot. It was annoying.

A horrible explosive noise ripped through the air and shattered in my mind. I clenched my teeth against a scream as I saw some weird sort of light flash up and flash away just outside the closest window. What the hell was that?

I moved closer to the window. Out of nowhere, an odd, contained clot of white light just appeared with another explosive crack. I'd never seen anything like it. Was it some kind of peculiar lightning?

But there was no rain. And the sound accompanying the light wasn't anything like thunder.

I was so rattled by the light, in so much pain from my headache, that it took a few moments to become aware of the almost unpleasant shivery sensation just under my skin. Which meant someone was casting a spell. All right. What was the point of it? To scare people, I supposed. I imagined it would do a pretty good job.

Where were these people getting these spells?

Feeling dizzy, I stepped back and sat down. And this was fortunate, as the next flash of light hit the nearest window, smashing the glass and warping the ironwork. A second ball of light quickly appeared thereafter, this time developing on the floor just inside the window and leaving a scorch mark. I imagined I could feel the strength of it against my skin.

All right, now I was starting to get scared.

So were others in the house. I could hear shouts and screams and heavy and fast footsteps. And was that something burning?

I could hear the door to our suite being thrown open. "Shintaro!" Fiona called. "Shintaro!"

"In here!" I answered precisely in time to another flash of light. That was unnerving.

Fiona ran in. "What's going on?" she demanded. "Where's Shintaro? Why aren't you doing something?"

"This is some kind of spell," I told her. "This isn't something a Pair can do anything about."

"Can't you do something? You can cast."

"If there's something that can be done with a cast, it's beyond my knowledge and ability."

"Where's Shintaro?"

"There's something wrong with me," I admitted. "Taro's gone to fetch Browne."

"In this?"

"It wasn't doing this when he left."

"What's wrong with you?"

"Don't know exactly."

"There has to be something you can do," said Fiona. "Please, Dunleavy. It's hitting the manor. We've got to stop this."

"I honestly don't know."

"Damn it!" She left as quickly as she'd come.

I closed my eyes and tried to concentrate. Was there anything I could be doing? Was there a spell I could use, one that wasn't an obvious choice but could be helpful with a little creative application?

Thoughts felt heavy, pressing hard against my headache.

Bailey was the next person to storm into my room, which shocked me almost as much as the light balls appearing out of thin air. "Please, Shield Mallorough," he said. "Under any circumstances, I would never presume to disturb you, but the manor itself is being destroyed. There must be something you can do."

Destroyed? "I'm sorry, but there isn't." I hated having to admit it.

"Where's Source Karish?"

"He's gone to visit Healer Browne."

"I will fetch him back."

"You can't go out in that."

"It's barely safer in here."

"There's no point. Karish can't do anything."

Bailey shocked the hell out of me by not answering before dashing out of the room.

All right, this was enough. I opened the overmantel of the fireplace in our bedchamber. I pulled out a spell book and flipped through the pages, trying to find a spell that might be anywhere close to useful. But when I tried to actually read the words, it made my headache and my nausea more intense.

Anger bubbled up in my chest. Damned kyrra powder. Browne should have told me my reaction to it could be so severe. I wouldn't have taken it. The circle probably hadn't even needed me. I doubt the absence of one person would have made a real difference.

So I put everything back and sat on the end of the bed.

Not long after, I heard the door of the suite being flung open. "Lee!"

"In here."

Taro strode in, followed by Browne.

"You're crazy," I accused him. "Running about in that . . . whatever it is."

"We didn't know it was focused around the manor until we got here. It seemed very far off at first."

"It's a cast," I said.

"Aye," Browne responded.

"Do you think it's Kent?"

"Probably."

So our attempt to warn him off had failed. Or had made him even more determined to act.

Browne flinched when the glass of another window was blown out. "Do you have any cave crystals?"

"No."

"Why not?"

I frowned. "Why would I? I gave them all to you."

Browne rooted around in her sack and retrieved a small bag. "I'll be back soon."

"You can't leave Lee like this," Taro objected.

"She can wait. I'm not sure the manor can."

"You're not leaving her like this."

"Don't you try that lord of the land demeanor with me, boy. You said you can't do anything about the lights. I can."

"There's a tsunami coming."

I looked at him. "What?" He hadn't told me that.

"I felt it coming on the way back." He turned to Browne. "She has to be able to Shield before it gets here."

"One disaster at a time, Source." And she left, ignoring Taro's demands.

"She's a healer, isn't she?" Taro ranted. "That is her primary responsibility, is it not?"

"To Fiona and her people," I said. "Maybe not us, so much." Besides, I'd lasted this long, and it sounded like the manor was about to come down around our ears.

"It's more important that you are at full strength. There is an event coming."

"I can Shield if I have to."

"It's stupid to force you to do so when you're at half strength, especially when a solution is currently walking about the manor."

There was another explosion of light. Gods, it was loud. And the air felt sharp, almost painfully so.

It seemed to be making my headache worse.

Taro started pacing.

"Stay away from the window." Getting hit by one of those spheres of light had to hurt like hell. If it wasn't fatal. Was it fatal?

Taro sharply changed the direction of his pacing.

And then another ball appeared in another window. The timing was frightening.

"There'll be no windows left in this damn place," Taro complained.

Which would probably be interpreted as another sign of bad luck.

And all of a sudden, the air wasn't so painful. "Ah," I said.

"What?" Taro demanded.

"It's working."

"What's working?"

"Whatever Browne's doing."

"There's still light flashing about," said Taro.

And people continued to shout and scream and run around, yet . . . "The air feels better."

"What does that even mean?"

"Can't you feel anything?"

He paused in his pacing, facing me, his hands clasped behind his back. "There is an odd crackling sensation against my skin. Is that what you mean?"

"Something like that."

He resumed pacing. "She needs to hurry up. That tsunami is getting closer."

The air changed again. There was something curving and almost smooth about it, like the shell of an empty egg. I lifted a finger to touch it, but there was nothing there. It confused me.

It was soothing, and my headache and nausea eased just a little.

"The lights aren't hitting the manor anymore," said Taro.

"I can hear them."

"The lights are still playing about the sky. They're just not reaching the roof or walls." He leaned closer to the window.

"Stay away!" I said as loudly as I could manage.

He ignored me. "It's bizarre. These balls of light appear, but only half of them actually form. It's like they're sheared into pieces. It's fascinating."

I didn't care. It was insane to be hanging by the window right then. "Please." To my worry and frustration, he refused to move.

The manor was still ringing with screams and shouts. I guessed no one else could feel the change in the air.

Fiona stormed back in. "You two all right?" she demanded.

"Where the hell is Nab?" Taro demanded. "Lee's a wreck."

"Are you?" Fiona asked me.

"No."

"If she were dying, she would say she was fine," Taro groused.

"I would not. I complain about things all the time."

"I'll see if I can find her. Right now I'm just trying to make sure no one's dead." And she was gone again.

In time, the lights faded out. The screams stopped, and the intensity of the footsteps pounding through the halls lessened. That soothed my headache as well.

"I think he's given up," said Taro. "Would his casters be able to feel whether the lights were getting through?"

I had no idea.

We waited. A long time, I felt. It was over. What was Browne doing?

Taro was pacing again, looking grim. He could feel the tsunami coming. I wondered if he was having to fight off channeling it. He was used to attacking events as soon as he felt them.

And finally, Browne came back. "Everything all right?"

"There's a tsunami coming, damn it," Taro snapped. "She has to be able to Shield."

"Nice to see you're so worried about her," Browne muttered, blowing her bangs out of her face.

That wasn't the issue right then; it wasn't what was important.

Browne dug around her sack again, this time taking out a small box, longer than it was wide and deep. She opened it and took out a small, shiny dark blue leaf. She held it out to me. "Put this under your tongue."

When I took the leaf from her, I realized it was hard, brittle, and sharp. That wasn't going to be comfortable to be putting under my tongue. However, as soon as it was in place, it began to dissolve.

And as it dissolved, its flavor crept out from under my tongue, sliding over the sides of my mouth and crawling onto my tongue. I, to the best of my knowledge, had never eaten rancid meat, but I imagined this was somewhat what it tasted like. "Zaire!"

Browne put a hand under my chin and pushed up. "Keep your mouth shut."

It was vile. Far worse than the kyrra powder.

"Swallow," Browne ordered.

I closed my eyes instinctively. The leaf had dissolved completely: my mouth was filled with curdled saliva.

"Swallow."

I swallowed. I couldn't help screwing my face up with disgust. "Is this some form of entertainment for you? Concocting remedies that taste that bad?"

"Yes, it is," Browne answered with sarcasm that was impossible to ignore. "That was for your head." She held out a small dark orange bottle. "This is for your stomach." She pulled out the cork. "It's going to taste spectacularly awful."

"Lovely." I took the bottle.

"Just one sip."

I reluctantly allowed a small amount of fluid to flow over my lip and into my mouth, reminding myself I was a Shield and had vast stores of endurance and discipline. It didn't actually taste as bad as the leaf. It was sour enough to bring tears to my eyes, but still superior to the flavor of the leaf.

"How long is this going to take?" Taro demanded.

Browne glared at him. "What is your problem?"

"A *tsunami* is coming," he practically snarled.

"There will come a point where he won't be able to keep himself from channeling," I explained. "And if I can't Shield, he'll die."

"And then so will she," he added. "We really don't have a lot of time, and if we're not ready it will be a mess for absolutely everyone. All right?"

Browne grumbled under her breath.

"How long will it take to work?" Taro demanded.

"It's different for different—"

"Are we talking hours? Days? What?"

She was still glaring at Taro, but her voice was mild when she said, "It should be under an hour."

Taro growled and paced.

I crossed the room to get my purse.

"You should be lying down," Taro objected.

"I want the spell components at hand." But to make him feel better, I returned to the bed with my purse, and once I had the ingredients organized the way I liked, I lay down.

While they tasted awful, Browne's medicines were effective. It didn't take long for the pain and nausea to assuage a little. "All right, you can start."

"Not yet," Browne objected. "I can still see the pain around your eyes."

"It's good enough."

"I'll be the judge of that."

No, I would. I looked at Taro. "You can start."

"Are you sure?"

"I am."

He took a deep breath and visibly relaxed, his shoulders lowering just before his shields dropped.

And, yes, it was harder than it should have been, and it brought my headache ringing back to close to its original pressure, but we were able to get the job done, and that was all that mattered.

I didn't like being watched while I channeled, but it seemed like it was happening more and more often.

So I put it out of my mind. "Thank you for all your work tonight, Healer Browne. You protected the manor and alleviated my discomfort. I don't know how to repay you."

"As far as I know, you're not required to."

Well, no, but that didn't mean I couldn't wish to demonstrate gratitude. I would have to think about it.

"I want to teach you the spells I used to protect the manor," Browne said, packing her supplies in her bag.

"Not right now," Taro objected. "She's exhausted."

"No, not right now," Browne agreed. "I will return in the afternoon. I will show you what I did. I'll want to speak to Her Grace, too. If Kent is prepared to engage in these kinds of attacks, there is more we should be doing."

"Like what?" I asked.

"I don't know yet." She rose to her feet. "Get as much rest as you can. We'll need you to be lively."

I packed my purse as Taro showed Browne out. Then I flopped back on the bed and stared at the canopy.

"How's your head?" Taro asked.

"Right now, I'm wishing it wasn't actually there."

"I think you should eat something."

My stomach did not like the sound of that. "I don't."

"You haven't eaten enough today. I'm going to see what I can get from the kitchen. Then you can sleep."

"I feel like all I've done is sleep," I complained.

"Well, you've been using your mind in unnatural ways, haven't you? And taking drugs. Of course you'll be knocked about. I won't be long."

I sighed. I closed my eyes. The headache and the nausea continued to ease, just a little bit at a time, but I couldn't relax. Our warning hadn't delivered a promising response. I didn't know what would. How could anyone respond to an unprecedented attack like this?

I had no idea. Probably no one else did, either.

Chapter Twenty-one

Browne returned to the manor the next afternoon, and I met with her in the front room. Being the person she was, she wasted no time and led me down to the cellar.

"I relied on the old standbys," she said. "North, south, east, west. It's usually safe to start there." She drew me into a corner that I presumed corresponded with one of the directions. She pulled away a sack of something—turnips?—revealing a small glass set into the floor. Inside it was a chunk of crystal from the cave. Wrapped around the glass was a length of red yarn. "It's fairly simple, really," she said. "I just hum the right note, which awakens the crystal. The glass picks up the note and the vibration carries back and forth between the glass and the crystal. This particular shade and make of yarn carries the influence far. So . . ." She hummed, and the glass filled with light. She pulled me to another corner of the cellar, revealing another piece of crystal within. She hummed, and not only did this glass fill with light, but a beam of light developed between the two glasses. She did the third, and then drew me back to the entrance of the cellar, where she had buried the forth. "We have to make sure we're standing outside the range of the beams before we close the square," she explained. "Or we'll be stuck inside until the cast fails."

"How long does that take?" I asked.

"I'm not sure, I couldn't stay to watch, but I would guess a couple of hours. I was able to leave shortly after treating you."

"Why would this keep you from leaving? It's just the cellar. And how did this protect the house from the lightning?"

"I also did it in the attic and around the manor. It shielded the entire structure."

"But you said you'd never come across anything quite like these crystals before."

"I haven't."

"Then where did you get the spell?"

She shrugged. "I just did what made sense."

"You mean you made a spell up?"

"Aye."

"Just on the fly?"

"It wasn't that difficult, really."

"How do you do that? Just make things up?"

Another shrug was the only response it looked like I was going to get. "Come with me," she said. "The others are collecting at mine. We thought it best to have a discussion."

"What? Right now?"

"Do you have somewhere else you need to be?"

"No, I suppose not." So I followed her out of the cellar and then out of the manor.

"No one was hurt, yesterday," Browne told me. "There wasn't even a lot of structural damage. News of that will reach Kent. He will try again."

"He doesn't appear to be endowed with any great focus."

"He's using the scatter approach. Spells. Physical attacks. There are ever more rumors about Fiona being incompetent, which I have no doubt Kent is helping to spread. And I think the fish are being poisoned deliberately."

"It seems like it, but that doesn't make sense. Why would he deliberately destroy a resource that contributes to the wealth of an estate he wants to take?"

"Possibly he can remove the poisonous element after he's successful."

"Possibly? So if there is such a spell, you don't know of it?"

"It seems to me that I'm not the only one creating new spells. We're going to have to catch up in some way."

"I wonder how she'll react to that." I didn't like it. And maybe Fiona would object to having tenants with that kind of power. I would, in her place.

"It's the one way we can help her. She has enough to worry about without dealing with Kent."

"You mean, the discord among the tenants."

"And that the land isn't settling to her."

I frowned. "I'm not sure what that means."

"The land is having difficulty adjusting to Her Grace, because she wasn't born here."

"I don't understand that." Or believe it, really.

"Spells are stronger here. They're coming back faster here than anywhere else."

I was aware of that theory. "What does that have to do with who the titleholder is?"

"Blood is a particularly powerful component in spells."

Aye, I'd heard that. "But Her Grace invoked the ritual making her the titleholder. I thought that was powerful."

"It is, but she was chosen from outside the immediate family. She wasn't a natural heir."

"The law doesn't recognize natural heirs. Titleholders can choose anyone they want."

"What the law recognizes is very different from what natural power recognizes. This title was kept in the immediate Karish family for generations. Source Karish was born here. The land may recognize Source Karish in a way it doesn't recognize the Duchess."

Westsea had wealth.

Westsea had political might, though that might be waning.

Flown Raven was a powerful place for magic.

Neither the Dowager nor the Emperor had been born in Flown Raven; neither carried Karish blood. They would probably have similar difficulties should they own the property themselves. Worse problems, possibly, than Fiona was experiencing.

The Dowager had run the estate when Taro's brother had the title, and she had tried to rule the estate when Fiona first arrived. She thought Taro had no spine of his own. She probably assumed she could rule the estate if Taro had the title. But the real question was whether she was acting on behalf of the Emperor, and if she was, why? What would she get out of it?

"Wait a moment. You said, earlier, that the marriage contract had some kind of spell supporting it, and that this was severed or something when I was called to the Academy."

"Aye."

"So why didn't Taro's call to the Academy sever his connection to the land?"

I watched her think about that. "His father held the title," she said. "And then his brother. Source Karish was already a Source when he became the heir. There was no severing event after that."

"He asked the Empress to sever him from his family after his brother died," I said. "He officially abjured the title. Doesn't that count?"

"I'd forgotten that." She tapped her teeth with a fingernail. "That might be enough. He may experience similar difficulties to Her Grace should he take the title now."

"Can we tell everyone that? It might make things easier for Her Grace."

"I want to think about that for a bit, make sure that kind of information would actually help her."

All right then.

We reached Browne's cottage. Her kitchen felt very crowded with all the members of the casting group within. They stood clustered around the large table, and on the surface of the table was a collection of bunches of dried blossoms and herbs, small pots of powders of various colors, cinnamon sticks, shards of wood, and pieces of crystal from the cave. "Thank you all for coming," said Browne. "I think we can agree that someone is attacking Flown Raven, and will attack again." She didn't mention Kent. I wondered if he had been discussed by the circle. "As many of the attacks involve spells, I believe it our duty to meet those attacks and hopefully stop any further assailments from happening. So, does anyone have any ideas?"

"Patrols," said Mitloehner. "There should be as many of us walking the grounds as possible at all times. When whoever is doing this hears of it, it will act as a deterrent."

"All of the grounds," Thatcher added. "Not just the perimeter of the manor."

That seemed to be a weak strategy.

"That's an enormous area," said Browne. "And people can't spare that kind of time away from their work."

"If we come up with a long yard way of calling each other, we could keep the numbers down." There was something about Thatcher's voice that made it clear they'd been disputing this before our arrival.

"We do not come up with spells," Mitloehner snapped.

"You don't have to work as hard as the rest of us, old man," spat Berlusconi. "You can afford to spend hours walking the grounds, day after day. We can't."

"There is no reason not to see if we can create a suitable spell," said Thatcher. "All spells had to be created by someone at some time."

"The First Landed spent centuries, maybe even millennia, crafting these spells," Mitloehner declared.

"We don't know that. For all we know, they made up three spells before breakfast every day."

"Perhaps they did, but we are not them."

"That doesn't mean we're less than them."

"It is likely they had an intensity of training we lack."

"There's no way to know that. They had all sorts of machines, machines grand enough to take them between worlds. What need had they for spells? It may have been nothing more than a hobby for them."

This was getting us all nowhere. Couldn't they have settled this argument before I'd been brought in?

And wasn't that arrogant? As if my time was any more valuable than theirs. But this was frustrating. Especially as I had nothing to contribute. Being useless was so annoying.

"She is our Duchess," Tye interjected. "It is our duty to do anything necessary to protect her and her people."

"Including creating spells that injure people?" Mitloehner asked. "Because that's what we're really talking about here. This isn't just about communicating. It's about fighting back. And it's not our duty to do anything like that."

"It is, actually," Browne said. "We're Her Grace's vassals. Part of our duty is to fight at her order."

"With spells? Create spells to kill people?"

"What else would you have us do? Kent is attacking us. And that no one has died so far is only luck. They were running people down with horses. They started fires. If they weren't actively intending to kill anyone, they certainly didn't care if they did. We can't let this stand."

"It's Her Grace's responsibility to protect the people."

Fiona was trying. She just lacked the tools necessary to do it. Any titleholder would. Even in the times when titleholders more regularly attacked each other, I would wager casts had played no part in it.

"She can't fight against this. Not alone. You know that."

Mitloehner didn't respond. He just looked grim and annoyed. The others were content to be spectators. Some were watching Browne with smiles, or frowns, or furrowed brows of thought. Others were looking down at their feet, prepared to let someone else make the decision and thereby avoid all responsibility for it.

I was uncomfortable. This was not what I'd had in mind when I started dabbling with spells. The thought of learning spells designed to hurt people appalled me.

I didn't know why, though. I'd killed a man with my Shields. I'd killed a man with a knife. Why did the idea of doing something similar with a spell feel so much worse? It didn't make sense.

I didn't want to do this.

The idea that anyone who could cast could then use those spells to kill was appalling. No real training. No authority making sure the skills weren't being abused. If such spells were being used in Flown Raven, they would be developed elsewhere. If not right then, soon.

People didn't kill each other a lot. Not like they had in earlier times. The deaths I'd been around had been weirdly high in number, because my life was just that special. But for the ordinary person, mortal violence was a thing of the past. The Imperial Guard didn't really fight so much as police, protect the royals, and collect taxes. But all that might change if people thought they could kill, unseen, from the kinds of distance spells could apparently allow.

No. This wasn't what was going to happen. It was too melodramatic.

"We're getting ahead of ourselves," said Browne. "We need to create a form of alarm. Then we need something to protect everyone. If we can accomplish those, well, we'll talk about other possibilities."

Aye, delay the decision. Procrastination wasn't helpful, but it made me feel better.

"What matters most is that we are on the alert when something happens," Browne continued. "Not that we're wearing ourselves out patrolling. As it is, we're sprinkled out throughout the estate. We have farmers and fishers and Shield Mallorough lives in the manor."

"So we are including Shield Mallorough in our plans," said Mitloehner.

"Of course."

Hm. No one had asked me.

"Then she must be properly inducted into the circle."

"I am not being inducted into anything," I objected.

"Then you can't be a part of this."

"Fine." I would find some other way to help Fiona. I was able to handle things on my own, sometimes.

"You don't mean that," Browne said to me.

I just looked at her for a moment. I knew my mind. It was irritating when people presumed to think they knew better than I. "I'll just go, now."

"You would desert the Duchess?"

"Of course not, but I won't be swearing any oaths."

"Then you can't work with us," said Mitloehner.

"Fine." Aye, we were going in circles.

"Stop," Browne snapped. "You're being stubborn for the sake of it," she said to Mitloehner.

He drew himself up to his full insignificant height. "I am in charge here."

That shocked everyone. Apparently they were prepared to give Mitloehner precedence as long as he didn't ask for it. Or, more accurately, demand it.

"According to who?" Thatcher demanded.

"I am the oldest," he said.

"So? Nab's the most talented."

"According to who?" Mitloehner echoed snidely.

"According to anyone with eyes."

And just like that, everyone was talking, mostly about different things, whether Mitloehner was in charge, whether Browne was the most talented, whether I should have to swear an oath, but also about four other topics I couldn't quite determine because everyone was talking over each other.

Except for Browne. She was watching silently. "I'm causing discord," I said into her ear.

"We've never had to deal with anything this serious before," she answered. "Not really. This is as good a time as any to hammer out these things."

It seemed to me that the only things likely to get hammered were skulls. No one was really listening to anyone else despite the fact that the volume was increasing from one moment to the next. When they were facing a threat was not the time to determine the rules. The rules should have been drafted when they formed the group, when everyone was calm and they had the time to discuss things thoroughly.

Nothing was getting accomplished. Talking was turning into shouting, and people were getting angry. It was ludicrous. If they were prepared to argue over such trivial matters, I could hardly trust them to devise a workable plan for protecting the estate.

Could I come up with one of my own? I wouldn't know where to start, but at least I wasn't scrambling for authority or trying to prove anything to anyone. That had to be a sturdier foundation on which to build than all this disarray.

Browne left the room briefly and returned with a small gong, which she rang and kept ringing until everyone shut up. "One thing at a time," she said firmly. Then she looked at me. "Please understand, Shield Mallorough, the casters from Kent refused to take the oath. They feared it would conflict with their oaths to their lord. Or so they said. And now look where we stand."

If that were true, and I had no reason to think that it wasn't, I could understand why they were concerned. That didn't change my position. "There is no benefit for me to belong to your group."

Their bewilderment amused me. Despite my earlier protestations, they really thought I should be honored to be invited to join their group. And maybe I should be. I just wasn't.

"I've seen you cast," said Browne.

"For me, it is just a curiosity. It's not necessary."

"I've seen you use it when it appeared very necessary."

Ah. Right. She had seen me cast when Taro and I had channeled. Damn it. But I said nothing.

"Do you find it impossible to imagine that there might be other situations in which the ability to cast might be necessary?"

"I think I understand your concerns, truly, but I am a member of the Triple S. I cannot swear an oath to anyone or anything else."

"Your Source did," said Browne. "To the Emperor. That's not normal, is it?"

I glared at her. "You know too much."

She smirked.

Taro had had to swear an oath he didn't mean to the Emperor. And the damned Emperor hadn't even promised anything in return, as he had to all the others swearing oaths. I had known a solicitor for a brief while, and he had told me more about laws than I cared to know or could possibly remember, but I did recall him saying that a one-sided contract wasn't a contract at all, and wasn't binding. I didn't know if oaths of fealty could be called contracts, and the fact that all of the oaths given that day had been made while the Emperor had clearly been casting some kind of spell probably threw all the legal implications out the window.

I'd never really talked to Taro about it. I hoped he didn't feel bound by it. He shouldn't, as he had been forced into it, he'd gotten nothing in exchange, and to be asked to swear at all had been inappropriate, but sometimes he had a rather ridiculous sense of honor.

"I'm not going to explain the reasons behind that event," I said. "And it doesn't change the fact that you can't induce me to swear an oath to you."

"You're learning from books," said Mitloehner.

"Aye."

"Not all of us have lived here all our lives. We have had the opportunity to learn casts used in other areas, casts that might not be in your books."

"Or in any books," Browne added.

"I am not going to condone any experimentation," Mitloehner insisted.

"I'm not talking about experimentation," Browne said. "Or not just experimentation. Spells have been passed down that have not been put in any books. At least, no books I've ever seen. And these are things we can teach her."

And one thing I had learned since leaving the Academy and entering the real world, there was a hell of a lot that books couldn't teach. The idea of having this stuff explained to me instead of stumbling along on my own was appealing. That wasn't enough to make me forget my responsibilities. "I will not take any oath that is intended to supersede my obligations to Source Karish or the Triple S. I will not move from that position."

"That's not unreasonable," Thatcher suggested to the others. "I must admit I prefer to rely on a Shield who isn't easily swayed by non-Triple S interests."

"Perhaps we could devise an oath that wouldn't conflict with her other obligations," said Browne.

"Why should she be treated any differently than the rest of us?" Berlusconi objected.

"Because she is different," said Browne. "She's a Shield. None of us can really understand what that means. Though, you know"—she looked at me—"we'd all be delighted if you chose to share with us about that."

And say what, exactly? I was born a Shield. I spent years in the Shield Academy learning how to read and write and figure and dance the benches and endure music and protect Sources. Since I'd left the Academy, my first and only real responsibility had been to Shield Taro. Mere words could not properly relay all that meant.

People were looking at me, apparently waiting for me to say something. I looked back silently.

"We can offer you assistance, instruction, and confidentiality," said Browne. "We will never speak to anyone of your membership in the group, any spell that you cast, or that you can cast at all."

"Everyone knows you can cast," I reminded Browne. No one could help knowing. She'd almost been flogged, publicly, for that very reason. "And I hate to tell you, but I'm pretty sure everyone in Flown Raven knows who you all are and what you can do. Any kind of secrecy is a fiction."

No one was surprised. I could see it in their faces. They did look annoyed, and I wondered if I had violated some secret pact. Maybe the casters pretended they weren't casting and everyone else pretended not to know about them, and mentioning the reality of the situation was considered to be in bad taste.

"We can ensure that no one knows you're a part of it."

"How can you promise that when you can't keep your own participation a secret?"

"From what we understand of you and your status, you aren't expected to be in any one place at any particular time. If anyone asks you where you were, you can tell them your activities involved Triple S business and they'll cease their questions."

It was irksome that a regular was aware of that handy ploy.

"I've seen the results of your casting a spell improperly," Browne whispered.

I glared at her. She knew I'd accidentally colored my hair green using a spell that was meant to color it black. "That was my first spell."

"The fact is that you really don't know what you're doing and that's likely to blow up in your face, causing you damage and perhaps damage to others around you. Are you prepared to risk that so you can stagger about in a dangerous discipline with no supervision?"

She had a point. I hated that. "Fine. I'll agree to be guided by you. Barring emergencies."

I noticed Chan was writing on a slate.

"What do you consider an emergency?"

"I or someone else is going to die."

"All right."

"You must agree that if this group, as a whole, decides on a course of action, you will comply."

"Only if that course of action pertains to casting."

"Of course."

"And it doesn't interfere with my duty to Karish, the Triple S, or the Duchess." Technically, I didn't owe any duty to the Duchess, but I wanted to be free to assist her, if she needed it and I could do it.

"Yes."

"Then, all right." I felt really uncomfortable with this, but I did not like the idea of this group coming up with spells that could hurt people without my being involved. I would be walking around getting paranoid about what they were doing.

"Good."

"What happens, though, when Taro and I are transferred?"

"What do you mean?"

Browne knew so much. About everything, it seemed. How could she not know this? "Our assignments are not permanent. They are meant to last only a few years."

"What is the sense of that?" Berlusconi demanded.

"To avoid the Pair forming inappropriate attachments to local people or groups."

"Sort of like what you're doing right now," Browne stated dryly.

"Precisely."

"My dear, you're such a rebel."

Snarky woman.

"We're going to have to come up with some kind of severing ceremony," said Browne. "I believe it would be safe to assume that we will want you to maintain confidentiality, but remove all other obligations. Does that sound good?"

"No," said Mitloehner, but everyone else seemed to ignore him. A few made sounds of agreement, while most of the others said nothing. No one else opposed the idea, though, not vocally.

"Tell us what you've got, Ivor," Browne asked Chan, and he rattled off all the elements of the agreement that we had come to, only in prettier language.

"Does that appear accurate to you?" Browne asked me, and I nodded. "Good. How shall we do this?"

"The usual," Davos shrugged. "Except you use these words instead. And I think you should be the one to speak them."

Mitloehner actually growled. Browne smiled, triumphant. I

realized I had just witnessed some kind of power struggle, and Browne had won.

Everyone withdrew to stand against the wall, creating a cramped misshapen circle. Browne broke out a box of short candles—always with the candles—and gave one to everyone in the room. Then Browne put an equal number of candles on the floor around the table in a drunken oval. Finally, she took out a candle that she set on the center of the table.

She went back to the cupboards and took out a small sealed jar. "This is karum," she told me. "It is made from fish oil."

"Some kind of medicine?"

"No, wine."

Oh, that was not good. Was there a superlative more emphatic than horrific? "We have to drink that?"

"It's quite good, actually. But more importantly, it is made by our hands from the fruits of this estate."

"You didn't have all this rigmarole when you were going to induct me before."

A few people glared at me. I supposed I shouldn't have referred to their secret ritual as rigmarole.

"When we were going to do that then, the induction was to be held at sunrise. That time has power. At this time, other steps must be taken."

Well, I'd had to consume some foul things in my time. I supposed I could manage this.

Browne held up the slate. "I will speak a number of statements, starting with 'you.' You must repeat them, starting with 'I.' As well, I will ask you questions occasionally, which you will answer in the affirmative. Otherwise, I will be giving you instructions."

"I understand."

Browne lit her candle and sat on the table in the middle, her legs folded. "I call the Order of Casters of Westsea," she announced in a voice that was too big for the room. "Share my light and show our bond."

Tye stepped forward and approached the table. "I am Penelope Tye of Flown Raven. I seek knowledge." She lit her candle off Browne's. "I share strength." She lit one of the candles on the floor. Then she stood still, looking at Browne.

"Do you welcome Shield Dunleavy Mallorough?"

"I do."

"Will you provide guidance as required?"

"I will."

"Will you guard Shield Dunleavy Mallorough from those who will do her harm?"

"I will."

"Who is Shield Dunleavy Mallorough?"

"My peer and comrade."

"We weave your strength into the whole."

Tye stepped back to her place against the wall.

Chan stepped out. He took the same actions and made the same promises and lit candles in the same order. He was followed by a third. Everyone in the room went through the same routine, until all of the candles in the room were lit, except mine.

It took a very long time. There was an undercurrent of something in the room, something I could feel, something building up. It was still boring.

And then, finally, Browne looked at me. It was my turn. The woman beside me took my arm and nudged me into taking a couple of steps.

"You are Shield Dunleavy Mallorough," said Browne.

"I am Shield Dunleavy Mallorough," I responded.

"Your highest bond is to the Source and Shield Service."

I hesitated a moment. Technically, that was true. Personally, I felt my bond with Taro was the most important of my life. Pointing that out would interrupt the flow of the ceremony. They might have to start over again. I really didn't want that to happen. "My highest bond is to the Source and Shield Service."

"Second in potency is your bond to Source Shintaro Karish."

That wasn't his entire name. Did that matter? "Second in potency is my bond to Source Shintaro Karish."

"Your wings fly third to the Duchess of Westsea."

Hm. All right. "My wings fly third to the Duchess of Westsea."

"But you are a being of many parts."

"But I am a being of many parts."

"And one such part you will bind to us."

"And one such part I will bind to you."

"Into the circle you bind your arts of casting."

I really didn't like that one. "Into the circle I bind my arts of casting."

"From within the circle you glean your well of knowledge."

"From within the circle I glean my well of knowledge."

"Its members you will guard from harm."

"Its members I will guard from harm."

"Its secrets you will bury within your mind."

"Its secrets I will bury within my mind."

"You will move as the circle moves."

"I will move as the circle moves."

"And should you tarnish your bond to the circle, your casting arts shall be stripped from you."

Hey now, no one had warned me of anything like that. I wasn't going to throw away my ability to cast just because there was some kind of disagreement between the circle and me. They certainly had no right to ask it of me. I held my unlit candle out to Browne, to be taken, not lit.

"As it pertains to casting in Westsea," she added quickly.

That was a compromise I could accept, except for one more thing. "And should I tarnish my bond to the circle, my casting arts shall be stripped from me, as it pertains to casting in Westsea, and excluding what is needed to protect Source Shintaro Karish."

"Done."

There was some grumbling in disapproval, but no one spoke outright. Browne held out the candle, and I lit mine with it. "Shield Dunleavy Mallorough is one of us. Greet her."

I had expected to feel the jittery sensation I usually felt when a spell was successfully cast. I didn't. Did that mean the oath was meaningless?

Everyone clapped, three times, almost in unison. It sounded kind of creepy.

"All right, then," Mitloehner said sharply. "Can we finally move on to why we came here in the first place?"

Browne scrambled off the table, blowing out her candle. "I hope you've all been thinking, because the next thing we get to fight about is whether we're going to design a communication spell."

It was going to be a long afternoon.

Chapter Twenty-two

"But this is insane," I objected. "Someone is attacking your people."

"It's important," Fiona told me placidly.

"How is a dance important?" I asked. "Ever?"

"A titleholder must attend public events, Dunleavy. It is one of the ways she shows her people that she values them, a willingness to spend her free time with them. It's one of the ways she shows them she's clear of mind and of sound muscle. And it lessens the distance between titleholder and tenant. They'll see her as human. That can be useful in hard times."

I would have thought the opposite would be true. Wouldn't people, during hard times, draw comfort from feeling their titleholder was infallible? I always felt better when I thought people knew what they were doing. But this wasn't my area of expertise. "Well, I hope you have the chance to enjoy yourself, at least."

"Not so fast." She clapped me on the shoulder. "It's important that they see you're a regular person, too."

I almost said I wasn't a regular person. "This is careless."

"I thought you didn't need to be in the manor to stop the earthquakes and the tsunami."

"No, I don't."

"So there's no reason why you can't go out."

I just felt dancing was trivial. When times were hard, wouldn't people prefer to know their leader was working?

"Sometimes it is best that we make an effort to have life go on as normal," said Fiona. "You live as a guest in the manor. One of your obligations is to assist me in making things seem normal."

No one had ever told me that. Did she just make that up?

"I haven't gone for the last few weeks, and if I remember correctly, you haven't gone at all. It's past time."

All I knew was that if I feared I was in danger of losing my livelihood, I wouldn't feel like dancing, and I wouldn't want anyone else to feel like dancing, either.

"Is it that you don't like to dance?" Fiona asked.

"No, no, I enjoy dancing."

"There you go. A good time will be had by all. Tell Shintaro he's expected, too. And I've got some lovely pieces of jewelry if you'd like to borrow some. I know all of yours was stolen." She gently touched one of my earlobes before giving me a smile and wandering off.

Sometimes the affairs of regulars baffled me.

That evening, two carriages took us, Taro and me, my family, Fiona, Tarce, and even Daris, to the assembly hall. Within the building, all of the injured from the fire and the gear used to treat them had been cleared away. There were already several dozen people there, dancing to the music provided by a handful of instrumentalists sitting in one corner. There was a long table along one wall, covered with finger food and jugs with small glasses.

"Are you all right with this music, Lee?" my mother asked.

"This music is harmless," said Taro.

"Thanks for answering for me, dear," I said sarcastically.

"I am the expert in this area," he responded without remorse.

I watched the pairs go through their predetermined steps. "Is all the dancing this formal?"

"Do you not know the steps?" Fiona asked.

"No, no. This dance is familiar to me. I just mean, if all the dancing is like this, the music will be fine." And I wouldn't have to stay by Taro's side all evening. A pleasant enough place to be, of course, but it might appear that I was snubbing everyone else. And I didn't like the idea of Taro feeling he had to watch me all evening.

Linder appeared out of nowhere, grinning broadly. His shirt was orange, which was a hideous color in general, but it looked good on him. He was cute. As annoying as the Dowager was in her attempts to lure Taro and me from each other, I had to admit she picked pretty tools for the task.

"Want to dance?" he asked Mika, who took his arm.

"Have a nice evening, people," Mika said before he was pulled away into the crowd.

"So I guess we won't be seeing either of them again tonight," Dias commented dryly.

Taro invited my mother to the floor, and a young woman came out of nowhere to invite Dias. Tarce turned to me. "Care to dance?"

Sure. Why not? I nodded and let Tarce lead me to the end of the sets, so we could blend in with the other dancers without causing disruption.

And during the first circular hey, Tarce smiled at me. A small, delicious curving of the lips that was entirely fake. I couldn't help it. I laughed. He flushed. I felt bad. "I apologize," I said sincerely. "But . . . what were you trying to do?"

We were separated by the steps of the dance and then brought back together. "Showing good manners," he answered. "You might give it a try."

"That wasn't about manners. That was flirting." Or an attempt at it. Why would he do that with me? "Is that what Taro has been teaching you?"

He managed to look even stiffer. "I don't know what you mean."

I hoped Taro wasn't teaching Tarce to flirt with absolutely everyone. I didn't imagine there were many who could get away with that. When Taro had done it to me at our first meeting, I'd been a little repulsed, and he was really good at it. Someone with less skill could get himself in trouble. "I really don't think that'll work on Radia."

"Do you normally speak of things that are no concern of yours?"

"Only when people try to pull me into them."

"No one is doing that, yet you seem to be everywhere, insinuating yourself into every situation. You overstep your bounds."

Hey, he was the one flirting with me inappropriately. Or something. What other situation could he be referring to?

And if I was doing too much, he was doing too little. "How have you been helping Fiona in this business with Kent?"

He expressed no surprise at my use of Kent's name. So he thought Kent was behind it all, too. "That's no concern of yours, either."

"It's the concern of all the people who live here."

"You don't really live here. You are merely stationed here for a couple of years, and then you'll be moving on. Nothing here, other than your responsibilities as a Shield, is any business of yours."

He was right, of course, but having let myself get drawn into all sorts of local matters, I would have to get used to defending myself. "So you're saying I should live in some sort of box, and the only thing in that box is Shielding. I'm to have no connections to anything else."

"I'm sure you have all sorts of Triple S mysteries to keep you busy. Why don't you focus on those?"

Obnoxious twit. "I suppose because I care about Fiona. She's an admirable person and I want things to go well for her. I can't imagine knowing her and being prepared to do nothing to help her during difficult times."

He glared at me. I did not regret what I had said. He wasn't as bad as Daris, but he was still a sort of leech. He seemed ready to let Fiona handle everything herself. That wasn't what family was supposed to be about.

To give him his due, he properly finished the dance and escorted me back to Taro. I wouldn't have blamed him for leaving immediately. "Are you trying to teach him to be charming?" I asked Taro once Tarce was gone.

"Some things are to be kept between gentlemen."

"It's not working."

He sighed. "I know."

A pretty young woman approached me. "I am Yanara Ren," she said. "Would you care to dance?"

"Certainly." And it was the beginning of a busy evening for

me. I didn't sit out a single dance for the first few hours, constantly kept on my feet by various tradespeople and occasionally my brothers and Taro. In fact, I was kept so busy that I
didn't notice some people imbibing the punch a little more
freely than they should have, nor the edge that was developing
in the conversation around us.

Then I heard, "Well, then, maybe Kent would do a better
job of it," from immediately behind me, and I walked out of
the formation to look at the woman who had spoken the words.
I couldn't really help myself; I was moving before I really
thought about it.

I didn't know what to say. Something along the lines of
"Really?" or "Again?" Didn't the oaths they made to Fiona
mean anything to them?

Maybe such oaths didn't. Maybe that was why the Emperor
had been supplementing the oaths given on the day of his coronation with a spell. Maybe people just played out certain
rituals at certain times as a bow to history, and didn't mean anything by it.

If that were the case, some of those who had given oaths to
the Emperor were in for a shock.

So I was just standing there, looking at this woman, my
dance partner asking me what was wrong, not knowing how
to express myself. It was one thing to be rude to Tarce. He was
an ill-natured layabout. I knew this woman slightly, and she
was a hardworking person. I wanted to defend Fiona, but feared
offending a tenant. That might come back on Fiona in some
way.

But then the woman noticed me staring at her, and she
turned to me with a frosty look. "Do you have something to
say, Shield?"

Fine. "Just curious," I said in the mildest voice I could sim-
ulate. "If you feel Her Grace is so deficient, and that Lord Kent
would be superior, why don't you seek a tenancy from him?
You have a valuable trade. Surely he would welcome you."

Her eyes narrowed. "This has nothing to do with you,
Shield."

"Of course not." I shrugged. "I just feel a certain loyalty to
the Duchess."

Her companion glared at me. "Your livelihood doesn't rely on her competence."

"Yours doesn't have to. You could have left when the others did, instead of poisoning the minds of those who've stayed."

"You can go, now," the woman told me coldly.

I raised an eyebrow and nodded before heading around all the dancers to reach Fiona, who was standing with my mother on the other side of the room.

All right, fine. I had nothing more to say, and I tried to avoid repeating myself. I just resented those two people spreading discord when everyone there was working so hard to have a good time.

I heard a shout, the words of which I couldn't decipher, and a small crash that was nevertheless loud enough to grab everyone's attention. The music screeched to a halt while heads turned toward the source of the upheaval. A thin young man was straightening from having been shoved against a table.

This was followed by a short silence as we waited for the man to express some opinion about what had been done to him. Instead, he charged at a slightly older man, who I assumed was the perpetrator. The two of them barreled into a couple of spectators before landing on the floor, throwing punches that didn't seem to land very well, and just generally grappling in an undignified manner.

A woman pulled on the shoulder of the man on top, clearly attempting to stop the fight. She ended up getting shoved away by a third man. She responded by punching that third man in the face. It was a good shot, too. He lurched away covering his nose.

And then the fight seemed to spread, drawing in more and more people as though some sort of contagion were involved. Many people pulled away to the sides, avoiding flailing limbs with expressions of disapproval, but others jumped into the fights with glee, and still others watched the mayhem and cheered. It was awful.

It was difficult to understand anyone, but after enough garbled and nearly incoherent shouts it was clear that people were fighting over whether Fiona was worthy of their support or not.

I saw Daris standing to one side, drink in one hand, grinning. Wench.

Then someone got the bright idea to start throwing glasses, platters and jugs at people.

"That's enough!" Fiona shouted. "Stop this at once!"

No one paid the slightest attention to her. It was disheartening.

She went to the nearest couple of fighting men, grabbed one by the throat and wrenched him to the floor, landing him flat on his back. She held him on the floor with a foot planted in the middle of his chest. She gave a hard look at his opponent when he tried to jump forward. "Get out."

He fumed, but after a moment he bowed and actually obeyed her. At no point on his way to the door did he get engaged in another part of the brawl.

"That was beautiful," I told Fiona.

She shot me a tight grin. "And what do I need to do with you?" she demanded of the man beneath her boot.

"I'll leave," he grumbled.

"If I see you throw another punch, I'll fine you."

"What if someone punches me first?"

"Duck."

He scowled, but he nodded, and when Fiona let him up he did as his predecessor did: he left without causing any more difficulties.

I fell a little in love with Fiona right then.

When I felt a hand on my arm, I jumped. When I saw it was Taro, I slapped him in the stomach for scaring me. "That was uncalled for."

"You're too close."

"I want to show Fiona my support."

"I doubt she'll want you to lose teeth in the attempt. Move back."

He had a point, so I let him draw me back closer to the wall. I kept my eye on Fiona, though. When she reached the next pair of fighters, she actually grabbed one by the nose and twisted. It was hilarious. And his opponent, she kicked right in the side of the knee. He just dropped.

But here was the thing. As fabulous as she was, there was no way she could work her way through all the fighters in the room. She would either get exhausted and suffer her own injuries, or someone was going to get a bone broken. Or die.

"Wait here," said Taro. I watched him wend his way to the musicians. He approached the trumpet player and spoke into her ear. She nodded and stood on top of her chair, put her instrument to her lips, pulled in a deep breath, and blew.

And what came out was the loudest, sharpest, most ear-piercing, blood-inducing note I'd ever heard come out of any instrument, ever. It hurt. Covering my ears with my hands didn't dull the noise at all. What did Taro think he was doing?

When the blare stopped, I lowered my hands with relief. Then I realized that had been only a pause, to allow the player to pull in a huge breath before sounding the note again. Son of a bitch.

I was not so wrapped up in my own discomfort that I couldn't see the effect the notes were having on everyone else. They seemed to penetrate whatever chaotic emotions the brawlers were experiencing. They started pulling away from each other to cover their ears and grumble. It took several long notes from the trumpet player—the poor woman was turning a deep, dark red—before everyone settled down, but eventually all the fighting stopped.

Fiona had another man pinned to the floor, this time with a foot on his throat. She didn't seem prepared to let him up.

The trumpet player stepped down from the chair and Taro took her place. He waited a few moments until he was sure he had everyone's attention. "My brother slept with as many people as he could get his hands on," he announced. "He used this estate as his personal bordello. He didn't care if he was interfering with committed relationships. He didn't even care if people were willing. And the women he left pregnant received neither respect nor support from him. My father emptied the coffers again and again, investing in business enterprises that failed, one after the other. Not a coin was spent on the maintenance of the estate. His mother was never here. She let bandits run wild all over the land." His lip curled. "And this is the family you wish to hold the title? What's wrong with you people?" He paused, but no one said anything, no one challenged him. "It's time you all went home."

People protested, but under their breath, and they started

moving toward the entrance. I was relieved. So many people fighting in a restricted space, it could have turned into a nightmare of spilled blood and shattered bones.

Fiona had released her man, and her expression was stony. I wondered what had angered her more: that the fight had erupted at all, or that Taro had been the one to successfully end it.

Chapter Twenty-three

The morning of the final test, I woke up with such a fist of anxiety in my stomach and such a weight on my chest, I could barely breathe. Any equanimity I had experienced throughout this ridiculous process was just gone. In its place, I felt panic. Because I considered, for the first time, the possibility that Taro might lose. It could very easily happen. He'd lost the first test. And this test was the last chance. So what if Taro lost? What would I do?

Resentment rose up in me. If Taro hadn't been hungover, he might have won the first test, and we wouldn't be going through this now. It would have been settled and we could have been directing all of our attention to something important. Like Kent.

That wasn't fair. I knew that. Calm down calm down calm down.

Taro could do anything he set his mind to. Except sing, because he'd been born with a tin ear. There was nothing he could do about that. Everything he could control, could work on and perfect, he did. He learned things quickly. He could do this.

I wished it was hours later, and this was done. I would be

able to relax. We could send the Prides home and never think about them again. And maybe I'd spend a few hours grilling my mother to make sure I wasn't the subject of any other asinine contracts.

I could not marry Marcus. It just wasn't possible.

What if Taro lost?

He wouldn't.

According to the contract, if Marcus won the challenge and I refused to marry him, I would lose my identity. What did that mean? It couldn't be whatever status I might have as a merchant's daughter. According to the law—and me—I'd lost that status once I entered the Shield Academy. But what else could it mean?

My name? Would that work? I couldn't see how. Somewhere there was a book that stated I, Dunleavy Mallorough, was born on the date that I was, in the place that I was, to the parents that I was. Could that be struck out? Would it matter if it were? I'd still know my name. The people who knew me would remember my name.

Perhaps I would lose my memory. That would destroy my sense of identity pretty thoroughly. And it might make me forget everything I knew. Maybe everything I'd ever learned.

Oh gods. Could it take away my ability to Shield? Did anything have the ability to do that? That was, as far as I was concerned, what I was. Being a Shield was more important to me than anything else. Without it, I was nothing.

I would be useless. Shielding was all I knew how to do, all I could be. And once I was rendered useless, Taro would be, too.

But no, that wasn't true. There were considerably more Shields than Sources. There were Shields who could protect a Source who was bound to someone else. I had done it myself.

A Source as well known and as talented as Taro would not be allowed to drift about unproductively. He would be assigned another Shield. I had never heard of such an arrangement before, but I had no doubt an exception would be made for Taro, he being who and what he was.

And I would be useless. I would be posted where Taro was posted, because we would still be bonded, and there would be nowhere else, really, that they could put me, but everyone would know I wasn't Taro's true partner. Regulars would wonder why Taro had two Shields, why they should have to support an extra person, and all it would take was one individual seeing Taro and his other Shield working together for the rumors to start.

Other members of the Triple S would pity me. Some might think I'd gotten my comeuppance. I was sure there were those who felt I didn't deserve a Source like Taro; I was too quiet and careful.

I'd almost rather be married to Marcus than useless with Taro. Though I'd be pretty useless with Marcus, too. I didn't know the first thing about trade.

Taro had to win this test.

A crowd had gathered in front of the manor: Fiona, my family, the Prides, too many aristocrats who didn't have enough to do, tenants in the same state. Daris wasn't there, which was no surprise, but Tarce was absent as well, which hadn't been his habit up until then. The Dowager wasn't there, but Linder was, purely, or so it seemed, to be with Mika.

"Attention, everyone!" Fiona called, and after a few repetitions of the words everyone shut up. "This is the third and final test of the Suitor's Run between Trader Marcus Pride and Source Shintaro Karish." There was a sort of cheer from the spectators, the parasites. "This will be a test of intellect and ingenuity, and as each party has won one of the previous tests, this shall be the deciding challenge." She went through the usual warnings about neither party interfering with the other, and mentioned that while people could follow the competitors, any attempt to assist would result in that competitor's loss, and Fiona intended to monitor that by having the most experienced members of her staff follow each candidate.

"Her staff," I heard Cars complain. "They are likely to support Karish in some way."

"Then you should have brought some of your own people," my mother retorted.

"We didn't expect this farce. We thought your daughter would honor her obligations."

I was pretty sure they hadn't. They probably just hadn't planned things out very well. Another strike against them.

"Two necklaces have been hidden," Fiona continued. "One for each contestant. They are identical. A soapstone pendant in the shape of a whale on a yellow leather braid. The first contestant to hand me one of these necklaces wins the test." She held up two pieces of folded paper. "Each combatant will receive a paragraph. The first task is to memorize and recite that paragraph without error. The paragraph will also hold the clues to the next stage of the test."

Ah, hell.

Taro was smart. He had to be, to be able to channel. He understood people, could at times manipulate them. He could deal with changes. Not always gracefully, as in the case of Flatwell, but he functioned well enough. And I was pretty sure the Empress had seen more in him than just a pretty face.

But he had been eleven years old when he was sent to the Source Academy, and had received no education before then. He could read and write, of course, but not with the ease others possessed. Asking him to memorize a written passage, especially in circumstances like these, was a horrible idea.

But no one could have known that. It was possible Taro hadn't thought of it himself.

"I will provide the passages to the parties simultaneously," said Fiona. "Once you have your document, you may go wherever you like to read and recite the passages. The member of the staff in your party will determine whether you have adequately recited the passage." After reciting the traditional rubbish about witnesses from the different directions, Fiona held out a piece of paper to each participant. "Now." The two men took a paper. "It's begun."

Taro and Marcus strode away in opposite directions. Bailey, my mother, and a handful of others followed Marcus. I, my brothers, Cars, Fiona's housekeeper Cekina and the majority of the spectators followed Taro. Damn it. I would have preferred a much smaller crowd. I have never known Taro to feel apprehensive about an audience, but the weight of all those eyes would have to make his task more difficult.

Taro led us just around the corner of the manor, which caused us to be out of sight of Marcus's party. I thought that was wise. Taro didn't need to see how well or badly Marcus was doing.

Taro opened the paper and winced as he read it. We watched him read it again and again, at one point speaking the words under his breath.

Everyone was silent. I realized how easy it would be to disrupt Taro's work simply by speaking loudly. Either Cars didn't realize this, or he had some spark of honor after all.

After a short while, Taro gave the paper to Cekina. He took a deep breath. "Aloft and beyond the bristled green . . ." He came to an uncertain halt. He started again. "Aloft and beyond the green blades . . ."

Damn it, they weren't even sentences that made sense. It was poetry. Or gibberish.

He started again. "Aloft the bristled blades of green . . ." He swore viciously and held out his hand. "I need to see it again."

"Hey now!" Cars objected. "There's nothing in the rules that allows that."

"There's nothing in the rules that forbids it," Cekina retorted, giving the paper back to Taro.

"This is not right!"

"If you care to make a complaint, Her Ladyship is still in the inner garden. I can tell you, however, that Her Grace was both explicit and thorough in her instructions to me."

I could see Cars seething, but he didn't leave and he made no further objection.

Taro read the passage a few more times. He gave it back to Cekina and tried again. He was able to get out a couple of sentences, but then he needed to look at the paper again.

I heard some movement around the corners of the manor. I couldn't have been the only one who did. I hoped that didn't mean Marcus had already successfully recited his passage.

> Aloft and beyond the bristled blades of green.
> Prostrate to the firmament
> Serenaded by the cries of throats of gray
> Adjacent to peaks of bitter froth
> A mouth of dark and secrets.

Taro looked at Cekina.
She shook her head.

"For Zaire's sake!" he snapped. "This is a ridiculous waste of time, it has nothing to do with marriage or trade or managing an estate or anything that is useful, and who came up with all this ludicrous drivel that merely distracts from—" He pushed his hands into his hair and pulled it back from his face. "All right. Fine. If this is the way you want to do it." He dropped his hands, squared his shoulders, closed his eyes, and took a deep breath.

> Aloft and beyond the bristled blades of green.
> Prostrate to the slate firmament
> Serenaded by the cries of throats of gray and white
> Adjacent to peaks of bitter froth
> A mouth of dark and secrets
> Look low.

He looked at Cekina.

She smiled and nodded.

"Thank gods," he huffed. "That was farcical."

I agreed. And while I was relieved he was able to recite the passage, the next step was going to be the more difficult. Deciphering that mess.

Except Taro seemed to have no difficulty picking a direction and striding out. Everyone followed. There was no sign of Marcus.

Taro took us through the gardens to the stone ridge that divided from the grounds immediate to the manor from the rocky cliffs of the whalers' world. We followed the narrow winding path through the ridge. Seagulls screamed and the waves of the sea were capped with white. Taro scrambled up the rocky levels on the other side of the ridge, taking us straight to the same cave in which Fiona and I had been chipping out crystals. To the spike in the ground was chained a small wooden box. Taro knelt beside it.

Taro had had no doubt about where he needed to go. Now that we were at the location, the descriptions in the poem were obvious. But I would have needed more time to figure it out. Taro had had some time to think about the clues while he was memorizing them, but had he really been able to actually think about what the words meant while trying to memorize them? That would have been a challenging split of attention to maintain.

Or, well, it could have something to do with the fact that occasionally he spoke in phrases that sometimes sounded like gibberish. I knew there was always a kind of logic to them. Sometimes, in High Scape, one Source would say something baffling, and the other Sources would clearly understand what was said, while the Shields were left in ignorance.

So perhaps the riddle had made perfect sense to him.

The box was the length of my foot, the width and the height the size of my palm. The part of the box to which the chain was attached was solid iron. Taro pulled on the chain, but it was secure. He sat back on his heels.

I heard a sound from beside me. I looked at Cars and saw the smirk on his face. Was he merely feeling triumphant about Taro's difficulty, or was there something about this box that suggested that Marcus, if provided the same test, would easily conquer?

Taro picked up the box again, sliding the tips of his fingers all over it, testing the strength of the corners and edges. He looked at the iron end again and frowned as he pushed against the surface.

Something about the iron would unlock the box?

Cars was still smirking. I noticed both Mika and Dias were intent in watching Taro. And the odd thing was the way they were moving their fingers, on the right hand, Mika up in the air and Dias against his thigh.

A box commonly used by merchants? If so, that was hardly fair. Marcus would have a clear advantage.

On the other hand, if Marcus had had to determine a location through poetry, he would have been at a disadvantage. He didn't know the area as well as Taro. Perhaps this sort of thing was an attempt to keep the challenges equal.

We could hear the rush of the waves, the shrieks of the seagulls, the whalers at work, as we watched Taro fiddle with the iron side of the box. I couldn't quite see what he was doing, just that he seemed to be sliding smaller parts of the iron around, and that he would tug on the chain at intervals, without success.

It was taking a long time. Too long.

Taro's eyebrows drew together in a frown, and I could tell he was clenching his teeth. Again, I wondered if the attention of all the spectators was slowing him down. I wanted to send them all away.

I closed my eyes. Maybe one less gaze would make things easier for him.

What would be the use of such a box? To hold coins? Important papers? It seemed too big for one and too small for the other.

Maybe the events of the day would mean I would have to learn.

Taro made a sound low in his throat and I opened my eyes to see him put the box down, rising to his feet.

"Ha!" said Cars, obviously thinking Taro had given up, and I wanted to slap him.

Taro didn't even look at him. He walked away from the mouth of the cave. For a breathless moment, I feared Cars was right.

Before I could say anything, before anyone could move to follow him, Taro picked up a huge rock, almost stumbling as he took his first steps with it in his hands.

"Hey, now!" said Cars.

Cekina held up a hand. "It is not a violation of the rules."

Taro dropped the stone and crushed the box.

"Hardly requiring the highest of intellect," Cars complained.

Dias grinned. "Got the job done, though, didn't it?"

Taro pushed the rock to the side. Among the shards of the box was a white handkerchief. Taro unfolded the cloth, revealing a tiny stone sundial, small enough to fit in the palm of his hand.

We followed Taro away from the cave. From the direction he was walking, I figured that meant we had to go back to the manor. This was getting ludicrous. Maybe part of the test was physical endurance.

So we all traipsed our way back through the ridge, back across the gardens, and around to the front of the manor and the sundial. There was no sight of Marcus. I found that unnerving.

Here was the thing. Flown Raven had fewer sunny days than any other place I'd ever been. What use was a sundial?

Taro examined the top of the small dial, running his finger-tips over the surface. He slid his palm across the face of the real dial. He frowned. He looked up at the gray sky. He held his hand over the large sundial, shifting it from place to place. Trying to create a shadow?

Apparently, that accomplished nothing for him. He stood back and inspected the little dial again, turning it over in his hands. Then he knelt and looked under the plane of the large dial, making a sound of triumph as he pulled out a small white bundle.

He set the bundle on the ground and unwrapped it, reveal-ing six flat pieces of wood, each the size of my palm. He spread the squares out on the cloth, and then he scrutinized each one, front and back and all of the edges. He picked up two squares and seemed to be trying to hook them together. That didn't work.

There were lines on the surfaces of the squares. I was too far away to figure out what they depicted, if anything. When I took a step closer to look, Cars growled at me.

Taro sat on his heels. He examined all the squares. He flipped them all over. There were lines on those sides, too. At times, he tried to fit two squares together, but that never worked.

It was taking too long.

Where was Marcus?

He laid them on the cloth, one right after the other. He ex-changed two, then two more. Then he shifted them all.

Come on come on come on.

He changed two more pieces. Then he picked up the first two and shifted the edges against each other. Something clicked.

Oh, thank Zaire.

Taro picked up the next square. It clicked against the sec-ond square in his hand. Then he picked up the forth, but that clearly didn't connect.

Damn.

He tried all the remaining sides of the remaining squares. None of them fit together. He put them all back down and pushed his hands through his hair.

Don't give up now.

He stared down at the squares, rubbing his chin.

It took all of my discipline to refrain from moving closer. Not to help Taro. There really was no reason to believe I could do any better. I just wanted to see.

Taro placed the fourth square immediately under the first. They snapped together. Taro quickly fit the fifth square under the second, and the sixth under the third, creating a larger, perfect square. He flipped the whole thing over. He looked at it for a few moments, then rose to his feet and headed back to the manor.

I had to see. I looked at the square. It was an overhead view of pairs of dancers. I flipped the square over. The first smaller square had a figure writing at a desk. The second, the same figure speaking to someone holding a musical instrument. The third, the same figure standing over what looked like a table of food. The fourth, the figure was being dressed in a gown. The fifth, her hair was being styled. The final square was a picture of a receiving line.

A sequence of events Taro would have to work out before getting the final scene. A ball. The ballroom.

I ran to catch up with the others through the nearest door, and Taro took us to the ballroom.

And damn it, Marcus was already there. He was kneeling before a black box of wood and iron. There were smaller pieces of wood scattered over the surface of the box, and he was trying to fit them together in some way. Whatever he was making, he was at least partially successful.

There was another similar box on the other side of the room. That was clearly meant for Taro. I could think of no other reason to have both combatants in the same room unless this was the last stop.

Besides, Fiona was there, too.

Marcus was clearly in the lead.

He looked up as we entered. I tried not to glare at him. I tried not to be angry at him. None of this was his fault.

His gaze settled on me. I couldn't interpret his expression. He stared at me for a few moments, and then he looked down at his hands.

Taro ran to the other box, sliding the last little distance on his knees. He scooped the little pieces of wood together and, to my surprise, he quickly and ably started fitting the fragments together without appearing to have to think about it.

I looked at Marcus. He was moving much more slowly, having to look at each piece and turn it over in his hands before finding where it would fit.

"Hurry!" Cars called to him.

"Quiet!" Fiona snapped.

From the base of what Taro was building, it was clear it was meant to be a three dimensional triangle.

"Marcus!" Cars hissed.

"I will have you removed," Fiona warned him.

I found myself watching Marcus more than Taro. He was slower than Taro, but he was still ahead, and still making progress.

I could not believe how quickly Taro was working. He was having no trouble at all. It seemed to me that the longer I knew Taro, the more amazing things I discovered about him.

But when I looked at Marcus, I saw that he had completed his cube. He pressed it into an indentation on the top of his box.

A thought flittered through my mind. I wondered how Fiona had managed to get all the trinkets for the tests.

Taro pressed his triangle into the top of his box.

Marcus pushed the top of his box open.

Please please please please please please.

Marcus reached into the box and held up a necklace. He jumped to his feet and took two steps toward Fiona. Then he halted, taking a closer look at the pendant. He snarled and dropped it, racing back to the box.

It wasn't the right pendant, not the one Fiona had described.

Taro, apparently keeping an eye on Marcus as he worked, tossed his pendant aside and knocked along the sides of his box.

Marcus resumed his place by his own.

Taro ripped out some kind of black cloth that had been attached to either the bottom or the side of his box. He pulled out another pendant. He looked at it carefully before rising to his feet. And then he strode to Fiona, holding out the pendant.

Marcus was perhaps two paces behind when Fiona accepted

Taro's pendant. "Shintaro Ivor Cear Karish wins the test, and therefore the Suitor's Run."

Oh gods. I closed my eyes. Thank Zaire. Thank Taro. Good, good man.

"Marcus!" Cars hissed.

Marcus was pale. His last chance was gone.

"Do you know what you've done to us?"

Of course he knew, idiot. Just look at him.

Without a word, Marcus turned on his heel and headed to the nearest door. That didn't grant him any relief, though. His father followed him, berating him the whole time.

My mother hurried off after the Prides. I couldn't think why. I hoped it wasn't to gloat. It didn't seem like her.

I jumped at Taro and threw my arms around him, knowing I looked ridiculous but feeling too happy to care. "You brilliant, brilliant man." How dare anyone think he was anything less than intelligent?

He leaned down and pressed his forehead against mine. I closed my eyes and wallowed in a feeling of contentment I hadn't experienced since this whole mess had started. I took a long breath and let it out slowly. Thank Zaire.

All of a sudden, there was a ruckus from the front foyer, and someone shouting for Fiona. We all followed Fiona out of the room.

Fiona's largest footman was cradling Tarce in his arms. Tarce's face was bloody, especially around the nose and mouth, and one of his eyes was swelling shut. He appeared insensible, hanging limply from the footman's hold.

"What happened?" Fiona demanded.

"My lord felt Lord Kent should know Your Grace has the support of the family," said the footman. "And that his entrenchments weren't going to be allowed to continue." He choked briefly, then cleared his throat. "I'm sorry, my lady. They dragged us away. There was nothing we could do. When my lord was brought back to us, he was—" He swallowed, unable to finish.

Kent was insane. There was no other explanation. How could he think he could have the brother of the titleholder beaten and get away with it?

And oh my gods, this was my fault. I had taunted Tarce about his lack of assistance to Fiona, so he had gone to challenge Kent. I felt sick.

Fiona was flushed with fury. "Get the healer," she ordered. "This is ending today."

Chapter Twenty-four

"Daniel," Fiona snapped out to a nearby footman. "Take a horse and talk to every land tenant you can find. Find Youko and Evan and send them out, too. Bring all the adults here. Ilya, you get all the whalers and fishers."

"What do we tell them?"

"Nothing. Just get them here."

That seemed a little risky. And kind of arrogant.

"Tell them to bring shovels, mallets, anything they can swing and jab. Anyone who's got a horse has to bring it. Go."

She charged toward her office. I followed her. We picked up my family along the way. Marcus and Cars came, too, looking a little more composed. None of us really had a right to be there, but Fiona didn't seem to mind. From one of the shelves in the wall she pulled out a large rolled map, which she flattened on her desk. "This is my best map of the area," she said. "This is the boundary between Westsea and Kent. I'm going to have everyone gather there."

"To do what?" my mother asked.

Fiona glanced at me before she answered. "I'm going to arrest Kent."

"You can do that?" Taro sounded as shocked as I felt.

"Aye."

"Then why didn't you do that before?"

"We didn't have the right kind of evidence that he was doing anything at all. But this time, he assaulted my brother. An aristocrat and the sibling of the highest titleholder in the region. I don't know what all the circumstances are yet, but it's enough for me to go after him."

"And then what?" I asked.

"He's too high a titleholder for me to make judgment on. I'll hold him here and send word to the Emperor. He should send Imperial Guards for him."

"But why do you need to assemble all of the tenants?" I asked. I could understand why she didn't want to attempt to arrest Kent on her own, he might resist, but surely she needed only a handful of others to get the job done.

"It's likely Kent's either expecting a response from me, or will learn of my approach before I can reach his house. His tenants might try to stop me."

"So you want your tenants to hold them off."

"Aye."

"You anticipate a fight."

"Only if he forces one."

I rubbed my eyes so I wouldn't have to look at anyone. This was insane. I felt like I'd been transported back a few generations. This sort of thing wasn't supposed to happen anymore.

Why hadn't anyone changed the law books? Did they not have to read them once in a while? Why would they not, when they saw a piece of legislation that clearly was no longer relevant, simply strike out the inappropriate clauses?

"This is just stupid."

Oh. I'd said that out loud.

"What do you expect me to do, Dunleavy?" Fiona demanded. "Just let all these attacks continue?"

"There has to be more reasonable methods."

"Using reason against the unreasonable is naive and dangerous. Am I supposed to wait until he kills someone?"

That was the thing. It hadn't gone that far yet. There was a huge leap from beating someone to killing them. There had to be a more moderate way to accomplish what Fiona wanted.

"My dear," I heard my mother say tentatively. "I don't know how these things work, but I fear you might start something with enormous consequences that you can't predict. This could turn into a real nightmare."

"It already is a nightmare," Fiona snapped. "Did you see Tarce? I don't need to be a healer to know his survival is not certain. I'm not going to let that go."

I hadn't realized he was that badly injured. "I . . . It's my fault," I admitted. "I was teasing him because he didn't seem to be doing anything to help you with all this." When would I learn to just shut up?

Fiona glared at me. I prepared myself to be verbally sliced. I deserved it.

"I don't know that you're one of the few people whose opinion can influence his behavior," she said testily.

"I spoke to him last night and he went to Kent this morning."

"Maybe yours was the pebble that sank the wood, but he had to have been thinking of doing something for a while."

"But you think my words might have been what tipped him over the peak."

"My brother doesn't always think things through."

Perhaps her brother wasn't the only one with that particular flaw.

"If my tenants feel I can't look after my own family, they'll feel I can't look after them, either. And they'll be right. This must be done."

I understood her reasoning. I agreed something had to be done. Just not this.

"So you're going to start some kind of battle between your tenants and his?" Taro demanded.

"I doubt it will come to that," she said. "I just want a lot of numbers so no one will want to interfere with us. It's just a precaution. There isn't going to be any kind of battle." She layered the last word with sneering sarcasm, as though Taro were ridiculous for using it. "I doubt his tenants feel any real loyalty to him."

"That's a risky assumption," my mother warned her.

"I believe I may know better than you how my tenants feel. How the people of this whole area feel."

So my mother could just mind her own business.

"And if any of Kent's tenants do try to oppose us, I've got some lots free. I'll offer land to them."

"You would take tenants loyal to another titleholder?" Mother asked incredulously.

"If they join me they won't be loyal to him, will they?"

"But how could you trust them?"

"I'll treat them far better than Kent ever did. That buys a lot of allegiance."

This was giving me a thick feeling of foreboding. Maybe Fiona knew exactly what she was doing, but it didn't feel like it. And this had the potential to go very, very badly. I wanted no part of it. I didn't care if I looked like a coward for saying no. Hell, I didn't care if I was a coward for saying no. I should say no.

And yet, I couldn't say no. Perhaps that made me a coward, too, just a different kind of coward.

"The Emperor will not let this stand," my mother told Fiona.

"The Emperor is a problem that will have to wait."

There was procrastination, and then there was deliberate blindness. This was the latter, I feared.

"Wait a moment." She pointed at Taro. "I saw what you did to Lila. With your—I don't know—you made her sink into the ground."

Ah hell. There were more and more people finding out about this, but I would have preferred that the Prides weren't among them. What would they do with that information?

"Could you do something like that with everyone in Kent?"

"Of course not," Taro answered.

Hm. I wondered if he could. If he came across them a group at a time. He had sunk a small group all at once not long ago.

"Why would you even want me to?" he asked.

"To keep them immobilized. Kent's the only one I really want."

"That's beyond my abilities."

"Damn it." Then she turned to me. "Or maybe I should be asking you? You're supposed to be the smart one."

"That is an inaccurate and stupid thing to say," I snapped.

Yes, she was under enormous stress, but there was no reason to slander Taro, who had done nothing but support her.

Taro glowered, he was angry, but he chose not to respond. She didn't apologize. Neither did I. Moving on.

"Browne and her casters have been developing some spells that might protect the estate from further attack," I said. Were we still pretending Browne wasn't a caster? Was that possible without being ridiculous?

"How about something that works as an offensive?"

"I know nothing about that." I was aware that the circle had been developing spells while I had been elsewhere. No one had told me what those spells entailed, what they did.

"All right, then," Fiona said with impatience. "You know, you all need to leave. You're all just distracting me."

"Fiona . . ." Taro began.

"Seriously, just get out. All of you."

We reluctantly trailed out of her office, but collected just outside her door. "We have to stop her," said Dias.

"How are we going to do that?" Mika demanded. "Lock her in her office?"

We all looked at the door in contemplation.

"Locks from the inside," Taro reminded us.

"Yes, but we could put her somewhere else."

"We can't restrain the titleholder," my mother murmured.

"It's for her own good," Dias suggested.

"And who are we to decide that?" Mother asked.

"And how long are we supposed to hold her?" I asked.

"Until she cools down," said Dias.

"I think confining her will only make her burn hotter," I said.

"We have to do something," Dias insisted.

"It's not our place," said Mother.

Dias looked appalled. "Not our place?"

She gave him a hard look. "Not our place. We are merchants. We know nothing about the demands and rights of titleholders and their tenants. It is one thing to try to talk her out of behavior we think she'll regret. To actively interfere with her prerogatives as a titleholder, that may set off a series of consequences we don't like, that we can't deal with. And it's entirely possible we're wrong."

"So we just wait here and drink tea," Dias complained.

"No. We go with her. We try to remind her who she is. But we don't try to stop her."

That felt to me like we were merely abdicating responsibility.

On the other hand, none of us were responsible for Fiona. It was arrogant to act as though we were.

So we waited. I felt useless. I felt like I was in the way. I wished I had some nervous habits so I could indulge in them.

A short while later, Browne came striding down the hall. She looked grim. "How's Tarce?" I asked.

She ignored me, rapping sharply on the door. "It's Nab, my lady."

"Come."

She entered, and I resisted the urge to follow after her. And then the urge to press my ear against the door.

We waited some more. It wasn't long before Browne was out again. "Please come with me, Shield Mallorough." And she was off again, not looking back.

I didn't care for being ordered about, but I followed her. "Tell me Tarce's condition."

"He'll live," she answered sharply. "But he has an injury to his knee I couldn't completely fix. He'll limp the rest of his life."

I caught myself before I could say he was lucky. He wasn't lucky. He'd been badly beaten. He would be impaired for the rest of his life. It wasn't enough that his life had been spared. He had a right to his life. It wasn't lucky that he'd been able to hold on to it. It should never have been threatened in the first place.

"So what do you need me for?"

"First, we're going to call the other casters. We're going to bring them here."

"We can't go racing all over the place to get them here."

"No, we're going to call them here."

"A new spell."

"Yes."

"I thought we needed them to be spread out over the estate."

"Aye, but I want them all to have as many of the cave crystals as possible. The more they have, the better they can barricade the estate. Which is why we're going to the cave to chip out as many crystals as we can."

"What about the crystals we already gave you?"

"They aren't enough. I'm heading to the attic. I need you to get as many tablespoons as you can. And a knife. An Ottawa blade, if you can."

"Thereby ruining the blade," I muttered, but I hoofed it to the kitchen. There were, of course, a slew of people preparing for the evening meal. Which probably no one was going to be around to eat. "Please excuse me, ladies and gentlemen, but I have to take all of your tablespoons."

"Excuse me?" the cook demanded.

Having served myself a few times, I knew where all the tablespoons were, so I headed for that drawer and gathered up two handfuls.

"With all due respect, Shield, we're going to be needing those soon."

I didn't know whether it would be wise to explain why I needed the spoons, so I didn't. "Where are your Ottawa knives?"

"We don't keep hunting knives in here, Shield."

"Actually," one of the young men said, wiping his hands on his apron and staring down at his feet.

"Orin," the cook said with disapproval.

"They're the best for dicing beef." He opened a cupboard and reached behind some large pieces of crockery. He held out the knife, handle and blade the length of my forearm, the edge of the blade falling into a sharp angle at the tip. It looked kind of evil. It looked kind of beautiful.

I took it from Orin carefully, as though the handle itself could cut me. "Thank you." I realized everyone had stopped working to stare at me. I gave them a weak smile before I got out of there.

When I reached the attic, Browne had already cleared a space in the center of the floor and rolled a dozen large aprin leaves, filled with moss soaked in red wine. The smell was unpleasant. I put the knife aside and, under Browne's orders, placed the spoons on the floor, end to end, creating a circle an arm's length in diameter.

As we worked, Browne told me the words of the cast, repeating them to give me the chance to memorize them.

Once we had enough moss rolls, we laid them in four rows within the circle, from edge to center. Browne poured salt over the four rows, and then laid four more rows just of salt. She picked up the knife and spat on the blade. "Be our focus, sharp and bright, fold the distance, so thoughts can touch. Draw from the sky, the clarity of words, help us seek, help us find, shorten the paths, our mind to theirs." She thrust the knife into the floor.

There were, from what I witnessed, many flaws with the spell devised by the circle to communicate with everyone.

For one thing, the words didn't rhyme and had no real flow.

It took two people to cast the spell.

It took too long to prepare.

And the information that could be related was basic and limited. All that could be communicated, really, was a visual of the casters' location, and the order to come.

Browne and I stood on opposite sides of the circle. Reaching across the circle, Browne placed a moss roll into my left palm, and then added salt. She put a roll into her own hand and added salt. She reached back across the circle again. Palms up, we linked the fingers of our left hands together.

"Morgan Gidean," said Browne.

"Morgan Gidean," I echoed.

"Vic Ramna."

"Vic Ramna."

"Faye Berlusconi."

"Faye Berlusconi."

"Olan Roddin."

"Olan Roddin."

And so we went through every name in the circle.

"Hear us," we said together. "Our minds to yours. Our lips to your ears. Hear us. Hear us. Our minds to yours. Our lips to your ears. Hear us." And so on.

As we spoke, I imagined the manor, concentrating on the front main entrance.

Soon, I felt a strange pressure on my mind. At first it was one thin layer of something—it felt like paper—covering my whole head. From the inside. And then, after a few moments, there were little breaks in the paper, pressing in.

It was a disagreeable experience.

That sensation, I realized, was caused by other minds contacting mine. More and more breaks in the paper. I assumed that each break represented one mind, which meant there were going to be roughly seventeen breaks in the paper. The paper protecting my brain.

Really didn't like the idea of that.

But I kept speaking in time with Browne. I was thoroughly used to the jittery sensation I felt when a spell was successfully cast, but the vibration that developed in my voice and in Browne's surprised me. The two voices vibrated in unison. That was just weird.

And then images of all the people we were calling crowded into my mind. There were no words for them in the spell to indicate that they were or were not coming, but I could feel a sense of compliance.

Browne stopped speaking and pulled her hand from mine. The images disappeared, and I was suddenly all alone in my head again. And a little dizzy.

"All right." Browne knelt down and scooped up the moss rolls and salt, dumping them into a small burlap sack. "They're all coming. Now we have to get those crystals."

We gathered up all the spoons and the knife and, having nothing in which to carry them, piled them behind a hideous settee. I'd come back for them later.

"We need big bags," Browne said. "As many as we can find. They have to be strong."

"Should be some in the cellar."

"Then let's go."

I glanced out the window, surprised to see that the sky was still light. It seemed to me that with all that had happened, it should at least be evening.

I couldn't wait for this day to be over.

Chapter Twenty-five

When Browne and I returned to the manor, struggling under the weight of potato sacks full of the cave crystals, there was a crowd of people gathered in the inner garden. Fiona was standing on a chair, trying to speak. The muttering of the tenants made it hard to hear her. That was nowhere near a surprise.

They were all holding the implements of their occupations, though. I wondered what they'd thought the reason was for being summoned. They couldn't have anticipated Fiona's intentions.

"This is necessary to stop the attacks," I was able to hear Fiona say.

"You don't even know if Kent is behind this," called out the hated voice of the Dowager Duchess. She was there to stir things up. I could expect nothing less. "You just want his estate. Westsea isn't enough. You just want more and more, and you're willing to throw the lives of these people away to get it."

"Of course, that's not—" Fiona began, but the Dowager ran right over her.

"There have never been any problems in Centerfield. You cared about your tenants there. But you have no trouble causing difficulties for the people here so you can blame Kent in a false justification to take his land."

I couldn't see the Dowager, but she certainly had a piercing voice when she wanted.

"I'm not going to try to kill people," I heard a nearby whaler say. He didn't shout it, there was no way Fiona or anyone any distance away was going to hear him, but his tone left no doubt about the sincerity of his words. "That's just stupid. I'll leave."

"And go where?" the woman beside him asked. "How many estates serve whalers? Lord Ducal gambles all the profits away. The roads are atrocious. Lady Sky is said to be mad. And then there's Centerfield."

"There has to be somewhere that the titleholder isn't expecting me to shove a harpoon through someone's stomach."

He had an excellent point.

"This is a proper mess, isn't it?" a voice said from behind us.

Browne started and then turned to glare at hulking Yonhap for sneaking up on us.

He was unmoved. "So what are you going to do about this?" he asked.

"This isn't our responsibility. We'll wait over there." She pointed. "We want the casters to meet somewhere discreet. Then we'll find somewhere to get to work. Her Ladyship doesn't want the other tenants to know about the crystals."

We moved to a corner of the manor. This incidentally enabled us to better see Fiona, Taro, a row of footmen, and the Dowager.

And Daris. What was she doing there?

"How much more can you be expected to take?" the Dowager was asking of the crowd. "No Karish has ever demanded this from you. No Karish ever would. He wouldn't have to. Kent would have never dared to threaten a Karish in this manner."

I wondered if that could be true. I could understand how it might be. People with long histories in a region were probably thought of as belonging to that region, as much a part of it as the trees, accepted as immoveable objects. A newcomer was weak and more easily blown away.

I really hated it when obnoxious people were right. It felt like it unbalanced the whole world.

I saw Younis, Thatcher, and Netan looking at the crowd curiously before joining us. "What's going on?" Thatcher asked.

"Her Ladyship has lost her mind," said Browne.

Well, that was a little blunt.

"Then why are we here?"

"I'm waiting for everyone to get here so I can tell you all at once."

"That's Olson," said Thatcher, looking over the crowd. "And Matt."

"And Cowell," Netan added.

"What the hell are they doing here?" Thatcher asked.

"The Kent casters," Browne reminded me.

That couldn't be good. "Point them out to me." They had no business here. They should be removed.

No, not removed. Restrained. We didn't need them running back to Kent and warning him. Though he might know already. The casters had to be there for a reason.

This was going to end so badly.

"This has nothing to do with you!" someone shouted.

This created a thick silence.

The Dowager flushed a hilarious shade of red, and I realized that last comment had been made by a tenant to the Dowager. That was beautiful.

"You do not address me, you filthy little cretin."

And there went all of her credibility. She was usually smarter than that.

Then Daris was laughing. If laughter could be said to be clumsy, hers was, stumbling from one pitch to another, stopping for a moment and then starting again. And she was swaying. She looked spectacularly drunk. "You're all so blind," she cackled, loudly enough to be heard by everyone. "It was so easy."

For a few moments, everyone waited for her to continue. She just grinned.

"What was easy, Daris?" Fiona asked.

Daris laughed.

And a few of my memories slid into place. Memories I wanted everyone to know about. "You poisoned the fish," I called out. "You helped start the fires and impeded those who tried to put them out." Daris didn't admit to this, but she didn't deny it, either. "What did Kent offer you?"

The laughter drained from her face. "More than my own family ever did," she said darkly.

Everyone started whispering. I didn't know whether the knowledge that Fiona was being sabotaged by her own sister would win support from her tenants or cause them to believe the whole family was a liability and should just be tossed.

Out of nowhere, a dark cloud developed around two men, little darts of blue light spearing throughout. I wouldn't have noticed it so quickly if I hadn't been looking in that direction. What was that?

And those two tenants starting screaming, in fear, and in pain. Those around them drew back quickly, staring in shock as the men scrubbed their arms, torsos and legs, as though trying to scrape something off.

The Kent casters were whispering. No one around them seemed to notice. Or maybe they just didn't realize that what they were hearings were casts.

"Browne!" I said, hoping she had an effective reaction to this.

"I have no idea," she responded.

If she had no cast to deal with this, and couldn't create one on the fly, I had no chance of using a spell myself. I had to think of another way.

The two tenants collapsed, still screaming, and another cloud developed on the other side of the crowd.

More and more clouds began to develop, enough that I could tell when one would appear by a slight warping of the air. I couldn't hear anything but the horrific screams.

The first two tenants were bleeding from the eyes and ears. It was sickening.

I noticed Taro stepping back sharply, pulling Fiona off the chair and back with him. So when the next cloud appeared, it surrounded only the Dowager. Her screams seemed to be filled with outrage rather than fear.

Taro's eyes were wide with shock.

Marcus and Cars came out of the manor, no doubt drawn by the screams.

So the thing to do was take the Kent casters down physically.

They were all bigger than I, but that didn't matter. Surprise was a fabulous tool.

I got a whole two steps before Thatcher caught my arm and jerked me to a stop. "Where do you think you're going?"

I really disliked it when people who had no right to do so thought to put hands on me. "To break their concentration." And maybe their noses.

"Fine idea," said Browne. "Cheon, you take Olson. Biden, Matt. Spencer, Cowell. Just bear them to the ground and cover their mouths."

The three casters ran into the crowd. None of them seemed to hesitate, seemed to realize or care that they might be bringing themselves to the attention of the Kent casters and risking being caught by one of the dark clouds.

Released, I tried to follow. This time, it was Browne who caught my arm. "Stay still."

"I can't just do nothing."

"I'm not telling you to do nothing. I'm telling you not to be stupid."

I fumed for a moment. I couldn't do anything with a cast, and I'd been prevented from doing anything physical. What was I supposed to do? Just stand there?

"Can you see any of the other casters?" I asked her. "The ones who put us to sleep?"

"No, but they might not be the only ones he recruited. There's no telling how many he's got."

So, possibly, there were other casters loyal to Kent, in this crowd, or hidden from view on Fiona's land, or waiting on Kent's land for some countermeasure from Fiona. And wasn't this a catastrophe?

How had these casters come up with a spell like this, anyway? How had they known they would be effective? The vision of how they would have developed such spells, how they would have tested them, made my throat clog.

I watched Biden launch himself at the slim young man who'd been identified as Matt. They landed hard. That had to hurt.

I saw Taro yank Marcus back this time, and another black cloud appeared, capturing nothing but air.

Thatcher snuck up behind Olson and caught him by the

throat, yanking him right off his feet and slamming him into the ground. Then he covered his mouth with his hand.

And was bitten for his trouble. He quickly pulled his hand away.

Not all of the tenants had run away. A whaler was standing firm, watching Thatcher and Olson. When Thatcher removed his hand, the whaler, expression resolute, thrust her harpoon right through Olson's eye.

I put my hand over my mouth and averted my gaze as I gagged. I could have been happy spending my whole life without seeing anything like that.

And then I realized that the harpoon had not actually pierced any part of the caster's person. The whaler had just thrust it into the ground beside the caster's face. Thank god.

So far, everyone who'd been hit with a cloud had either died or was clearly close to it. There had to be a way to make the deaths quicker.

Or how about stopping their deaths altogether?

The Dowager had collapsed and was trembling on the ground as though suffering a seizure. Taro jumped to her side, kneeling, reaching out.

Marcus pulled him away. I couldn't hear what either of them said, but they were clearly shouting, Taro struggling to reach his mother, Marcus holding him back. Marcus was taller and larger than Taro. The trader won.

The air before me warped and seemed to whine. I watched Browne remove a crystal from her sack, hold it out, and hum.

The black cloud and the gleam from the crystal didn't react well to each other. They kind of exploded in my face. I felt no pain but I was blinded for a few moments.

When I could see, all the clouds were gone. The three Kent casters were on the ground. So were a dozen tenants, either twitching or, I assumed, dead. Browne knelt by the nearest, feeling the person's wrist and leaning far over to put her face next to his. After a moment, she stood and moved on to the next victim.

Taro, finally released by Marcus, was crouching on the ground beside the Dowager, who had finally died. He wasn't touching her, but he was holding his hand over her face. Not close enough to feel her breath, if she were breathing, or to do anything useful. I wasn't sure what he was doing. I couldn't read anything from his face.

She had been the last of his immediate family.

Fiona was going to need to hold another mass funeral. Too many in too short a time. Her run as titleholder had been plagued with disasters. I didn't blame anyone for feeling the way they did. This was a mess.

Fiona rubbed her face. For a moment, she appeared beaten and weary. Then she firmed her jaw and squared her shoulders, looking around at who remained.

"Farmer Cox," she called out, and this was the first of a string of names she listed. "Please carry the fallen to the ballroom. Find some people to help you. Cekina." She looked at her housekeeper. "Make sure family members can see the victims. Bailey, arrange for the Kent casters to be taken to the court room. I'll trust your judgment concerning their restraints. Dune, take Lady Daris and lock her"—she had to think about that for a moment—"in the small tack room. Lerana," she said to the whaler. "Take your harpoon to the court room."

Fiona remained while the others leapt to do as she ordered. She stood there while many of the tenants who had run away crept back. I guessed they hadn't gone far.

Fiona crossed her arms. "Well?" she challenged them all.

None of the tenants seemed to know what to say. They glanced at each other and grumbled nearly inaudibly. But they tightened their grip on their tools and they didn't leave.

"Source Karish, Shield Mallorough, Healer Browne, I would appreciate it if you would all come with me." She strode into the manor.

I went to Taro, who was still kneeling beside the Dowager. I pushed back some of his hair from his temple. "Do you want help carrying her in?"

"No," he said, his voice flat. "I don't . . ." He seemed unable to continue.

"I'll take her in," Marcus offered.

Taro seemed to think about it for a few moments before nodding.

I patted his shoulder. "I'm going to go see what Fiona wants."

"No, I'm coming." He rose to his feet. "Fiona needs us for something. I don't think she would ask me if it weren't important."

"I don't think Fiona is in a position to consider the feelings of anyone else right now."

"I have no reason to spend more time with the Dowager dead than I would alive. It's just her body."

I didn't for a moment believe that was what he really felt, but it would be heartless to press him.

I exchanged a look with Marcus before he knelt down to pick up the Dowager's body. He was gentle with her.

He was a good man.

Taro took my hand and wrapped it around the crook of his arm. I let him lead me back into the manor and through to the court room.

The three casters had been tied onto dining room chairs, backed against each other in a tight triangle. The whaler stood in front of one of them, staring at him as she leaned against her harpoon.

That caster seemed to find her intimidating. I didn't blame him.

It wasn't long before Fiona entered the room, heading straight for the Kent casters. She circled them for a few moments, just looking at them. The caster facing me watched her stoically. "Have you ever read the Titleholder List of Authorities?" she asked them. None of them responded. "They say I'm allowed to kill anyone who threatens the lives of my people."

Ah, another piece of legislation that had outlasted its usefulness. In High Scape, people broke into the homes of the titled all the time, often armed, and when caught it was expected that they would be turned over to the Runners, not killed.

Sometimes it felt like Flown Raven and the surrounding estates hadn't moved through time with the rest of the world.

But, then again, these people weren't just trespassers. They had actually killed people. So that made things a little less clear to me. I was just so uncomfortable with the idea of Fiona killing people, intentionally, with a clear head.

"I'm sure you know," Fiona continued, "that execution is the usual punishment for murder. But I am the magistrate in these parts. I can sentence you any way I wish. I could put you in the deepest hole I can have dug out. A hole too deep to climb out of. A hole too narrow to lie down in. Or even sit in. You would only be able to stand, no matter how exhausted you got. And I would never let you out. I would have food dropped in on you every other day or so and you would stand there and soil yourself and eventually go mad."

The caster facing me looked terrified.

"Lord Kent will not allow you to do anything of the sort," one of the others announced. His voice shook a little.

And there it was. Further proof that Kent was behind all of Fiona's troubles.

Fiona chuckled. "You cannot be under the delusion that Kent cares about any of you. You know as well as I that no one matters to him unless they are of use to him. You've failed. You're nothing to him."

"We didn't fail. We killed some of your people and terrified the rest. No one will support you now."

Fiona squinted at him as though puzzled. "You really don't know him, do you?" she asked. "He's not quite balanced. The things he's done in just the last couple of weeks, they prove he's lost all understanding of what he's permitted to do by law, all understanding of the logical consequences of his actions. He attacked the same tenants he was hoping to take responsibility for. He burnt down their homes and spoiled their produce. He beat a lord almost to death. Do you really think he cares about you? You're just tools to him. He sent you here to attack my people right in front of me. And you were caught. Of course you were caught. And he knew you would be caught. He threw you away while he kept his more important casters back on his land." She leaned close to the stoic one, her face a finger width away. "Because he does have other casters, doesn't he? Casters I've never seen before." She backed up a bit and resumed circling. "He tossed you at me, so I could do anything I wanted to you. The question is, what do I do with you?"

"Throw us in a hole if you want. We'll get out of it. You can't imagine what we can do."

"Why aren't you getting yourself out of this situation, then, if you're so all-powerful?"

An excellent question.

And telling, I thought, that none of the casters would answer. "You're going to kill us. Get on with it."

"Do you know what a Pair can do?" she asked.

What? Where had that come from? What did we have to do with anything?

"More than the Triple S would tell you. More than Pairs will tell you. But I've seen things. And, oh, the things they could do to a body, should they feel like it."

Hell. Shut up, woman. Was that why she had asked us to come?

I couldn't tell whether they actually believed Fiona or not. I didn't care. I was furious. We didn't need people adding to the ridiculous rumors about us that were already out there.

I tried to keep my expression bland. Whatever Fiona was doing, right then and there wasn't the time to correct her, to suggest in any way that I didn't support what she was doing.

"But you know," Fiona said. "There are some things you just have to do yourself. And, of course, I don't need to kill you, right now. I just need to make you wish you were dead. Until you tell me what I want to know. And if you tell me quickly enough, I'll have Healer Browne take care of you. She's quite good. So, Whaler Fenn, if I could have your harpoon."

The whaler handed it to Fiona.

Fiona turned the harpoon in her hands, end over end. It was a fairly long and heavy instrument. She clearly wasn't comfortable with it. Her husband would have been. He had gone whaling, occasionally.

"This is used on whales," Fiona said. "But I wonder what it could do to a person. What if I shoved it through your eye?" Fiona had clearly been inspired by the whaler. "Think that would hurt?"

One of the casters gasped. He was the one Fiona chose to stand before. She placed the tip of the harpoon against the top of his cheek, right under his left eye. "Wouldn't take much of a slip, would it?"

She couldn't really shove a harpoon through a person's eyes. Please, show me she couldn't.

"I wonder if you could cast so well, missing one of your eyes."

The caster swallowed loudly, but kept his mouth shut.

"How many casters does Kent have?"

None of the casters said anything.

Fiona shifted the harpoon just a little, bringing the tip infinitesimally closer to the caster's eye. "How many?"

We waited. I looked at Fiona. I couldn't believe she would actually do it. That would be torture. Torture was disgusting.

I wasn't going to stand there and let her do that to him, to any of them. My interference would infuriate Fiona. It might endanger everyone. I didn't care. This was not going to happen in front of me.

Had Lila felt pain when Taro sank her into the ground? I'd never thought about that possibility before. Taro had done that to a lot of people. Had that been torture?

I felt nauseous.

"Tell me what I want to know," Fiona ordered.

We waited. I slid a footstep closer. The idea that I could actually stop Fiona should she decide to carry out her threat was unrealistic, but I couldn't just stand there and watch, as though I approved.

The caster was flushed. He was breathing too quickly. I could see him swallowing again and again. But he didn't speak.

I wondered why. Was he afraid of Kent, or was some part of him sure Fiona couldn't go through with her threat?

After another long, silent moment, Fiona swore and stepped back. I let out a long breath. She couldn't do it.

She went to the next caster and held the harpoon to his face. "What else is Kent planning?"

But everyone knew she couldn't actually torture them. She had given herself away. She knew it, too, and it wasn't long before she gave the harpoon back to the whaler with an expression of resignation. "Have them stripped down," she ordered. "Then tie them back onto the chairs, the chairs a body's length apart. And gag them. A handkerchief stuffed in the mouth, another tied around it. I'll decide what to do with them later."

Thank Zaire. I didn't know what I would have done if Fiona had actually gone through with it. Just thinking about it made my chest burn.

"It'll have to be something else," Fiona growled, and she left the room.

Chapter Twenty-six

Not knowing what else to do, I followed Browne back out of the manor to the inner garden, still lugging a sack of crystals about. There were many members of the circle waiting, but not all of them. That was annoying. How long were we supposed to wait?

"Where are Morgan and Vic?" Browne demanded. "And Eun?"

"They're refusing to come," Tye reported sullenly.

Browne scowled. "Does no one honor their oaths anymore?"

"Be reasonable, Nab. No one anticipated anything like this."

"That's irrelevant. No one can anticipate everything when they take an oath. They know at the time that they're taking that risk."

"What's the plan?" I asked in a voice flattened to hide my impatience. We didn't have time for recriminations.

"We're each going to take a handful of crystals. We're all going to return to our homes, planting the crystals along the way. I trust you all brought glass and yarn." Almost everyone nodded. Hefez wrinkled his nose. He had clearly forgotten. "Get each crystal ringing before you leave it. Keep your last crystal for your home. Hopefully, by the time everyone's done, almost all of Her Grace's land will be protected."

"But that will keep everyone inside," I pointed out.

"That's why we'll have to wait until we think everyone who is going with Her Ladyship is beyond the border before we start planting the crystals."

And hope no one needed to be sent back.

"I think you should stick to the perimeter of the manor," Browne said to me. "Don't bother with the attic."

"I'm not staying here," I objected. "I'm going with Her Ladyship."

"You're needed to guard the manor."

"My Source is going with the Duchess." I had no doubt of that. "I go where my Source goes."

She scowled at me, but she made no further protest. "Fine. Penelope, the manor is yours. Here." She opened her sack. "Take as much as you can carry. You as well, Shield. We might need them."

I put a small handful in my purse. I didn't want the purse to be too full. I needed to be able to grab things quickly.

Fiona stormed out of the manor, addressing the tenants, who were pale and nervous as they fiddled with their implements. "You, you, you, you, you and you. We have mounts for you. You and everyone who has brought a horse, we will be riding to Kent manor."

Three servants were handing to the people who would ride head spades, fishing gaffs, and mallets. I didn't like contemplating what I was supposed to do with the fishing gaff I'd been given. The hook at the end of it looked vicious.

"The rest of you," said Fiona, "follow as quickly as you can. I don't want you to fight anyone if it can be avoided. I am hoping your mere presence will be intimidating. You outnumber Kent's tenants. Do only what is necessary to get by them. I don't want you to endanger yourselves needlessly, or injure anyone if it can be avoided. I just want you to get to the manor. Are there any questions?"

"What are we supposed to do when we get there?" a man called out.

"Just watch."

Witnesses, perhaps?

To prevent Kent's tenants from interfering?

To brag about how many loyal tenants she had?

Horses were being brought out. Fiona mounted one immediately.

"Give us a candle mark before you start," Browne told the other casters. I followed her to the horses. Taro had emerged from the manor and climbed onto a horse. I scrambled up after him.

I wasn't sure whether any of the things we could do would be useful. That was unpredictable. I only knew that there was no way I was going to wait at the manor where I would have no means of knowing what was going on. Clearly, Taro felt the same.

It didn't surprise me at all that my brothers came out to join us. They seemed the sort. What astonished me was Marcus's appearance.

"This has nothing to do with you," Fiona told him.

"This is completely insane," he said. "I didn't know this sort of thing still happened."

Fiona didn't dispute that. "Then one would think you'd refrain from participating."

"I can't just cower in a corner, or slither away, when people I know are doing something this mad."

He glanced at Taro, then glanced quickly away. I wondered if pride was a factor here. Taro was doing it, so Marcus must.

Fiona shrugged. "If you wish. It'll be dangerous."

"I understand."

"Up behind me, Trader Pride," Browne offered.

"Thank you, but I came here with my own horse." He jogged over to the stable.

My mother was standing near the door, looking annoyed, her arms crossed. Cars stood beside her, looking equally unimpressed.

After every horse had acquired a rider, Fiona kicked hers into movement and the rest of us followed.

My arms tightened around Taro's waist, my cheek resting between his shoulder blades. Did Kent know we were coming? If Browne and her group could communicate over a distance, so might the Kent casters. Perhaps they'd come up with a better way. There might be a legion of more violently inclined casters waiting for us on Kent's property. We should have brought more of the circle with us.

The Triple S had never trained us to do anything like this.

They would have been horrified to know what we were doing. I wondered if I could get away with not reporting this. When the inevitable rumors reached their ears, I could claim ignorance. Or, at least, lack of participation. Of course, Source Karish and I hadn't been involved in some anachronistic battle between two insane titleholders. What could that possibly have to do with us?

If we didn't end up dead. I closed my eyes briefly. This was so, so stupid.

There was no one waiting for us at the border between Fiona's land and Kent's. As we rode farther into Kent territory, in daylight, it was unnerving to see that there were no tenants working. They had gathered somewhere. They were waiting for us, in some unexpected place.

At this point, I realized none of us had thought to ask what we were going to do once we reached the manor. And Fiona hadn't thought to tell us. Unless we, too, were just supposed to stand around as witnesses.

None of us knew what the hell we were doing.

And then I saw what might have been the first line of Kent's defense. A wide, deep ditch had been cut into the soil. Looking either way didn't bring the end of the ditch into sight. It would have taken ages to create. There had to be an easy way to cross, or the tenants would have been barred from the manor, but I couldn't see any kind of bridge.

This had not been there when Taro, my brothers and I had sneaked over. Had it been dug by hand or created by a cast?

"I could jump this," said Taro.

"Not with me on the horse, you won't," I objected. "And don't even contemplate leaving me behind."

"I doubt any of the rest of us could manage it," Fiona admitted.

A squeeze to my forearm was all the warning Taro gave me before lowering his shields. I swallowed back an oath before erecting mine.

Still, Taro was getting ever more willing to create events. I found that disturbing.

The horses went crazy, bucking and jerking at their bits. Three tenants lost their seat and the horses ran off. Fiona swore as she ruthlessly pulled on her reins, drawing her mount's head too far in to allow it to move much.

The ground shook only slightly, but soil dropped down from the sides of the ditch. Taro didn't push the sides of the ditch together, which I would have expected. He just let the dirt fall in, the result being a low, flattened area that looked much easier to traverse.

Fiona looked at Taro, one eyebrow raised.

"Earthquake," he said.

"Very convenient."

"No, not really."

Fiona didn't look convinced, but she chose not to question it further. She spent a few moments looking at the indentation and prodded the horse to step into it. The horse's hooves sunk a little into the dirt, but not enough to either hamper or spook it. She crossed to the other side easily. Those of us who had been able to hold on to our mounts followed, the others left behind to chase after their horses.

The next barrier was the jagged outcrop of rock that surrounded the manor. The gap was filled with, I would guess, farmers. Kent had had the same idea as Fiona. Tenants were standing ready to fight with nothing more than hoes and pitchforks. It was disgusting.

Fiona charged ahead. The gap was small; I wasn't sure one could actually ride through it safely at anything faster than a trot. But either Fiona hadn't realized that, or she didn't care. Four of the tenants ran away. I didn't blame them at all. It was what I would do in the same circumstances.

Fiona swung her head spade. She hit the first man she came to right in the face and I saw blood spurt from his nose. I couldn't help wincing, couldn't help imagining what that would feel like.

More farmers ran away.

Then Taro and I were upon them, followed by most of the others. I refused to swing my gaff at anyone. Taro, I was pleased to see, didn't use his, either. This didn't seem to be a liability for our side. The rest of Kent's tenants ran away.

Thank gods. They weren't complete idiots.

And so we cleared the second barrier.

It wasn't long before I could see the manor. There didn't appear to be anyone outside it.

Wouldn't this have been a better place to dig that ditch? It would have been much easier; they could have surrounded the whole manor.

Maybe he'd thought the ditch unsightly, which it was, and he hadn't wanted to have to look at it.

Maybe he didn't know what he was doing, either. I had no reason to believe he had any experience in this sort of behavior. Maybe he was just making things up as he went along.

So that would be all of us, then.

Fiona's horse squealed. Its head was pushed to the side by something invisible, a painful looking angle. This didn't stop its forward motion. The poor animal seemed to bend in on itself, pushing Fiona forward. And then Fiona slammed against something invisible, too, sliding to the ground.

Fortunately, sort of, we had been letting Fiona ride ahead—she was the titleholder—so the rest of us had some warning. Not a whole lot. Two tenants ran into the barrier before everyone managed to stop.

Browne was off her horse the instant she could stop it. She ran the few steps to Fiona and knelt beside her.

"I'm all right," Fiona said.

There was blood gushing from her nose.

Browne touched Fiona's nose.

Fiona slapped her hand away.

"It doesn't look broken."

"Of course, it's not broken. Go check on the others."

I dismounted and, hand out, walked slowly to where the invisible barrier seemed to be. At first, I felt nothing more than a faint brushing against my fingertips, but as I pushed in, the barrier solidified into something hard. When I knocked on it, there was actual sound.

A disturbing thing, to feel and hear from something I couldn't see. Even worse, I could place my hand against the barrier, and lean on it, and it supported my weight. That was just bizarre.

Most alarming of all, Kent's casters had come up with their own kind of barrier. One that seemed to be more effective than ours.

One of the tenants who had run into the barrier had knocked

himself unconscious. The other appeared unharmed. The horses were another matter. Fiona's was slumped on the ground. Another was kind of meandering around nonsensically.

I had heard nothing to indicate Browne knew the first thing about healing animals.

Kent sauntered out of the manor, and he didn't have to take many steps before his smirk became obvious.

Fiona carefully moved forward until she could touch the barrier.

Kent strolled over to her, halting when there was only a body's length between them. He crossed his arms. "You've come uninvited on my land," he said. "You may leave now."

"After all you've done? Try again."

"I don't know what you mean."

She didn't respond to that. I approved.

"I do know you are completely unable to care for your people, Westsea. When I go back to the Emperor with news of how you've let thieves and bandits overrun your lands, he will make the appropriate order. Why, I've heard that your own brother was badly beaten right under your nose. Tell me, is he dead, yet?"

Bastard.

"We know you're behind all of our difficulties, Kent," Fiona told him. "Your people have admitted it."

He shrugged, apparently unconcerned. "I have no control over what others say. You may not have noticed this, but most people aren't very smart."

So he was just going to deny everything. Interesting choice.

Taro dismounted and walked up to Fiona. "What will stop you?" he asked Kent.

"This is none of your business, Source."

"This involves my family's land."

"You have no family. You had all bonds severed by the Empress."

Taro couldn't refute that. "All right, then. I love the color of Fiona's eyes. The sky calls to me. That's all I need. I'm flighty. Ask anyone."

Kent frowned at him in confusion. That was possibly the first genuine expression I'd seen on him.

"You attacked my people," Fiona accused him in a low voice. "You have killed them."

"I did nothing of the sort."

"Your casters came on my land and used spells against my tenants."

He widened his eyes in an insincere mockery of shock. "Tell me you don't believe in such fancies. Tell me you're not so foolish."

"We know they belonged to you."

"If any of my tenants have been claiming to dabble in casting, I will of course expect you to bring the law to bear on them."

So he really was prepared to throw them away. I would have wagered they hadn't known that. Were any of them within earshot? Were they listening to this?

"And what about this?" Fiona pressed against the barrier.

"I see nothing."

He was interesting, in an aggravating sort of way. Deny deny deny. There was a sort of power in refusing to concede to any point. There was really no reasoning with a person like that. You could only keep talking, with him calmly refusing to admit to the value of your words, until you hit him or walked away. And with the barrier, Fiona couldn't hit him.

"No matter how the Emperor feels about me, he's not going to give you control over the very people you have been terrorizing."

He just smiled. "You've left your people all alone. How irresponsible, at a time like this."

Had he sent his tenants to attack Flown Raven? Would they be stopped by Fiona's people? Were farmers now stabbing each other with pitchforks?

I could see it happening in my head. People with no real idea of the significance of what they were doing, shoving the tines into vulnerable flesh, killing their neighbors, dying at the hands of those with whom they'd had no argument less than a month before.

And because of what Fiona had threatened the casters with, I couldn't avoid envisioning one of those steel prongs piercing someone's eye.

Shields weren't supposed to have that kind of imagination.

"You will cease this harassment," Taro declared to Kent.

"What can you mean?" Kent asked in all innocence.

"You will not attack any more people."

"I haven't attacked anyone."

"What do you think would happen," Taro asked Fiona in a light tone, "if I eliminated his house?"

Fiona seemed confused. "He'd repair it."

"I didn't say damage. I said eliminate."

"Are you going to try a cast?" Kent asked with a smile and obvious confidence.

So casts couldn't get through the barrier.

Taro grinned. "I'm no caster. Casting isn't the only way to get things done. How do you like your garden?"

Kent appeared puzzled.

"Get your people out of the house."

I knew what he planned. I wasn't even surprised. More like resigned.

Kent crossed his arms and tilted his chin in a gesture of defiance. He looked like an adolescent.

"Ready, Lee?"

"Really bad idea, Taro." I just had to say it.

"Oh, no, it shouldn't be difficult at all."

That wasn't what I meant and he knew it. He was going to do it anyway. Damn him. His shields went down, so of course mine went up.

Kent didn't even deign to watch. He stood there, arms crossed, looking at Taro, amused. Well, at least there would be some entertainment in watching his alarm and astonishment.

Gasps all around as the whole manor sank into the ground by an arm's length, stone cracking, the steps crumbling, the lowest windows shattering. I heard some shocked shouts from within. Kent's eyes widened before he wheeled around to look at his home.

Heh.

"Get your people out, Kent," Taro ordered.

Kent said nothing. He ran toward the manor, freezing as Taro let the building sink another arm's length.

"Get your people out."

Kent whirled around. "You won't continue as long as there are people in there."

Oh, that was just a whole other level of despicable. How was it that no one had killed this man in his sleep?

Taro did not let Kent's behavior stop him. He had the building sink farther.

The dilemma was sorted for us as a cluster of people came out of the building.

"Damn you, get back in there!" Kent ordered.

He was loathsome.

Taro didn't hesitate again. The manor continued to sink. The stone continued to crack. In moments, all of the windows had popped out of their casements. I could hear wooden beams twisting and collapsing. There were cries still coming from within. Two of the servants ran back into the house. I was pretty sure it wasn't to sacrifice themselves. They exited a few moments later, each assisting an elderly person. They were followed by a handful of others.

Please let everyone get out.

"Stop this!" Kent shouted at Taro. "I order you to stop this immediately!"

"Stop what?" Taro asked disingenuously. "Say there, what's happening to your house?"

"You're doing this!"

"This is a startling, discrete event the likes of which no Source can possibly create. It's simply a freak accident."

"You're lying!"

What an incredible accusation for him to make.

"I gave you an order!"

"I'm sorry," said Taro. "Are you a member of the Triple S council?"

Kent threw himself at Taro, and bounced back off his own barrier. That was kind of hilarious.

The roof disintegrated into shards of tile. Fragments of glass glittered in the grass. Two more servants jumped out, this time from windows.

"Do something!" Kent roared at them.

One knelt, pouring a scrambled mess of items on the ground. He picked a small bag up and dumped something in his hand. He scattered small white pieces I couldn't identify in the grass. His lips moved. Nothing happened.

The next servants to escape the building had to do so through third-story windows. Fortunately, the third floor was much closer to the ground than it had been originally.

"Everything is in there!" Kent screamed. "My coffers! My accounts! My seal!"

I didn't care.

The manor was collapsing in on itself, the ground inflicting unnatural force on the walls. The noise was incredible. Soil was being pushed up into small hills, and all around the manor the ground was buckling. At this point, no one was doing anything other than watching a phenomenon that would no doubt be burned into their brains for the rest of their lives.

It was astonishing how quickly an entire building could be made to disappear. It wasn't long at all before there was nothing left but a significant stretch of turned soil. The heavy silence pressed down on my shoulders.

Taro raised his shields. I lowered mine.

Movement in my peripheral view had me looking about. All of Fiona's tenants had caught up with us. They were all staring with their mouths dropped open. Just . . . damn.

"There is no way we're going to be able to hide this as anything other than you doing something unnatural," I said to Taro.

"Aye."

"This is going to come back and kick us in the teeth. Hard." There were already so many rumors about Taro doing unnatural things. Healing. Hints that he could cause events. And now this, in front of a huge audience. This was going to tip suspicion into full-fledged belief.

"It is indeed."

I sighed. Hell.

Chapter Twenty-seven

With a roar, Kent leapt at Taro. This time, he was not impeded by any barrier. It made me wonder if the spell had somehow been attached to the manor, and with the manor gone, so was the barrier. Interesting.

Fiona raised her head spade so the blunt end of it was pushed, by Kent's momentum, into the Earl's chest. He howled and drew back.

I couldn't understand why she didn't use the blade instead. That might have ended things right then.

But maybe she didn't have it in her to actually kill him. As far as I knew, Fiona had never killed anyone before. That would be a difficult step to take.

"This is my game," she said to him. She twirled her spade. She was more comfortable with it than she had been with the harpoon she'd handled in the court room.

"You would attack me while I'm unarmed?" he demanded with ridiculous affront.

She laughed. "Are you serious?"

After everything he had done, he had the nerve to cry foul? Smack him in the head with that thing, Fiona.

"Give your spade to him, Trader Pride, if you please."

"I'm quite sure everyone who matters would be prepared to swear he already had one, my lady," Marcus responded.

"I am better than this man in all things," said Fiona. "Including honor."

Rather than hand it to him, Marcus threw it at him. Kent jumped back to avoid being hit by it, then had to bend down to pick it up. As soon as he had it in his hands, Fiona swung at his head. He barely managed to block it.

"Do your damned job!" he shouted.

Who was he talking to?

But then a caster jerked into action, and spilled more ingredients onto the ground. Two others joined him.

"For Zaire's sakes!" Browne muttered with disgust. "Jump on them!"

I saw Taro stiffen in his readiness to obey. I caught his arm and pulled hard. "You shouldn't be distracted." He may have to shift soil again. "There are others who can do this."

Marcus and my brothers were the first to charge at the casters. One of the casters blew from his palm what looked like a shower of flour. Marcus's horse stumbled and kind of shrieked and curled in on itself. My brothers stopped dead.

"Why did we come here if we're just going to stand here and watch?" Taro hissed at me.

He had a point, but we'd already done something valuable. We'd pretty much destroyed Kent when we destroyed his manor. That wasn't just his home. Even screwing every coin out of his tenants and rebuilding wouldn't replace all that he'd lost.

Every scrap of evidence that Kent was a legitimate titleholder had been destroyed.

Interesting.

Kent jabbed at Fiona's stomach and she awkwardly blocked it. These couldn't be the best weapons to be fighting with. Though it seemed oddly appropriate, in a way. It was a whaling tool, after all. And Fiona seemed to handle it with greater dexterity than Kent.

Then again, he was considerably larger than her, with, by far, the greater reach.

I was tempted to sneak up behind him and crack him on the back of his head with my gaff. As far as I was concerned, he had abandoned all right to fair consideration with his past behavior. What stopped me was knowing how much Fiona would resent it. It would be significant if she conquered him alone, to her and to her tenants.

"You can't really think you can overcome me," Kent sneered. "I have height and muscle on you."

Fiona didn't say anything. She just swung again.

"My family has been protecting this land for generations. Unlike you."

And yet, his manor had been demolished in a matter of moments. Hers was still standing.

"When the Emperor hears of this attack on my land, he will give your title to me."

"The Emperor demanded Fiona pass the title over to me," Taro whispered into my ear. "He offered the Kent estate as consolation."

I was stunned. "How did you find that out?"

"Fiona told me. She showed me the letter."

"Do you think Kent knows?"

"No idea."

And then, out of nowhere, my eyes were bombarded with black smoke, followed by the sensations of long, thick needles piercing my pupils, my ears, my nose. It was all I could see, all I could feel, and then I drew in breath. Charcoal filled my mouth. I choked when I tried to talk.

For a moment, I couldn't remember where I was.

Just as suddenly, the cloud was gone. Browne was kneeling at my feet, crystals scattered in the grass about me. I had to blink a few times. I glanced about and saw that I seemed to have been the only one surrounded by the cloud. "Why the hell are they going after me?" I demanded. "You're the one with all the skills and experience with casting. Don't they know that?"

Don't shriek, girl. Calm calm calm.

Browne shrugged.

I looked at the Kent caster and realized there was now a collection of them, all of them spilling spell components on the ground and muttering. Every person who tried to get too close winced away as Marcus had. They were protecting themselves, but I had no idea how.

I heard a strange kind of yip from Fiona. I looked over in

time to see her jerk her left hand back quickly. Struck by
Kent's spade, I supposed. It didn't stop her from striking out at
Kent's face. He ducked.

Then he hissed. "You fight as badly as you rule," he said.
"Such arrogance, thinking you can take over an estate of such
depth and variety with no understanding of it. You condemned
the tenants to fear and poverty. And you are either too stupid or
too ignorant to see it. Or maybe you do see it and you just
don't care."

He might want to stop talking. I could hear him wheezing
a little. Unless he really thought he could dishearten Fiona
with his accusations. He hadn't managed to do that before.

Taro approached the Kent casters. "Taro!" I shouted use-
lessly.

He stopped well short of the area where Marcus and some
of the others had encountered difficulty. He threw his gaff at
the closest caster. It seemed to fly unimpeded by any barrier,
which I found confusing. Then again, the flour had settled to
the ground. I supposed the barrier existed only while the flour
was suspended in the air.

The caster ducked, but Taro hadn't been aiming at her head.
It struck her solidly in the ribs. She shouted and curled in on
herself before collapsing to the ground.

"Good shot!" I shouted at Taro. He grinned in response.

It looked like Fiona was getting frustrated with the time the
fight was taking. She turned the spade in her hands and shoved
the blade into Kent's stomach, just off center. He grunted and
jumped back, pressing a hand to his abdomen. I couldn't see
any injury, but Kent was wearing only a thin shirt. It would
have offered no protection.

I heard horses. My eyes followed the noise. Some of Kent's
tenants, from the looks of it.

I watched them approach and split around us.

The mounted Westsea tenants charged at the mounted Kent
tenants.

The mounted Kent tenants galloped away.

All right, then.

Browne ran closer to the Kent casters, pulling a handful of
crystals from her purse and throwing them. Like the spades,
they seemed to sail through whatever barrier the casters had

erected, landing in the grass at their feet. I supposed the barrier was meant to stop spells and nothing else, unlike the first barrier. That was a serious vulnerability, but perhaps the first barrier had really relied on the manor for its strength, and the Kent casters simply couldn't create a barrier of that sort of power on their own.

Just like everything else, spells had their limits.

I couldn't hear what Browne did next. I could only see bright piercing flashes of blue and white that hurt to look at. It didn't seem to harm the casters at all, but they stared in open-mouthed shock. Browne ran at them brandishing her own spade, and the barrier appeared to have been eliminated. At least, she was able to run right up to the casters, and they seemed too shocked to respond, because she was able to clock one in the face before they thought to move.

And then I saw the mounted Kent tenants were galloping back. What the hell?

The mounted Westsea tenants galloped out to meet them. I couldn't help feeling proud of them. *They* hadn't run away.

The clash of horse on horse was gruesome. Some of them were crushed as they were knocked off their feet, and once they were on the ground they tripped up other horses. I could imagine their legs snapping. And I didn't think I would ever be able to forget the sound of the poor animals squealing.

What was I doing here? This wasn't supposed to be my life.

Some of the Kent tenants broke free from the melee and rode toward Taro and me, bearing clubs. Fear leapt up into my throat. I raised my gaff. This was so, so stupid. I was going to get my head caved in.

The man intending to attack me wasn't sneaky about it. He raised his club high and I could easily predict its path. He probably didn't know how to fight, either.

I stopped the progress of the club by lifting my gaff over my head. The gaff was damned heavy when held that way, and I could feel the vibration all through my arm. I didn't know how often I could do that.

Taro struck the same man in the stomach, causing him to shriek. Then I hit him in the head. I was already tired. I couldn't imagine how Fiona and Kent could be still going at it. Not that I had the opportunity to look at them again.

"Help me!" I heard Browne shout. I couldn't look at her, though, to see to her difficulty. Because I felt a sudden sting in the back of my head, the pain of which caused me to lose my breath, and I kind of collapsed against Taro. I couldn't feel my hands. I was pretty sure I'd dropped my gaff.

My sight cleared in time to see another Kent tenant raise his club to us again. I lifted my hands, knowing it was stupid as I was doing it. The bones in my arms would be crushed. I couldn't help myself.

My little brother Dias crushed the back of the tenant's head in with a mallet. I saw the tenant's eyes widen in shock. Then I saw Dias's eyes widen in shock.

I was pretty sure my brothers had never been in this situation, either. In fact, I would wager I had more experience in real violence than they did. Though I doubted they'd managed to reach adulthood without a fistfight or two, that wasn't the same as having to worry someone was going to get killed. I hated the fact that they had been dragged into this.

Behind him, I saw Browne had fallen on the ground, and a caster was trying to stomp on her with his feet and swing at her with a club, while she kicked at his shins. I was pretty sure the only reason the caster was having difficulty was because of his unfamiliarity with the awkward and weighty tool.

Marcus tackled him, and that was the end of that.

Fighting really was a whole lot less elegant than history scrolls would have one believe.

All of the Kent casters had been tied and gagged—so much was going on without my noticing—with their own clothing, which left them pretty much naked. I'd hazard something like that was never part of their expectations on their journey to Kent. I wondered what Kent had promised them to lure them into his service.

I wondered how he'd found them in the first place. While I had encountered some casters who had been stupidly obvious about trying to use spells, most strove for discretion. So how had Kent come to know about these people? How long had they been in Kent? Were they part of some larger group that was training to use hurtful spells?

One problem at a time. Worry about the people trying to kill you right now.

Kent shouted. He was very red and sweaty, his steps clumsy, his swings of the spade less focused and controlled. Fiona looked exhausted, but there was still more certainty in her movements. She jabbed high, she struck low, and Kent seemed forced to spend most of his strength and attention on avoiding her blows, rather than going on the offensive.

Perhaps she was stronger than him after all.

She clipped him in the nose. He jerked too far back, almost losing his balance. So she kicked him in the groin, and almost every man around me groaned in reaction. Kent curled over and stumbled a bit, and Fiona shoved him to the ground.

She fell on him, hard, using her weight as a weapon. Her knees dug into his stomach, and he cried out. She placed the handle of her spade across his throat and pressed down, hard.

Kent's body heaved, his legs kicking out. He tried to buck Fiona off, but she clung on. I watched Kent's face turn a disquieting shade of dark red.

Was she killing him? He deserved it, he really, really did, but I would prefer it happened accidentally.

If he did die, I was pretty sure he wouldn't be the only one. I looked about and saw tenants, both Fiona's and Kent's, lying unmoving on the ground. Browne was kneeling by one, moving her hands over him, before rising from him with a grim expression.

I couldn't believe all of this was still legal.

It took longer than I thought for Kent's kicking and squirming to stop. When it did, Fiona continued to press down for a few moments. Then she climbed off him. "Healer Browne," she called.

Browne's examination of the Earl was brief, as though she really couldn't be bothered. "He breathes," she announced.

Fiona nodded and looked at where the mounted tenants from Westsea and Kent were still riding into each other, swinging implements, and the tenants on foot swinging fists.

"The fight is over!" Fiona shouted. "You can stop!"

They kept hammering at each other.

Taro sighed. "Lee?"

Well, there was really no point in trying to be circumspect anymore. "What do you have in mind?"

"Just the ground, a little. Enough to spook the horses and get everyone's attention."

So he caused a minor earth tremor. Most of the horses bucked their riders off. Most of the fighters on foot seemed to panic and scatter. When all the fighting had stopped, Taro let the ground settle.

What now?

"Bell, Everett," Fiona called. "Please tie him." Two of Fiona's tenants jogged over and bound Kent in the same manner as had been used on the casters. He would be outraged if he knew he was being subjected to such indignity. I liked that. "Mathis, I'm going to ask you to donate your horse to carry Kent back. You'll have to lead him."

"Of course, my lady," said Mathis.

"Pick three men to go with you, in case he wakes. You can hit him if he gives you any trouble."

"Yes, my lady."

"Healer Browne, tap whoever you need to look after the injured. Take care of Kent's people, too."

"Yes, my lady."

"With my authority as magistrate," Fiona announced loudly, "I am placing the Earl of Kent under arrest, to face judgment from Emperor Gifford."

"You can't arrest him!" one of Kent's tenants objected.

Fiona raised an eyebrow at him. "Of course, I can."

"And what are we supposed to do?" another tenant demanded.

"That has nothing to do with me."

"He has no family that we know of. Who's his heir?"

"I have no idea." Fiona found her horse and climbed on.

"You're just going to leave us like this?"

"You're not my responsibility." And with those words, she kicked her horse into a trot.

That seemed cold to me, but really, what else was she supposed to do? They had fought her people, did their best to kill them. Any thoughts of taking them on as tenants herself had obviously dissipated.

Taro, Marcus, my brothers and I found horses and followed Fiona.

Was that it? Three weeks of hell ended in a fight that lasted less than half a candle mark? Was that really how these things worked?

When we reached the border between Kent's land and Fiona's, we encountered a blue glow that seemed to stretch from the ground to high in the air, and as far as I could see to the left and the right. I sighed.

"What the hell is this?" one of the tenants asked.

There was a single person who didn't know about that element of casting? I was almost shocked.

And I wondered how everyone would react. It was one thing for Browne to use casting for healing. Even people uncomfortable with any kind of casting at all might be willing to let that slide. They could even pretend to know nothing about it. After all, healing was a learned skill. The average person would know nothing more about healing than they did about casting. It was easy to pretend to oneself that nothing odd was going on.

And when the Imperial Guards had come, and tried to flog Browne, it had been easy to interfere. There had been only four Guards, who were arrogant and careless in their search for casters, who had alienated everyone so much the tenants probably would have supported anyone the Guards chose to persecute, especially a harmless woman who had lived among them all her life.

But this, this was different. No one could ignore it. And people would have to make decisions about how they were going to feel about casting, how they were going to feel about the people who used casts. That could be dangerous.

It was like all of our secrets had been bared at once. That was going to kick us in the teeth, too.

The barrier eventually faded. "Everyone follow me," Fiona ordered, and I wondered why she thought we wouldn't. It became clear when we began to reach people's houses. Fiona didn't take a straight line back to her manor. She twisted and looped around every building, slowly.

Kent roused then. "What are you doing?" he demanded.

Fiona didn't look back at him, but she answered, "Showing everyone you lost."

"Release me immediately," he commanded, as though he were in any position to get people to do what he wanted.

I couldn't help snickering.

"The Emperor won't let you have Kent."

"I don't want Kent," Fiona told him. "The whole stretch of it needs to lie fallow. I don't have the time to deal with land that won't produce anything for years."

The tenants who hadn't gone with us, the parents of young children, the elderly or infirm, those who simply weren't prepared to do anything but their most basic, absolute duty for Fiona, watched our procession, some of them laughing at Kent's state of undress.

"This is a dishonorable way to treat another titleholder," Kent chided Fiona angrily.

She did turn briefly, then, to shoot him a look of pure astonishment, but she said nothing.

When we reached Fiona's manor, she ordered that Kent be restrained in the tack room, with Daris. I wondered if Daris was still drunk. Maybe she was unconscious. Maybe it wasn't the best idea to put them together in a place that had sharp implements.

Fiona herded my brothers, Cars, Marcus, my mother, Taro and me into her office, where she pulled out some small crystal goblets and a decanter of something a golden brown. "I can't thank you enough for your support," she said, filling the goblets. "Especially those of you who have no real connection to me. You didn't have to risk yourselves like that. I want you to know that it's appreciated. And you were an excellent lesson in loyalty for my vassals. One they won't soon forget."

I hoped these challenges to Fiona's authority were over, because I didn't know how Fiona would fare if they weren't. She was a stronger person than I, but I didn't think it would take much more to make her snap. When good, smart, strong people hit their emotional limit, the results could be nasty.

Chapter Twenty-eight

The next day, my mother told me that she was planning to propose a minor partnership—whatever that meant—to the Prides.

And this offended me. "We had to go through all of that and you're just going to give them what they want, anyway?"

"I offered the same to Cars when he first came to us, but he refused it as it didn't include everything the original contract had. I imagine he'll feel differently about it now."

"But why?"

"I know you feel my behavior was dishonorable, that we continued to enjoy the fruits of the contract after you were sent to the Academy. This is not true. Our actions were entirely legal."

The two terms weren't mutually exclusive. In my opinion, it was quite possible to be a legal ass. "Then why are you doing this?"

"Marcus has shown great merit. I think him a fine man. I would like to avoid seeing him suffer from his father's actions. And despite their current misfortunes, they still have connections that might be of use to us."

It was disturbing to me that I couldn't know which of

those motives was the genuine one, but the idea pleased me. I had been impressed by Marcus, too. I didn't want to see him destitute.

Hester entered the room. "Holder, Shield, Her Grace has instructed me to inform you that Lady Daris is in the process of being exiled from Flown Raven, and it is desired to have witnesses to this event."

Why? To inflict some humiliation on Daris? Not that I had a problem with that. Daris had had no difficulty serving humiliation and more on her family.

I looked at Mother. She rolled her eyes and shook her head, so I went to the stable by myself and joined the crowd, which included both tenants and local aristocracy.

I noticed Radia lingering at the front of the assemblage. I made my way to her. No one objected to my doing so, and so they shouldn't. I was short enough to be seen over by almost everyone. "It might not be good for you to be here." I indicated her cane. "It could get rowdy."

"I wasn't going to miss this. Lady Daris has been an embarrassing annoyance from the moment she stepped onto this land."

I could hear Daris shouting before I could see her. She was swearing up a storm. Some of the oaths were ones I had never heard of, and some didn't make sense. I knew she wasn't drunk because Fiona hadn't allowed her any alcohol. I had heard that people who regularly drowned themselves in alcohol were actually less coherent and agile when they were sober.

Hiroki was carrying Daris from the stable to a waiting carriage, both arms around her waist and holding her off her feet as she tried to kick and punch at him. Hiroki was barely holding on to his balance. Daris was shrieking. There was absolutely no dignity involved. I bit back a smile.

As this was going on, other servants were carrying trunks from the manor and tying them to the back of the carriage. There was a lot of baggage. I wondered if it could cause the carriage to tip over.

Fiona was not there. That was surprising.

"Where is she going to go?" I asked Radia.

"She's going to be dumped in Savinj, apparently."

"That's in the middle of nowhere."

"That's as far as Fiona is willing to send her carriage and men."

"But it's just going to be her and her belongings dropped on the side of the road."

"That's what I hear."

Huh. That was severe, though I agreed that Daris deserved it. I wondered how she was going to manage. Did she have any money of her own? Did she have any friends? Did she have any useful skills if she had neither of the former?

It wasn't much longer before trunks and Daris were loaded into the carriage, no less than four footmen being sent with her, presumably to make sure Daris actually made it to Savinj.

I wanted to wave farewell. I decided that wouldn't be dignified.

It was then that I noticed Tarce in the crowd, leaning heavily on a walking stick. I gestured at him. "I'm aware this is none of my business," I said, "but I'm going to ask anyway. What do you plan to do with him?"

"Nothing."

"He's jumping through a lot of hoops for you."

"People don't change, Shield Mallorough. Not really. If I were to give him any encouragement, he would consider the task accomplished and revert to his former ways. I have no interest in spending time trying to improve him."

"You're a steadfast person."

"Yes, I am."

Hester tapped my shoulder. "Her Ladyship would like to see you in her office."

"Of course. Thank you."

Both Taro and Fiona were in the office. "We've been going through the Dowager's things," she said. I raised my eyebrows at that. "When she died," she explained, "all that she had became mine, because Shintaro removed himself as an heir and she didn't choose anyone herself."

Taro's posture was rigid. He'd been reticent since his mother's death, and I had no idea what to say to him. I couldn't comfort him with reminders of what a wonderful person she had been, how much she'd be missed. And he hadn't talked about her. I wanted to make him feel better but I didn't know how.

Fiona spread a collection of documents over her desk. "We found these hidden—well, it doesn't matter where they were hidden. They're all letters from the Emperor." She flipped one over so I could see the seal.

Except . . . "That's not the Imperial seal."

"This letter was written while he was still crown prince. This one is dated about fifteen years ago."

"That's—" I didn't know what that was. Except disturbing. The Dowager and Gifford had been communicating that long ago?

"I showed these to Shintaro, and we both felt you should see them." She put the letter down. "I'll leave you two alone."

I sat in Fiona's chair and picked up the first letter.

"If I remember correctly," Taro said from his post by the window, "that was written shortly after my father died."

The letter was very short. After elaborate salutations, the Emperor had written: *I am not prepared to intercede with Her Majesty on this matter. Frankly, it is not in Our best interests to have the Westsea title settle on you, and you are not named as an heir. However, I am sure the new lord will come to rely on your excellent guidance. We would welcome any news on how he is faring in his new role.*

"He's talking about your brother, right? The new lord."

"Aye."

"Your mother wanted the title to go to her instead."

"It seems so."

"But she's not a Karish." Wasn't. Wasn't a Karish.

"Of course she is." He'd forgotten, too.

"Not by blood."

"What has that got to do with anything?"

Blood was powerful for spells. Blood could tie people to land.

But had the Emperor known that? So long ago?

I turned to the next letter. It was even shorter, a single line: *It is expected that a young man, recently bestowed with a great inheritance, will indulge in wild celebration.*

Taro's older brother had been everything Taro was reputed, incorrectly, to be. He'd slept with who knew how many people. He'd abused alcohol and powders. He'd ignored his responsibilities. And he'd done that throughout the almost fifteen years between acquiring the title and dying. He hadn't been just a young man enjoying new wealth and freedom. He'd been a lifelong parasite.

The next letter said: *We are not in a position to accommodate you. At this time.*

Which suggested to me that he thought he would be able to accommodate her at a later time. When he was Emperor?

The next: *We are certain Westsea is safe in your capable hands.*

Aha. So the Dowager had been as good as ruling Westsea herself. She had expected to continue to do so when Taro took the title. Instead, he had abjured, and the Dowager had been unsuccessful in running over Fiona. So she'd started campaigning for Taro to take the title back. At least, that was how I remembered the sequence of events.

Only a few letters stretched over the next several years, all very short, all commending the Dowager on her skill with managing Westsea.

And then a letter just after Taro's brother's death: *We are sure your second son will need as much guidance as did your first.*

The next said only: *That is unfortunate, but not unexpected, given your son's prior responsibilities.*

That was when Taro had abjured the title.

The next letter was dated shortly after the death of the Empress, and it said: *We are and will always be indebted to you for your unique assistance. However, We must be circumspect in our actions at this point.*

"What would your mother have done for the Emperor?" I asked Taro.

"I don't know," he responded, his voice low. "But I am alarmed."

The last letter said: *We agree that control of Westsea would be advantageous, but We are not able to dictate resources to its procurement at this time. You must do as you see best.*

Had the Emperor really been the one to send Lila to Flown Raven, or had the Dowager arranged it while telling Lila she was acting on the orders of the Emperor? Just as she kept telling Taro it was the Emperor who wanted him to have the title. Maybe his interest in Flown Raven was not, as we'd thought, about getting access to its power for casting. Maybe he had sent the Imperial Guards to cause difficulty for Fiona, because that was what the Dowager wanted.

The Dowager was dead. Was that going to make a difference?

I collected all the letters and shuffled them into a neat pile.

Taro left without saying anything, which was very unlike him. Following him probably wasn't the best idea, but he had been alone a lot recently. Not off gambling or risking our lives steeplechasing. That was a problem. He wasn't like me. A lot of solitude wasn't good for him.

And it wasn't as though he went anywhere far or obscure. He'd sat on the front steps, his shoulders slumped. If he wanted to be alone, he shouldn't have made himself so easy to find.

I sat beside him and said nothing for a while.

I didn't know if I was making him feel better or not.

Once the silence had made me uncomfortable, I said, "I'm sorry."

"No, you're not."

"I am."

"She was an awful, awful woman."

"She was your mother."

"It's stupid to feel anything for her."

"Feelings are never stupid."

"You don't believe that."

"It's something I've learned." I was sort of lying. Sometimes, I felt people's emotions were disproportionate to their cause. But Taro's current feelings were not an item in that category. His mother was dead. Her character was irrelevant.

I couldn't imagine how it would feel to lose one's family. It didn't matter that I was an adult, and that I rarely saw them: I was sure that if every member of my family died, I would feel lost.

How could I make him feel less lost? Make him feel less alone? I leaned against him.

"I'm sorry," he said.

"For what?"

"If I'd kept my mouth shut and denied Marcus's challenge, the contract would have remained void, and we wouldn't have to get married."

None of this was his fault, not really. "It won't be so bad." At least I wasn't going to have to marry Marcus. "There will no doubt be a certain cachet attached to being the person to wrap the chains of matrimony around the Stallion of the Triple S."

He glared at me. "I can't believe you're still laying that on me."

I grinned at him, unrepentant.

"I like your brothers better," he claimed. "Maybe I should marry Mika instead. I'd wager the spell would accept the substitution, given he's part of the Mallorough family."

"He wouldn't have you. He's madly in lust with Linder."

"He has excellent taste."

"That he does."

We sat there, watching what movement there was, mostly the house staff crossing to and fro performing one task or another. They all saw us, and many nodded or tugged a forelock, but no one spoke to us. After the chaos of the past few weeks, it was restful. Pleasant.

At around dusk, Dias clattered down the steps. "I've been looking all over for you," he complained.

"You couldn't possibly," Taro responded. "We've been here for ages."

"Well, I didn't know you'd be lazing around on the steps, did I?"

"I'm quite comfortable here," Taro informed him.

"But we've got chocolate."

That made me smile.

He took us to our suite and locked the door behind us. Mika was sitting on the floor, of course, surrounded by covered dishes and plates. There was the promised chocolate, and Mika was sipping wine. He raised his goblet in a toast. "All hail the betrothed couple."

I rolled my eyes and said, "Really, what is it with you and the floor?"

"Are you the type of person who needs to be told something twice? Sister, I'm so disappointed."

"You really think you're cute, don't you?"

"Surely you're not implying that I'm not."

I sat on the floor. I never really found sitting on the floor

comfortable. I'd rather sprawl on a settee. I accepted a goblet
of chilled wine and wondered where my brothers had gotten
it. I hoped they had paid for it. Members of the Triple S could
requisition goods. So could their partners, as long as they remained partners, and children, until they were adults. That was
it. But many regulars didn't know precisely where the line was
drawn, and my brothers might be able to get away with procur-
ing goods without paying for them.

I didn't ask, though. That would be rude.

"So," Mika said as we cut into beef—no fish, thank Zaire—
and potatoes. "Start talking."

"Excuse me?" Taro asked.

"Where did you go that year you disappeared?"

Well, that was blunt.

And neither of us said anything.

"Clearly you haven't had enough wine." Mika reached over
to pour some more red for Taro.

Taro put his hand over his goblet. "I won't have my mind
dulled again."

"Are you trying to get us drunk so we'll tell you what you
want to know?" I accused them.

"It's not so much that we want to know," Mika objected. "I
mean, aye, we want to know. Things have happened to you.
But it is more that I think you need to tell us."

"There was a light about you, after your Matching," Dias
added. "It's much dimmed, now."

I didn't know what to think about that. I didn't believe I was
the sort of person who exuded any kind of light. That just
wasn't my nature. But I had certainly become disillusioned
about certain things. Except Taro. He was the only force in my
life that had never let me down.

Suddenly, I felt tired. Bone weary, my limbs weighed down,
my eyelids heavy. I wanted to curl up on my bed and pull the
covers over my head and just not think about anything, sleep
until everything was normal again.

Mika tucked a few strands of my hair behind my ear.
"You'll feel better."

"I have no way of knowing that. I'll probably regret it."

"You'll have no reason to," Mika promised.

He didn't know what I had to tell him. Breaking into an

office and destroying a family's business, while horrific, was nowhere near as bad as killing someone.

"If you were to disappear, we'd like to know where to start looking."

I looked at Taro.

He looked back, giving me no indication of what he thought I should do. Prat.

The weight on my chest suddenly grew heavy and hard. It made it difficult to breathe, though that made no sense. I wasn't ill. There wasn't anything physical pressing against me. It was all just emotion. It was a bad, bad idea to base decisions on emotion.

But I was tired and I couldn't breathe.

So I told them. About killing Creol and how we did it, about killing a Reanist during the attack on the aristocrats at Yellows' manor. Looking for Aryne, and who she was.

And this was when Taro, who had been letting me do all the talking, made a contribution of his own, one I'd known nothing about.

"The Empress decided to preserve Aryne's status as a possible heir," he announced. "A sort of second plan, should Gifford prove to be . . . inadequate."

I stared at him. "She thought Aryne was useless!"

"She certainly wasn't impressed. But she wasn't impressed with Gifford, either. She had great concern over his opinions, his companions, his actions and his plans. She predicted that he might not live very long."

"He was threatening his own health?"

"No. She thought someone was going to kill him."

Hell, how callous was that? I'd never thought her a warm and friendly person, she had obviously been raised to be obeyed and had expected blind compliance, but I'd never thought her so hard-hearted, either. This was her son she had been talking about.

"As far as she knew, he had no children, and she was confident he wouldn't choose an heir until he was much older. Apparently, it's never wise for a monarch to choose an heir too early, as that heir might be tempted to hurry along the monarch's death. Should Gifford die without an heir, she wanted it to be possible for Aryne to ascend to the throne."

"But Aryne isn't being educated to do anything like that." Aryne was clever and seemed able to judge people very well, but I really hoped there was more than that to being a good monarch.

"The headmistress of the Source Academy is bringing in people to instruct Aryne in politics, diplomacy, military strategy, and so on."

"The headmistress knows who Aryne is?"

"No. I asked her to make sure Aryne received a unique education. She doesn't know why I asked."

"Oh." I was shocked to find Taro had that kind of influence.

"But she doesn't know the code," said Dias.

The code the heir needed to know in order to inherit.

"It's not a code. It's something more elaborate."

That made sense, given what was to be inherited.

"And I know it."

We all gaped at him.

"You could be the next monarch," Dias breathed.

Technically, that was true. In reality, I didn't think that would be allowed to happen. Taro had the undeserved reputation of being unreliable in anything other than channeling. And, if people didn't think he was all that smart . . .

Taro scowled. "I am a Source."

"So's Aryne," I reminded him.

"Not a very good one."

"What has that to do with anything?"

"She may become skilled with training, but I really, really doubt it. She couldn't even teach."

Which would leave her engaged in maintenance, cooking, or caring for the children of the Academy. These were all useful and necessary tasks, but to have to do it in one of the academies meant one had failed to become a viable Source or Shield. And such a person might be serving or cleaning up after someone who, only the year before, had been a fellow student. I couldn't imagine how awkward that would feel. I wouldn't like Aryne having to accept that. Still. "I don't think that means she should be, you know, ruling us all." In fact, the idea kind of horrified me. Aryne had suffered a lot of abuse for much of her life. I wouldn't blame her if she used whatever power she might acquire to punish the world for her pain.

"I was told to use my judgment."

We spent more time staring at him.

That was a frightening amount of power to be vested in a person who really didn't have the training or experience to hold it.

He shrugged with palpable discomfort.

"Do you think the Emperor knows?" Mika asked.

Taro's eyes widened. Clearly, that was a possibility he'd never considered.

What would the Emperor do if he knew, if he found out? Would he send us to the end of the world? To Taro's birthplace, hoping my Source would be overwhelmed by the natural events? Maybe the Emperor hadn't really cared about the title at all, had merely felt the title would be another tie that wasn't, ultimately, really important to him?

Or would he kill us?

Our secrets were even worse than I'd known. I almost wished Taro hadn't told me.

But then, it must have been horrible for him, carrying that secret alone.

I didn't know what to do. It was as though my mind had slowed down, so slow thoughts floated away before I could grab them. I didn't think I could make a decision to save Taro's life.

I was so tired, staring down at the floor, feeling suspended from reality. It took me a while to realize Taro was speaking, a while longer to understand he had taken over the duty of reporting our crimes to my brothers.

I expected Mika and Dias to deliver expressions of disgust and walk out, to refuse to talk to us, talk to me, for the remainder of their stay.

Instead, Dias took my hand and placed it on his thigh, covering my hand with his. An odd gesture, but one that drew me from my daze, gave me a firm connection to the world again. And it made me feel safe in a way that I'd never felt before, even with Taro.

We were silent for a while after Taro finished speaking. Mika was frowning. Dias was staring into space. I had no idea what they were thinking, but then I'd never had any skill at reading people. Taro was the one with greater talent in that area.

Then Mika snickered. "Who would think our severe and sensible sister would lead a life of such adventure?"

I could do nothing more than stare at him in shock. That was his response to everything we'd gone through? What the hell?

Taro shoved Mika hard enough to push him right over.

And my brain was still so slow that I found myself protesting, "I'm not severe!"

Dias patted my hand. "It's reassuring to know that you'll always leap to the most important issue in any situation."

"You're annoying," I murmured.

"Ah, I love you, too," he retorted.

And then the sense of relief I'd been too pessimistic to truly anticipate flooded through me. It almost made me dizzy.

And it brought tears to my eyes. What was wrong with me? I'd never been so close to crying so often since I was an adolescent.

"I have to admit, this is more serious than I'd expected," said Mika, having straightened from Taro's attack. "But I'd rather know all the details than be ignorant."

"Why?" Taro asked. "Sometimes I wish I were ignorant."

"A trader needs to know everything about everything, good and bad, in order to make the right decisions. Everyone does, really, but in my experience, people do prefer to work with their eyes closed. Father's been able to take advantage of that, in the past."

"And what do you think is the right decision?" Taro asked.

"We won't tell anyone else."

Dias didn't object to Mika speaking on his behalf.

"We can be discreet. Well"—he glanced at Dias—"*I* can be."

Dias sketched out a rude hand gesture.

"We know things you don't. About more than trade. Now that we know what you've been up to, well, we can ask better questions. We have a lot of connections spread all over the continent. We could be useful."

"Useful for what?" Taro asked.

"Warnings? Maybe? If we hear something with the slightest connection to what you've just told us, we can relay it to you. You've run against some powerful and diverse people. The Emperor, no less. I think you'll need all the information you can get your hands on."

"Information is power," Dias added.

As plans went, it was weak and full of holes, yet it was still reassuring. How odd.

"You haven't touched the chocolate," Dias commented.

I frowned at him.

"We're done with the angst, aren't we?"

Our trials were "angst"?

Then he grinned. I supposed he was trying to be funny. He wasn't quite achieving the mark, but I could appreciate the effort. I could use a smile.

I popped a ball of chocolate into my mouth.

My brothers left not long after, and although it wasn't late, Taro and I went to bed. I didn't expect to sleep. I thought worry over what I'd told my brothers would keep me awake. Instead, I was sucked into deep slumber the moment I closed my eyes.

The next duty was attending a series of funerals, the final one in observance of the Dowager's death. It was the one with the smallest attendance. The Dowager had had friends and connections, but apparently none were in the area, and there didn't appear to be many tenants interested in seeing the Dowager honored. The only servants in attendance were the ones who had worked in the Dowager House, and some of them seemed sincerely devastated. It reminded me how strange people could be.

Taro, the Dowager's closest family, refused to carry a trinket that represented her, to throw into the fire. I didn't blame him at all. I thought he was being dutiful to a degree the Dowager didn't deserve, hadn't earned, just to attend the funeral at all. And I didn't think he was at all eased by the ceremony, which was supposed to be the point of it.

He remained withdrawn for days, and hid in our suite. All I could do was watch and hope he rose up from his dark mood on his own.

I received a note from Marcus, in which he asked if he could meet with me. I hadn't seen a lot of him, and I understood he had been part of the negotiations going on between his father and my mother. I had been happy to avoid anything concerning that process, but I wasn't comfortable just ignoring Marcus until he left. Cars? No problem. But Marcus, well, I actually kind of liked him.

Though I would never, ever admit it to anyone.

We met in one of the parlors. I sat. Marcus wandered through the room, from window to fireplace to an end table, at which point he picked up a small button box and immediately put it back down again. He was clearly uncomfortable.

"Your mother offered us a partnership," he said.

"She told me she would."

"She didn't have to."

"There must be something advantageous about it."

"Well, yes. I suppose. But she—your family, they don't really need us."

I shrugged. "From what I've learned, fortunes can rise and fall. And I imagine there's no such thing as having too many friends."

"No. I suppose not."

His voice was a little vague, as though he really wasn't paying attention to what we were saying. "Are you all right?" I asked.

"Yes. I'm just a little—well, I came here expecting my life to go a certain way."

"And now it's taken a sharp right. I thought you'd be relieved."

"Except now, my father is thinking that with this alliance with your family, a marriage with me will be more appealing to one of the families who rejected us before."

I was appalled. "You mean, your father still wants to—" Breed him like a stallion?

"Aye."

"I can't—I'm sorry."

"So am I. He will be furious when I refuse. He might even disinherit me."

My eyebrows flew up in shock.

"It was one thing to comply when we were desperate. I won't marry just to improve a position that is already, well, good enough."

To hell with courtesy. "I don't like your father."

He smiled. "I can see why you wouldn't."

"What will you do if he does disinherit you?"

"Find a position with another family."

Did he have a fair chance of accomplishing that, a member of a merchant family that had been enduring years of misfortune?

I found myself wishing I could think of some solution for him. And that was a useless wish. I didn't know anything about such things.

"It's not done yet," he said. "And my father may regain his reason once we begin to experience the benefits of our connection with you."

It seemed a faint hope. I'd seen nothing of Cars to suggest he was a reasonable person.

"But that isn't why I wanted to speak with you. I just wanted to apologize for all of this."

"None of it was your fault."

"I could have refused. Like you did."

"I think your willingness to do whatever it took to protect your family is an admirable trait. Inconvenient, but admirable."

Sometimes, I could learn new things.

"And now you must marry Shintaro."

"Aye."

"Is that so very awful? I understand that you love him."

"I do love him. But marriage has little to do with love."

"True enough."

"And I never thought I'd ever do it. I resent being forced to do it."

"I can understand that."

Of course he could.

"My father and I will be leaving shortly." He held out a hand. "It was a pleasure to meet you."

I shook it. "You, too." It hadn't been, but I was sure I would have enjoyed his company in other circumstances. "Take care."

They left later that day. I was relieved, despite my appreciation for Marcus's character. I didn't want there to be even the most remote possibility that I would have to end up marrying Marcus, after all. The past few weeks had been so unpredictable, I didn't trust things to remain stable.

My emotions were mixed when I received the news that
Kaaren and my father had arrived. My father had been just as
responsible as my mother for the mess with the Prides. On the
other hand, I'd had more recent contact with my mother than
my father, and she'd managed to irritate me. A lot.

His first words to me, when we met in Fiona's office, were,
"I'm sorry."

For some reason, tears threatened my eyes. Again. What
was wrong with me?

"Though if you have to get married," he continued, "at least
it's to a fine man."

"And such a pretty one," Mika added.

Taro raised an eyebrow at him.

"I'm not hearing any demurrals," said Mika.

"Surely you didn't expect any," Taro retorted.

"Taro is extremely truthful," I added in the most somber
tone I could muster. I was thrilled to hear him speaking at all
in something other than a distressing monotone.

My father narrowed his eyes at me. "You've changed."

It sounded like an accusation, and I had no idea how to
react to that.

"It's good to see," he said then.

And suddenly I felt a little offended. Like he was suggesting I had been something inferior before. Which made no
sense. If I hadn't changed after all I'd been through since last
seeing him, there would have been something wrong with me.

Bailey actually knocked before entering the office, though
he didn't wait for an invitation to come in. "Good afternoon."
He turned to Taro. "There is a display taking place in the inner
garden, my lord. I believe it might be interesting to you."

"What kind of display?" Taro asked.

Bailey merely smiled.

Really, he wasn't nearly as stoic as stories with characters
in his occupation would seem to suggest.

As we followed Bailey through the manor to the rear, it
seemed to me that the building felt empty. This was unusual.
There were always servants running around, doing things. But
I saw and heard nothing. At least, not until we reached the rear
entrance.

I'd never seen so many people crammed into the garden,

even for the funerals. Whalers, fishers, farmers and tradespeople, with more coming as I watched.

My first reaction was a spurt of panic. What stunt were they pulling now? Hadn't Fiona been through enough? Couldn't they just perform their tasks and let Fiona perform hers?

But as I looked at them, trying to pick out angry expressions, wondering who I had to worry about the most, I realized that the mood of the crowd didn't appear to be hostile. There was a lot of chatter, but no shouting. I couldn't hear any threats or complaints.

The chatter stopped when Fiona strode into the garden from around the manor. She looked calm, self-assured. I must have been getting to know her rather well, because I could see tension in the way she held her shoulders.

Four people separated from the crowd. Two men, two women, lean with years of hard work. By their tools I determined that they were a whaler, a fisher, a farmer and a tradeswoman. They stood in front of Fiona, about a man's height away.

"I don't know what tenants at other estates do," the whaler announced in a loud voice that still failed to reach all of the spectators. His voice didn't resonate. "But here, we choose representatives to speak on our behalf in certain situations, mediate disputes, determine where surplus supplies go when there are others in need."

In other words, some of the responsibilities that were within Fiona's domain. I would be offended if I were Fiona, but the Duchess's expression was one of polite interest.

"To be chosen to represent one's assembly," the whaler continued, "is a great honor bestowed upon one who is considered by most to be wise and trustworthy. We"—he gestured at the three people beside him—"have been so chosen."

So, that meant what? Was there some ancient rite enabling tenants of their stature to oust their titleholders?

I was losing my patience with ancient rites.

"Things have been difficult," the whaler said. "We have lost lives, homes and produce. We are angry. We have held you responsible for our misfortunes."

Which was wrong, in my opinion, but Fiona merely nodded, as though she were willing to accept the charge.

"Although many of us have struggled with the idea of someone who is not a Karish governing this land, we are forced to concede to Source Karish's argument, that the most recent of Karish titleholders did not shoulder their responsibilities as they should have, and that it is because of this lack that we have felt forced to create our own means to govern ourselves."

The whaler looked down at the head spade in his hands. "We all have great respect for Source Karish. He has demonstrated he is an able Source, and he has been willing to engage in tasks outside of his regular duties." The whaler suddenly grinned. "He even tried his hand at whaling, though his efforts were less than adept."

Many in the crowd chuckled. Taro accepted the ribbing with grace. It wasn't as though he had wanted to learn to hunt whales. He thought the pursuit dangerous and insane.

"But Source Karish wasn't raised here. Not truly. We are aware he was given no exposure to the tasks and demands of running the estate. We are aware that being called to the Source Academy has greater significance than merely being called to the Source Academy, that it severs family ties and responsibilities. That you then refused the title"—the whaler gave Taro a bit of a hard look, which suggested to me he still hadn't quite forgiven my Source for his decisions—"is also, we think, more than just a choice; it had far-reaching effects. Effects that can't be reversed."

Couldn't they? If Fiona decided she no longer wanted the Westsea title, she could give it to Taro, couldn't she? Or was there something else going on that I knew nothing about?

"We have to concede that we have no reason to believe similar events wouldn't have occurred if Source Karish had taken the title, and great reason to believe that perhaps he might not have been able to address those events effectively."

This time, the look the whaler sent Taro was apologetic. Taro raised his hand slightly and shook his head. No hard feelings.

"Given these circumstances . . ." He stepped closer to Fiona, holding out his spade in both hands, horizontally, as though he were offering a sword or a scepter. "We welcome you, Your Grace, to our lives and homes."

Fiona accepted the spade with the same spirit of solemnity in which it had been offered.

I smiled. This was good.

The whaler bowed and stepped back, and the fisher stepped forward, offering her fishing gaff with both hands. "We welcome you, Your Grace, to our lives and homes."

A little awkwardly, Fiona balanced the spade on her forearms so she could accept the gaff.

The farmer offered a goad. "We welcome you, Your Grace, to our lives and homes."

This was so much more meaningful than the oath of fealty they had sworn not long ago. Then, they had merely complied with Fiona's demands. This, this was something the tenants had devised, had offered up on their own initiative. This was fantastic.

The tradeswoman's offering was a mallet.

Fiona managed to hold all of these implements without looking ridiculous. "Thank you," she said. "I'm honored with your trust."

Not the prettiest rhetoric I had ever heard, but it seemed to satisfy everyone.

I felt like applauding.

And I experienced a feeling of settlement that I hadn't even noticed I'd been lacking since coming to Flown Raven. It was nice.

Imperial Guards arrived a few days later, to pick up Kent and his casters. I hadn't gone near Kent during his incarceration. I had been told he'd spent hours shouting threats, then promises. He'd tried to starve himself, but had broken down once he was hungry enough. He'd tried to hang himself but had only rendered himself unconscious by the time he was discovered. At that point, apparently, he'd lost all will to do anything, leaving the various tools in the tack room untouched.

Good. I didn't care. He deserved to have the worst life could throw at him.

As for the casters, they had spent much of their incarceration gagged. That couldn't have been pleasant. It must have been effective, though, for I heard nothing of them managing to cast any spells.

No one hung around to watch the Guards take Kent and his casters. The Guards sent to investigate the use of casting in

Flown Raven had been arrogant and condescending and stupid, and they'd tried to flog Browne. No one wanted to attract the attention of these Guards.

Having Kent gone, that made everything seem a little more settled, too.

I couldn't get too comfortable, though. We still hadn't heard anything from the Triple S. Word of what Taro had done had surely made it back to them, but days passed without a single piece of correspondence from them. I didn't know what that meant. Maybe they didn't believe what they were told. Maybe they did, but had more important things to worry about. Maybe all of the councilors had died and the resulting chaos meant the information had been lost. I didn't know, and I hated that.

And then, so quickly, it was the day of the wedding. I almost couldn't believe it. The idea of it was just so bizarre. I'd never thought I'd ever do anything like this. And it was yet another ritual. I hated rituals.

At least everyone had agreed to cut the three-day ceremony to something under a few hours. Less demanding, and less to go wrong.

Except, that morning, when I put on the dress, I found it didn't fit.

It was a lovely gown, more elaborate than any I'd ever worn. The green sleeves fell over my wrists and hung to the floor, wildly impractical. The neckline was nice and high, a simple collar around my throat. The bodice was supposed to wrap closely around my torso from neck to lower stomach and the small of my back. The front of the skirt fell to my feet, while the back trailed several useless feet behind me.

The most astonishing thing about the dress was the intricate embroidery covering the front panel and flowing down in a few lines along the sleeves and the skirt. I couldn't imagine how it had been stitched so quickly. The thread was white, and had clearly been inspired by the design of my white Shield's braid. It was the first time I'd worn clothing that wasn't marred, in some way, by my braid.

It was a lovely dress, and it didn't fit. The bodice was hanging noticeably loose.

"How is this possible?" I pressed the front panel to my stomach. "He just made this. He measured it only a few days ago." Though, now that I thought about it, I remembered it had felt just the slightest bit loose then. I hadn't told the dressmaker. I had wanted to be able to breathe on my wedding day. Fainting would be undignified.

"You haven't been eating much, the past couple of weeks," Taro said.

He was wearing a black tunic, black trousers, black boots. He had also had a cape inflicted on him, green silk, pinned to his right shoulder with one silver broach and to the left side of his waist with another. It looked a little ridiculous, poor man.

"It's not like I've been starving myself."

"You've practically been living off coffee and tree tears."

Hm. Unfortunately, the dress didn't look nearly as good hanging as loose as it did. But there was nothing to be done about it.

"Your hair looks sleek."

Hester had skill with dressing hair. The shape of my face meant having all of my hair tied back wasn't flattering. What she had done was smooth most of it into a coil at the back of my head, with the locks closest to my face left free to fall in the lazy curls she had burnt into it. It didn't look too bad.

"Should I tell you that yours does, too?" I asked him. "It always does."

He just shrugged. Usually, he didn't care to hear compliments from me when it came to his looks, though he showed no difficulty in accepting them from others. Someday, perhaps, I would ask him why.

As ready as we were going to be, we went down to Fiona's office, to tell her it was time to start the fiasco. We found her staring at a letter, looking shocked.

"What's wrong?" Taro demanded sharply.

"Nothing," she answered almost absentmindedly.

"Oh," said Taro, a little confused, like he'd been ready to charge to her rescue and was surprised to learn it wasn't necessary.

"This is from the Emperor." She raised the letter a little.

"He didn't take the title from you, did he?" I demanded abruptly.

She chuckled, but it was a short sound of derision. "The opposite. He's given me Kent."

I thought about that for a few moments, but thought didn't make it any less confusing. "That doesn't make sense." The Emperor didn't like Fiona. Why would he give her a new estate without demanding she hand in the old?

"He's collapsed Centerfield, Westsea, and Kent into one estate," Fiona added.

"What does that mean?"

"There are a whole lot of legal implications," she said. "Mostly, it just means there's only one title for all of them. I'm not the Countess of Kent. My Centerfield title no longer exists. I'm just the Duchess of Westsea, and Westsea covers all of the estates. I can speak with only one voice at council. All estates will be taxed identically. And so on."

"But why would he do that?" Taro asked.

A whole slew of disparate pieces of information fell into place. "The Emperor isn't after you to take the title anymore," I said to Taro. "It was your—it was the Dowager who wanted you to have the title. And now—" She was dead.

"All right, he doesn't care about the Westsea title," said Fiona. "That doesn't explain why he's willing to give Kent to me."

"The Earl didn't have an heir," Taro reminded her.

A lot of titleholders didn't bother with heirs, it seemed to me. Shortsighted.

"The logical thing," said Fiona, "would have been to give it to one of his cronies. Unless . . ."

And she said nothing more.

"Unless what?" Taro prodded.

"The Earl was right. I haven't been paying enough attention to the maneuvering in the court at Erstwhile. There's a reason Gifford is giving Kent to me; it's to his advantage in some way. But I don't know what that is."

"You could refuse to take the earldom, couldn't you?" I asked.

Fiona snickered. "Why would I do that?"

And my understanding of Fiona took a sharp step to the left. She wanted the earldom, regardless of the difficulties it might bring. That was surprising. And disheartening.

But the largest part of my mind didn't care. The most important effect of the Emperor's decision was that, finally, Taro would be left alone. Finally.

Fiona let the letter drift back to her desk. "Well, then," she said in a brighter tone. "It's time to get you two married." Then she frowned at me. "Do you need to get that dress adjusted a bit?"

"I'd rather not take the time." I just wanted to get the whole spectacle over with.

She shrugged. "Let's get it started, then."

A lot of effort had been put to arranging the garden into a traditional wedding arena. A large circle was outlined with thousands of tiny white rocks, into which had been mixed tiny shards of black sea shells. White sand was sprinkled within the circle. From the same finicky process, two paths had been created, stretching from the outer edge of the garden to the edge of the circle.

To one side there was a collection of white tables and chairs where guests would be emptying Fiona's barrels and larder. Musicians were already playing nice bland music that was unlikely to make me crazy in front of everyone. The spectators— a lot of them, servants and tenants and local aristocrats—were already arranged between the paths.

Fiona stood in the middle of the circle, a thick black belt pulling her blue gown to her waist, two strings of red beads hanging from the leather. There were two small stools, the sort so low that one's knees almost touched the ground. I had seen them before, with the merchant who had given to Taro and me our harmony bobs. On the ground there was an unlit candle and an empty copper bowl.

Taro and I joined Fiona in the circle.

My father and siblings were on one side of the circle, just outside the ring, and Tarce, Taro's closest relative in the area aside from Fiona, was propped up on a crutch on the other.

The music stopped. The guests fell into silence. All I could hear was the wind, the sea, and the screaming of birds. The sky was overcast. The wind was cool. Just another normal day in Flown Raven.

"I am Fiona Keplar, Duchess of Westsea, and as such I am

given the authority to create the bond of marriage between two parties. Does anyone object?"

No one did, of course.

"What is your name?" Fiona asked me.

"Dunleavy Mallorough." My name, stripped of title.

"What is your name?" Fiona asked Taro.

"Shintaro Ivor Cear Karish."

"Who offers Dunleavy Mallorough for marriage?"

"I do," my mother called from the other end of one of the paths. She walked up the path to the circle, protecting the flame of a lit candle with the palm of her hand. She hesitated at the edge of the circle. "I seek entry into the marriage circle."

"Granted," said Fiona.

Mother stepped into the circle and then knelt before the unlit candle. "The Malloroughs offer our protection to the Karishes." She lit the candle, than took two steps back, still remaining within the circle.

"Who offers Shintaro Karish for marriage?"

"I do." Tarce awkwardly approached the circle, trying to manage both his crutch and a silver jug. "I seek entry into the marriage circle."

"Granted."

Tarce stood beside the empty bowl and poured water into it. "The Karishes offer our good health to the Malloroughs." And then he dropped the jug with a loud clang that flipped the bowl over, spilling the water to the ground. He flushed. I felt badly for him. He'd been going through a kind of hell recently.

"Dunleavy, do you have a spouse now living?"

"I do not."

"Shintaro, do you have a spouse now living?"

"I do not."

"A marriage is a bond recognized by law securing a connection between two families, so they may share blood and property. It cannot be created without the full knowledgeable consent of two adults of sound mind. Do you, Dunleavy, consent to this marriage?"

"I do."

"Do you, Shintaro, consent to this marriage?"

"I do."

"Do you, Dunleavy, understand that as a result of this bond, you will be unable to create any other marriage bond without dissolving this one?"

"I do."

"Do you, Shintaro, understand that as a result of this bond, you will be unable to create any other marriage bond without dissolving this one?"

"I do."

"What do the next generation bring to the union?"

"A book of poetry," Kaaren called out, holding up the volume. "We bring to the union our knowledge, our experience, and our thoughts." She didn't enter the circle, but took several steps around it.

As Tarce, instead of a parent or uncle or the like, was of Taro's generation, the only person on hand of the next generation was Stacin. Poor young, shy Stacin, so somber in his little blue tunic and blue trousers, carrying a small bowl, with Cekina beside him to make sure he didn't drop the bowl or wander off in the wrong direction.

When Stacin reached her, Kaaren smiled down at him. The two had spent a lot of time together, so Stacin wouldn't be overwhelmed in Kaaren's presence.

"What do you have, Stacin?" Fiona asked in a warm tone.

"Fruit," Stacin said quietly.

Dried fruit, meant to bring to the union sustenance, muscle and discipline.

Kaaren leaned down and gently took the bowl from Stacin. She held out the small book. He frowned at it and looked at his mother.

"Take the book, love," his mother told him.

He slowly did so, and once it was in his hands, Kaaren lightly touched his head before resuming her place with the rest of my family. Cekina led Stacin away.

Fiona gestured at the stools. Taro and I sat down.

Taro's stool collapsed immediately, and he managed to stay on his feet with a twist and an oath. People twittered, and for a moment Taro looked like he'd follow the original oath with a string of aristocratic invectives. Instead, he rolled his eyes, tossed the ruins of the stool aside and sat down on his heels.

So, no, dignity wasn't going to be a part of this public ceremony. How very like my life as a whole.

But I shouldn't sulk. At least it wasn't Marcus on the other side.

"Marriage is a serious endeavor," Fiona announced. "It should not be undertaken without the intention to respect the other's family as one's own. Do you take the Karish family to be your own, Dunleavy?"

"I do."

"Do you take the Mallorough family to be your own, Shintaro?"

"I do."

"Will you hold your connection to the Karish family above all other connections, Dunleavy?"

"I will." Though not to the Karish family, per se. I was aware that Taro had some relatives named Karish whom I'd never met. My connection to Taro, though, was, of course, the strongest one I had.

"Will you hold your connection to the Mallorough family above all other connections, Shintaro?"

"I will."

The bindings on my hair snapped, my hair tumbling to my shoulders and into my face.

I sighed.

"Will you protect the Karish family against all who would bring them harm, Dunleavy?"

"I will."

"Will you protect the Mallorough family against all who would bring them harm, Shintaro?"

"I will."

Fiona pulled the knife from her belt. "Do you offer your blood, Dunleavy?"

I held out my hand, palm up. "I do."

She sliced my palm. "Do you offer your blood, Shintaro?"

"I do."

She sliced his palm. Then she pressed our palms together. "As blood flows from Dunleavy to Shintaro, from Shintaro to Dunleavy, respect and support flow from the Malloroughs to the Karishes, from the Karishes to the Malloroughs."

Fiona gave one of the strings of beads to my mother, the other to Tarce. "Bind the beads as you bind your families."

And then the strings, both of them, broke apart, all of the beads sliding to the ground and pinging off in a dozen different directions.

There was a moment of silence, and then someone said, "It's like you're cursed."

"Or the marriage is," someone else muttered.

"I don't care as long as the wine hasn't gone rancid," added a third.

Then someone hissed and everyone shut up.

It wasn't that I didn't believe in curses, just that I didn't think that was what was going on right then. Taro and I were getting married. Of course it would be a farce. I was at once frustrated and amused.

My mother and Tarce just looked at each other, for a moment, clearly unsure what to do. Then my mother moved forward, taking the end of Tarce's denuded string and wrapping it with hers.

Once they were done, Fiona took the final product and draped the strings over my wrist and then Shintaro's. "Dunleavy and Shintaro, you are now married."

Normally, the two parties would have decided on one family name to use, and that would have been announced. There was no way I was going to take the Karish name, aside from Taro they had all been monsters, and there was no way I was going to suggest Taro take mine. His entire request to the Empress had been to be severed from taking the Westsea title without having to give up his name. I wasn't going to ask him to give it up now.

People applauded.

It all felt ridiculous. And this wasn't the end of the affair. There was to be dancing and drinking and eating, and given our luck so far, a table would collapse or someone would be poisoned or someone's crazy ex-lover would try to kill someone.

"If you would follow me!" Fiona called out. "We'll move on to the fun part of the proceedings!"

People cheered and there was a great wave of movement.

Except my family. And Taro.

Or, more properly, my family.

It was interesting, the power of words, the enormous change they could create. And they didn't always need to be part of a cast to do it.

Dias shocked everyone by sort of jumping on Taro, arm around my Source's shoulder. "Welcome to the family, big brother!" And because Dias was actually bigger than Taro, he had to lean down a little to kiss my husband's temple. "Can I borrow some money?"

Taro snorted and tried to shove him away. Unsuccessfully. And then, before my eyes, they degenerated into some kind of weird wrestling . . . thing. Had they both turned into thirteen-year-olds?

My father smirked, my mother sighed. "I'd hoped Shintaro might have been an influence for maturity."

"Instead of the other way around." Taro was no grappler, but I had a feeling Dias was being a little careful with him.

Taro's hair had become undone and one of his broaches had snapped off. He was grinning and his eyes were shining.

I felt a knot in my chest loosen, and I couldn't help smiling.

My father, displaying great care and agility, managed to get close enough to put a hand on the back of the neck of both Taro and Dias. Dias released Taro immediately. It took Taro a few more moments to understand the signal, but he eventually let Dias go.

"Not in front of the tenants, children," Father scolded them. Then he kissed Taro on the forehead. "Welcome to the family. There's room for another son."

Taro was practiced at hiding his thoughts and feelings behind a bland expression on his face, and he was clearly trying to do so right then, but it was obvious he was almost overwhelmed by this invitation of inclusion. I silently berated myself for once more failing to understand something Taro had needed. The fact that his blood family had neglected and deliberately excluded him had created an injury he had always carried. I'd never considered the possibility of proposing he join mine.

Wasn't that the best reason to marry someone?

So, I could feel content with that.

A handful of weeks of tension and worry—panic, really—was finally soothing out. I was able to give something to Taro that he had always lacked, and I no longer resented the fact that I had to do it. Fiona's title was firmly in her hands, and no one was going to try to take it from her. And the Triple S, they seemed to be leaving us alone, at least for a while.

It felt like I could breathe again. Everything seemed calm. My imagination, I knew, was fairly limited, but it looked to me like no one was going to be going crazy anytime soon.

So, it was all good. Finally.

THE ULTIMATE IN FANTASY FICTION!

From magical tales of distant worlds to stories of those with abilities beyond the ordinary, Ace and Roc have everything you need to stretch your imagination to its limits.

Marion Zimmer Bradley/Diana L. Paxson

Guy Gavriel Kay

Dennis L. McKiernan

Patricia A. McKillip

Robin McKinley

Sharon Shinn

Steven R. Boyett

Barb and J. C. Hendee

M12G0610

**Explore the outer reaches
of imagination—don't miss these authors
of dark fantasy and urban noir who take you
to the edge and beyond . . .**

Patricia Briggs	**Anne Bishop**
Simon R. Green	**Marjorie M. Liu**
Jim Butcher	**Jeanne C. Stein**
Kat Richardson	**Christopher Golden**
Karen Chance	**Ilona Andrews**
Rachel Caine	**Anton Strout**

Penguin Group (USA) Online

What will you be reading tomorrow?

Patricia Cornwell, Nora Roberts, Catherine Coulter,
Ken Follett, John Sandford, Clive Cussler,
Tom Clancy, Laurell K. Hamilton, Charlaine Harris,
J. R. Ward, W.E.B. Griffin, William Gibson,
Robin Cook, Brian Jacques, Stephen King,
Dean Koontz, Eric Jerome Dickey, Terry McMillan,
Sue Monk Kidd, Amy Tan, Jayne Ann Krentz,
Daniel Silva, Kate Jacobs...

You'll find them all at
penguin.com

*Read excerpts and newsletters,
find tour schedules and reading group guides,
and enter contests.*

Subscribe to Penguin Group (USA) newsletters
and get an exclusive inside look
at exciting new titles and the authors you love
long before everyone else does.

PENGUIN GROUP (USA)
penguin.com